CROOKED MAGIC

The Land of Enchantment #2

KATHLENA L. CONTRERAS

flyingtigerpress.com

ACKNOWLEDGEMENTS

I get a lot of my inspiration from songs, so I'd like to thank Sting for "The Shape of My Heart" and Bruce Hornsby for "Rainbow's Cadillac".

No book is complete without acknowledging my biggest inspiration and fan, my husband, Bob. And of course my awesome first readers, Laura Phillips-Carlson and Lara LaVonne Jordan. Thank you all for all you do.

PROLOGUE

Everyone around the table was shouting. The Lieutenant Governor shouted at the Senate Minority Leader. The President Pro Tem shouted at the Speaker. The governor's aides shouted at the senators' aides.

David Gray wanted to put his head in his hands, close his eyes and make the whole damn mess go away.

"Governor." Lianne, Gray's advisor, bent over his shoulder. "He's here. The consultant we talked about. I told him—"

"Who the hell are you?" On the other side of the table, the Minority Whip glared down the room. He looked like an angry turkey, face red, wattles quivering, small eyes behind his glasses outraged. "How did you get in here?"

God, was this a reprieve? Faces turned. The shouting died down. A man stood just inside the conference room door, smiling as if amused.

"That's him," Lianne whispered. "Mr. Moraihn."

Gray waved her and her perfume away. "Mr. Moraihn," he said, raising his voice to be heard by the man by the door. "I'm sorry, but this isn't a good time. I appreciate your coming, but I'll have to get back to you.

My aide—"

"Oh, no," the man interrupted. "This is the best time."

He had a hint of a brogue to go with his sandy hair and freckles. He was by no means a big man, and wasn't doing anything but standing quietly, but something about him sent a warning prickle up the back of Gray's neck.

"Kris," the Lieutenant Governor snapped, turning to her aide. "Call security for an escort."

The stranger's sharp blue gaze leapt to the young woman. "I don't think so," he said.

Kris stood frozen, phone to ear, lips parted as if to speak.

Gray turned to her. "Kristen—"

The young woman didn't move. Not even her eyes. She might've been a figure from a wax museum, except for the terror in those eyes.

Another of the aides, a young man, grabbed her arm. "Kristen? Are you okay? Kris!" He scrabbled his own phone out of a pocket, then yelped and dropped it. The phone slumped into a puddle of molten plastic.

Gray shoved to his feet. "What the hell?"

The people at his end of the table scrambled out of their chairs, babbling. Those on the other side craned their necks or stood to see what was going on. Voices cursed and questioned.

The stranger took a step forward. "Quiet."

The voices stopped as if a Mute button had been pushed. The air suddenly shimmered, almost as if it were no longer air at all but some perfectly clear crystal.

Gray brought fingertips to forehead. Was he having a

stroke? He turned slowly. No one else in the room moved. No one but Lianne, his advisor. Her long nails bit into his arm through his suit jacket.

"Mr. Moraihn is the one..." Her voice quavered. She swallowed. "He's the one who—"

"Just Moraihn," the man said. "I'm the one who will stop the impeachment proceedings against you."

Gray's cheeks went cold and his gaze darted to the men and women around him, a roomful of people prepared to destroy his career.

"Don't worry," Moraihn said. "They can see and hear nothing of what we do." He spun an empty chair and sat.

Gray remained standing. He breathed hard, but couldn't seem to get enough air. He looked from Moraihn to Lianne and back again.

"How?" Gray said. "Are you some kind of hypnotist? Is that what's going on here?"

"Nothing like that." Moraihn picked up an abandoned pen and turned it in his fingers. "What would you say if I told you magic is real?"

Gray gave a strangled laugh. "I'd say you're out of your mind."

Moraihn's lips quirked up. "Out of touch for a time, yes. Out of my mind? Hardly. Let me show you."

He studied the pen he held, slowly raised his hand and opened his fingers. The pen hovered in midair, then shot across the room, toward Gray.

No, Gray thought. Lianne cried out and made a grab for him.

The pen struck him. Pain blazed in his chest. He yelled and clutched at it. The pen clattered to the floor at his feet, leaving behind a blot of ink that stained his shirt. Blood oozed out, red within the black.

He clawed his shirt open, fingering the puncture beneath. Ink crept across the skin of his chest. He tried to wipe it away but it continued its spidery crawl, forming familiar shapes. Numbers?

No. How—? No. Gray scrubbed at his skin. The numbers remained as if tattooed. He backed up, horrified noises pushing through his throat.

"Oh God." Lianne's manicured fingers reached and flinched away again from Gray's chest. "Oh God."

Moraihn got to his feet. He waved a hand at Gray's chest. "You have my number. Call me when you're calmer. When you've had time to…what is it you say?…to process this. We'll discuss what I can do for you." He smiled again. "And what you can do for me."

He walked toward the door and vanished into it.

CHAPTER 1

The hardest thing about being a wizard was knowing when you should use magic—

And when you shouldn't.

So far, Amethyst Rey had avoided having to use it much at all. She drummed her fingers on the dining room table and scowled at her laptop screen. She had a very bad feeling that was about to change.

"Damn," she said.

Caramela, her pit bull, trotted over, plunked her big, blocky head on Amethyst's knee and gazed intently up at her. Amethyst gave her a reassuring pat. Caramela hated it when she cursed the computer.

Talys, in the kitchen, slanted her a look out of eyes the silver of polished steel. A tank top and shorts—both black, as usual—showed off the barrel-chested, slim-hipped build of a Navajo Indian. His black ponytail and broad, good-looking face completed the image, though he wasn't Navajo at all.

In fact, he wasn't even human.

"Another demanding client?" He raised a finger that dripped dish suds. "Wait. Let me guess. Mrs. Parnell has decided the pattern of the window you just installed doesn't precisely match that of her showpiece Maria pot."

Mrs. Parnell was, Amethyst suspected, *nouveau riche*. French for 'pain in the ass.' Amethyst had been tempted more than once to tell her to get another stained glass artist, but Talys always found a way to make her laugh at the situation. Like the whole Maria pot thing. Mrs. Parnell had to make sure absolutely everybody knew she owned an honest-to-goodness, black-on-black Maria pot, yes, *the* Maria Martinez, the famous early 20th century San Ildefonso Pueblo potter.

"No," Amethyst said. "Worse than Mrs. Parnell. Look at this."

Talys dried his hands on a dishtowel and came around the breakfast bar.

He leaned over her, one hand on the back of her chair, the other braced beside her on the table. She could always sense his presence, like knowing where the sun was behind clouds. But when he was close, like this, it was a sort of doubling. A wizard's sense of her familiar, along with his physical presence, the warmth of his body, the warm scent of his skin…

She gave her head a shake and made herself pay attention to the article on the computer screen.

Petroglyphs Mysteriously Mis-Plotted
By Rose Gutierrez
Albuquerque Journal Staff Writer

Surveyors recently discovered the Indian petroglyphs at the heart of the Camino subdivision controversy were in fact not within the boundaries of the proposed development. Tribal leaders of the Isleta, Sandia and Laguna Pueblos have contested the findings. Lawyers for the pueblos have petitioned the courts for a restraining order to halt work, citing the cultural and archeological value of the ancient rock drawings...

He straightened. "Yes, and?"

"Those damned wizards have to be behind it!"

"I scarcely see how you came to that conclusion."

"This fight has been going on for years," she said, stabbing a finger at the screen. "That developer tried every angle. No go. Not with the petroglyphs there." She raised her arms like a priestess invoking miracles. "Then the wizards return," she intoned. "And lo! The petroglyphs are right where the developer wants them. Doesn't that seem just a little too convenient to you?"

"Perhaps, but—"

"There is no 'but,' Talys! If wizards can shove aside something as irreplaceable as those petroglyphs for somebody's profit, what else will they do?"

"Exactly what wizards always did. Work their will in the world. Support or topple established power structures. Create new ones."

Her stomach clenched suddenly around the tamales she'd had for lunch. "Are you serious?"

"Why are you shocked?" he said. "The world went on for centuries—millennia—in that fashion. Your little American experiment with representative government only came about after wizards had nearly all vanished, when ordinary folk began to believe that they could also control their destinies."

He'd been with her for over a year, but sometimes she felt she didn't know him at all.

"So you're saying it's okay for wizards to trample over other people. Just because they can do what other people can't."

He shrugged, an elegant gesture for such big shoulders. "I'm simply stating fact. Those with power use it. Those without, follow—or wisely get out of the way. Part of the human condition, from what I've observed."

She took a long breath, swallowing her temper. "And when someone with power runs into someone else with power who doesn't particularly agree with that philosophy?"

"I sense the incipience of some rash and foolish act from which I shall be compelled to dissuade you."

"After some wizard who's been out of the world for however-many hundred years decides to stomp through my town screwing things up? Damn right I'm about to do something rash and foolish."

He gave her a long, level look. "And how much of this is attributable to the fact that it was you who restored the wizards' power?"

Her temper went out like he'd sprayed it with a fire extinguisher. She got up and turned to the window.

His arms came around her from behind. "You are not responsible for their actions."

"If I ignore what's going on, I am." She sighed and rubbed her face. "No matter how much I might want to."

He just held her a moment, then bent his head to

nuzzle her neck. Since he'd taken human form, this—the form he inhabited, to be specific—seemed to be his preferred method of distraction.

"No, no, no," she said. "That will *not* work this time."

He moved to her ear. "What won't work?"

"Talys—" She turned, braced her hands on his biceps to gain a little space and scowled up at him. "We've got to do something about this." She waved in the general direction of the computer screen.

"No, we don't." His hand slid under her shirt.

She caught it and took it out. "Yes, we do. Besides, you're the one who's always badgering me to use magic."

He sighed. "You've a knack," he said, "for ignoring my suggestions until the most inopportune moments."

She put on an innocent look. "That's not true. I use magic to open the garage door. And keep the bread fresh. I use it for that, too."

"And to start wizards' wars, it seems," he growled.

"Oh, come on. It's not that bad."

He released her, holding his arms wide as if in surrender. "Very well, love. Gather your purse. If you're determined to make life difficult, we may as well get it over with."

New Mexico's summer monsoons had touched the mesa's thin grasses with green. Snakeweed bloomed sulfur yellow against tiny, lime-green leaves. A lone hot air balloon drifted south beneath a sky of deep, crystalline blue. On the other side of the Rio Grande valley and the glittering spill of Albuquerque, the Sandia Mountains' slate-blue hump loomed against the eastern skyline.

A few miles to the west, one of the Albuquerque volcanoes shouldered up out of the mesa. Much closer, by the front bumper of Amethyst's Subaru, in fact, a survey stake lay flat in the grass. The high-altitude sun had faded the stake's orange flag and turned it brittle. Another stake, this one fluorescent green, flicked in the breeze about a hundred yards off, on the other side of a jumbled, rusty pile of basalt. A few car-sized blocks of stone scattered the space in between. On the nearest, a hand was pecked through the dark desert varnish to the paler rock beneath, greeting or warning.

The rocks pulsed with…something. A sort of heat, or a low, subliminal hum. Amethyst turned slowly, head tilted and fingers extended as if the sensation were something she could touch.

"Do you feel that?" She frowned. "Magic, but it feels…old. Asleep. How can that be?"

"The magic is in the stones themselves," Talys said. "These stones are sacred to the Pueblo peoples of the Rio Grande." The sky reflected in his sunglasses. "They are alive, almost sentient from the energy given them over the centuries."

"I never knew before."

On one block, a figure danced with upraised arms under an uneven orb that might have been a gibbous moon. An owl's face, or maybe a human's, gazed east, toward the mountains. On a higher rock, a star with a face and two hands peered down. Amethyst smoothed the hair on the back of her neck.

Caramela snuffled along the ground, for once seemingly oblivious to the magic. Maybe it was so old, it faded into the background for her.

"Okay," Amethyst said. "Then the only magic I'm picking up is what's in the rocks. So what are we looking for?"

As far as experience with magic, Talys was definitely the senior partner here. She had a little over one year, while he had…centuries? He'd always avoided telling her exactly *how* much more.

"Did some wizard physically move the rocks?" she said. "Did they fox the surveying equipment—or maybe mess with the surveyors' minds, or what?"

Talys' ponytail stirred in the breeze, glossy black strands sliding against the black of his shirt. He squinted and shook his head, looking rather Special-Ops in his tight-fitting t-shirt and black cargo pants. All he needed was an ankle holster with a semi-automatic.

"Mind-magic is difficult and generally requires close proximity, even physical contact with the subject," he said. "Within those limitations, a compulsion or binding could indeed achieve the desired effect."

Amethyst shuddered. Memory intruded—Jas Harker's dark eyes holding hers, the feel of his fingers in her hair—

She stopped the thoughts. Shot them dead in their tracks, in fact. With a .45 with hollow-point bullets.

"Illusion," Talys went on, "making things appear

other than they are, must be maintained. Physically altering the environment—say, by relocating the offending stones—requires a great deal of power. Possible, certainly, but strenuous, and the type of thing we couldn't help but notice." He picked his way through the scattering of basalt and tufts of sand sage. "I sense no fresh magic, therefore I'd assume that documents were most likely altered to show the petroglyphs in the preferred location. A subtle, elegant solution."

"Which suggests that someone well-connected hired the wizard, since they'd have to have access to the plats." She frowned. "But the rocks are here." She pointed at the ground. "No matter what the survey shows, they're *still* here. If somebody did slip down to Planning and Zoning to whisper incantations over the plats, how does it solve the problem?"

"Once scrutiny is relaxed and public interest has dwindled," he said, "other documentation of these artifacts could simply vanish. A few days with the aid of heavy machinery," he snapped his fingers, "and their existence is erased indeed."

"It can't work that way."

"Yet your legal system depends upon documents, does it not? What recourse is available without it?"

She raked a hand through her hair. "But Talys, how is even a wizard going to find every piece of paper relating to these petroglyphs?" She counted on her fingers. "Newspaper articles. Scholarly studies. Geological surveys. Magic isn't omnipotent, for godsake."

"Granted. Yet we can't know the entirety of the

measures that might be involved."

She kicked at a survey stake, thinking. "Good, old-fashioned undue influence and all? Maybe a nice curse or two, and some those compulsions you mentioned. Better than bribery." She rubbed her forehead. "God."

Caramela had strayed farther than she should. Amethyst called her. She trotted back, her wide, pink mouth open in a pit bull grin. Amethyst patted her muscular side and looked around. Miles to the west, a grey veil of rain slanted down. She could see a long, long way.

"You know," she said. "I feel really exposed up here."

"I would suggest a ward rather than illusion. Better to deflect attention entirely." He studied her. "I hope you realize, love, the moment we meddle here, our opponent will know another wizard has been at work. I'd prefer to leave him guessing as to *which* wizard. A ward is passive, and thus less likely to leave traces."

"Damn," she said under her breath. She did *not* like the idea of leading an angry wizard to her doorstep. "Okay, a ward it is, then."

Amethyst plucked a dry sand sage stalk and marked a pattern of lines in the pale dirt. She spat, stirred and dipped a forefinger into the spot of mud.

Talys made a noise. "Interesting. I've not seen a spell of misdirection of that sort in, oh, perhaps two thousand years. Primitive, but binding and effective."

Yikes. Maybe up his age by a factor of ten?

"Yeah, well, my brain is full of such second-hand gems." She marked the same lines in mud on Talys' forehead, then her own, then on the bumper of her

Outback. Caramela was already pretty well camouflaged by her color and low profile. "Courtesy of possession by several dozen wizards' shades."

He grinned. "Every cloud has its silver lining, eh?"

"Right," she muttered.

Here, where the smooth sweep of mesa folded down to the edge of the volcanic escarpment, the land dipped and rolled. The terrain seemed a better candidate for open space than for home lots. But open space generally didn't generate much profit.

"So the rocks were here first," she said. "Let's make sure they get to stay that way."

"You need only fix the symbolic values, the relation of the stones to the boundary points of the land in question."

"Like fixing coordinates in a spreadsheet. Too bad we couldn't just Google the subdivision and do the magic remotely."

He tilted his head. "It may be possible. Indeed, it's likely. If you know how."

"Which I don't," she sighed. "So we do it the old-fashioned way."

The mesa rolled toward the dark hump of the volcano. She nudged a chip of basalt with her toe, then picked it up and pressed her thumb to the darker, varnished side.

Talys took a quick step toward her. "Amethyst—"

Then he was there with her, touching the magic. She felt him ready to restrain her power, but he waited, poised.

Magic ran along her nerves, through her veins, hot

and tingly. She suddenly tasted dirt and rock. The deep, slow pulse of the earth thrummed just beneath hearing, something she could feel more in her bones than ears.

She opened her hand and a spiral showed on the stone, the image perfectly smooth as if laser-cut.

"That should take care of illusion or bewitchments anyone might set."

He took it, turned it in his fingers then nodded. "This is very like the magic already here. Yet if found—"

She took it from him, scuffed out a shallow trench in the sand among the tufts of grass, dropped and covered the chip.

"Good luck with that. Now. What do you think about letting the rocks watch out for themselves?"

He plucked at his lip, considering. "You are determined to do this."

"Yep."

"Very well," he gave a resigned wave of the hand. "Then proceed."

A flutter of nervousness went through her. *A little late, don't you think?* she scolded herself and paced to the opposite end of the basalt pile.

The rocks here had tumbled long ago. The tip of one showed among the grass and sage like the prow of a sunken ship. Amethyst pressed her hands to two adjacent planes, pushed power from her center and down her arms. She lifted her hands. Two prints remained like afterimages. Wrapped around the rock was a face with a bar of eyebrows with the stone's corner as a nose.

Amethyst stepped back and admired it. "That should

help keep the bad guys away."

She moved to the opposite side of the rock promontory.

Sleepy and ponderous, the ancient magic roused at her touch. Some called animals to the hunt, some fertility to crops and people. Some honored the spirits, another celebrated the beauty of a desert flower. Amethyst touched each, reminded the magic of itself, of its place in the world, of its stony permanence.

"Very good," Talys said. "Very good indeed." His smile shone, white in his dark face. "Old magic possesses the value of permanence, as does earth magic. Here you've taken advantage of both."

She hadn't used a tremendous amount of power, but more than usual. She crouched and rested elbows on knees, cold and drained.

Talys' footsteps crunched across the ground, then he cupped the back of her head. Energy flowed into her. The weakness diminished, but the sense of openness to everything around her remained. Magic connected to everything. When she used it, the barriers between herself and the outside world thinned to transparency.

She felt the distant thunderstorm's electrical tension, a collared lizard in a cool nook in the rocks dreaming of succulent bugs. She tasted the lemony-mint scent of some desert plant, smelled the gassy exhaust of a small plane overhead, heard a toddler's tantrum in a house at the edge of the mesa. Drawing on Talys' energy, she pushed the world outside again.

"Whew."

She took his offered hand and let him pull her to her feet. Her thoughts settled into their usual channels, like a river after a flood. She opened the car door. Caramela hopped into the backseat.

Magic breathed on the back of her neck. She turned. The tumble of rusty-black stones watched her, awake and aware. And perfectly obvious to anyone who came to see why, exactly, his spell wasn't performing as advertised.

"You know, I'm pretty sure we've just pissed someone off," she said. "Possibly several someones—the wizard plus whoever hired him."

"No doubt, but you forget one thing." Talys placed a hand on his chest. "Me. Even a strong wizard will be reluctant to confront one accompanied by a familiar. My knowledge, my non-mortal nature, not to mention my enhancements to your power provide you with formidable superiority."

"Not to mention your bashful modesty," she said.

The back of her neck prickled with warning. She rubbed it. *Imagination*, Amethyst told herself and climbed into the car.

CHAPTER 1.5 - OPPOSITION

H e stood at the edge of the table land. The wind of an approaching storm plastered his shirt to his thin body, tangled in his short, dark curls.

He called himself Stregone—*warlock*. Not the name given him at birth, but it fit, and he'd worn it since before his people had discovered this continent. A wizard had stolen that name for a long while, left him drifting mindless and powerless. Then another gave it back to him, along with his power. Like a man under an enchantment, he'd reawakened into a world changed beyond his imagination. A world where ordinary mortals flew, and spoke over long distances, and scried far scenes in glass. A world where his power had been rendered redundant.

Or so he thought. For a time.

The stones rising from the dry ground watched him, their ancient, unfamiliar magic muttering like the distant thunder. A stern-browed face glared at him from the nearest. Two hands flanked the face: *stay away*.

Last time he'd been here, the stones had slept. His employer had wished them moved—or removed. He'd laughed, knowing well enough to leave them alone. People nowadays had strange notions of wizardry. He possessed other spells, which did much quieter work. Not the sort of thing that would awaken the magic here.

Not far from where he'd parked his own vehicle, tire tracks flattened the grass. Footprints, one set large, another small, and those of a dog, made patterns in the floury sand. He followed the tracks. Short grasses and weeds scratched at his boots. A rattlesnake buzzed beneath a grey-green bush. Stregone reached out a thought and silenced it.

No magic here that was not old, no magic that did not fit. Yet there were the stones, awake and watchful.

He returned to where the other car had been parked. He called up his powers and grimaced. The magic now was like this age—loud and fast. It grabbed and towed one along, stripping barriers and defenses, flattening any attempt at finesse. Often his spells went wild. He disliked feeling like an apprentice once more, struggling with his craft. Yet he worked a finding. It felt like a proper finding should. He cast it over the tire tracks.

Nothing. He should have felt a tugging, a pull that would lead him to the vehicle that had made those tracks, to the person who had driven that vehicle.

He frowned. Huge raindrops splatted him like bird droppings. He waved them away. Clearly his powers were in order this time. Someone must have cast a spell of bafflement.

Stregone closed his eyes, bowed his head and called up more power. Sweating, he released his counterspell, then his breath. His arms ached. He found his fists clenched, relaxed them and opened his eyes.

He might as well have cast the magic into a void. A

chill crept up his back. Could his opponent be so powerful?

He opened his senses to the magic. The old magic of the stones rose like a hunched, shadowy presence whose roots stretched backward through the depths of centuries. His own spell made flickering gaps where his imperfectly meshed power fractured the magical ether. Nothing else, nothing but the spell on those tracks, magic that lay in the dirt like a lizard's discarded tail.

His eyes narrowed. Staring down into the busy glitter of the city, he picked at knots of questions. Why awaken the stones, then scamper off and hide? If someone powerful enough to thwart his spells wished to warn him off, a more direct approach would have made more sense. Why protect the stones at all? What good were they in this age? Who would care to preserve their antiquated power but—

Stregone raised his chin in sudden realization.

The wizard who'd been here could, of course, be anyone, perhaps the ancestors of those who'd carved the figures on the stones, who'd set the ancient magic. But those, he suspected, might lie in wait to confront the one who defiled their sacred place. No, this was a marking of territory. The magic worked said, *This is mine. I was here first.* He knew of only one wizard who could make that claim.

His gut tightened around certainty. He'd confronted that one once before, shortly after he'd reawakened. And been bested. Stregone was not the sort of man to be thwarted without consequences. Others, wizardly and commonplace, had learned that to their grief.

He climbed into his vehicle. He took the phone from the console, spoke his message and pushed "send".

A message came back: **Who?**

He replied: **I have a guess.**

Take care of it. Project needs 2 move.

He was beginning to weary of an employer whose ambitions extended no further than amassing wealth. Stregone might, if he were cunning and careful with his knowledge of his rival, find a more appreciative buyer for the information.

He tapped a finger on the steering wheel then sent back, **You did not pay me for that.**

He waited. Finally, the message came: **Come here. We'll talk.**

Oh, yes. They'd talk. But Stregone would also be talking with someone else. And a certain young wizard would quickly find her life a great deal more complicated.

❖❖❖❖❖❖

From: 870.9786: Stregone says another operator n area. Project halted. Pls advise.

From: Ragman: Do you have vital info?

870.9786: No.

Ragman: Can Stregone locate new operator?

870.9786: Maybe??

Ragman: Do not contact. I will meet w Stregone.

870.9786: My project?

Ragman: Will attempt to mitigate probs, but need that info.

870.9786: Thx. Will have Stregone contact you.

❖❖❖❖❖❖

To: TGarret@daggetinc.com

From: Ragman@ndns.net

Subject: Specially skilled operator

Mr. Garret:

We recently discussed your interest in gaining a valuable new resource that will give your company an unparalleled competitive edge. A promising individual has come to light. I will call to discuss your terms and requirements, and if you decide to move forward, will make the appropriate connections. My assistant will call to set an agreeable date and time. In the meantime, please keep in mind that other parties have also expressed an interest.

HHR

❖❖❖❖❖❖

The man in the overcoat sat at the counter sipping a cup of coffee, a half-eaten bagel and cream cheese in front of him. The waitress called orders to the kitchen, the cook set plates under the heat lamps and called orders back. The clink of knives and forks on dishes, the background music turned up too loud to stay in the background made nearby conversations impossible to hear. The place was no Starbucks; no wi-fi, no trendy twenty-somethings with their smartphones and iPads and Bluetooths. Just a counter with the kitchen on the other side of a hand-through. A few much-patched booths sat under a row of windows that let you see everyone passing by on the sidewalk outside. Perfect for keeping an eye on things.

The man sitting at the counter next to him was stocky and nondescript, except for the old acne scars that pocked his cheeks. He folded the stock section of the newspaper and stabbed a sausage on his plate.

"Can I take a look at that?" Mr. Overcoat gestured at the stock page. "I bought some stock in this tech startup in Albuquerque and want to check it."

"Albuquerque?" The other man said and slid over the newspaper. "Jesus. Dink town in middle of the desert. What the hell is there?"

"You'd be surprised," Mr. Overcoat said. "This thing is really going to pay off."

Mr. Scarface shook his head. Mr. Overcoat slipped a thick manila envelope into the folded section of the newspaper, which he pretended to study for a while.

"My shares are down," he finally said and slid the paper back.

Mr. Scarface put a hand on it. His eyebrows climbed. "Too bad. Looks like mine just went up. Maybe you should get into another industry."

"Like shipping and transportation," Mr. Overcoat said. "Nothing fancy. If I was a customer, all I'd want was my stuff delivered undamaged."

Mr. Scarface gave a grunt of a laugh and tucked the paper into his coat. "I'm sure you'll get what you want."

Mr. Overcoat angled a knowing smile at the other man. "I'm sure I will."

CHAPTER 2

"I hate not knowing!" Amethyst blanked her phone and sat back in the passenger seat. A week, and still nothing on the newsfeeds about the petroglyphs. "There's got to be some way to find out if the spell I set worked."

Louisiana Boulevard unrolled ahead like a gemmed necklace studded with topaz, diamonds, rubies; flashing, weaving, changing against the soft evening darkness. Traffic lights blinked from green to red, cars streamed in and out of the mall parking lots.

"If you suggest driving to the west side to have another look about," Talys said, "I shall take you home and tie you to the bed."

"Like you *could*, Mustang Man."

He raised one black brow and slanted her a look. "Is that a dare?"

She grinned. "Depends on what you plan to do afterwards."

Talys glanced in the rearview mirror, flicked his signal and changed lanes. She wondered where he learned to drive. Although since he'd actually *been* a car for some time, she guessed it wasn't much of a leap.

"Very well," he said. "If you insist."

She opened her eyes wide, pretending alarm, and raised her hands as if ready to fend him off.

Amethyst Rey.

Her name came as clear as if someone had whispered it from the backseat. She whipped around, any impulse toward laughter gone. The street behind them was thick with the glare of headlights, the glow of signs and streetlights.

"Did you hear that?" she said. 'Hear' wasn't the right word, but there wasn't one better.

"What was it?" Talys wasn't alarmed. Just…curious. Interested.

"My name. Someone's thinking my name. Someone close by."

He peered into the mirror once more. "Ah. I'd perceived we were being followed."

"You—" She pushed a breath through pursed lips. No point arguing about why he'd neglected to mention it earlier. She shot a narrow look back. "Well, let them follow *this.*"

She reached for the magic. A coil of Talys' silver energy held her back.

"Wait," he said. "I see some value in discovering who should be so presumptuous. Don't you?"

"I don't know." She dug through the junk heap of spells in her mind. One conjured a doppelgänger. Another used light to baffle and bewilder an enemy, perfect for the circumstances. A third made the hunter follow his own tracks until the spell was dispersed—or until the hunted decided to put an end to the hapless circling.

She sighed. "I guess you're right."

"Confidence, love," he said, flipped on the signal and turned left onto a side street.

The stores in the strip malls on either side of the street gave way to a back alley, then the windowless, metal-roofed blocks of what must've been warehouses or industrial buildings. The street dipped down and the busy flow of traffic on Menaul disappeared.

"I changed my mind. This is *not* a good idea."

"Patience. Just a moment more, I think."

He flipped the car into a U-turn, pulled to the curb and twisted off the lights.

Amethyst pulled her seatbelt out, let it snap back.

Talys reached over and put a hand over hers. "Be still."

She knotted her hands together in her lap. Headlights appeared up the street, one—no, two cars.

"Shit," she said.

The lights paused, then the car in front came on, drove past and also turned around, pulling in a few yards behind them. The rearview mirror suddenly reflected a bar of light across Talys' eyes. Headlights shined in the passenger side mirror, too. The second car stayed where it was, half a block or so up the street. Headlights glared through the windshield, then swung off at an angle.

Damn, damn, damn. Now they were blocking the street. So could Talys do evasive driving, too? She wasn't sure she wanted to count on it, although she'd seen him execute some mean moves when he'd been a car.

Her heart beat so hard she was dizzy. "What now?"

Talys gave her a curious look and put on his sunglasses. "Why are you frightened? You're a wizard."

"Because up until last year, I was just a regular person, and regular people freak when cars follow them and then block them in. Habit, y'know?"

He chuckled and glanced in the side mirror. "Ah. I see. Simply remain calm, love, and all should be well."

"Yeah, right," she muttered.

Amethyst squinted into her own mirror. A figure approached, silhouetted by the headlights. She could tell only that it was male, and sort of bulky.

Talys buzzed down his window. With the light from the two cars' headlights, there wasn't any problem seeing the guy when he leaned down. He looked maybe in his mid-forties, Anglo, his cheeks marked with acne scars.

"Hey," he said.

"Hey," Talys said. "What's up?"

The slang jarred her, but Amethyst kept herself from giving him a look.

The guy must've seen something in her face, because he said, "Sorry, didn't mean to scare you. I'm looking for the Naked Furniture warehouse. Do you know where it is? I must've taken a wrong turn."

"Oh," Talys said. "I doubt that."

The guy gave a lopsided grin that showed movie-star-white teeth. "Well, I guess you might be right." He leaned an elbow in the window frame and looked across at Amethyst. "Actually, Ms. Rey, there's somebody who wants to see you. I'm here to take you to meet him."

"Who's that?" Amethyst said.

Talys spoke over her. "I'm afraid we have to decline the invitation."

"No, I don't think you will," the guy said.

A tap came at the passenger side window. Amethyst jumped and spun. Another man stood there, though she could only see his chest and arm. And a gun. With a freaking *silencer*.

"You both look like smart people to me," said the man at the driver's window, "so I'm sure you're thinking, 'I wonder what all they've got in the other car?' Right?"

Panic squeezed her chest. Talys didn't touch her, didn't even glance at her, but she felt him, felt a sense of calm and soothing wrap around her like a comforting arm.

You're a wizard, he'd said. Okay.

She riffled through spells. One would take the man's power of movement, leave him frozen and helpless. Another would open a void that would swallow him. Eeek. No. Not even under the circumstances. All she wanted was *out* of the circumstances—

She knew exactly the spell for that. Amethyst took a breath, clamped one hand around Talys' wrist, splayed the other on the dashboard and hauled up power.

Outside the car windows, everything went dark and silent. A sense of enclosing walls replaced the open air of the city night. A smell of old oil wafted in.

"By the dark gods of all the underworlds," Talys snarled and grabbed her as she slumped in the seat.

Her ears rang. Retinal ghosts from the headlights flickered when she moved her eyes. Her guts felt crushed, the marrow of her bones sucked dry.

"Sorry," she croaked. Her head lolled.

He made a furious noise and flung out of the car. He came around, jerked open the passenger door and scooped her up in his arms.

The fluorescent light overhead stuttered on, illuminating the familiar clutter of Amethyst's garage, the scarred old workbench and pegboard above it. The door that let onto the laundry room banged open ahead of him. He carried her up the garage steps, into the living room and plopped her down on the couch then stalked off.

Caramela padded to the couch and studied her out of worried, amber eyes. Her thoughts pushed into Amethyst's mind, wordless, layered with worry and concern and the scents she smelled of stress and fear. *I'm okay now*, Amethyst thought to her and raised a shaking hand to scratch her bulging jaw.

In the kitchen, the refrigerator door opened and closed. Same with the silverware drawer. There was the clink of a plate on the countertop, a sound of chopping. Talys came into the room carrying a plate and a glass of orange juice.

Standard operating procedure when a wizard worked big medicine was to refuel afterward or face the consequences. And zapping them out of the middle of deep doo-doo and into her own garage counted as major big medicine.

She downed the juice first—quick energy. Talys knelt beside the sofa with a plate of apple and banana slices, good, simple sugars, easily digested. She devoured it all.

Talys chewed curses in what sounded like several

different languages.

"Why are you so mad?" she said. "What was I supposed to do?"

"So you transported us, as well as a large, immensely heavy object, not a street or two over, but several miles across town. Mass and distance do matter in magic, Amethyst. Newtonian laws of physics don't revoke themselves as a special courtesy to wizards, and the more you defy them, the greater the cost in power."

"Excuse me, did you not see the *gun*? And like Mr. Acne Whiteteeth said, they probably had some more firepower trained on us in the other car. Sorry if I thought the best thing was to just get the hell out of there."

"You do realize, of course, that you've just given them a dazzling display of your power. I doubt we've seen the end of this."

"Seems to me that giving them a display of my power will make them think twice in the future." She stopped. "Wait. They were looking for me." Her mind clicked over what had happened. "They know what I drive."

He sat back and regarded her out of his silver eyes. "I wondered when you'd get there. I suppose this isn't a good time to tell you I told you so."

"Oh, no, no. You're not pinning this on me. Not when—" She stopped again. "Shit."

"Yes?"

Her insides were doing unpleasant things, and she was pretty sure it wasn't all due to the magic she'd just used. "Someone knows what I am. And they're trying to get me." She shifted her jaw sideways. "Finking bastard."

Talys looked somewhere between wary and bewildered. "Who?"

"Jas Harker, who else?"

"That's quite a leap, love."

"Really? How else would they know to look for me?"

"There's no evidence—"

"That they were looking for a wizard?" she said. "Tell me they were looking for a stained glass artist, then."

"I agree it's highly unlikely."

"Then did someone go out to the petroglyphs and track us down? You promised what I did couldn't be traced back to me. And, *and*," she said, another idea suddenly occurring. "The gun, Talys. Wizards don't need guns. These guys were civilians."

He sighed. "If you're looking for the culprit who might've—what is the term? Blown your cover?—you have a number of choices besides Jas Harker. You've already confronted other wizards."

She made a disgusted noise. "Yeah, every one I've met so far." She bit her lip, thinking. "Why would a wizard tell a civilian about me? It doesn't make sense. Not unless he has a personal motive."

She sat up and put her feet on the floor. Her head swam, and she still felt like her stomach was sucked to her backbone. She ignored both.

"Amethyst—"

"What do you want me to do, Talys? Just wait and see what happens next?"

"Of course not but—"

"Then what?"

He ran a hand down his face. "Very well. What do you have in mind?"

Good question. She hadn't heard a whisper from Jas in over a year. Although a suspicious number of high-end stained glass commissions had been coming her way. Did she really want to upset the status quo?

She puffed out a breath, leaned forward and pulled her phone out of her back pocket.

"What," Talys said, covering her hand with his large, brown one, "are you doing?"

"What does it look like I'm doing?"

His lips thinned with annoyance. "Like you're preparing to increase your difficulties."

"Maybe." She slid hand and phone from his grasp. "But if I'm going to go looking for bastards, I might as well start with the one I know."

"Should I point out that most businesses closed several hours ago? Or will that spoil your sense of justified outrage?"

"Let me put it this way. That never stopped me from getting through to him in the past."

Amethyst thumbed on her phone. Talys heaved another sigh, but didn't argue. He closed his eyes and cocked his head as if listening. She swallowed a flutter of nervousness and brought up the dial pad on her phone.

She'd deleted Jas' contact a long time ago, feeling a certain savage satisfaction when she did. So it was a little unsettling to realize that she still remembered his direct number. What did that say?

The phone rang, then rolled over to voicemail.

Damn. She sat listening to the silence after the greeting, trying to decide whether or not to leave a message, then finally shrugged and ended the call.

"Okay, okay, you're right," she grumbled.

"Perhaps," he said, "you'll be thinking more clearly in the morning."

"Thanks a—"

Her phone rang. *Magus Corporation*, the caller ID said. She gave Talys an *I told you so* look and answered it.

"Amethyst!" Jas Harker's voice said. "I saw you called. What a surprise. I'm delighted to hear from you." He really did sound delighted, too.

"Yeah," she said. "So. I guess we need to talk."

His laugh came over the phone line. "Direct as ever. I was looking forward catching up. It *has* been awhile."

Not damn long enough. Somehow, it didn't come out.

"Very well, then." In spite of her silence, he still sounded his usual, good-natured self. "Why don't you come here."

She glanced at Talys. Eyes still closed, he shrugged.

"When?"

"Mmm… Say around six tomorrow? I should be free then."

"Fine."

"I'll clear you with security."

"Yeah. Thanks. Bye." She ended the call before he could say goodbye himself.

Talys opened his eyes. "Yes, I can understand how you'd be beguiled."

Beguiled. Ouch.

"He's pleasant, seemingly open," he continued. "Offers a meeting in a sufficiently public setting to assuage suspicion, while at an hour late enough to accommodate discretion. No use of magic whatsoever." He nodded. "Yes, very nicely done."

"Believe me," she said. "It always was."

"You didn't mention me, I notice."

She snorted. "You're coming."

"What about security?" His eyes were teasing.

Amethyst set her jaw. "I guess they'll have to be flexible."

CHAPTER 3

"I'm very sorry, Ms. Rey, but I only have you cleared to go up." The Magus Corporation security guard, a clean-cut, craggy-faced fortyish man, glanced at Talys, who was dressed in his usual black—suit, shirt, tie and all.

Oh, and the sunglasses, of course. And the ponytail. An American Indian MIB.

"I'm sorry," Amethyst said. "I must've forgotten to mention my friend."

"Let me call up to the top floor and see what I can do," the man said.

Amethyst smiled, took Talys' elbow and strolled away to wait.

The Magus Building lobby displayed its old fairy-cave perfection. The sculptures scattered around the lobby radiated grace and calm. The granite-boulder fountain opposite the elevator filled the space with its chuckles and murmurs.

She steered Talys toward the front doors. "That's where my window would've gone." She pointed at the green glass curtainwall above the doors. "About six feet above the doors and four across on either side."

He nodded. "I saw the sketch. Lovely."

"Ms. Rey?" The guard strode toward them. "You're both cleared to go up. Mr. Harker is waiting for you."

Into the elevator and up 25 stories, techno music playing over the speakers. It was the tallest building in the state of New Mexico. Of course, since it belonged to Jas, it would be.

The elevator door opened and there was the corridor, jade green carpet, soft dawn walls, paintings. Reception area at the end, but no receptionist.

The hallway spilled into the skylit reception area. Jas came toward them from a right hand hall, green-patterned tie loosened, shirtsleeves rolled up. Black hair, dark eyes, pale face, brows with that charming mismatched quirk, just as good-looking as ever.

It was the first time she'd seen him since—

Since she'd thought he was just a man. No. She wasn't going there.

"Amethyst," Jas said, completely ignoring Talys. He extended a hand to shake.

Was he kidding? After what he'd done? She gritted her teeth and gave as brief a shake as possible.

She nodded at Talys. "This is Thomas Aturj."

Jas finally looked at Talys. Or rather, looked *up* at Talys.

"Mr. Aturj." He offered his hand again.

Talys was bolder than she was. He kept his hands clasped in front of him. Behind the black sunglasses, his face didn't show a flicker of expression. He'd make a great Secret Service agent.

Jas gave a wry smile and turned the rejection into a

gesture of invitation. "This way."

Down another green-carpeted hallway, past empty offices. Jas stepped through a cherry wood door and ushered them inside.

He'd remodeled. And he had good taste, she had to give him that. Watercolors in frames made with the honeycombed tubes of cholla cactus skeletons graced the walls. A waist-high, hand-built jar with runnels of green glaze stood in one corner. There was a writing desk in cherry, a matching credenza and computer armoire. Three chairs in muted green upholstery sat in front of the Coke-bottle green window-wall. Near the chairs, a teapot and three cups sat on a round table.

How sweet.

Amethyst sat. So did Jas. Through the window, the bulk of the Sandia Mountains loomed over her shoulder like a giant granite eavesdropper.

Talys didn't sit. He came and stood behind her chair, blocking out the mountain.

Jas' black brows twitched up. "Your familiar, I presume. He's changed a great deal since I saw him last."

Last time—the only time—Jas had met him, Talys had inhabited a '69 Mustang Mach I. The reminder of the circumstances of that particular meeting didn't help her temper.

"He has a name."

"Oh, yes. 'Tom Aturj.' A little obvious, wouldn't you say?"

Thaumaturge—magic user. It figured Jas would be one of the few people who'd get the joke.

"*Magus* Corporation," she shot back.

Jas chuckled and leaned forward to pour tea. "I suppose we can't resist teasing ordinary folk."

She took a long breath. "Who've you been talking to?"

"I thought it was only your familiar who'd been watching too many mob movies." Jas took a sip of tea. "Could you possibly narrow it down?"

She shook her head and gave a disbelieving laugh. He was always just so damn smooth.

"Some guys stopped us to give us an invitation. Interestingly enough, they knew my name and what I drive. Seems somebody wants to meet me."

Jas put down his cup with a clink. "Who?"

That wasn't quite the reaction she'd expected. "After they flashed the gun, I didn't stick around to ask."

"A gun. Idiots," he said then gave her a look. "You didn't ask the gentlemen who accosted you who sent them?"

She kept herself from cringing. Of course, that would've been the most sensible thing to do.

"That was the least of my worries at that particular moment."

He looked like he was trying not to roll his eyes. "Then why come to me?"

"Come on, Jas," Amethyst said. "Do you really want to make me come out and say it?"

"I see," he said. "I was to be the villain who'd set the hounds on your trail. Hmm." He turned the cup on the table. "I didn't realize I'd sunk quite so low in your eyes."

"What did you expect?"

His chest rose with a silent breath. "I swear to you, I'm not your enemy. I never was."

"Sure, that's why you—" She clamped her lips on the rest. *Why you* lied *to me, why you strung me along and then...*

She hadn't realized how angry she still was. Why should it matter? Except... It still hurt, what Jas had done.

She started over. "So what does that make you then? My friend?"

"If you like."

"That didn't work out too well last time, did it?"

"Amethyst—" He pushed out a breath. "All right. No, I haven't given you away. If you can't take me at my word, I'm sure you'll realize your exposure would hardly be in my best interests."

She grunted. True enough. She had a strong suspicion his wizardry had a lot to do with the success of his company, but she was also pretty sure she was the only one who did. He wouldn't want to give her a reason to blow his own cover.

"So who *would* have an interest in outing me?"

He waved a hand. "*Who* is immaterial. What you should be asking is *why*."

"Okay then, why?"

He leaned back, propped an elbow on the chair arm. "Let's take Magus Corporation as an example. Think about the business I'm in."

"Data security and firewalls. An Internet search engine." She shrugged. "So?"

"If someone could gain control of this organization,

what else would he stand to gain?"

"Access to your clients' data. Their finances. Their computers, networks, the data of companies *they* do business with. Their customers. Even the government, I guess. Damn."

He nodded. "'Damn' indeed. Two hundred, even a hundred years ago, a wizard could do damage enough to the local social and political structures. But the sphere of influence of even the most powerful was limited. Today, with the entire globe interconnected... Well, you saw what happened to the economy recently."

"And the Internet," she said, appalled. "Power grids."

"Exactly. All that lovely interconnectivity. All someone needs is a resource to help them gain to access it."

"A wizard." She frowned, thinking about the petroglyphs. "Wait. I'm confused. You were talking about wizards doing things to mess with the system. Where do I come in?"

"You were a programmer. Follow the logic. Say I'm an ordinary man—an ordinary man of position and power. I'm under pressure in some way. Say I've learned of a resource that will give me a considerable edge. What do you think I'll do?"

She cursed under her breath. "Whatever it takes to get it."

He held out a hand, palm up. "Exactly. At the risk of bringing up a sore subject, now you understand my situation last year."

When he tried to ensnare her. No, she would *not* get

sidetracked. This was too important.

"So are the wizards making a power grab?" she said. "Or regular people who think they can use us?"

"In your case, assailants with guns suggest the latter. But I have to admit, I'm more concerned about the former."

Information clicked into place. "Someone is after you, too."

"Not after me personally, no. What I am—that, I believe, isn't known beyond this room. But it appears someone has his sights set on my company."

She leaned forward, lifted a teacup and handed it up to Talys. He took it. Unbending a little, or was he simply following her lead? She picked up her own and sipped. Orange spice herb tea, her favorite. She ought to be annoyed, but couldn't quite manage it.

"Someone's attacking your company with magic?" she asked

"Yes."

"Who?"

He lifted his shoulders. "They'd best hope I don't find out."

"What—" She hesitated.

"What are they doing?" He gave her a brief, knowing smile. "So far, they've tried only minor incursions. Electronics enchanted as scrying media. Compulsions and bindings placed on trusted employees. When the spells encountered the wards I have on the building, we were left with some melted smartphones and confused people."

She looked up at Talys. He still didn't show any

expression. But she didn't sense surprise, either.

"So what do you do?" she asked Jas. "Engage in battles of wizardry on the floor of the stock exchange?"

This time it was a real smile, the kind that made his eyes crinkle. "Over the years, I've learned the value of keeping a low profile. Of course, eventually someone will begin to wonder why Magus Corporation is proving impervious to their efforts, but by then…" He gave a dismissive lift of the hand and drank tea.

He'd do whatever it took to eliminate the problem. Did she blame him? What would she do once she found out who'd outed her? The thought unsettled her stomach.

"You think it's the same people who are after me?"

"I don't know. What I want you to think about is how far an individual or an organization might be willing to go to secure your abilities."

"Including you?"

He shifted in his chair and avoided her eye. "Not this time," he said quietly.

Jas? Have a conscience? Could it be?

"So why are you telling me all this?"

He gave the same wry smile as when Talys had refused to shake his hand. "Oh, I don't know. Perhaps I'm repaying a debt."

She gave him a skeptical look. "Then thanks. Now Tom won't have to dangle you out the window by your ankles to find out who you told about me. Whew. What a relief."

Jas laughed. "It can't be nearly as great as my own." He paused. "In all seriousness, Amethyst, I recommend you guard yourself. I don't need to remind you that even wizards can be vulnerable."

Talys didn't move or make a sound, but a pulse of something went through him, too quickly to identify. Jas must've sensed it, too, because his gaze shifted to him.

Amethyst stood. "Fortunately," she said and put a hand on Talys' arm, "I'm a little less vulnerable than most."

Jas also stood. "Understand the last thing I need is someone else to contend against."

"Yeah, well, I'm taking your word on that."

"I'm grateful for that. I'll even be daring and suggest that you might need another friend."

"Don't push it, Jas."

* * * * * *

Amethyst leaned an elbow on the car's armrest. "So. What do you think?"

Talys glanced in the rearview mirror, flicked his signal and changed lanes. "An interesting question, if a bit open-ended," he said. "I think Mr. Harker is trying hard to return to your good graces."

"Well, he won't."

A corner of his mouth quirked. "No need to say so on my behalf, love. I don't feel the least bit rivalrous. Although I wouldn't venture to presume he feels the same."

"I didn't appreciate the way he ignored you."

Late sunlight moved across his face, drawing cheekbone and jaw and brow in high relief. "Oh, I assure you, he wasn't ignoring me. His behavior spoke quite eloquently of my status in his eyes."

"What about all that watch-your-back jazz? D'you think he was just blowing smoke?"

He glanced in the mirror again. "Do you?"

"If it hadn't been for last night, I would've said 'yes.' But... Were wizards a commodity before?"

"Certainly they were valued highly," he answered. "They were, however, also feared."

A muscle between her shoulder blades unwound. "My point exactly."

"But the landscape has changed a great deal in the last few centuries. Wizards are greatly diminished in number. They were nearly extinct for a time. People now don't fully comprehend what a wizard is capable of."

"Obviously," she said. "The only problem is, what happens if these guys don't get the message I'm not interested in playing?"

He tilted his head, considering. "I suspect you'd be unwilling to isolate yourself in a tower in the depths of a forest or in a fortress buried within ramparts of mountains." The light changed and he accelerated onto the eastbound I-40 onramp. "Not that either would prove much of a barrier to four wheel drive or a helicopter."

"You're kidding. They really did that?"

"Some did. Those who tended toward solitary study, as well as the overtly meddlesome ones. Those interested in power for its own sake." He shrugged. "That, or do as our Mr. Harker has done. How did he phrase it?—keep a low profile. It grows tiresome, both psychologically and magically, to constantly maintain one's guard, and as he pointed out, wizards do, indeed, possess vulnerabilities."

"So we're back to square one. Somebody is after us— well, me, I guess—and we don't know who." She raked a hand through her hair. "This stinks. I really hate the idea of going around spelled up every which way to Tuesday just to be left alone." A cold thought hit her in the gut. "Talys, what happens if they decide to use leverage? They could go after my family. They could go after Melodie and Marl."

Melodie Odham was Amethyst's best friend since their days in the IT program at UNM. Marl was Melodie's husband of six months.

"Ordinary folk have found means to harm our kind," he said. "But it's scarcely easy." He made a considering moue. "All things being equal, perhaps flaunting your power did serve a useful purpose."

"Good to hear you say so."

He gave a dry chuckle. "However, until we can identify our adversary, I fear you will, indeed, need to spell yourself up every which way to Tuesday."

CHAPTER 4

Amethyst knew she should be inside, talking and laughing with Melodie and Marl and Talys, but was she? No. She was out here, in the dark, without a jacket, doing what she could to protect her best friend and her family.

The sound of a party came from some other block, the *whoomp* of the bass line pulsing in the air. A few fallen leaves lay scattered across the grass, so many upturned hands pale on Melodie's back lawn.

Amethyst pushed the material world to the back of her consciousness and quested for any sense of stalking or seeking, the whisper of her name in any mind, any thread of magic.

Nothing. Yet.

She bent her head and reached for the magic. If those guys knew who she was, they'd already know who her friends were. What she needed were good, solid wards and guards.

She molded a spell that protected against fire and weapons, though she had to jigger it a little. She was pretty sure anyone bent on assault would use bullets instead of the blades and arrows the spell was originally designed to protect against. She shaped a ward that took ill-intent and turned it back on itself, flinging the energy of anger or aggression or harm back on the perpetrator. The meaner he was, the more reactive the ward.

As a rule, Amethyst wasn't into hurting people. But she'd make an exception if somebody decided to go after anyone she cared about.

A fan of warm light appeared on the patio beside her and the sliding glass door whisked open.

Melodie stepped out juggling a couple of plates. "Hey, what are you up to out here?"

Amethyst wrenched out of the magical ether. "Oh, I…" She realized what she must look like, standing in the middle of the backyard like some Druid priestess. "To be honest, I'm working some spells."

Melodie froze. The plates she held quivered. "Um, I hate to say this, Wiz, but the last spell I saw you work didn't come out too well."

Amethyst cringed. The party. The one where the little glamor of love she'd cast on Caramela sort of…well, *spread*. It had been pretty embarrassing for all involved.

"That was last summer. I didn't have as much practice then," she said. "Besides, wards and shields, I know. When you're a wizard, you get those down fast."

"Uh-huh." Melodie put a plate in her hands. "Why is that not reassuring?"

Amethyst sat in a patio chair. It rocked under her. "Sorry. I should've told you what I was doing, first. But I think I'd better do it anyway."

"Well, take a break and have some of my awesome, irresistible Death by Chocolate cake."

Amethyst smiled. "If only chocolate could solve problems as easily as it distracts from them." She inhaled the aroma and cut a bite.

Melodie plopped into her own chair. "Like someone wants to send you on an all-expense-paid trip to the Roswell Alien Autopsy facility?"

Something halfway between a choke and a laugh popped out. Then died. She hadn't thought about that— that someone wasn't as interested in hiring her as studying her.

"You don't think—"

"God, Wiz, I was kidding." Melodie's old nickname for her, when they were competing for top spot in their classes. Neither of them had realized then how appropriate the name really was. "Seriously, maybe whoever sent those guys really did just want to talk to you."

"You're forgetting about the *gun*, Mel."

"I know it looks bad—"

"Just a little."

"But did you ever think that whoever it was might be afraid of *you*? Or the guys they sent might've been. I *know* you—you're my best friend. But if I didn't, what you can do would scare the hell out of me. When I really stop to think about it, it *does* scare me, because I'm pretty sure magic is more than just making people fall in love with your pit bull and chasing off asshole party crashers."

Amethyst shook her head. "But if they're afraid of me, why risk pissing me off? Why not just approach very politely and offer enough money to stuff a mattress with? No. I think what they were doing was trying to get the upper hand. Scare me first, keep me off balance."

She didn't say anything about possibly messing up someone's plans for the petroglyphs. Maybe that's what the guys with the guns were all about: somebody registering their displeasure. Except if that was what was going on, you'd think they'd be more persistent about trying to intimidate her. The calm of the last couple of days was ominous.

She put down her uneaten cake and raked her hands through her hair. "What really worries me is what they might try to bring me in out of the cold."

Melodie swallowed hard enough to hear.

"Yeah," Amethyst said. "Now you know why I'm setting those protective spells."

"You know," Melodie said, "this secret identity stuff isn't nearly as cool as it is in the movies."

Amethyst made a rude noise. "If it was secret, I wouldn't be having problems right now."

Melodie gave an acknowledging grunt. "How many people have you told about yourself?"

"Exactly two."

"Three," Melodie corrected. "Tom knows, too."

Melodie didn't know that Talys was more than just her boyfriend. "Right," Amethyst said.

"Then how did these guys know you're a wizard?"

"Exactly what Tom and I were discussing." Amethyst made patterns in the icing of her cake. "And short of going out and saying, 'Here I am, take me,' I don't know how to find out."

"You have, you know, magical powers, right?"

"All the spells I know are pre-industrial, and anyway, magic is like every other force. You have to direct it. How will I find whoever's looking for me? They're going through third parties."

"So then yeah, let 'em catch you," Melodie said. "You're a wizard! Don't tell me you can't say some magic word to make locked doors spring open and yourself invisible. For all I know, you can do magical teleportation."

"I can. Don't look at me like that, because it's not easy, and you'd better know where you're going. Besides, you know as well as I do, they don't need to grab me. All they need is a good hacker on the payroll to make my life totally miserable."

Melodie poked at her cake. "What you need for a start is a good firewall for your data." She made a sound that might've been evil twin to a laugh. "Too bad you're not on speaking terms with Jas Harker. Think of what Magus Corporation could do for you right now."

Was Melodie psychic, or was it just Amethyst's guilty conscience?

"Uh-huh." Melodie's eyes narrowed.

"'Uh-huh' what?"

"You forget I have two teenaged stepdaughters, dear. I recognize that look of being caught in some hideous misdeed."

"Promise you won't yell."

"Better just tell me and get it over with."

Amethyst took a deep breath. "I went to see Jas."

Melodie's lips went to a thin line. "Jas, as in the

attempted rapist?"

Oh, crud. "I need to explain that."

Melodie took a bite of cake, chewed and swallowed. "Now, I want you to know, that was a shout I was swallowing. Because I have a feeling this is going to get a lot more complicated than I thought it was."

Here we go. "He's one too, Mel. A wizard."

"A wizard. Jesus Christ almighty God."

"Sorry. And—well, it wasn't exactly rape he tried to do."

"Not exactly. How reassuring."

She touched Melodie's hand. "When it happened, I was going to tell you the truth. About the magic and everything. I really was. Then you just assumed…well, about the rape, and it wasn't that far from what actually happened, and…"

Melodie waved a hand. "Judging from your subsequent opinion of the man, he obviously did something despicable."

Amethyst folded one arm over her middle. She did not want to go into the gruesome details. But Mel deserved to know.

"We kissed." She paused, wet her lips. "And he laid a binding on me. I couldn't do…anything. Not even think."

Melodie breathed a curse. "And you're actually speaking to him? How can you when he'd do—something like *that?*"

"I think he regrets what happened."

"Don't tell me you trust anything he says."

"Maybe some of it. Tom thinks he has a point,

anyway."

"At least you're taking Tom along with you to meetings with assault-prone ex-beaux. Good."

Amethyst waved her fork. "Why does everyone think I'm incapable of taking care of myself?"

"Because in your present state of duress, I think you'll do something desperate and dumb, like ask the suave Mr. Harker for help."

"I hadn't considered it." Not quite yet, anyway.

"Has it occurred to you that he's the one behind all this?"

Amethyst blew through her lips. "Come on, Mel. Why do you think I went to go see him?"

"So now you believe he isn't."

Streetlight scattered orange flecks and leaf shadows across the lawn. The distant party thumped away. A dog barked a couple of yards over.

"I don't know. I suppose he could be, but it just seems so…" She gestured vaguely. "Too baroque or something. And he was awfully convincing."

"He was last time, too, if I recall."

Sad but true. "In a different way, though. This time… He can't have just been playacting."

"You don't…" Melodie cut a careful bite. "That is, old feelings aren't coming into play, are they?"

"Please. Give me some credit."

Melodie looked up. "You fell hard for the man."

"Yeah, and took a hard fall afterward. I'm here to tell you, I didn't call him up because I missed him."

Melodie looked like she was choking on curiosity.

Amethyst sighed and waved a hand. "Yes, Jas is still charming. But he's also still a bastard. He'll have to do a lot more than serve my favorite tea and provide a little information before I'll change my mind about that."

Chapter 4.5 – Opposition

To: JPittsco@PI4U.com

From: ragman@ndns.net

Subject: Info packet

Dear Mr. Pitts:

You will receive today by private courier an envelope containing photographs, personal data and other relevant information. I am interested in creating public pressure on this person. After appropriate measures have been employed, please see that an invitation for contact is delivered. Enclosed as well is an advance check for your services.

HHR

To: ragman@ndns.net

From: JPittsco@PI4U.com

Subject: Info packet received

Dear Sir:

Got it. I can use the witchcraft angle. LMAO. I know just the people who will go for it. Should be able to get results fast. Thanks for the advance. I'll send weekly time and expense statements, as usual. Get in touch if there is anything else I can do.

Jim Pitts

CHAPTER 5

"I feel like the heroine of a slasher film, and a shadow with an upraised knife is gliding along the wall behind me," Amethyst said in a low voice, glancing across the store toward the register. Helen, the owner of the glass shop, was busy wrapping the glass she'd already selected.

"That," Talys said just as quietly, "is a thought to which you'd best not give energy. Concentrate instead on perpetuating a state of peace."

"Peace," she said. "Right."

She slid out a square of clear glass with green and blue flecks, like a fixed spray of confetti. It was fun. But Mr. Evans wasn't the sort to go for fun. He'd said he wanted something traditional, and that meant a window with nice, sober cathedrals in single clear colors. Maybe, if she wanted to try to push it, something textured. A hammered effect, or crinkled.

Talys shook his head—hard to say whether at her skepticism or the glass. He'd met Mr. Evans, too.

"Trust your power to protect you," he said quietly. "How many ordinary folk will be willing to persevere when confronted with it?"

"The ones who are just cocky enough to believe it's

like any other kind of power. If they throw enough money and influence at the problem, resistance will go away."

"Then they'll soon learn differently."

She shot him a look. "Ever hear of an arms race?"

He frowned. That said he'd been thinking along the same lines. She was grateful she had him as a spell transceiver. Not to mention a driver. Magic—especially the kind that worked on the senses, like spells of diversion, confusion—had to be constantly renewed, and it was damned hard to drive and keep it going. Wards were a little easier. At least with them, it was a matter of setting the magic into the object to be warded. Nevertheless, the ward had to be renewed periodically.

She sighed. For now it was just a matter of finding the right shade of blue glass. That was a problem she could actually do something about.

"Perhaps this one?" Talys said.

The glass was a deep, ultramarine blue. "Perfect. Why didn't I get you involved in the business sooner?"

"Determined to retain your independence," he said. "A trait common in the self-employed. Not to mention wizards."

She carried the blue glass to the register. "This should do it."

Helen wrapped that one as well and rang everything up. She took Amethyst's credit card and swiped it through the machine.

"It's not taking it. Do you want to try another?"

"That's strange." Amethyst put the card back in her wallet and offered her debit card.

Helen ran it and shook her head. "This one, too." She handed back the card. "There must be some kind of trouble with the network."

She had a bad feeling about this. Putting on a smile, she pulled out her checkbook. "I guess I'll have to resort to old-fashioned paper."

She did enough business here, Helen would probably put the merchandise on a tab, if it came to that.

Talys gathered up the glass, tucked it under one arm and opened the door for her.

"'Trouble with the network,'" Amethyst muttered. She pushed the 'unlock' button on the key fob and opened the back of the Subaru. "This is just a little too coincidental for comfort."

He arranged the glass in the plastic crate she kept in the back of the car for that purpose. "Mmm. Nevertheless, a simple explanation remains possible."

"You're just saying that to make me feel better. I'm still checking it out when we get home."

She opened the car door and rubbed her eyes. Ward. Distraction. Even with Talys' concentration and direction, the actual power came from her. And it got tiring. Like being somewhere where the wind blew all the time, or in a house where the TV was never turned off: a constant, low-level demand on her resources.

She dropped into the passenger seat. No whisper of her name came into her mind on the way home, thank God and the magic for small favors.

Talys made the left onto Flint, her street. The car purred up the hill, passing familiar houses—flat-roofed, pueblo-style homes, and a few with inexplicable Swiss chalet gables and diamond mullion windows. (She'd never been able to guess what the developer had been thinking with those. Swiss chalets? In Albuquerque?) Past the house with the pop-up trailer in the driveway that had never, in the five years she'd lived in the neighborhood, been camping. That awful rental house's barren front yard and the primered old pickup parked on the dirt.

A lot more cars were parked on the street than usual. Someone must be having a party. They topped the little hill and Amethyst's house came into view.

She blinked. "What's going on?"

The sidewalk was filled with people. No, not just people—people carrying signs, like protestors. What could there possibly be to protest on a working-class neighborhood street?

Talys growled, actually growled, like an animal. "They're in front of your house."

They were. Men in conservative haircuts, women in below-the-knee skirts, maybe a dozen of them. She couldn't read the signs, but she saw a cross on one. Gary Griego, his girlfriend, Emily, and Gary's dad stood in their yard next door, staring. Heather Purdy, the neighbor on the other side, was too.

Talys didn't slow to turn into the driveway. Gary waved, and his dad, Oscar, walked toward the sidewalk as if to meet them. Heather, on the other hand, went bouncing out into the street waving her arms as if booty shorts and a low-cut tank top possessed the literal ability to stop traffic.

He tried to swerve around her, but Heather just kept coming. Of course Talys had to put on the brakes then.

She tapped on the window with bubblegum-pink fingernails. "Tom! Amethyst! What's going on? Who are all these *people?*"

"That's her!" A woman pointed at the car. "The one in the picture Brother James showed us. *Witch!*" she screeched, still pointing at the car—at Amethyst.

"*What?*" Amethyst gasped.

Talys cursed. She felt like she stood in the middle of an explosion. But the explosion was inside her.

"They can't—!" she stammered.

"Heather!" Talys bellowed. "*Get back!*"

He almost never shouted like that. It made the hair on Amethyst's nape go up.

Heather, still babbling, didn't get back.

Amethyst fumbled with her purse. Where the hell was her phone? She damn sure couldn't magically whisk the car out of the middle of this crowd.

The people who'd been on the sidewalk surrounded the car now, a gabble of voices, shouts.

A man pressed a cross to the window. "The power of the Lord will drive out evil from our midst!"

"Witch!" a woman screeched. "We don't want you in this town!"

"Devil worshipper!" another yelled.

"But I'm Catholic!" Amethyst said.

A young man with a shock of blond hair pressed his phone to the window. "Hey, witch. Show us some magic."

A sign slapped the windshield: *The face of the Lord is*

against them that do evil. Something—only a fist, hopefully—thumped the car.

Heather had disappeared somewhere behind the crowd.

Amethyst's mouth tasted like metal. Her hands shook on the touchscreen of her phone. *How am I going to get us out of this?*

She didn't realize she'd said it aloud until Talys said, "Don't do anything. I shall take care of it."

He shoved the door open. Another young man in a button-collar shirt who'd been shouting through the window staggered back, off balance. Talys stood up like Godzilla rising out of Tokyo Bay. The women hurried back to the sidewalk. The men stood their ground.

Talys grabbed the nearest by his collar and shoved. The guy went down hard on his butt in the street.

"Get out of my way," Talys snarled, "or I shall be happy to deal with all of you."

"Devil!" one of the women shrieked from the sidewalk.

Through the windshield, she saw him give a thin smile and a slight, mocking bow. "At your service." Dressed all in black, with his sunglasses and black ponytail, he certainly looked the part.

A man fell to his knees and started praying. Two more joined him. The others moved to stand in front of the women.

Amethyst finally managed to punch in 9-1-1 on her phone. "There's a bunch of people in front of my house. They're all around my car," she babbled to the dispatcher.

"We can't move, we can't get to the house."

"Tell us how it feels to confront the might of the Lord," the blond guy said. His phone was still pressed to the window.

Amethyst looked at it. Whoever was on the other end watching the streaming video would be looking at a blank screen about now. All of a sudden, she could think again, breathe again, as if the magic had burned out panic. The operator on the phone wanted the address.

"10368 Flint Avenue, Northeast." Her voice wasn't shaking now.

Talys stalked around the front of the car. The man pocketed his phone and scrambled backward. On her own phone, the operator was telling Amethyst to stay on the line.

Talys climbed back into the car, put it in reverse.

"They've backed off," Amethyst told the operator. "But they're still there—still in front of my house."

No response.

"Hello?"

Nothing. She dialed again. Still nothing, not even a fast busy or a recording. "Shit."

Talys swung into the driveway. The people all stood in a knot on the sidewalk, most of them praying. Much less unnerving than shouting. The neighbors were nowhere in sight. The garage door trundled open (no one would know she didn't have a garage door opener) and shut behind them.

She dropped her phone back in her purse. "My phone dropped the call, but I think they heard the address."

Talys' lips went to a thin, hard line. He swung the car door open. "Try your call again inside. In the meantime, however, I would suggest you set some magic upon the windows to prevent breakage. And upon the roof to discourage fire."

"*Fire?* They can't…wouldn't…"

He climbed out of the car. Grabbing her purse, she scrambled out after him. She was shaking again.

He opened the door to the laundry room and ushered her in ahead of him. "Trust me, love. I have seen this sort of thing before."

No doubt. Screaming peasants, pitchforks, torches and all. Maybe even a witch-burning or two.

"But Talys. This is the United States." That hadn't stopped the witch-burners. "It's the twenty-first century."

"And those people have been inflamed beyond all reason. When hate and fear rule, terrible things are done."

"Inflamed. By who? *Why?*"

She hurried into the house. Talys strode into the living room, apparently securing the rest of the house. Amethyst eyed the living room window like a despot prepared for assassination. The magic she used on her stained glass windows to prevent breakage would work there just as well. With the alley behind the house, she'd have to do the back windows, too.

Talys stood on the tiled square by the front door, looking down at something. "Amethyst," he said.

"Hang on." She touched the magic, the ether that surrounded the physical world like a fiery, heaving sea, that ran through it like lava through the veins of the earth. It mapped the shape of her thoughts, molded itself to her will. When she was in it, working it like this, she could see it. Now it coated the windows with a vibrant electric blue with yellow overtones, shimmering, alive.

As it had in the car, the magic did something to her, as well. A sense of power burned away fear, desperation. She was no frightened woman terrorized by fanatics. She was a wizard, and damned if she'd hide, trapped in her own house.

The phone rang, the landline she was still dithering about cancelling. Looked like it was a good thing she hadn't. She strode back into the kitchen, snatched it up.

"This is Oscar, next door. You all right? Should I call the cops?"

Oscar was a good, solid guy.

"I already called them, thanks," Amethyst said. "And Tom's enough to make them think twice." She hoped.

"Okay, but who—?"

The line went dead.

She just held the phone for a minute. Punched the "talk" button a couple of times. She could, of course, try the corded phone in the bedroom. But what was the point? Setting it down on the countertop, she turned to face Talys.

He held out an envelope. Plain. White. Her name typed across it. No address.

She clenched her fists. "What the hell is that?"

"It appeared to have been pushed under the door. I suspect," he said, "it may go some distance toward explaining today's inconveniences."

Sometimes Talys had a truly British way of understating matters. She snatched the envelope and ripped it open.

Ms. Rey, the letter within read. It, too, was typed. Problems can be solved. You will be contacted soon.

"Contacted! What, are they going to lob a rock with a note tied to it through my living room window?" She said something foul, wadded up the letter and hurled it at the wall. "Problems! *Problems!*" She hugged her arms, shivering. "This—this is blackmail! Terrorism! 'Cooperate, or else—'" She ground her teeth, hanging by her fingernails onto the impulse to blast something with magic.

Talys came and put his arms around her. He didn't speak, but comfort and ease came flowing into her. She wrapped her arms around him and squeezed.

"I want the sonofabitch behind that note," she said. "And when I've got him—"

She didn't want to think about what she'd do.

CHAPTER 6

Amethyst folded her arms and stared at Talys across the roof of the car. "So what's the plan?"

"Get in, love," he said, his voice echoing in the dusty dimness of the garage. "I'll tell you as we drive."

"And the barbarians in front of the house? What about them?"

Talys raised a brow. "Are you attempting to tell me that you are wholly without means of coping with such an annoyance?" He got into the car.

Amethyst just clenched her fists. Finally, she took a deep breath and dropped into the passenger seat. "I'm sorry." She stared out the windshield at the dim garage. "I'm scared."

Talys laid the backs of his fingers on her cheek. "I know you are. But allow me to suggest that the best way to avoid being frightened is to face your fear."

"Easy for you to say."

"Because it is true. I might also remind you that you're scarcely defenseless. Even if you decline to harm your enemies."

She sighed. "I was going to whine about stuff like this happening to me, but you're not going to let me, are you?"

"Have I ever?"

She snarled at him, ran through the spells in her mind and settled on a solid, boring camouflage spell.

"Okay," she said. "Let's do it."

She called magic that had once let some tribe creep past enemy raiders.

The garage door rolled open. The protesters still walked up and down the sidewalk with their signs. A couple of young men stood at the edge of the driveway. Amethyst narrowed her eyes and sent heat into the concrete under their feet. Not a lot, just enough to get uncomfortable after a moment. One guy picked up his foot, rubbed it through his shoe and moved away. His friend followed.

Talys backed down the driveway and into the street. It was eerie, riding in a car that no one even glanced at. She kept waiting for the protesters to turn, point and start shouting again. If another car came along the street, she'd have to kill its engine to keep it from running into them. *If* she could find any spells that would affect the internal combustion engine. There weren't very many wizards left by the twentieth century to have created such spells.

Halfway down Flint, and the protesters disappeared behind the curve of the hill.

Amethyst let her head drop back. "Okay, let's hear how we're going to find whoever sicced the Fundamentalists from Hell on me."

"The note will tell us." Talys made a left onto Eubank. "Such things hold—how shall I describe it?— vibrations, spoor, so to speak, of the one who wrote and held it." He gave a smile that showed a lot of teeth. "It should lead us to her—or him—quite handily."

A nervous flutter started in her middle. She pulled the crumpled letter out of her purse and held it between both hands. A jumble of impressions came through her fingers: a vague flurry of everyone who had touched it, a stronger impression of malicious purpose.

"Do you feel the one who wrote it?" Talys said. "Use a finding spell to trace it back."

She searched her mind and found a spell that wrapped itself around her and pulled.

"Yow." Holding the letter, she closed her eyes.

Following a magical homing beacon was a strange experience. No little blinking dot on a GPS screen here. If anything, it was more like being a fish on a line, towed forward no matter what lay between. She sat back, followed the tug and let Talys worry about traffic and the best streets to take.

"More and more to the right," she said.

Talys made an acknowledging noise.

She opened her eyes. An apartment parking lot barricaded with a tall, steel-barred fence slid by on the left. On the right, a fourplex gave way to little old homes with cracked stucco and security-screened front doors. A little boy, immaculately dressed in white shirt, pressed slacks and small dress shoes, pedaled a Big Wheel along the sidewalk. A woman in a neat blouse and skirt walked from a faded car to one of the front doors.

"Where are we?" Amethyst asked.

"Between the fairgrounds and the air force base. The War Zone, as I believe it is sometimes called. Kindly attend to your wards."

From what she saw, the neighborhood only looked poor. "It's mostly only bad at night."

"Nevertheless," he said, and made a right.

Security bars seemed to be the preferred window treatment, so Talys' concern probably wasn't unjustified. An awful lot of vehicles were parked in front yards under the watchful eyes of those windows, too. What if the letter was leading them toward some meth-head in an abandoned house?

A left. Another left, then a right, and they were into a commercial area. Slightly seedy strip malls interspersed with houses converted to offices or retail fronts lined the street. Barred windows were the norm here, as well.

That tugging feeling grew stronger. It almost felt like someone was trying to pull the letter from her hands.

"Hang on," she said. "We're almost—" The pull was directly to the right. Her right ear rang, and something tickled at her right cheek. "Here. Pull in."

Talys pulled into a tiny parking lot that had nearly decomposed into gravel. The house it fronted had been divided into a duplex which was now two commercial spaces. The one on the left bore a hand-painted sign that read in big, blue block letters on white, *Maria's Salon*. Underneath, pink script read: *Hair Nails Pedicures*. The small sign over the door on the right hand unit bore only a name: *James Pitts, LLC*.

Presumably a professional of some kind. The question was, what kind? And exactly how professional could he be?

Talys' lips twisted in distaste. "I still feel you should allow me to handle this."

She had a strong desire to do just that. "Maybe."

She slipped the letter into her purse and shrugged the purse strap over her shoulder. She should feel pretty much invulnerable, especially with Talys backing her up. But 29 years of non-wizard habit was hard to overcome.

"Do I have the guard magic right?"

He turned his head as if catching a scent. "Very little can touch us through that. Only a wizard stronger."

"Thanks a lot, Talys," she said. "Let's hope Mr. Pitts isn't that."

Out of the car then and up the cracked cement steps to the door, Talys right behind her like a big shadow in black slacks and polo shirt. That gave her enough courage to open the door.

A bell jingled. It was dim and cool inside and had the vague, sweetish smell of old houses. A couple of square, patched vinyl chairs sat in the dimness beside a small table scattered with magazines and sections of newspaper. A narrow door led into another room where a man sat behind an enormous desk.

"Hi," he said, got up and came around the desk to the office door. He was tall, with a shock of bristly, reddish-blond hair and close-set, bright blue eyes in a long face. "Can I help you?"

Amethyst's mouth tasted like she'd been chewing on the contents of her change purse.

"I sure hope so." She put on a smile. "I'm Amethyst Rey."

His face went slack for a moment. Then his eyes flicked from her to Talys. "I'm sorry. Did we have an appointment today?"

"No-o-o-o," she said. "I don't think so."

He hesitated. Probably deciding the best tack to take.

"Ahm—yes," he said. "Come in." He motioned them into his office. "By the way, I'm Jim Pitts."

Amethyst lowered herself into a chair in front of his desk. The chair looked like a derelict from the Seventies, upholstered with threadbare, coarse-woven brown-and-orange fabric. A CRT and computer keyboard perched on one corner of the desk. A little portable tube TV sat on a stand behind it. As he had in Jas' office, Talys remained standing behind her.

Mr. Pitts' eyes flicked again. "You're welcome to sit down, sir."

Talys might've been carved in stone.

"Usually," Amethyst said, "he prefers to stand."

A muscle twitched in Pitts' cheek, but he kept the mild, pleasant expression on his face. "Coffee?"

"No thanks, Mr. Pitts." *Here goes.* "I'd rather talk about the people you sent to harass me."

"Now, Ms. Rey, really—"

She pulled out the letter in its envelope, slapped it on his desk. "This came from you."

He wet his lips. "That's quite an accusation."

"But here we are. How do you think that happened?"

He shrugged. "You looked me up on the web? Maybe somebody gave you a referral."

"Yeah, like the lunatics in front of my house who

wave signs and scream at me."

He shook his head and *tsked*. "Sounds like you need a private investigator. You came to the right place." He rummaged in a drawer. "Would you like a schedule of fees?"

Behind her, Talys said, "She'd like the answer to her question."

Pitts looked up at him. "That sounds threatening. I'm sure you didn't mean it like that."

The hair on Amethyst's neck prickled. "Things have not been going well lately. It seems somebody decided to take a bulldozer to my life, and we're not happy about it."

He snorted. "Come on, Ms. Rey. Things don't just happen to people. People make their own problems."

And you're just the guy to make them happen. "I'm sure you know that harassment is illegal. If you won't help me, I guess I'll to have to call the licensing board and the police."

His smile this time was wide and toothy. He shoved the phone toward her. "Here you go. Need the numbers?"

She stood. The magic seethed around her, molding her skin like a campfire's heat on a cold night. "Those fanatics believe in witches, Mr. Pitts. Do you?"

He threw back his head and laughed, a short, sharp bark.

He'd arranged everything that happened today, and now he had the *cojones* to laugh?

She took in the magic and let a little seep into the visible light spectrum. Shadows shifted over the walls. The florescent light overhead sputtered and went out.

Pitts snapped forward in his chair. "What the hell is going on?"

Talys stood behind her, unmoving, amping up her protective magic.

She could play dumb, too. "That's what I've been trying to find out."

Pitts shoved to his feet. Light and shadow moved across his face; soft green and blue and violet. A faint smell of ozone hung in the air.

"Get the hell out of here." His hands, big, with scabs on the knuckles, shook. "Get out!"

Power moved through her like liquor, just as intoxicating. "I'll be happy to, just as soon as I find out who hired you to harass me."

"I don't give a rat's ass what you want." He snatched up the phone. "You wanna talk to the cops, baby? Just stick around." He started punching in numbers. "You and Tonto there are in *my* office threatening *me*, and let me tell you, that ain't harassment, that's assault."

A call on the phone? Oh, please. That was way too easy. "Come on, Mr. Pitts. I won't even say who told me."

He jabbed the disconnect button a few times—no surprise there, since he wouldn't hear a dialtone. He slammed down the handset and came around the desk. Talys moved and was suddenly between them, a black-clad wall.

"I won't tell you shit," Pitts said. "You keep fucking with me and you'll find your life a whole lot damn harder than it is now."

That was, of course, an empty threat, since it was up

to her what—if anything—he'd be able to do after this interview. Really, someone as angry as he was could pop a blood vessel and end up—

Amethyst stiffened. Oh God. What was she thinking?

"No." She faltered backward, toward the door. Talys cast her a fast, questioning look. She swallowed hard, steadied herself. She had to finish this. "Don't threaten me, and don't screw with me. You tell whoever hired you that."

She snapped a thought into the air. Every light in the place blazed on, a radio blared, the TV on its little scarred table popped on, squawking, his computer dinged, his mobile phone weebled a frantic little tune. She kicked up the voltage a little more. Sparks spat and everything fell silent. Blue smoke and stink of burning wires curled into the air.

She walked out the door.

Talys came out about the time she reached the car. She sent the office door slamming behind him. The bell gave a distressed jingle she heard all the way outside.

He stalked down the steps without so much as glancing back. "Amethyst! What are you doing?"

She opened the car door. "Going home. I've had all of this I can stomach."

He caught the edge of the door. "Are you mad? After what this blackguard has done?"

He said 'blackguard' like the vile insult it once must've been.

"Let go of the door, Talys. I'm not going to stay here and do exactly what he would in my place. *I won't be that kind of person.*"

His hand moved to her shoulder. "No. But I shall finish this. This cannot be allowed to continue."

How easy that would be. Talys wouldn't even tell her what he'd done unless she asked. Which of course she wouldn't.

"So not only would I be a bully, I'd be a bully and a coward, too gutless to do my own dirty work. No, we're getting out of here with our virtue intact."

His fingers tightened. "You do know, of course, it won't end here."

Sighing, she slid into the seat. "I know. And I have a feeling that when whoever's doing this ups the stakes, I'm not going to like myself much anymore."

CHAPTER 7

Ah, yes. The stakes. Her bank accounts. A phone that actually provided contact with the outside world. Her *life*, for godsake, since possible new commissions were likely getting one of those 'This number has been disconnected' messages.

Her current clients were probably listening to the same message and thinking about the progress payments they'd made, wondering if they'd ever see the window they'd paid for. It would *not* look good to contact them and say, 'So sorry, I'm afraid I'm having phone problems. That's why I'm talking to you through an image in your morning coffee.'

No. Definitely not.

Amethyst peeked out the front blinds. A half-dozen or so zealots rotated duty in front of the house. Still. They'd taken a break overnight, but shown up bright and early this morning.

"This is insane," she said and let the blinds snap back into place. "What do these people think they're doing? What's the *point?*"

Talys sat with his bare feet on the coffee table and a printed newspaper open in front of him. The Internet was out, too. She wondered where he'd gotten the paper, since she certainly hadn't ventured outside to find one.

"The point is, I'd wager...what is the term?... to *soften you up*," he said. "Give you time to consider how difficult things have been made for you, and how much more difficult they might yet become." He cocked his head as if considering. "I shan't trouble you more by sharing what occurs to me."

"How thoughtful of you," she said. She shook her head, trying to shake out some pretty bad thoughts of her own. "So what I want to know is, are these people for real? Maybe they're actors hired by that guy Pitts. I can't believe people now would actually do stuff like this."

Talys rattled the newspaper. "You haven't been paying attention to the news, then, love. I'm afraid this isn't that great a leap from burning popular children's books and staging ugly marches at soldiers' funerals."

"Great." She folded her arms and scowled. "So no matter how obnoxious and irritating they are, that means they actually believe in what they're doing."

"It would appear so," he said. "Unlike you, I might add."

She bristled. "You want me to do something? Fine." She turned and marched for the front door.

Oscar Griego from next door, wearing an old-fashioned sleeveless undershirt and hitching up his pants, beat her to the protestors. A faded tattoo showed through the wiry white hairs on his forearm. Another showed on a still-impressive bicep. The little group in front of her house clustered together and fell back.

"Hey," he shouted at them. "What's your problem?"

A tall older man with cold, grey, deep-set eyes pushed forward. "This woman is a witch, did you know that?"

Oscar faced the man—lay leader, preacher, whatever—like a scarred old pit bull squaring off against a German Shepherd dog. And you just knew the Shepherd didn't stand a chance.

"What you doing here, anyway?" Oscar said. "You like picking on ladies? That the kind of fella you are?" He turned and caught sight of Amethyst. "Where's that boyfriend of yours? If I was him, I'd be down here kicking some ass." He didn't bother lowering his voice.

Why did the cavalry that showed up all seem to be from Custer's regiment, ready to piss off a whole tribe of well-armed Indians?

"You're all *loco en cabeza.*" Oscar twirled a finger by one temple. "You think she flies around on a broomstick? *Brujas!* Witches!" He blew through his lips in disgust, turned his back on them and stalked over to Amethyst. "I called the cops on 'em yesterday," he said to her. "But you see what we pay taxes for? Nobody shows up!"

A bad feeling crawled through her belly. "I thought I read somewhere it's illegal to picket in residential areas."

"If it isn't, it should be. Who put the wild hair up their tight butts, anyway?" Sometimes Oscar's Army career really showed.

"That's what I was coming out here to find out," Amethyst said.

A warm, firm hand fell on Amethyst's shoulder. "Oscar," Talys said behind her. "Everything under control here?"

"Hey, Tomás," Oscar said. "Why you letting a girl do a man's job? Let's chew the fat with God's chosen there. Maybe talk some sense into them, heh?"

The air was positively drenched in testosterone. "Guys—" Amethyst started.

Neither paid any attention to her. Talys shook Oscar's hand and the two men turned to face the protestors.

The women sifted out the back of the group, leaving a knot of five or six men facing Talys and Oscar. The shouting started.

The women jittered farther away. Oscar jabbed the tall guy in the chest with a finger, then all of a sudden, they were shoving back and forth. Talys got between Oscar and the tall man. Gary, Oscar's son, came outside, a hovering presence. A door banged to the left.

"Hey!" a woman's shrill voice shouted.

Amethyst turned. Heather, well-filled-out tank top, low-rise shorts and all. Could this get any worse?

"What's goin' on here?" Heather demanded. "I'm tellin' ya, y'all better just go on home, because I've called the police."

Yes. As a matter of fact, they could get worse. The tall man shouted back at Talys. What with all the other shouting going on, it was hard to hear what he was saying, but it sounded Biblical. Oscar was trying to get around Talys to have another go. Angela, Oscar's wife, crossed the lawn like a frigate under full sail, shouting in Spanish.

Heather's drawl got really thick when she was mad, and with the old guy toe-to-toe with Talys, who she had a thing for, she was mad. Angela Griego's calling down of the wrath of God in Gatling-gun Spanish was easier to understand.

Amethyst waded into the fray. "Come on, you guys. These bozos aren't worth it. Let 'em stand out here and sunburn."

Heather pinned down the women. "You should be ashamed of yourselves. Just ashamed! People like you wear bedsheets where I come from. And where I come from, we don't take too kindly to that sort messing with our friends!"

Amethyst looked up. It was early in the day for thunderstorms, but a few clouds were already piling over the mountains, like puppies out of a basket.

So how about a nice bolt of lightning? Maybe to the water tank the next block over. That shouldn't hurt anybody, and lightning was known to travel as far as ten miles...

She touched the magic. It was all flows and swirls and eddies, the reflection and source of everything alive, of the churn of air and water, the slow grind of the earth. It ran over her like current through a computer chip, racing along pathways within her, melding with her nerve impulses, molding the shape of her thoughts and carrying them outward into the world. Talys whipped around.

The lightning struck, a finger of blinding white. Thunder crashed an eyeblink later. A young girl in the group squealed and flinched. Even the men started and faltered. Lightning struck again, again, *crack! crack!* Talys stepped away from his opponent and gripped her arm.

The protestors muttered and the girl whined, "Mom, did we make God mad? I don't like this!"

At least the kid had a conscience.

"I don't either," Amethyst said. "Come on, Tom. Let's go inside before we get hit."

And just like that, Heather was hurrying back to her house, Oscar and Angela to theirs. Gary had already disappeared. The protesters milled, then scattered for their cars.

Bang! the thunder went again. *Okay, now,* she thought to the magic. *Thank you very much, but that's enough.*

Talys towed her up the walk and hustled her through the door. Thunder cracked again, rattling the windows.

"Quiet down, quiet down," she muttered to it, then to Talys, "How do I stop it?"

He took her hands, folded them to his chest. "Like this…"

The magic took a different shape, boiling and jostling up within her, then sliding down, up and down, a generator churning but not discharging. That prickling sense of…of purpose, of attraction faded, but the boiling seethe didn't. Of course not, because it was in her, too, not just in those clouds over the mountains.

She looked up at Talys. "That was me? That was coming from *me?*" The last word squeaked.

"Came through you, rather. Your emotions gave it rather more potency, however. Lightning, love…" He shook his head. "Perilous. Weather is a chaotic system, easily influenced. Not such a simple matter to control."

He made it sound like a teenaged girl. "I thought

storms and lightning were the traditional purview of wizards," she said.

"Certainly. Although they frequently dealt with the effects for years afterward."

She pulled her hands from his, dropped onto the sofa and held her head. "God."

The cushion beside her dipped with his weight. "Amethyst. For the moment, the situation with these people is an annoyance." She made a rude noise, but he went on, "Should it become more than an annoyance, should it become threatening in any fashion, I *will* take action."

She braced her hands on the sofa cushions. "Why are you telling me this?"

He had the sunglasses off, and his eyes were as cold and hard as metal. "Because your restraint borders on the unreasonable."

"So what if it is?" she said. "*What bloody damn difference* does it make, Talys?"

"It makes a difference because you will not be left to yourself. If some ill befalls you—"

"You're left vulnerable," she broke in. "I know."

He regarded her silently a moment. "I was going to say, you won't approve of my subsequent actions. Why are you so certain my concern is only for myself?"

"Because you won't leave me to *myself!* You won't let me deal with this the way I feel I need to."

"When your preferred tactic is to hope that ignoring the problem will make it go away?"

She shoved to her feet. "Don't tell me that, Talys. I

went out there. I was going to talk to them. What do you expect me to do?"

He just gave her another of those stares. "Use your power. Take control of your situation."

She snapped a curse and turned away.

He put a hand to his head, a frustrated, human gesture. "I wish you had joy in the magic. The sense of possibility, of freedom, of creation. Why do you see it only as a burden?"

She took three deep breaths, swallowed the wad of emotion in her throat. "I-I'm afraid I'll do wrong. I'm afraid I'll hurt someone."

His brows made a perplexed kink. "Magic won't change who you are."

"You don't understand! I *like* this power. I like how it makes me feel. I can do whatever I want. I can make those people out there disappear. Forever. I can make their cars blow up. Close their hate-spewing mouths. Rip every thought out of their heads and leave them drooling—"

Talys had been trying to interrupt her. He took her hand, drew her back down on the couch. "Hush, love. Hush. I do understand. I was in your mind for a time, remember?"

She shook her head. "All the wizards I've seen—the ones I learned those spells from—they're the same. Heartless. Arrogant. Like Jas, what he did to me. He wanted me tame, to use my power, and he didn't care about *me*. About what I wanted. What I felt."

"Yet he seems to rue that decision."

"You're defending him?"

"I'm attempting to make you understand that wizards are subject to the same frailties as other mortals. The same frailties, and the same nobilities. You've met but a handful of wizards, love. You've yet to realize that they can be equally great and good, as mean and vicious."

"You told me wizards are contentious. In the beginning, you warned me—"

"Yes. And I warn you still. Did your mother not warn you when you were a child? Take no gifts from strangers. And yet as some ordinary mortals can be evil, are you evil?"

"But I'm not an ordinary mortal," she said. "How long will it take 'til I'm like the wizards I've met, Talys? A year? Ten years? A century?"

He smoothed her hair. "When I chose you to bond with, it was because of your youth. I knew you couldn't be the predator that had devoured so many others. But I've always been particular about the wizards I choose to partner with. I've known human-kind long and long. I know what mortals ordinary and otherwise are capable of. And I refuse to increase the power of any who might do harm."

That stopped her. The choking distress ebbed, the fear that one thing larger and more powerful than she— magic—would consume her.

She sighed and leaned against him. "So," she said. "Short of turning them into horned toads, how do we get those people off my sidewalk?" She rubbed her temples. "How am I going to unlock my life?"

"You are capable of dealing with some of these

difficulties without magic," he said.

"Sure I am. If I wanted to hack the phone company and the bank. I have enough trouble already, thanks. Plus it's been a long time since I hacked anything. Meanwhile, computer security has come a long way."

She tugged at her hair. If only she knew how to put magic together with computers, all her problems might be solved. If only there were someone who...

Damn. She shoved herself back into the cushions and bit her lip. Damn, damn.

"I can't be that desperate."

Talys, for all his sensitivity to her, looked confused. "Pardon?"

Well...yes, she could be that desperate. Although maybe it was more acceptable to think of it as simple pragmatism. A much more sensible thing to do than to go around tossing magic like balloons full of fresh, slurpy cow manure.

"Ugh," she said.

"'Ugh'?"

She pushed off the sofa, marched into the kitchen and dug her phone out of her purse. She thumbed it on automatically, which was stupid since it didn't work. She stuffed it back into her purse. Fortunately, wizards didn't have to go over the local phone network. For that matter, she could probably get along reasonably well without electricity, too, although keeping the refrigerator running could get old fast. Water might be more problematic, if that got shut off, too.

Talys appeared in the doorway, filling it with black-clad brown muscle. "Tell me," he said on a sigh.

"I have to see Jas. He's the only thing I can think of that won't just be a Band-Aid on this whole mess."

Talys' brows shot up. "No, indeed. But at what cost?"

Amethyst ran a hand down her face. "For one, Melodie will be sure to chew me out good."

He quirked a smile. "I was thinking more on the order of what payment Mr. Harker will wish to extract."

No kidding. "Then I'll just have to remind him exactly what he owes me, won't I?"

CHAPTER 8

Amethyst had just about all she could stand of people yelling at her. If nothing else, magic at least let her avoid that unpleasantness. Taking Talys' hand, she zapped the two of them to their destination.

The green glass curtainwall of the Magus Building blinked in, replacing the living room's closed blinds. A wavery reflection in the glass showed Amethyst her own image, a thin, dark-haired woman holding hands with a big, Native American man in Special Ops black. Behind them stretched a kaleidoscope image of parking lot, cars and trees.

She waited for Talys to tell her they still had other options, she could apply her own resources to the problem—problems, plural—etc. But he didn't say anything. Damn. She really wished he wouldn't trust her assessment of the situation so completely. Or maybe his own assessment coincided. Damn, twice.

Still holding Talys' hand, she turned and marched for the front doors.

This was twice in one week now she'd pushed open these tall, green glass doors. It wasn't a good feeling. It felt craven and crawling and degrading.

Then again, Talys wasn't holding her by the shoulders and saying, 'Are you crazy?', so the alternative had to be worse. Or maybe it was just her pride talking. How many women wanted to reopen a relationship with their devious, conniving, ex-almost-sort-of gentleman friends?

Well, maybe the ones who enjoyed the adrenaline rush.

The fountain's splash and burble echoed across the lobby. The tap of their footsteps on the river-pebble floor laced between.

This time security sent them right up. Sylvia, the receptionist at the top-floor desk, recognized Amethyst and greeted her with a smile, eyed Talys appreciatively and escorted them to Jas' office.

Jas rose and came around his desk to greet them, hand extended, with that eye-crinkling smile of his. Damn him. She wanted to jam her hands in her jeans pockets, but unfortunately, that wasn't the best way to begin a plea. So she shook his hand and took the chair he offered. He didn't offer to shake Talys' hand this time, but Talys did deign to sit. The sunglasses, however, remained on.

Tea and sandwiches were waiting on the table. Jas poured.

"Help yourselves," he said.

Amethyst took a sandwich and offered one to Talys. He held up a hand and shook his head. Apparently there were limits to his graciousness.

"I notice you took the express this time," Jas said, leaning back in his chair and comfortably crossing an ankle over one knee.

"The—? Oh. Zapping here. How did you know?"

"I felt the pulse of magic. You should've told me. I'd've let down my defenses for you to come to my office."

Amethyst sipped tea. It tasted of jasmine and rosehips this time. "It seemed presumptuous."

That was a perfect opportunity for gloating. Fortunately, even if he *was* a devious conniver, Jas was too gentlemanly to gloat. In fact, he was acting positively Japanese, taking a moment to sip tea and take a bite of sandwich.

"You mentioned having a problem," he said. "I presume what we discussed the other day has taken a turn for the worse."

"Um…yes. I guess 'worse' might about cover it."

She looked down into her tea. Little ripples fled outward across the surface, bounced against the gold-rimmed edges and shivered back in again.

"Subtle little disasters?" he asked. "Commissions inexplicably going south, unfounded rumors, that sort of thing?"

It wasn't remotely funny, but a laugh popped out. "Not so subtle, and the rumors are uncomfortably founded on truth." She replaced her teacup on the table. "It doesn't look like there's magic behind it. As far as I can tell, it's all good, old-fashioned undue influence. I can treat the symptoms." If she wanted to be unscrupulous. "But I don't think I'll be hassle-free until I get to whoever's causing them." She braced herself and plowed on. "The most effective strategy would be to track this person back through the datastream and let them know *I* can reach *them*, too." She folded her hands and wet her lips. "But I don't have the resources to do that. Or the knowledge."

"How far has it gone?" Jas said.

"Well, the check I wrote to my glass supplier should be bouncing any time now, and I expect them to start holding witch burnings in effigy on the front lawn by this weekend, at the latest."

"On what front lawn?"

"Mine."

He laughed, then stopped and said, "You are joking, aren't you?"

"I wish."

A frown replaced the grin. It wasn't an expression she'd seen often on Jas' face. It wasn't the sort of expression one wanted to see on a wizard's face, either.

"What have you done to remedy this?" he said.

Talys turned his head to look at her as well. Waiting to hear what she would say? Or warning her? With that stony expression, she couldn't begin to guess.

"I tried yesterday to find out who's behind it," she said.

Jas raised his brows. "And?"

She gave a stiff shrug. "My leads declined to oblige me."

He gave a disbelieving laugh. "You're a wizard, Amethyst. They can't decline to oblige you."

This was the root of the whole problem that had turned a promising romance into something found under the plastic trashbag at the bottom of a garbage can at the end of a summer week.

"Well, yes, actually they can. I asked, they refused to answer, and I am not about to begin using magical thumbscrews or thought scans or whatever on innocent civilians."

One of Talys' brows twitched. Granted—one of those civilians hadn't been all that innocent.

"If I may be blunt," Jas said, "you'd rather swallow your pride and come to me for help."

And here she'd thought he was too much the gentleman to mention it.

"That's about the size of it." She shoved her chair back and made to stand. "I should've known—"

"Amethyst, wait." He reached across the table, caught her wrist. Talys stirred aggressively and he let go again.

She made it the rest of the way to her feet. "Why? So you can sit there and whittle me down to size?"

Talys still sat between them, hands on knees, and as best as she could tell through the sunglasses, keeping an eye on Jas.

Jas was perched on the edge of his chair as if to spring up. Glancing at Talys, he stayed put. "That wasn't what I meant to do."

"Then what did you mean, Jas?"

He pressed his eyes with thumb and forefinger. "Amethyst, please. Sit down. I can't talk while you look like you might blast me through my windows, chair and all. Please."

Why plead with her to stay? She didn't mean anything to him—anything, that is, in the sense of a healthy relationship. He'd made that clear enough last year.

But *she* needed *him*, and he *could* do something for her.

She dropped into her chair, crossed her legs and turned sideways. Through the green-tinted windows, the city spilled down to the river then rose up again on the other side. Traffic beetled along the interstate, winking in the sun.

"What I meant," Jas said, "was that I wouldn't have expected you to come to me until…" His lips went to a line and he shook his head. "Perhaps under any circumstances."

"It's business," she said. "And we're both businesspeople, right? I'd rather do business with you than start mauling people."

He sat back once more. "Business. What do you propose?"

"I still have the patterns for the window you wanted. If you buy the materials, I'll build it, free of charge." She drummed her fingers on one knee. "And you said you're having trouble, too. If you need help, I'll help you. Within limits, of course."

"Of course," he murmured, maybe sardonically. "If we decide to enter into an agreement, what do you have in mind?"

"I need to ward my presence in cyberspace somehow, so they can't access me there. And I need to fix what's already been tampered with." She fiddled with the edge of her napkin, carefully folding the corner. "I thought about trying it, but I'm afraid it might cause more problems than I have now."

"Without a doubt," Jas said.

"I don't know if this person can be tracked back. I don't know how careful they're being, how much they're laundering their communications."

Jas shrugged. "Unless they're doing it all personally—face-to-face, via courier and so forth—they'll have to go through the network. Phone, mail, it doesn't matter, it'll run through a computer. What do you intend to do once you've found them?"

She turned her napkin, folded another corner. "As Mary Poppins said, I guess it'll be time for a spoonful of medicine."

He flashed a grin. "I think it was sugar."

Jas knew musicals? Somehow she just couldn't picture a wizard sitting in front of the TV watching Julie Andrews whirl across London's rooftops with her umbrella.

"Whatever. But I'll have to get my point across somehow."

He traced the rim of his teacup with one finger. "You understand I must protect my own interests."

She would not dribble out of the chair and go slinking out. She knotted her hands between her knees. "Of course."

"I don't say I won't help you," he said. "I owe you that much."

This was making her dizzy. Was that a 'yes'?

"So," she said. "What do you have in mind?"

"I'll provide the resources to reach this individual. But once I do, the actions taken and the magic used will be yours. I'd recommend a magical worm. You'd be leaving your calling card and making life difficult, both at the same time.

Talys still looked stony, but something in the way he tipped his head back slightly suggested he might be pleased.

"As you already mentioned," Jas went on, "you'll need to protect your data. You don't want to lock yourself out of the network, just block malicious intent." His lips tucked in a smile. "Magus screens are an excellent defense against identity theft, as well. The best around."

What did you call a situation in which you felt abjectly grateful to the man you were supposed to hate? Ticklish? Awkward? Absolutely mortifying?

"Thank you." She wanted to ask what he was going to do, and when. But that would sound greedy. "What should I do?" she said instead.

He gave her a sort of sidelong smile as if he knew exactly what had gone through her mind. "Nothing right now. You're having problems at the bank?"

She rolled her eyes and nodded.

"I'll put those matters to right first, then. You should have access to your funds again by tomorrow at the latest. I'll call you when I have more."

She let go a breath and sat back in her chair. Wow. She'd never thought about it: if he could so easily manipulate her records in various computer databases, he could've made mischief a long time ago. And hadn't.

Which meant two things: one, there was a very high probability he *wasn't* causing her present difficulties, and two, he actually might *not* be her enemy. Maybe she could downgrade him from bastard to jerk. Or was it upgrade?

Leaning forward, she folded another corner of her napkin. It was beginning to get quite small.

"Thanks, Jas. Well…" She reached for her purse. There wasn't anything else to say that wasn't sappy, maudlin, embarrassing or all three. "I guess I'd better let you get to work. Let me know if I, um…if there's anything I can do."

He stood. "I will."

He couldn't mean that to be as disconcerting as it sounded.

Talys stood. Jas extended a hand. Surprisingly enough, Talys shook it. Was that a little subtle male challenge on Jas' part? *Dare you refuse to shake my hand with what I'm doing for your lady?* She wondered if Talys was applying his rather fearsome grip. If he was, Jas pretended not to feel it.

Jas turned to Amethyst. He drew breath as if to speak, but then only held out his hand.

She took it. Somehow, it felt like more than just the polite gesture of shaking hands, more than sealing an agreement. It felt like a change, like that first, tangy whiff of damp earth and aromatic desert vegetation that says rain is on the way.

But was it the kind that washes away the dust and cools the heat of a summer day, or a black storm that sends sheets of water rampaging down to fill streets and homes and golf courses with muddy, raging water?

CHAPTER 9

The phone rang. Amethyst put her handful of silverware on the lilac-and-green placemat. *Thanks, Jas,* she thought, grateful for the fact that the phone was ringing at all, but felt all prickly. She answered the call.

"Okay," Melodie's voice said on the other end of the line. "We're almost to your street. What's going to happen?"

Amethyst leaned her elbows on the kitchen counter. Afternoon sun slanted through the window, shining on the immaculate countertop and spotless sink.

"Just drive up the hill like usual. When you get close to the top, you'll see the protestors. The main thing is to try to ignore them as completely as you can. Tell Marl that, too. I mean, don't run over them or anything—"

"Are you sure?" Melodie asked.

Amethyst grinned. "Don't tempt me. Anyway, the magic depends on misdirection, and if you're focused on them, you might draw the attention of someone with enough sensitivity. Just pull into the driveway and come through the side gate. I don't want to try to get too fancy with the front door."

"You know, I hate to tell you this, but this is

ridiculous. Dinner at friends' shouldn't have to be staged like a ransom drop."

"Well, *mi amiga*, that's why you're here tonight."

Melodie started to say something, then interrupted herself. "Marl just turned onto Flint. See ya in a minute."

Amethyst put her phone down and called, "Talys?"

"Ready," he called back from the living room.

She hurried in. He already stood by the window, looking out. Joining him, she slid an arm around his waist. It was like plugging into a power source, except the swirls of energy, the blink and flash of light were magic.

Yep, there was the ever-present sign-carrying group, back up to strength again since it was after working hours. Apparently earning a living had to take precedence over the Lord's work. The protestors turned to look down the street as Melodie's sleek little Insight appeared.

Amethyst dipped into the magic, formed a replica of the car, the whirling of its hubcaps, the glint of sunlight on its glass and metal, whirring up the street and past the house. The real car she faded from sight. It didn't exist, it was a grackle stalking across the sidewalk, the glare of concrete in the sun. A bubble of silence enclosed it, containing the slam of car doors. Marl and Melodie were ants scurrying across the driveway. Marl turned as if to look at the people on the sidewalk, but Melodie grabbed his arm. His head snapped forward again and they disappeared from sight around the corner of the garage.

Talys took his arm from around her waist (when had he put it there?). "Well done, love."

She wound her fingers in his. "It wasn't much." She

frowned. "They won't see the car in the driveway? Eventually?"

"I am capable of ensuring the spell remains in place." He tugged his cuffs (black, of course) and headed for the kitchen.

Amethyst peeked out the blinds once more then followed.

Talys whisked open the sliding glass door. Melodie only looked bemused, but Marl was shaking his head like a dog with a foxtail in its ear.

"I don't believe it," he said with no trace of his usual quiet drollery. He braced one hand on the back of a dining room chair. "We drove right by them. They didn't even look. Like we didn't exist. And when the car door closed, I was sure…" He shook his head again and for the first time, really looked at Amethyst. "It wasn't real before. What you said—what you can do."

Lowering herself into a chair, even Melodie laughed a little shakily. "I have to admit, that was a little more graphic than what I've seen you do before. Maybe I should stop calling you 'Wiz'."

Amethyst sat in the chair next to her. "I'm sorry."

Talys moved around the kitchen, opening cabinets and the refrigerator, putting things on the counter.

Marl smoothed back his hair—not that it stayed smoothed. "I did say I wanted to see some magic." His lips quirked. "I suppose I expected it to be more…flamboyant, or something of the sort. Not something that tips reality on its ear."

"Pray," Amethyst said, "that you never see the

flamboyant sort."

He raised his brows in an expression somewhere between alarm and interest.

"Because about the time you do," she explained, "is the same time you start asking yourself where you are and what you're doing in this handbasket."

That got him to laugh. Suddenly he was the same old Marl, the man with the deadpan humor that could catch the unwary like a tripline in the grass. She shuddered to think of what he must be like in the courtroom. His opponents probably never knew what hit them.

"Anything to drink, all?" Talys asked. "Tea? Coffee? Perhaps something stronger?"

"It's not too early for a glass of wine, is it?" Marl asked.

Melodie shook her head. "None for me. I'm debugging code."

Talys brought wine in a garnet and purple hand-blown glass, one of Amethyst's "company" glasses.

Taking the wine, Marl asked him, "How on earth did you cope when you learned about her?"

Amethyst bit the inside of her lip. How would he answer that?

Talys shot her a teasing glance. "I was brought up to expect such things. It seemed quite natural."

Interesting. Somehow, she'd never thought of him as young, as learning, being taught…by whom? Or what? Were familiar spirits ever young and ignorant? Were they even born in any fashion? She did know he could die (if that was the word) if the form he inhabited was destroyed before he could move into another. Which implied that the spirit—Talys himself—could be destroyed, too. How exactly that might be accomplished, she didn't know. And didn't ever want to find out.

"Okay," Melodie said. "Show me this code. Then I'm off the clock."

Everyone trooped down the hall into Amethyst's front bedroom-slash-workroom.

Melodie went in first and looked around. "Ooh, you cleaned up. Just for us?"

Amethyst made a face. "One needs company occasionally. Otherwise why put things away when you'll just have to get them out again?"

Wine in hand, Marl stood in the middle of the cluttered room, gazing around. She had the distinct impression he was trying not to look appalled. Talys took a seat at the desk—it had the biggest chair.

Amethyst opened the doors to the computer armoire. Sheets of code were taped to the inside of the doors.

Melodie gravitated over and studied them. "These are worms."

"Yep," Amethyst said.

Melodie turned to eye her. "Where did you get them?"

Amethyst leaned down and flicked on her laptop. "Jas gave them to me."

"Jas? Jas Harker?" Marl said.

Either Melodie hadn't told him the new revelation about Jas, or else he knew and still couldn't believe Amethyst would have anything to do with him.

"Okay." Melodie sank into a chair. "Things are getting complicated again."

"This whole situation is like the Hydra," Amethyst said. "I cut off one head and three more grow in its place. It's only going to get worse unless I find the source of the trouble, and I needed Jas to do that."

Melodie opened her mouth but Talys said first, "Indeed, not the most attractive, but potentially the most efficacious solution."

Melodie shook her head, more mutinous than accepting. "So Jas applies the considerable resources of Magus Corporation to get to the root of the problem. And fix it, I presume."

"He fixed my data," Amethyst said. "I get to fix the one who messed it up to begin with."

"Hence the worms," Melodie said. "And you want me to take a look at this worm of yours, make sure it'll work and that it won't get caught in a virus sweep or bang up against a firewall."

Amethyst nodded. "It's been a long time since I did any real coding."

Melodie cocked a brow. "And probably never anything like this."

"No." Amethyst folded her hands in her lap. "Never anything like this."

Melodie and Marl exchanged a look, then Melodie grinned. "Let's see if I finally get to quit calling you 'Wiz'." She elbowed Amethyst out of the chair and sat down at the computer.

The laptop wasn't state-of-the-art—it took more than

the usual artist's income to manage that—but it stayed as current as Amethyst could afford to keep it. It helped that she could put together her own hardware. Leaning over Melodie, she tapped at the keyboard and brought up the code.

Melodie studied it a while, scrolling up and down. "'Wayland Archer,'" she read. "You've got a name? Great! So who is he?"

"Don't get excited," Amethyst said. "He's not an 'Ah-ha! The culprit at last!' kind of guy. He's just some guy who works part-time at an electronics store in Okemos, Michigan."

"A hacker?"

"Apparently so."

"Well then, who's he freelancing for?"

Amethyst made a face. "That's where the trail ends. Whoever put him up to it made sure they didn't leave tracks."

"That suggests someone who knows what they're doing," Marl put in.

That's what Jas thought, too, but it didn't seem like a good idea to say so in the present company.

"Seems like it," Amethyst said.

Melodie frowned at the screen. "If you got a name," she said slowly. "You might be able to find out who's behind him. Do some phreaking, find out who he's calling."

"What matters is that they're discouraged," Amethyst said. "If they're put on notice that the door swings both ways, and I'm something a little more dangerous than the usual resource available to the highest bidder."

Melodie slid Amethyst a glance. "If Jas could dig up a name for you, seems like he could've done more than give you worm code to use as a template."

"We're attempting to minimize entanglements," Talys said.

Entanglements. What a perfect word. Not to mention that Jas wanted to minimize entanglements, too.

"I'm glad to hear that." Melodie turned back to the computer screen, studied it a while then pointed to a line of code. "What's this? You're referencing video locations."

"If he tries to access his own data, for example online banking or purchases over the Internet, I've programmed an animated amethyst to appear on his screen," Amethyst said. "Remember that old gem screensaver, where the clear faceted shape would roll around the screen? This is the same thing, but purple."

Melodie chuckled. "A calling card."

"Right. And if anyone tries to access my code, it shatters. So does his data."

Melodie peered at the screen. "Except I don't see that here. I hate to say it, Wiz, but this isn't the sort of thing to strike fear into the heart of a harasser. I mean, he might be creeped out that you tracked him down, but if the worst he gets out of it is a screensaver that activates at inconvenient times—"

"No. I didn't program a virus into this worm, because the virus will be magic. The worm will just carry it where it needs to go."

Melodie's eyes went wide. "And so even if he has the

best virus protection software around…"

"Unless the hacker also happens to be a wizard, he won't be able to pin down the problem. Because the code won't show anything beyond a little hacker toy."

Marl blew up his cheeks like a trumpeter and let out a breath. "Somehow I think I should've stepped out of the room about five minutes ago. As a representative of our legal system, I don't think I should be hearing this."

"Should the matter arrive before a judge," Talys said, "I believe your vow to tell the truth would be sorely tried in any case."

Marl gave a short, uncomfortable laugh. "True. But I feel I'm about to become an accessory."

"Marl—" Melodie began in a tone of disgust.

"Wait, Mel," Amethyst said. "You're right," she said to Marl. "I shouldn't have brought you into this. I'm sorry. I didn't think."

"When a woman is being stalked," Marl said slowly, "the most the law can do for her is to issue a restraining order." He puffed out another breath, ran his hand over his hair again. "And some of them end up dead before we can go any further."

Melodie stabbed a finger at the screen. "Well, then this is a restraining order. And you can't expect her to sit here like a princess in a tower while the barbarians slaughter their way up the stairs."

"Actually," Amethyst said, "it's closer to a booby trap, but I'm pretty sure those are illegal, too."

Marl nodded once. "They are."

"So what else is she supposed to do?" Melodie said.

He held up his hands. "Hon, I know—"

"Please," Amethyst said. "Marl's absolutely right. Ethically, this is closer to the law of the jungle than the law of jurisprudence. And if nothing else, wizards do seem to operate by the former." How depressing.

Melodie grabbed her wrist and shook it. "Come on, Wiz. This is self-defense." She rounded on Marl. "Isn't it? If some kook was taking a prybar to her door, she could do what she had to. Right?"

Marl looked from one to the other of them. "Well…yes. Depending upon the circumstances."

"And wouldn't you say they're rather dire?" Melodie said fiercely.

"You can't get mad at him for his integrity," Amethyst told her.

Melodie shot her a sour look. "So I suppose you're going to climb up to the stake all clad in glowing white while they pile the wood around you."

"Hardly," Amethyst said. "Besides, Talys and I already discussed the improbability of wizard-burning."

"Okay," Melodie said. "How about full disclosure then?" She turned to Marl. "Will that satisfy the legal and ethical requirements?" She scrolled down through the code, moused the cursor in place and began typing. "'Mess with…Amethyst…Rey at your…own risk,'" she dictated, then asked Marl, "Will that do it?"

Amethyst nodded. "They'll still know I can get to them. It might be enough to make them think twice."

CHAPTER 9.5 – OPPOSITION

Music blared through the bar. Low-hanging lights over the tables illuminated drinks, hands, the dull red glow of cigarettes while leaving the faces of the patrons dim and obscure. A waitress whose breasts strained her halter top swung through the crowd, a tray full of drinks raised over her head.

Two men sat at one of the tables, one with his overcoat draped over the back of his chair. The man he drank with knew him as Robertson. He was, after all, the son of Robert.

"Look at this." Robertson offered a phone. A purple gem rolled around the screen, alternately splintering then revealing the text: *Mess with Amethyst Rey at your own risk.*

The other man—Char, he called himself—watched the waitress like a mugger sizing up a mark. His forefinger drew a pattern in the condensation on his glass.

He waved away the phone Robertson held. "I have no use for such things."

"Well, the rest of us do," Robertson said. "And let me tell you, this is one annoyance I'm ready to have stopped."

One of Char's ash-colored brows twitched. A little

flutter of fear beat under Robertson's breastbone. What was there to be afraid of?

Except it gave him the creeps, the way every time he met the man, it was like running into some old, forgotten acquaintance. He'd recognize the plain, unlined face, but the minute he walked away, he'd be damned if he could say what Char looked like, or even exactly how the conversation had gone.

"Who is this person, this Amethyst Rey?" Char said.

The music, the voices cranked up drunk-loud, should've made his quiet words impossible to hear. Somehow, Robertson had no problem at all.

"One of you people," Robertson said. "She was fucking with someone's business in New Mexico. He wanted her out of the way. I figure, hey. Get her out of his way, bring her in and make her useful at the same time. I even had a—" He started to say 'buyer' but changed his mind. "I had an employer lined up." He swigged his gin. "Then I couldn't deliver. I had some pressure put on her, and she does this."

He tapped the phone. It belonged to one of his subcontractors. *Ex*-subcontractors. The ball-less puss had bailed the minute he realized his little hacking job had been tracked back to him.

That had given Robertson the creeps worse than Char's disappearing act. It was the first time he'd run into one of these people who could do their shit on tech. It'd also make her more valuable than the rest of them. The commission he could charge on her— He gave his head a shake.

"The guy who owns this phone can make the bug go away," Robertson said. "Then the next time he logs into some account—any account—it comes back again." He picked up his glass, set it down again without drinking. "She's scared the crap out of everyone I've sent to deal with her. I'm running out of reliable people. It pisses me off. But if she thinks she can piss me off and I'll just forget about it…" He shrugged.

Char turned his glass and began a new design. "She enchants your devices. She is young?"

"Twenty-nine or thirty, somewhere in there."

Char made a noise. "That one." He shook his head. "I will not contend with her."

Robertson's antennae went up. "Why not? She'll kick your ass, or what?"

Char gave him a look that made the hair stand up all the way from the back of his neck to the backs of his hands. "Presumptuous, Robert's son."

"Look, I'm only trying to get an idea of what I'm dealing with, okay? If I need to call in more muscle, I'd better know."

Char pinned him with that serial-killer stare. Cold prickled under Robertson's collar, then the wizard sat back and nodded once. Robertson took a breath like he hadn't been breathing a second ago. He probably hadn't.

"She has more power than it seems she should for one so young," Char said. "Enough to have vanquished the wizard who had overcome any other he faced. Afterwards, she might have gone about confronting rivals, but instead she does nothing. A wizard powerful enough to do nothing worries me very much indeed."

Robertson frowned, thinking. "So we find a weak spot. Or make one."

Char tilted his head. "A bane, perhaps. Something silent and subtle, that attracts random mischance."

"So don't you guys have way to avoid random trouble?"

Char sat back and toyed with his glass. "Oh, yes. But it is not a thing most wizards will waste effort on. Why, when we can simply draw to us what we wish?"

Robertson suppressed a shudder. "So will you do it?"

"Such magic takes as much effort to weave as to ward against. And to cast a bane on another wizard... Risky."

"If she's as powerful as you say, seems it might be useful to make her a little less so."

Again, Char gave that thinking pause. Dealing with these people was a test of patience.

"Perhaps," Char said. "I will consider it."

Robertson held in a sigh. The waitress was heading back to the bar. Robertson liked the way her hips and bare midriff moved as she carried her tray.

"You find her appealing?" Char said.

Robertson gave a short laugh. "Yeah. I wouldn't mind having her under me."

Char's lips quirked in something that wasn't quite a smile. He raised his hand, and the waitress came to their table. "Another, please," he said.

The waitress smiled and took Robertson's empty glass. Char offered his. She took it, caught her breath and locked eyes with the wizard.

"Do you have a break coming?" he asked her.

Those amazing tits of hers rose and fell with her breaths. Without breaking from Char's gaze, she nodded.

"Good," he said. "I'll meet you outside."

"Yes," she breathed and hurried to carry the empties to the bar.

Char turned back to Robertson, that same not-quite smile on his face. "Too bad," he said. "I, too, find her appealing."

He got up and walked out, leaving Robertson to pay the tab.

CHAPTER 10

Attrition had whittled down the marchers on the sidewalk. Only the hard-core remained, including the mean-looking grey-haired guy—the Prophet of Doom, Amethyst called him.

She suspected the men and woman with him were family, and that they were more afraid of him than anything else. The ones who'd dropped out probably had to change churches.

"Gah!" Amethyst said. "What is it going to take to get rid of these guys?"

Talys looked up from his book. "I presume that's a rhetorical question."

"Maybe not," she muttered.

"Does that mean you're prepared to use some of the more, ah, abstruse magic you learned?"

The phone rang, sparing her the need to ponder the answer.

"*Hola*, Amethyst, this is Oscar. Hey, we're setting up a neighborhood watch group. Wanna come for the first meeting? I'm barbecuing."

"Neighborhood—? Oh." The persistent group on the sidewalk bothered more than her. "Sounds like a great idea. When?"

"In about ten minutes. Gary's setting up the grill now."

"Okay, see ya." She ended the call and turned to Talys. "Think a little neighborhood solidarity might do the job?"

Talys grinned and picked up his sunglasses. "It might," he said, "at that."

Amethyst put on her favorite hat—the one with the stampede string so the wind wouldn't blow it off. In New Mexico, that was important. Talys disappeared into the kitchen and returned with a paper grocery bag.

"Tortilla chips and your pico de gallo salsa," he explained. "And drink. We oughtn't arrive empty-handed."

"Oh. Yeah." The fact that she hadn't even thought about it showed how distracted she was these days. "Thanks."

She opened the front door, and the marchers zeroed in on her like angry yellow jackets.

Pretending to ignore their chanting and praying, she crunched along the simulated dry streambed that curved through the native vegetation in her front yard. Most was past its summer prime, but the yellow-rimmed fire wheels of gaillardia still splashed color below the sulfur blooms of dwarf chamisa.

Oscar had apparently decided to set up the meeting in his front yard. He sat in a collapsible canvas chair with a built-in awning drinking a Miller Lite. Gary, his son, made a production of lighting the barbecue. He was scrunched down, studying the burners. Amethyst guessed he was trying to hide.

"Hey, Amethyst," Oscar called, saluting her with his beer. He also pretended there was no disturbance on the sidewalk forty feet away. "Whatcha want to drink? Beer? Soda pop?"

Talys brandished his grocery bag. "We brought lemonade."

"*Bueno*. Gary, go inside and get glasses, heh?"

Gary seemed more than happy to escape the spotlight.

"And bring that plastic table from the patio," Oscar called after him.

One of Talys' brows quirked above the rim of his sunglasses. "Fire against fire, Oscar?"

Oscar grinned, showing a silver-capped front tooth. "Sure, why not?"

"Hi, y'all." Heather, carrying a big Tupperware bowl, brushed past the protestors.

A flock of five blond boys followed. The oldest, maybe eleven or twelve, wore an expression of too-cool boredom and carried an enormous Hobby Lobby bag with sticks and sheets of paperboard poking out of it. The middle boys looked either excited or embarrassed, and the littlest one frowned fiercely at the protestors.

Heather walked into Oscar's yard, slipped off her sandals and wriggled bubblegum pink-painted toes in the grass. "Mm, mm, mmm."

Amethyst had to stifle a laugh.

"There's not enough cool, green grass in this town," Heather said. "I do miss it." She nodded at the boys. "These are my sister's boys. Boys, say hello. This is Mr.

Griego, and this is Miss Amethyst and Mr. Tom."

"Please to meet you, ma'am, sir," they all mumbled dutifully in accents thicker than Heather's.

The youngest boy stared wide-eyed at Talys. "You an Injun?" he squeaked. "A real one?"

Talys bowed. "Born on the Navajo reservation."

His accent and the bow didn't seem particularly Navajo.

Heather blushed and took the child by the shoulders. "Now, Joe! What a question!" She turned to Oscar. "Is there someplace the boys can paint?"

Amethyst eyed the Hobby Lobby bag.

"Sure, sure." Oscar heaved himself out of his chair. "You got something that needs to go in the icebox?"

"Potato salad with peas."

This was definitely going to be a multicultural barbecue. Or was it multiregional?

Heather handed the bowl to the oldest boy. "Now, be polite, and make sure you do what Miz Griego tells you, hear? Help her with the signs."

Signs?

Oscar herded the kids to the front door. "Gary!" he called into the house. "Bring out that table!" He came clumping back and dropped into the chair. "That kid," he muttered. "'But, Dad,'" Oscar mimicked. "'A barbecue in the front yard? Why?'" He shook his head. "He needs a stint in the Army. But Mama says no way."

Mama was Angela, Oscar's wife.

Down on the sidewalk, the marchers sang a hymn.

"Have a seat, Amethyst, Heather," Oscar said. "We

don't get together enough. Time we did."

Amethyst perched on the edge of a white resin chair. Talys came to stand behind her, but he had one hand in the pocket of his black cargo shorts and a beer in the other. A far cry from his attitude with Jas or the odious Mr. Pitts.

"Wouldn't it be better to plan strategy in private?" she said quietly.

Oscar drank his Miller Lite. "Demonstrating strategy is better." He beamed at the marchers as if imagining some pleasant scene.

"Oh, much better," Heather said and patted Amethyst's knee. "Just you wait and see."

Talys chuckled darkly.

Uh-oh.

More neighbors showed up. Amethyst only knew them as The New People in the Jaramillo's Old House. Heather introduced them as Fiona and Ralph.

"Rafe," Ralph corrected her. "The British pronunciation."

Heather dimpled and apologized, and Amethyst suspected she knew exactly how the name was pronounced.

Ralph—*Rafe*—wore a vaguely Jamaican-looking crocheted hat and Fiona wore dreadlocks and organic cotton clothing.

Mr. Wesley arrived, a tall black man with slight slouch and grizzled salt-and-pepper hair, heavy on the salt. "Mrs. Wesley sends her apologies. And this." He offered up a raspberry cheesecake with fresh raspberries. "Says each to his own faith." He made a skeptical face. "We gonna do something about this?" Without looking, he waved a hand at the singing group on the sidewalk.

"That's the plan," Oscar said, cracked open another beer and handed it to Mr. Wesley.

Heather stood and took the cheesecake. "I'll just take this inside and check on the boys."

"Ask that son of mine where the hell that table is!" Oscar shouted back over his shoulder.

"I'll thank you to watch your language!" the Prophet of Doom yelled.

"I'll thank you to mind your own goddamn business, you tight-assed sonofabitch!" Oscar yelled back. He grinned like a hyena scenting dead meat.

The Prophet turned away and sang louder.

The Griego's front door opened and Heather and Angela came out. The white paperboard and sticks had been transformed into protest signs. The one in front read *NEIGHBORS AGAINST HATE*. The initial letters were big and bold and in red, and spelled out...

"NAH," Amethyst read aloud. A hysterical laugh tickled uncomfortably. She choked off most of it. Talys squeezed her shoulder and looked like he was trying to avoid erupting into laughter himself.

Carrying the belated table between them, Heather's nephews trooped out the door and handed out more signs. One read *Bigot-Free Zone*. Heather thrust a sign into Amethyst's hand: *Aren't The Witch Hunts Over?*

The oldest boy's sign said *Neighbors Supporting Neighbors*. The boys marched past her to the sidewalk, tromped up and down in front of the Griegos' yard, singing something like, "Uhh-uhn, Uh-uh-uhn." It sounded like an orc marching chant. The protestors sang louder than ever. The kids grunted their orc-chant.

Heather glanced at her watch. "They should be here any minute."

"Who?" Amethyst said. She didn't want to know, but thought she'd better.

"Action Seven News," Heather said and crossed her legs. Her pink-painted toes wriggled in delight again. "If the police won't come, we just have to take things into our own hands, don't we?"

Amethyst gazed on her with newfound respect. "What do you do for a living?"

Strange. In the months Heather had rented old Mr. Meadows' place, Amethyst had never asked.

Heather swirled a sprig of mint in her glass. "I'm a publicist."

"There, love, you see?" Talys said. "When you publish your memoirs, you know exactly who to turn to."

My Life and Times as a Wizard, Amethyst thought.

"Hey, great," she said without enthusiasm.

"Boys, come back into the yard now," Heather said.

The kids came and sat in the grass around her, still holding their signs.

Most of the protestors looked unhappy: ashamed, embarrassed, awkward. Their singing faltered.

"Raise up your voices!" the Prophet of Doom said. "These people have been corrupted by the evil in their midst. We must show them the light!"

Rafe and Fiona, getting into the spirit of things, held hands and sang John Lennon's "Imagine."

Talys joined in his rich baritone.

Mr. Wesley chuckled. "I think your welcome's wearing thin," he called. "Better throw in the towel."

Heather looked around as if checking out a set design, then nodded once in satisfaction.

The Channel Seven news van came into sight like a rescue ship breaching the horizon. The van parked and two guys got out. One slid open the side door and shortly reappeared with a minicam.

Amethyst scrunched down in her seat. Maybe disappearing like Gary had wasn't such a bad idea. But if she used illusion, it would work on everyone, friend or foe. She could probably fox the video camera, though.

Talys squeezed her shoulder again. "Hush," he murmured.

"Yes," Heather answered in reply to some question from the news crew. "These fanatics have been harassing the whole neighborhood for just *days*. I mean, who cares if some neighbor is a witch. Doesn't the Constitution guarantee freedom of religion?"

A dispute was taking place among the protestors. The Prophet and one of the other men argued, and some looked around desperately as if wishing *they* could disappear. The cameraman panned over them, then up to Oscar's front yard. The lens stared at them—Amethyst, Talys, the rest of her neighbors. A spark of cold went through her.

"Oh, Talys," Amethyst murmured. "I don't think this

is a good idea."

"It's a great idea." Oscar tipped his head back and grinned at the camera. "After this, you won't see those creeps around here."

The cameraman and reporter descended on the protestors. Everyone but the Prophet distanced themselves. Two or three shaded their eyes the camera. Pretty soon the news crew stood on Oscar's defiantly lush, green lawn.

Oscar, Angela, Mr. Wesley, Rafe, Fiona, Heather and her five nephews ranged around Amethyst. Talys stood with his hand on her shoulder. She wasn't sure whether to be uplifted or mortified.

What would they do if they knew those people down on the sidewalk were absolutely, literally correct?

CHAPTER 10.5 - OPPOSITION

The house was dim, the living room lit only by blue twilight coming through the window and the glow of a TV screen. The woman on the sofa watched the evening news. Her son slouched beside her. His black hair hid his eyes, and the game in his hands gave soft beeps and trills. The sofa was only two years old, in a brick red and cream pattern a little like the rug on the wall, the one Grandfather had woven. The TV was a new flat panel, and had TIVO. Her husband had a good job as a heavy equipment operator at the Navajo Transportation Department, so they could buy these things.

"Siege in a Northeast Heights neighborhood," the reporter intoned. "Christian fundamentalists picket the home of an Albuquerque practitioner of the Wiccan religion. We're here at a neighbor's home, where a march and barbecue in support have been organized…"

The screen showed a group of white people carrying signs with Bible sayings. Then it flashed to the green grass and shady trees of someone's front yard. Blond-headed children clustered around a pretty woman. The men and women on the lawn held signs of their own. The camera zoomed in on them.

The woman gasped, pressed her hand to her mouth.

The boy raised his head.

She grabbed for the TIVO controller on the coffee table. "Get Grandfather!" she said. "Hurry!"

The boy hesitated, confused.

"Go!" She pushed the record button.

The boy dropped his game on the sofa cushion and ran out.

Maybe she was wrong. She'd caught only a glimpse of the man on the screen.

She'd watched the recording six times when the boy came back with her father. He was dressed in jeans and a red checked flannel shirt. His hair was knotted in the traditional style, and threaded with grey. Her father didn't ask questions, but he would wonder. To answer those questions, she made room on the sofa for him and pressed the "play" button on the remote.

She'd started recording where the old Spanish man raised his beer to the camera. The camera moved to show a young white man and woman, then to a dark-haired Spanish woman sitting in a white plastic patio chair. She looked nervous and uncomfortable. A tall, broad-chested Navajo man stood behind her, dressed all in black. Familiar. Impossible.

"Hey," the boy said. "That's Uncle Frank! But—" He felt the tension in the room and fell silent.

Her father sat stiff and still, his hands on his knees. "Let me see it again."

Once more, she reversed the recording. It came to the part showing the man who looked like her brother, and she paused it.

"I can't tell, Father," she said. "But I think it's him. It looks like him. His face, his hair, his shape."

"It's not him," her father said.

"I know. It can't be. But..." She trailed off.

Her father stared at the image frozen on the screen. "My son didn't smile that way. He didn't wear those kinds of clothes."

The boy's round eyes moved between them and the TV screen. "Mom," he said as if trying to reason with her. "Uncle Frank died. You told me."

No one said anything, not even about the boy using the name of the dead. The man on the screen gazed back at them through his dark sunglasses, a slight quirk of amusement on his lips.

"My son died," her father finally agreed. "That isn't him. His body, but not him."

"No," she said. She put her head in her hands. The hospital had lost Frank's body. When the time came to take care of it, it was gone. Nobody could find it. It was horrible. "No," she said again.

Her father's hand fell on her shoulder. "We'll find out. Maybe I'm wrong."

She didn't raise her head.

"The people at the TV station can tell us how to find this man," he said. "I'll tell them my son has been missing, we've been looking for him."

She didn't know about such things. "What if they won't tell you?"

"I have songs," he said. "Songs that will return what's lost."

"You sang those songs last year, when my brother—"
She couldn't go on.

He gestured at the TV: at Frank's image.

Many people nowadays didn't believe in the old
songs' power. But she'd seen them work. They'd worked
here, now, with Frank. "And then?"

Her father was rarely angry. She saw anger in him
now. Watching so silently, the boy must've seen it too.

Her father didn't answer right away. "My son died,"
he finally said. "When I see what looks out of his eyes…"

He took the remote from her and pressed a button.
The TV screen went dark.

CHAPTER 11

Amethyst let the blinds snap down. "You know, I don't mind getting yelled at now that we're down to one lunatic, but it's still embarrassing when company comes over."

Peeking warily out the front window had gotten to be a habit—or maybe a compulsion. At least the marchers were down to only the Prophet of Doom. The problem was what he lacked in acolytes, he more than made up for in vehemence.

Talys tugged his sleeves straight and put on his sunglasses. "Even when company consists of the inimitable Jasper Harker?"

She scowled at him and checked the living room one more time: everything vacuumed, dusted, pillows in place on the sofa, the stained glass panel on the wall glowing with its usual eldritch light.

"Why," Talys said, "are you so nervous?"

She threw up her hands. "I don't know!"

He settled into a chair. Caramela came wagging up to him and offered her tug toy. "You said he's visited in the past."

"Yeah. When I wasn't here," she muttered.

"You might have insisted on meeting him elsewhere."

"And give him the satisfaction of arguing with him? Then he'd *know* how I felt about him seeing my house."

Talys chuckled and gave the tug toy a yank. Caramela growled and yanked back. Amethyst wished she could be as unconcerned. But she ended up drifting back to the front window.

Jas pulled up to the curb in his emerald green Infiniti. It was low, sleek, and exuded Jas' own smooth style. She knew a color like that didn't come stock. But if you could drop six figures on a car, she supposed a custom paint job was no big deal.

The Prophet strode toward him, brandishing his sign-du-jour (*Woe unto them that call evil good, and good evil*) and shouting something—Amethyst could hear the shouting, but not the words. She fidgeted, not sure whether to be embarrassed or wickedly delighted.

Jas just stood on the sidewalk with a hand in one pocket of his slacks. He faced mostly away, so she couldn't see his expression. She imagined an amused quirk to his lips—his casual, unalarmed posture suggested as much. Finally, he spoke. Getting too close to Jas, the Prophet spoke. Jas took his hand out of his pocket and replied.

"Uh-oh." Amethyst shifted from one foot to the other. "Maybe I'd better go out there."

"Mmm?" Talys gave Carmela's tuggie a shake.

A pulse of magic rippled the ether. Suddenly the Prophet dropped his sign. His hands went to his throat. His eyes went wide.

"Shit." Amethyst lunged for the front door, flung it open.

The Prophet careened across the street to his car, his fingers clutching his throat. The only sound that came from him was a high, thin whine. Jas only watched him, arms folded.

Amethyst hesitated on the front porch. Whatever was wrong with the Prophet didn't seem to affect his ability to drive—his old Chevy sedan stuttered, gunned, then screeched down the street, trailing a cloud of blue smoke. Jas watched him go, then ambled up the driveway to the front door. He was, indeed, smiling, but the smile was self-satisfied.

Amethyst frowned. "What did you do to him?"

"Good afternoon, Amethyst," he said. "How are you today?"

She gave an annoyed snort. "Okay, fine. Hi. Now what happened?"

"I simply told him if he had nothing constructive to say, he ought to say nothing at all." He shrugged. "It appears he has a poverty of thought."

The magic he'd used clung to him like a static electric charge.

"You—" She stammered, trying for something besides obscenities. "Dammit, Jas!" she finally managed.

He cocked his head. "A good curse can work wonders. You should try it yourself sometime."

"You can't do that!"

"Why not?" He snapped his fingers. "Poof. Problem solved."

"Yeah, but it was *my* problem. That isn't how I wanted it solved!"

"Does it matter? He was harassing you."

She clenched her fists and clamped her jaw on the impulse to scream. "He's a civilian. He can't fight us. It's bullying."

"Amethyst, what do you call what he was doing to you? Did you do the man any harm? Did you provoke him? I don't understand what you're angry about. I only intended to be helpful."

He really didn't know. Talys stood in the doorway behind her, looking unconcerned—as if he'd known that Jas would do something.

She pressed her fists to her forehead. "Gah!"

Talys stepped onto the porch and coaxed her hands away from her face. "Come, love. It's done, and done for the best. I doubt you'd rid yourself of the man any other way."

"Thank you, Thomas," Jas said without a trace of sarcasm.

One of Talys' brows twitched. "No need to thank me. My concern is for Amethyst."

"I should never have let you come over," Amethyst told Jas. "You were the one who didn't want entanglements. Then you use magic in my front yard!"

Jas' hand came up as if for a placating touch, then fell. "A curse is passive magic. You felt it because you were standing right there. Otherwise, it won't leave traces."

"I *know*." The information lay mixed in the junk heap of spells in her mind. It was just that she'd been mad enough to forget. She pushed out the anger with a breath. "Forget it. Come in."

Caramela stood in the middle of the living room, her feet planted like a sumo wrestler. She raised her hackles from collar to tail and growled. Jas stopped just inside the door.

"It appears she scents the bane about you," Talys said.

"Obviously," Jas said.

More dominance displays. And not the dog's. Amethyst swept past them. She caught Caramela by the collar and hustled her into the backyard, trying not to relish the sight of a wizard brought up short by a snarling pit bull. She kissed Caramela on the head, closed the patio door and hurried back into the room.

Jas had stopped in the middle of the living room and stood gazing at the stained glass panel that dominated the long wall.

"Now *that* is a fine piece of magic." He stepped closer to the panel, closed his eyes and turned his head as if sniffing wine. "A making, wasn't it?" He gave a low whistle. "If your power can create an object of that size and detail, what are you doing wasting your time on hand work?"

"Don't you start."

She stomped back into the kitchen. She should have left Caramela in. Give Jas something to think about besides insulting comments.

There was silence from the living room for a moment. Then hesitant footsteps followed her.

"Certainly your handiwork is equally impressive," Jas said.

She didn't turn, just took glasses out of the cabinet and filled them with ice. She sighed. *Okay*, she thought. *He's trying.*

"Thank you." She lined up the glasses on the countertop. "Would you like something to drink?" That came out grumpily. She tried again. "Iced tea, lemonade? Or I can make coffee." The coffeepot was up on the top shelf of a cabinet, but she did keep coffee around for those who drank it.

Talys stepped into the kitchen. "I shall get the drinks."

She squeezed his hand in thanks.

"Iced tea, please," Jas said.

He glanced around the kitchen, at the other stained glass pieces. Amethyst had made insets for the top cabinets, and a decorative panel hung in the window by the breakfast bar. He leaned on the counter to see it better, blue morning glories twining around a central section of clear glass.

"I made that in my MA program," she explained.

"And the cupboard doors?"

She wrinkled her nose. "They were stained this Seventies dark walnut and had awful yellow bullseye plastic inserts. I refinished them and did the glass not long after I bought the house."

"Very nice." Jas took a glass from Talys.

"Your windows are in here." She led Jas through the laundry room, down the two steps into the garage. "They're too big to assemble in my workroom." She tried not to see the oil stains on the floor, the workbench older than she was and rusty cans of paint on the shelves.

"No need to apologize," he said.

The apology she'd tried not to make had obviously come through. She rubbed the back of her neck. Talys, leaning in the doorframe, shrugged.

Jas seemed interested only in the window on its makeshift worktable, a piece of ¾ inch plywood screwed down on sawhorses. The window itself was the design they'd worked on over a year ago: a green pool with brightly colored koi swimming among ripples. Between the white-painted plywood behind it and the single fluorescent shop light overhead, it wouldn't show to its best advantage. He circled the worktable, hands clasped behind him.

He stopped. Amethyst waited, but he didn't move, didn't look up, didn't say anything. A nervous flutter started in her middle. Whatever else he was, Jas was still a client. Well, sort of. He had to be happy with the work, anyway. And right now, he didn't look happy.

Talys folded his arms, also waiting.

She bit her lip. "Is there a problem?"

The question, the whole scene echoed in her mind. At least Talys was here this time. Jas wouldn't assault her with magic—or with anything else, for that matter—and get away with it.

Jas raised his head. "I'm afraid I have to call in the favor, Amethyst."

The flutter turned to a tremor. "What do you mean?"

He faced her. "You offered to help if I needed it. Well, I need it."

"What about the window?" she said. "That was the agreement. You help me, I make the window. No charge." She gestured at the pieced-together puzzle of glass. "There it is. Like I promised."

He spread his hands. "I know."

Heat ran into her face and her eyes narrowed. "Is this some kind of trick? What are you up to this time, Jas?"

In the doorway, Talys straightened.

Jas barked a humorless laugh. "I wish it were. I'm no happier than you are, Amethyst. But they've come at me where they can hurt me most."

She folded her arms. "And you'll tell me what that is, right?"

"They've done exactly what I helped you do. They've done something to get through the firewalls I install. I have half a dozen large clients prepared to sue me for data breach."

She just stared at him. "Mary Mother of God, Jas, you own a computer security conglomerate. And you're a wizard!"

His lips thinned. "I am. I am not, however, a systems designer or a programmer."

"And you don't have about a hundred of 'em working for you?"

"How many of those do you expect can do magic? Or recognize it when they see it?"

She opened her mouth for another retort.

"You can read code," he said first. "And you can see what's between the lines of that code. You can tell me how they're breaching my firewalls. Once I know, I can take countermeasures."

"So get your people to walk you through the code while you look over their shoulders. You don't need me."

He sighed. "Ordinary folk or wizards, I don't intend to make my nature public knowledge. Which leads me to my second reason for coming to you."

She definitely wasn't going to get out of this.

"You're a known quantity," Jas said. "I'm—as yet—not. I'd like to keep that advantage as long as possible."

She gave a disbelieving laugh. "So I get to go around with a great, big target painted on my forehead. Gee, thanks, Jas."

Talys' upper lip quivered and he made a sound deep in his throat.

Jas made a frustrated gesture. "Do you honestly think I'd throw you to the wolves? If nothing else, it's in my interest to ensure your safety."

"And you certainly—" she began hotly.

"That is neither your responsibility nor your concern," Talys said over her.

Jas shrugged. "Perhaps not. But if she agrees to help me, I'll have to make it my concern." He hesitated. "I wouldn't have asked if you hadn't offered." He came around the worktable, hands held out. "Please, Amethyst. I swear to you..." The magic suddenly wrapped his words, making them more than words; making them truth. "I am not lying. I'm not creating an excuse."

"Excuse." She pounced on the word. "For what?"

"For...for..." he stammered. "For drawing you in."

It was the first time she'd seen Jas anything but

smooth and collected. The words of his hasty patch were still wound with magic—truth, but not quite true.

He looked so exposed, so utterly caught out she suddenly felt sorry for him. *Or maybe,* the thought whispered, *you don't want to think about where the truth might lead.*

"Okay, okay. I believe you. And I *did* promise to help you. Conditionally."

"Nothing to compromise your morals." The old smoothness was back. "Of course."

Amethyst tapped her foot. "Okay then. But first take the curse off the Prophet."

"Who— Oh." Jas gave her a hard look. "You're completely unreasonable."

"I agree," Talys said.

Magic obviously did something to people's brains. Or maybe this was clear proof of how power corrupted.

"Maybe," she said cheerfully. "But if we're going to be the good guys, we have to act like it. And good guys don't beat up on people who can't fight back."

Jas puffed up his cheeks and blew through his lips. "I'll have to find him to do it."

"I know some good finding spells. Want me to show them to you?"

"No," he said. "Thank you."

This might actually be—dare she think it?—fun.

"Cheer up, Jas. Being good has its own rewards."

"And when we eventually confront our opponents?" he said. "Will you be so delicate then?"

CHAPTER 12

"Y**ou're** *what?*" Melodie said.

The noise and bustle of Expo New Mexico surrounded them—Amethyst and Melodie, Talys and Marl—with a strange bubble of privacy. Amethyst should've just kept her mouth shut. But she didn't want to have to hide things from her best friend again. She hated lying. It was exhausting, and it made her feel lonely and grimy.

"When Jas agreed to help me, I promised I'd help him if he needed it. What was I supposed to do? I don't need any more enemies. And I could argue that I need some wizardly friends."

"Friends!" Melodie snorted. "Somehow I don't think Jas Harker and the word 'friends' belong in the same context."

They turned onto the tree-lined Avenue of the Governors, only relative relief from the crush at the main entrance. The Midway rose to the left in a whirl of spiderweb machinery and flashing lights. To the right were the exhibition halls and Tingley Coliseum, and beyond that the horse barns and animal exhibitions, the Indian Village and Villa Hispania.

Girls in short shorts and midriff-baring tops walked

with *vato* boyfriends in wife-beaters and drooping jeans. Kids in silly hats ran by clutching cotton candy like Olympic torches. Big Spanish families ambled by at *Abuelita's*—Grandmother's—pace. A voice, blurred over a loudspeaker, carried over the squeal of children, the clang of bells, the amplified whisper of Andean pan pipes. The greasy, decadent smell of fair-food sent out tendrils to ensnare them as they passed—funnel cakes dusted with powdered sugar and cinnamon, green chile cheese dogs on a stick, smoked turkey legs.

"That's a little harsh, hon," Marl said. "Jas did come through for her."

"Sure," Melodie said. "What I ask myself is *why?*" She shot Amethyst a glance. "Which is what you should be asking yourself, too."

"What would I do without a caring friend to point out the obvious?" Amethyst said.

Marl chuckled. Melodie elbowed him in the ribs.

"Look at Tom," Amethyst said. "Does he look worried?"

Talys, scanning the kaleidoscope of activity through his sunglasses, strode along dressed in his usual black, from his baseball cap to his flip-flops. "I have no need to worry. She's quite capable of protecting herself."

Amethyst tucked her arm in his. "Besides," she said. "As long as Jas wants my help, he'll have to behave. We already have that settled."

Melodie made a face. "I'm so relieved."

"Turning to more cheerful subjects," Amethyst said, "do you want to see the rodeo tonight?"

Marl shrugged. "I can take a pass on that, but we talked about seeing Huey Lewis and the News."

Talys' brows climbed above the frames of his sunglasses. He mouthed the name at Amethyst.

Marl gave a wave of the hand. "I know, I know. 'Eighties geezer band. What can I say. I'm a geezer."

Melodie bumped him with her hip. "You are *not* a geezer."

"If we're going to the concert," Amethyst said, "I'd better call Jas and postpone 'til tomorrow."

Melodie opened her mouth, then made a noise as if she'd been pinched. "Look how good I'm being!" she said brightly. "I'm not making a single comment about— Okay, Marl, stop!"

Amethyst laughed. With Talys, she headed for a bench along the thoroughfare to make her call. A knot of Native American boys, two of them dressed in dance costumes, long fringed kilt, fringed sash, moccasins and all, dodged in and out of the crowd. One wore a pair of alien antennae with bobbing green-glitter balls at the tips. The bells on their moccasins rang a frantic, jumbled rhythm.

She smiled and pulled the strap of her little purse over her head so she could open it. She dug out her phone and tapped in Jas' mobile number. The boys, confronted by an impenetrable clot of people, veered onto the grass, laughing and shoving each other. Amethyst squeezed back onto the bench and pulled her feet out of harm's way. One boy glanced aside at them. He stumbled, and the laughter disappeared from his face.

Talys took a step forward.

Amethyst, too, reached out a hand to the boy. "Are you okay?"

"Come on, Daniel," the boy with the antennae said, still running, green-sparkle balls bouncing. "We're gonna be late!"

The first boy's eyes were huge in his round, brown face. His friends yelled at him again, and he went pelting after them. His face turned toward Amethyst and Talys once, then he disappeared into the crowd.

Amethyst shrugged and held her phone to her ear. "Hey, Jas. It's Amethyst. What? I can't— Oh, yeah. We're at the fair. In fact, I called to see if we can reschedule. Okay. I appreciate it. I'll talk to you later."

She ended the call.

Melodie and Marl waited at a photovoltaics company booth, looking at brochures. Melodie turned with an arch look. Amethyst braced for the worst.

Melodie only said, "Anything in particular you want to see?"

Amethyst checked the time on her phone, then stuffed it back in her purse. "First I want to get one of those green chile cheese dogs, then I'd like to see the Frisbee dogs."

"I'd be curious to see the dance that so flustered those boys," Talys said.

Curious about the reaction of the boy who'd almost run into them, she guessed.

"How about you?" she asked Marl and Melodie. "Want to go see the dances at the Indian Village?"

"Sure," Marl said. "Why not."

The center of the Indian Village was a sand-bottomed bowl for dancing. Bordering the area on three sides were booths offering food and gifts, everything from dreamcatchers and beadwork to fantastical kachina dolls and fine Navajo silver and turquoise work.

Families lounged on blankets in choice shady spots. Down on the dancing grounds, three men pounded out a rhythm on a skin-covered drum. Amethyst felt the beat like her own heart.

"No dancers with alien antennae," she said.

Talys only shrugged.

He seemed unconcerned, not even really curious. But Amethyst sensed...what? Determination? Something as subtle as a heightening of attention?

Melodie headed for a booth displaying Pueblo pottery. Marl followed, but Amethyst hung back.

"Talys?" she said. "What are you looking for?"

"Mmm?" His broad, brown face turned one way, then another. "Nothing, really. Merely looking."

Looking, right. Marl and Melodie moved to the next booth, this one selling beaded belts and other leather goods.

"Is it that boy?" Amethyst took a leap. "He seemed to recognize you."

Now Talys did face her. "Why do you say that?"

She'd first known him as the cocky, pushy, infuriating spirit inhabiting a '69 Ford Mustang. She'd transformed him into a sword to fight the worst fight of her life. And then...then, when she thought he'd been destroyed, he reappeared like this—as a man. No, she reminded herself.

As a spirit inhabiting a man's body.

All the questions she'd had then came rushing back: where, exactly, had he found a body to use, and how did he go about inhabiting it? Talys had promised he wasn't a thief. And she'd never asked any further than that. Maybe she should have.

She stuttered now, not wanting to accuse. "You—" She gestured at him. "Well, you're obviously Navajo." He'd said as much himself, and he had a Navajo's barrel-chested, slim-hipped build. "That kid could've been, too. So…"

"So," he said.

Melodie and Marl browsed a few booths down now. The drummers started a new rhythm, faster and more aggressive than before.

Amethyst grabbed his arm. "Come on, Talys. Don't do this to me. You know how much I hate it."

He covered her hand with his, raised it to his lips and kissed the fingertips.

"Don't try to distract me," she said.

"Do you fear my past will come back to haunt us?" he teased.

"Something like that."

"No need to worry, love. There are pasts and pasts. My own has nothing to do with anyone who might have known this face." He turned her hand over and brushed his lips along her wrist.

She tried to ignore the tingle starting in her stomach. "Yeah, but—"

"Wiz!" Melodie leaned out from the line of people at

the nearer booths and waved at them.

Amethyst sighed. "We need to continue this conversation."

He gave one of his enigmatic smiles and guided her toward Melodie.

Melodie pulled her to the booth when she got close. "Didn't you say you were looking for cabochon garnet earrings? Look."

Amethyst dutifully looked. Talys stood behind her, a seawall against the ebb and surge of fairgoers. She even bought the earrings (they *were* what she'd been looking for).

A prickle of watching brushed the back of her neck. Turning, she slipped the earrings in their little Ziploc baggie into her purse. It was a good excuse to step away from the press of people at the booths, to run a glance over the people behind her. Kids rolling down the grassy berm. Three middle-aged Anglo women, tourists or transplants, dressed in Santa Fe chic—boots, broomstick skirts, bolero jackets and lots of turquoise topped with wild-colored cowboy hats. A Native American woman with an older man, father and daughter, maybe.

The watching tingle disappeared. Amethyst turned her head as if searching for a lost scent. Nothing. Imagination? After all, she hadn't heard the whisper of her name in anyone's mind this time. And even if—*whoever*—was still stalking her, she couldn't imagine him making his move in the middle of the New Mexico State Fair. Things could get too messy.

Still, it wouldn't do to be careless. She called up a

ward. It had to be general, magic to thwart and confuse random ill-chance. A ward against something specific, say fire or physical harm, would have been better, but she couldn't ward against every possible threat. The spell appeared to her wizard's eye as a shimmering bubble of purple light around them.

She frowned. It wasn't quite right. It was thin somehow, and wanted to fade. She made a troubled noise.

"What is it?" Talys murmured.

"Look at the magic. It seems…distracted. Like it isn't quite listening to me."

He tilted his head. "Ah. Yes. The dances, the songs…a great deal of tradition hangs heavy in the air here, magic honed for centuries. It's been changed, its full power broken and dampened for performance to outsiders, but it still produces echoes. Any magic you attempt to work must vie with this old power." He took her hand. "Here."

The warmth of his energy coursed up her arm and through her, then out again. Talys' silver infused the ward. It settled and steadied.

The drummers finished their performance, and the White Mountain Apache dancers filed onto the dance grounds. They stamped and chanted. Amethyst leaned against Talys on the grass. Marl and Melodie sat beside them, sharing fry bread. The dance stirred magic now and again, lazy swirls that dissipated like whirlpools on a flowing stream.

Uneasiness breathed down her neck. The sense of eyes returned, a breath across one cheek.

Pretending to shift her position, she straightened, searching. Spectators filled every gap around the dance grounds; at the far end, a raised stage held audio equipment, judges. Too many faces turned this way. Too many eyes too far away to see where, exactly, they looked. She shifted again.

Talys' arm circled her waist. "What's the matter, love?"

She shook her head slowly. "I...don't know." She reached her awareness into the magical ether. The press of life was a bubbling stew that buffeted her attention every which way. "I think we should go."

She leaned, touched Melodie's shoulder. "It's getting a little crowded for me. We're going to step away for some air. We'll meet you by the entrance after the dance."

"Okay," Melodie said.

Talys stood, pulled her to her feet and threaded them through the clusters of people. Away from the dance grounds, it was quieter. With the dance going on, fewer people browsed the booths. Still, the sense of too much noise, too many voices, thoughts, emotions, *life*—

Blind, deaf, numb, she stumbled.

Talys caught her. "Amethyst? Are you well?"

She folded her awareness tight. The everyday world came back: the trampled grass under her feet, the buildings around her, the brilliant blue sky, the sharp, high-altitude sunlight. She took a breath, then another. "I keep *feeling* something, so I tried to find it..."

The arm around her stiffened, then he chuckled. "So you touched the magic?" He tsk-tsked. "Never open your wizardly senses in a crowd, love. It's a recipe for sensory overload."

They stood at the edge of the Indian Village. The Navajo hogan stood behind them a short distance, an eight-sided structure of timbers chinked with mud. People passed, some hurrying to catch the dance. A fair security cart hummed by. The two officers riding in it looked as relaxed as the rest of the fairgoers.

"Thanks for telling me," she said.

"I thought—"

"Frank!" a woman's voice called behind them.

The voice was close. Automatically, Amethyst looked. The woman, a Native American, was maybe three or four yards away, moving toward them. A man walked with her. His hair, streaked with grey, was done in a traditional knot. Was it the same man and woman she'd seen a few minutes ago? Maybe. She wasn't sure. There'd been too many people.

"Frank," the woman said again, reaching for Talys. "Is that you?"

Behind the sunglasses, confusion puckered his face. Feigned, of course—Amethyst felt no confusion in him.

"I beg your pardon, madam." His accent was more pronounced than usual. "I fear you've mistaken me for someone else."

Her face fell. She took a step back. The man touched her briefly on the arm, then moved forward.

His brown face was hard, lined, expressionless. He held out a closed hand, fingers facing down. "Then this is for you."

Now Talys was perplexed. He hesitated, then held out his hand. The man opened his. Four small, ivory beads fell, tiny in Talys' big palm. Then the man began singing.

It was a high, ululating song full of words Amethyst couldn't understand. But anger was there, and grief.

Power rang there, too. Magic leapt up in answer. It spun, ripped around her, dark, hungry, enraged. Amethyst threw out a shield. The magic blew through it, over it, around it, oblivious to her defense.

The darkness gathered, rose, swept toward Talys.

She shouted, threw herself, body and power, in front of him. The maelstrom engulfed him. She swept her arms up, fingers crooked. Her own magic, desperate and furious, slashed at the storm, claws of panicked purple against an invisible, elemental wind. She might've been flailing her hands at an ordinary wind.

She called more spells, fendings, protections, spells to baffle and confuse the magic. The silver fire that was Talys flashed, shredded like tissue in a tornado.

"No!"

She opened herself wide to the magic. It poured through her, an unbearable pressure. She snatched at the silver bits. Darkness whirled them away. Darkness crushed them.

Talys collapsed. Amethyst cried out his name and tried to catch him. He was too big, too heavy. His hand fell open and the white beads rained down. His sunglasses bounced away. She was on her knees, hands splayed on either side of his body. His baseball cap lay on the ground beside his head, upturned and empty. His eyes were open.

Open, empty like the hat. The silver in them was gone.

"Talys!" she screamed.

She grabbed his face, dived with wizard's senses into his eyes—Native American dark. Nothing. Blankness. He could leave his chosen form, like a hermit crab creeping naked from its shell. He'd done it before, at great risk. This time he'd been torn out.

She swept the magical ether around her. Nothing. No warm, silver energy that was Talys. (Silver motes struggling in the dark wind, devoured—) *No.* He had to be here. Had to be somewhere. She searched, frantic.

The silver flicker, the spirit that was Talys, sucked out of the form he occupied, torn apart, flung away—gone. Nowhere—not in the ground, the air, the trees; not in the people around her, not in anything she held. Not even in herself.

Gone.

Gone.

Her heart beat too fast. She couldn't breathe, couldn't get enough air.

"You've killed him."

She looked up to see who'd said it. People stood all around. Round eyes. Open mouths. The Indian man and woman still stood there. The woman's hands were pressed to her mouth.

"You killed him," the voice said again. Her lips moved. She felt her voice in her throat. She said it, the terrible words, the words that couldn't be true.

Other voices babbled, called, cried out. Someone shouted.

Tears ran down the woman's face. Her mouth worked, but nothing came out.

Talys wasn't growing cold yet—it was too soon for that. But Amethyst took her hands from—from this shape that was no longer him.

She stood. Power thrummed in her as if her skin held no muscle, no bones, nothing but power. Shadow spread outward, crept across the asphalt, stained the air around her. The ground under her feet hummed to the same pulse that filled her. A prickle of static raced up her back and down her arms, a purple webbing of witchfire. The sharp smell of ozone suddenly filled the air.

The woman cried out and fell back. Expression flickered into the man's face at last: fear.

Amethyst reached out and stilled the two with a thought. Her teeth squeaked together she clenched them so tight. Pain in her jaw lanced into her temples. Heat pulsed behind her eyeballs. She tasted copper and iron.

"You killed him!"

Ice crystallized out of the warm fall air. Grass withered and crisped. Cracks appeared in the pavement, branching and multiplying from the epicenter of her feet. The beat of the power increased, fast and hot and aggressive as the drums earlier, burning her inside and out, gathering, current in a thunderhead before the bolt leaps—

Someone gripped her arm. "Amethyst!"

She whirled, teeth bared. Her vision was a pinpoint, red seething darkness all around. Melodie's face filled her view.

"Amethyst." Melodie's voice shook. "You have to

stop this." Her eyes were round, dark, the pupils dilated with fear. "Stop it," Melodie said. "Understand? You can't do this here."

"They killed him," she said again. Her lips moved, but she didn't feel her voice this time. More voices were crying out now. A girl or a woman squealed, a high, foolish sound. Amethyst couldn't stand it, and it stopped.

"Listen to me," Melodie said.

She couldn't listen. Too many voices shouted and cried and screamed. Power roared in her head. The seething red closed in on the tiny spot of light.

Out of the noise, Melodie's voice cried, "Get her phone!"

"*What?*" That was Marl.

"Call Jas Harker! She just called him, the number will be on her call log. It's in her purse, Marl, hurry!"

"But—"

"Just do it, please! You two, get the fucking hell *out* of here, now, do you understand me? What's wrong with you? *Leave!*"

The hands on her arms moved to her face. They shook her.

"Amethyst, talk to me. I'm here. I'm with you. Tell me what happened."

She didn't want to talk. The magic would say everything. It danced, trembling at the end of her power, a landslide ready to rumble down, to crush, to smother, to destroy—

Another power reached out. The onrushing magic slowed, shivered, stopped. She snarled in rage, but arms came around her, a cheek pressed against hers, a voice spoke in her ear.

"That's enough now." Jas' voice.

Jas? The magic turned soft and enveloping, cool fog soothing fire. She struggled, struck out, physically and psychically. He caught her hands, and the magic simply flowed around her blows.

He smoothed her hair, kneaded her shoulders. "Your friends are here. They'll be hurt, too. Let it go, Amethyst."

She struggled to pry away the resistance to destruction. Horror, pain, rage—the magic would make them go away. The magic would sweep her up, carry her off, burn away everything. She wouldn't have to think, to feel—

Jas' magic pressed into her mind, blunting pain, stilling thought. She wanted to fight it, but couldn't think why.

The world bloomed again, light and color and sound out of that terrible red blackness. Talys sprawled on the ground, half-hidden behind Jas' shoulder. Melodie and Marl, faces aghast. The Indian man and woman, clutching one another. A circle of staring people.

Jas turned, but kept an arm around her waist. He glanced down, and the cracks in the pavement drew together like healing wounds. The grass remained dead, but he laid illusion over it, making it seem only trampled green.

The mind-magic he'd used on her had turned her into a videocamera. Events followed one after another without meaning. She saw, heard, but didn't experience.

"What did you see?" Jas asked Melodie and Marl in a low voice.

"Tom, lying on the ground," Melodie said. "And she was looking at them—" Her eyes cut to the Indian man and woman. "—like—like she—"

"Yes," Jas snapped. "What else?"

Melodie's teeth chattered. Marl wet his lips, then answered. "Shadows. Something like electricity…" His voice, too, was unsteady. He pulled Melodie closer to him.

Jas nodded and let out a breath. "No pyrotechnics, then," he muttered. "Good."

"How…" Marl began. He tried again. "I just called you. How—"

Fair security rushed up. The golf cart squeaked and jolted to a stop. The men took one look at Talys, and one snatched the radio and gabbled into it. The other jumped out and hurried to lean over Talys. In another minute, two Albuquerque PD officers in shorts appeared, running. One started clearing the area, the other bent over Talys. Jas stepped back, pulling Amethyst with him.

She planted her feet. "No. *No.*"

The cop moved toward them. Jas raised a warning hand. Amethyst struggled, but somehow Jas drew her back.

The other cop checked Talys' pulse. "What happened here?" she said.

"They killed him." Her voice was a frayed thread. The only words she knew. The only words she would ever know.

The cops scrambled for gear. "Who killed him?"

Sirens wailed over the distant clang of the Midway, the drift of music. Amethyst stared at the old man, harmless-looking in his pressed cowboy shirt and new jeans. Tears finally started, running hot down her cheeks. "They…they…"

Jas shushed her. There was sudden commotion, shouts. Sirens yowled, coming closer. Cops and security converged on the Indian woman and the old man.

"He was my brother!" the woman cried. "Lightning hit him. He died last year!"

CHAPTER 13

Amethyst escaped to the living room. Only Caramela followed—she crept up onto the couch and laid her big head on Amethyst's thigh. Silent comfort, asking nothing of her.

Streetlight slanted through the gaps in the blinds, striping the living room carpet pale orange. The air was thick with the smells of chili and corn tortillas, cumin and cinnamon. Voices came from the dining room—Dad and Mama, Marl and Melodie. And Jas. The rest had left, Heather in a sober black dress. Oscar and Angela. Gary and Emily, sad and quiet and sympathetic. Friends, customers she'd grown close to. Uncle Martin and Aunt Estrella, cousins and spouses and kids. Even Alex Junior, her older brother, and his wife and baby had flown in from San Diego. Too many people to smile at and thank, to talk to, to be polite and sane with—

She wanted to crawl into bed and disappear. To get away from this house that was too full—and still agonizingly empty.

"But why won't they let her have his body?" Mama asked someone.

"They weren't married, Tonia." That was Dad. "She has no claim."

"The body has to go to next of kin," Marl said. "And if they don't choose to communicate with an unofficial partner..."

None of them spoke loudly. To ordinary ears, the voices would've been just a murmur, a word decipherable here and there. Amethyst's wizard's ears heard anyway. Probably Jas was the only one who'd know how well and how easily.

"If he *was* part of their family," Melodie muttered.

"The dental records proved he was," Jas said.

"Next of kin!" Mama said. "'Frank Tsosie,'" she mocked. "He wasn't Frank Tsosie. He was Tom Aturj. He changed his *name*. You don't do that if you're on good terms with your family."

"If he'd been struck by lightning, he might've had amnesia," Marl said. "Were you able to find out the cause of death, Jas?"

Amethyst already knew how Talys died. A body can't survive without a life-force to animate it.

Jas didn't answer for a moment. Yes, he knew she could hear. "It was listed as undetermined," he finally said in a low voice.

A fork or spoon tinkled. "*Not* lightning," Melodie said.

"They should've let her go to the service," Mama said.

"If they followed traditional beliefs, I don't know if there would've been a service," Marl said. "Navajos have a lot of taboos surrounding death."

"I know they have different customs. But it's cruel,

not letting her say goodbye."

Amethyst had already tried to explain. It didn't matter. The body was just a body. She'd been able to love him because he was a man, but it wasn't *Talys*.

There was the rattle of ice in a glass. "I'd hate to see her put through that service," Jas said.

Melodie and Marl knew exactly what he meant, of course. Dad and Mama didn't. Yet. It was so hard to remember the things she shouldn't say and do in front of them.

"At least she'd have some closure," Dad said. "She'd stop—"

Silence for a moment.

"She'd stop looking for him," Mama whispered.

"Oh, no," Melodie said. "What's she been doing?" She, too, whispered.

"I don't think she's willing to admit he's gone," Jas put in. "That is, she knows he's dead, but she's hoping to find…something left behind."

"Those people, the father and sister, insisted he died a long time ago," Melodie said. "At least Amethyst is trying to keep him alive."

"Denial," Jas said. "I'm not looking forward to anger."

"No," Marl said with quiet fervor.

"You two, *be quiet*," Mama said. Amethyst couldn't remember the last time she'd heard her so angry. "She needs people to stand by her now. Not worry about how she'll behave."

Marl spluttered an apology.

"Please, Mrs. Rey, forgive me," Jas said. "I have no intention of abandoning Amethyst."

Jas must still have that lulling spell on her. She should be infuriated. Or maybe grateful, who knew? She only felt...as if she'd been snuffed out. Like Talys.

Grief rose again, twisting. The pain in her reached out—she couldn't stop it. Magic growled and muttered like a distant thunderstorm. The light in the stained glass window on the living room wall rippled. Petals dropped from flowers in the arrangements that covered the coffee and end tables, the top of the entertainment center. A smell of dust and ozone bloomed in the room. Caramela whined and pawed her: *Please*, that paw said. *Please don't.*

A chair scraped the dining room linoleum.

"Jas?" Melodie said.

"I'm just going to check on her. No, that's all right, stay here. I'll be back."

His power came first, a sudden tangle that blocked her from the magic. His shadow appeared on the carpet, spilled by the light in the kitchen and dining room, then came the cush of his footstep.

"Amethyst?" The light behind him illuminated an angle of cheek and jaw, a sweep of black hair, the curve of shoulder and arm.

Her cheeks were cold. She wiped them. She couldn't remember beginning to cry.

He hesitated, then sat beside her. He didn't make the cushions dip as much as Talys had. She turned her face away, pressed her cheek to Caramela's head.

"You have to be careful," he said quietly. "If you

haven't already told your father and mother about yourself, they won't be able to understand now."

She shook her head against Caramela's.

His hand touched hers. "You have to try. You have to get a grip on your power. You're frightening people. You could hurt them. At the fairgrounds, you'd gathered enough energy to level the place. You don't want something like that to happen again."

"*My power*," she ground through her teeth. "It's worthless. I did everything—everything I could. Nothing worked. Nothing."

"The man was a shaman. You can't fight shamanistic power with our kind of wizardry. It's older. It works by different rules."

She pushed herself upright. "It ripped him right out of his body! Ripped him out, tore him up and threw away the pieces! How did they even know about him?" Her mind whirred like a wind-up toy. Ideas clicked and turned and fell into place. "You knew about him."

His fingers tightened. "No. Don't do that. It won't help."

"No one else knew." She groped for something, anything that would make sense. Did Jas have a reason to get rid of Talys? Jas had promised he didn't intend to draw her in again... She didn't know, couldn't think. Everything was jumbled.

"The woman said he—the body Tom inhabited—was her brother," he said. "The moment that shaman saw him, he would know what he was looking at. And it wouldn't be a man."

She clenched her fists. "You should've let me kill them."

"If you had, it would destroy you."

"Who cares." She dropped each word.

"Every person in this house cares." He paused. "Tom would care, don't you think?"

"Yes," she said in a suddenly small voice.

But she didn't know *why* he'd care. As a familiar protecting his wizard? How many wizards had he linked with over his long existence? What did he feel when they died, beyond vulnerability? While she felt...she felt...like an arm or leg had been hacked off and the artery was gushing blood.

"It was my fault. I knew something was wrong. I thought—I thought it—the wrongness—was for me. Not him." She breathed, trying to get air through her constricted throat. "Why? Talys didn't do anything to them! She said her brother died last year. She knew he was already gone. Why do they care about a body? What good is it to *them?* They think it's filthy. They'll put it in a hole somewhere in the desert and cover it up with rocks. But Talys—Talys—"

"I know, I know."

"I couldn't stop it." The tears poured out again, but she didn't sob. "Why not? Why couldn't I save him?"

He worked at her knotted fingers. "It *wasn't* your fault. A shaman's power comes from the spiritual plane. From the otherworld. Ours comes from the magic here. The shaman's would've passed like a ghost through any spell you worked."

The tears stopped. "The spirit world," she murmured. "Talys was a spirit." She raised her head. Jas sat close, almost as close as Caramela. She felt his warmth, too. "Where did he come from?"

"I don't know. Familiars have never been common in my time."

A layer or two of the suffocating grief peeled away. "What if he wasn't destroyed?"

Jas shook his head.

She thought of the dark wind, tearing, whirling away bits of silver. "What if—what if he was only...driven off...somewhere?"

Jas was still shaking his head. "Amethyst, don't."

"It happened before," she said stubbornly. "He was carried away, and I thought—"

He put an arm around her shoulders and jiggled her. "Don't do this to yourself. This isn't the same. The binding is broken. You know it is."

That was the spurting artery: the binding left dangling with nothing at its end. No familiar. No Talys. She didn't want to cry again. Not with Jas there. But it hurt so much—

"Violita?" Mama's voice came from the kitchen doorway.

Jas withdrew his arm, released Amethyst's hand.

Mama came into the room. Against her black dress and dark hair, her face looked paler than her usual adobe rose complexion. Her brown eyes were sad and sympathetic. "How are you?"

Dad joined her. He wasn't a tall man, but he was

solid, with an air of calm dependability. His dark tie and black suit jacket were gone. He wore a pearl grey shirt. Amethyst was glad. All-black clothes were Talys' signature. She didn't want to see anyone else wearing them.

"Come on, Caramela," Dad said. "Make room."

"No need." Jas stood.

Dad nodded with obscure satisfaction. Mama took Jas' place, took Amethyst in her arms and pulled her head to her shoulder as if she were six years old.

Dad laid a hand on her cheek. "Holding up okay, Thistle?"

Her parents had purple nicknames for her: Mama's little violet, Dad's prickly thistle. Dad's had always been more appropriate. She tried to smile, gave a one-shouldered shrug and a nod.

"Good." He patted her cheek and asked Jas, "Got a minute?"

"Certainly," Jas said.

Dad led the way to the front door. It opened on a breath of rain-scented night air, let in the hum of a car driving up the street, then closed again on them.

Amethyst let her attention follow them. Distraction, that was all it was. Something else to think about. In the dining room, Marl and Melodie's voices faded to the background murmur they really were.

"I expect you to be careful with her," Dad said. She couldn't hear them with her ears at all, only through the magic. "She's in a lot of pain," he went on. "She doesn't need anything else to deal with. I think you know what I mean."

"Yes," Jas said. "I do. It's been a long time since I lost anyone that close to me, but I hope I'm a good enough friend to understand what she's going through."

"I'd appreciate it if you stayed a good friend." Dad emphasized the last word.

"Of course."

Dad was the best. He took care of her the way Talys did—the way Talys had—

Tears surged up.

"Oh, Violita," Mama said. "Oh, *mijita*."

"I let him down." Amethyst's voice cracked. "He counted on me, and I failed him."

Mama put a hand over Amethyst's mouth. "Shush, Violita. I don't want to hear that talk. Tom wouldn't have either."

The tears sank away again, and she sagged against Mama's shoulder. "What do I do now, Mama? What do I do?"

Mama only rocked her.

CHAPTER 14

The shaman's dark wind filled her mind. Amethyst couldn't think, couldn't remember. People talked to her, she answered, but it was like her voice belonged to someone else, someone who understood what was said to her, what was happening.

"No, Mama, it's okay. Go on home. I'll be fine."

"I'm still worried about you, *mija*. Come home with us. Stay a week or so. You know how happy it would make your papa."

Amethyst wanted Dad to be happy. But she couldn't stand everyone watching her like a crystal vase wobbling on a shelf.

"Hey, Amethyst, honey." That was Heather, on the porch with a foil-covered dish. "I brought you a chicken green enchilada casserole. Just in case you don't feel like cooking."

Amethyst didn't say the refrigerator and freezer were filled with spaghetti, beef stroganoff, shepherd's pie, tamales, chicken noodle soup (as if what ailed her was no more than a bad cold). She couldn't eat any of them.

And Melodie's calls and visits: "Why don't you come over for dinner, Wiz?" "Want to go to Balloon Fiesta this weekend?" "Marl and I are taking the Rail Runner to Santa

Fe. We'll have some lunch and do the galleries. We'd love it if you came along."

How many days before the doorbell rang again? This time she opened the door and found Jas outside.

He looked her up and down and his lips settled into a grim line. "How are you?"

She thought she should be annoyed. Pretending to act the way she normally would seemed to convince people. "You came to my house to ask me that?"

"You don't answer your phone."

"Maybe I've been busy. You could leave a message."

Jas folded his arms. "I have. Several."

She didn't have the energy for this. "Then sorry. Did you need something?"

He tilted his head as if considering. "Why don't you show me the window. I haven't seen it in a while."

Amethyst rubbed her forehead. "Jas, I'm really not feeling well right now."

"I know." He took her arm, stepped inside and shut the front door. "But go get dressed and let's take a look at the window."

Get dressed? She looked down. She still wore her pajamas. Heat crept into her face.

"I'll be right back," she muttered, pulled free of his grasp and hurried down the hall to her bedroom.

The bed was a rumpled pile. Clothes lay on the floor. She flung through the strewn mess, dragged on jeans and a wrinkled t-shirt that didn't reek of stale laundry. Her hair—well, she wasn't going to get in the shower with Jas in the house. Besides, what was the point? She did the best she could with a brush, put it in a ponytail and went out again.

She found him in the garage, looking down at the window, hands clasped behind his back.

Amethyst followed his gaze. Dust hazed the rich colors. The copper foil was already beginning to show dark, oxidized spots.

He looked up. Something moved through his gaze. "Ready? Good. Let's get some lunch."

A flicker of real irritation did rouse this time. "I'm not hungry."

"We'll go to the office afterwards," he went on. "I still need you to look at that code."

She sighed and resisted the urge to close her eyes. "Jas, I'm sorry, but I'm really not up to it."

"It'll do you good, give you something else to think about. Besides, you don't want to owe me two projects, do you?" he said, smiling.

Sudden rage swept her. "I don't care about your goddamn projects! You deal with it, okay?"

His smile fell away. "Stop indulging yourself, Amethyst. You have obligations. Pick yourself up and meet them."

"You—you sonofabitch!" she spluttered. "*Indulge* myself! What, d'you think I'm staying home to eat ice cream and watch TV? Do you have any goddamn *idea*—"

"You're not the only one in the world who's lost someone."

"Just my familiar! Who I also happened to love!"

His dark eyes went cold. "I've lost more people I

loved than you can imagine, little girl. Wives. Children. Friends. Do you want me to tell you how many I've watched die? I can heal injuries and illnesses, but I can't stop aging." He gave a humorless laugh and shook his head. "If you can't deal with this, I don't know how you'll cope over the next few hundred years."

"Who cares? What business is it of yours? I never asked for any of this." She waved her arms. "I'm done, understand? Finished! Go away and leave me alone!" The words spilled out. She wasn't making any sense, but it didn't matter.

He came around the work table and caught her by the arm again. "You're coming to the office and looking at that code as you promised. I went far out of my way for you, Amethyst. Now you're going to repay the favor."

She cursed and took a swing at him, but he raised an arm and blocked her.

He spun her and pushed her against the garage wall. "Is that what you want?" he said through clenched teeth. "Fine. Let's get it over with, then. You're still angry with me, are you?"

"I'm sick of you screwing around with me," she spat. "Sweet-talking me, lying to me, trying to con me into doing what you want. Well, the hell with you!"

He released her and spread his arms. "I was raised not to hit women, but I don't mind matching magic with you."

She shoved him away and stormed toward the half-finished window, already hearing the satisfying crash it would make when she kicked the sawhorses out from under the plywood work surface. He caught her shoulder and pulled her back. She whipped around, fist cocked, his chivalry be damned.

The garage disappeared.

He released her and stepped back. Amethyst snarled a curse and dropped her fist. He'd zapped them into some office—windowless walls in a soft sage green, low-pile carpet in utilitarian grey, workstation. Probably in the Magus Building. She didn't bother trying to zap herself back out again. She'd have to wrestle with his shields while he hit her with some other kind of magic. She made to shove past him.

Jas took her by the arms and thrust her into the chair in front of the workstation. He was slender, nowhere near Talys' bulk and height, but stronger than she would've thought.

"If you don't like me sweet-talking you, I'll simply tell you. Stop acting like a child in a tantrum. Look at the code."

She glared up at him. "Then bring it up, goddammit. I'll look at it." Damn sure looking was *all* she was going to do.

He leaned over her and tapped the keyboard. The screen lit up. Jas straightened again, raised his hand palm-up. A paper-wrapped sandwich appeared there. He slapped it down on the desk.

"Eat that. Pick up the phone when you're finished and tell me what you found." He walked out and shut the door behind him.

Amethyst clenched her fists on her knees and fought

the impulse to either scream or throw the sandwich at the door. Or both. Who the hell did he think he was, calling her *little girl*? Calling her a *child*. She glared at the lines of code. He thought he had some bad juju in his system now? Wait 'til she was done with it.

She scrolled through the code, then backed out and started poking into other files on the tree. She could open all of them. Had Jas screwed up and left her logged in under his security level? She doubted it. Which meant he was trusting her with full access to the system.

Amethyst folded her arms and scowled at the screen. "Damn you, Jas," she muttered.

She clicked on a file titled *Breached* with a date of about a week and a half ago. A list of organizations came up, along with the datasets compromised and the method of infiltration. Some of the companies she didn't feel very sorry for, but damn… The ASPCA? Doctors Without Borders? The Nature Conservancy?

"Shit." She sat back in the chair and kicked at the workstation's leg. "You bastard. I *have* to help you now, don't I?"

❖❖❖❖❖❖

"You ate," Jas' voice said behind her. "Good."

Amethyst wrenched around. Her neck kinked, and she winced and rubbed it. "Dammit, Jas!"

He leaned in the doorframe. "When I didn't hear anything, I thought I'd better come check on you. I anticipated having to come down here and put out fireworks an hour or two ago."

Hours? She rolled her head and shoulders. The mustard on the sandwich wrapper was dry. Two water bottles—one empty, the other half-empty, sat beside her on the desk. Where the hell had they come from? *Three guesses, Amethyst.*

"Did I ever tell you you're one damn despicable excuse for a human being, even if you are a wizard?" she said.

His lips twitched. "Once or twice. I take it your conscience got the better of you."

"Not that you'd know anything about that."

"Not a bit. I'm a pure pragmatist."

"Obviously," she said.

"That's why I picked up take-out, so we can eat in my office. You look like hell."

She folded her arms and shoved back in her chair. "Gosh, thanks for that, Jas. I tried to spare your fine sensibilities, but you wouldn't take 'no' for an answer."

"You know I never do. Now come on." He stepped to the side and gestured toward the door.

She toyed with the idea of making life difficult for him. She might not be able to zap through his shields easily, but she could zap herself elsewhere in the building and make him come looking for her. Or—

Oh, never mind. He'd only enjoy it.

She stood. "Do *not* zap me. If you do, I'll fry every piece of electronics in this building."

"No one here will give you a second glance. You look like one of the programmers."

She sailed past without looking at him then stopped in the hallway outside. She had no idea where they were in the building. He caught up with her as if he didn't know perfectly well she was lost and walked on, just enough ahead to lead the way without making it obvious. Why did that annoy her as much as when he was pushing her around?

Wait. She actually *was* annoyed now. In fact, she'd also been furious, concerned, interested…when the last time she'd felt much at all was when Talys—

She stopped the thought. Better to just be annoyed with Jas. Especially when he was right.

They rode the elevator to the top floor. Amethyst wondered if Jas did something, whether technological or magical, because it didn't stop on any other floors. Most of the desks in the executive reception area were empty, although she caught a glimpse through office doors of a couple of harried-looking people pounding away on presumably down-to-the-wire projects. They greeted Jas absently and went back to work. He opened his office door.

The aroma of Chinese food greeted her. Several P.F. Chang's bags waited on the table in front of the big windows. Outside, a blue and purple twilight gleamed. Squares of light glowed in the neighboring buildings, investment bankers or engineers putting in a long day. Surprisingly enough, the food made Amethyst's mouth water.

She shot Jas a suspicious glance. "So is this just coincidence? Or did you know how much I love P.F.

Chang's?"

"I'll go with coincidence. Have a seat. You can tell me what you found after we've eaten."

The whole scene echoed some of her first meetings with him. A strange pain twisted somewhere between her stomach and heart. She swallowed hard and took a sip of the tea he poured, a fragrant green.

"Why is it you're always trying to feed me?"

He slid across a plate loaded with double-fried noodles, pepper steak, almond and cashew chicken, then peeled the lid off a container of hot and sour soup. "Am I?"

She poked her chopsticks in his direction. "Yes, you are. Why?"

He occupied himself with another box for a moment. "I don't think I should answer that. It sounds like one of those 'does this dress make my butt look fat' questions."

A laugh popped out. She scowled and clamped her mouth shut. Holy Mary. She was laughing at his jokes now. Disgusting.

"Do *not* say I'm skinny, or I'll—"

"Fry every piece of electronics in the building. Yes. I know. Am I allowed to say you don't seem to be eating properly lately?"

"That's it." She pushed to her feet.

He took a spoonful of soup. "I thought you loved P.F. Chang's."

"Not enough to be insulted while I eat it."

He put down his spoon. "That was an observation by a concerned friend. I'm sorry you can't tell the difference."

Tears suddenly muscled into her eyes. She put up a hand to shield them and turned away. "Don't do this to me now."

"What am I doing?"

"I can't trust you!"

"No. You can't."

She spun back. "What the hell is that supposed to mean?"

"Amethyst…" He sighed and pinched the bridge of his nose. "It means I don't expect you to. But that won't stop me from behaving as a friend." He dropped his hand. "I don't think you realize how vulnerable you are."

"I've lost my familiar. You think I don't feel vulnerable?"

"Then why are you playing Persephone pining away in the Underworld?"

Amethyst drew a breath to protest, then let it out again. The world hadn't stopped just because Talys had— She gritted her teeth. Had died.

"Are you saying what happened to Talys—" Logic dragged her in a direction she didn't want to go. She sank into the chair. "No."

Across the table, Jas sat silent, reply enough to her thoughts.

"I thought I stopped them with that warning. I didn't, did I?" She just breathed, fighting tears. "So they killed him." Her voice broke. "It was magic, wasn't it? They worked some kind of vile spell to bring that shaman. I thought it was just something that happened. Something— something terrible that happened. But after everything else, I should've known."

She pressed her fists to her forehead. He reached across the table, pulled her hands away. She tried to break free, but he wouldn't let her.

He shook her a little. "This isn't your fault. What else would you have done? Tamely submitted?"

She stared across the plates of food growing cold, her wrists caught in his grip. She felt sucked down into darkness, like the only thing that kept her from going under was that grip.

"Is this why you guys are the way you are?"

He gave his head a shake, his dark brows quirked in puzzlement.

"Wizards," she explained. "Is this why you'll do—whatever it takes to get something? Because if you don't, somebody will do it to you first?"

"Not all of us," he said softly. "No."

"Because I'm thinking, maybe if I'd just hurt someone really badly—"

"No, Amethyst." He bent his head a moment, then looked up again. "You have to realize how old some of us are. Things were so different four hundred, seven, eight hundred years ago. When killing an enemy or a rival was a matter of simple survival. When most people never knew when an enemy might ride over the hill and slaughter your brothers, rape your women and carry off your children to slavery. The morals weren't the same. You protected your own. As long as you did that, you owned the moral high ground."

"But who am I threatening?"

"Most wizards won't understand you," he said. "They'll see only that you have enough power to be a threat. The fact that you don't use that power as they would makes them only more uneasy."

What am I supposed to do? She didn't want to ask him.

He watched her a moment, then let go her wrists. He slid a spoon across. Automatically, she picked it up and dipped it into her soup.

Jas watched her. "Eat a little. Then tell me what you saw in that code."

She managed to get a sip of soup, salty and tangy, past her lips, then squeeze it down.

He ate in silence. Somewhere along the line, he did some kind of magic on the food: a wisp of steam rose from her plate. Her choking distress ebbed. She wondered if he did something to her, too. Or maybe it was just the usual grey dullness creeping up on her again.

The chopsticks made it easier to take tiny bites, but she finally couldn't take any more.

She laid down her chopsticks and spread her hands on either side of her plate, steadying herself. "It's a magical Trojan Horse. The code looks harmless—as I'm sure you've already been told—but once it's accessed a system, it transforms into something that opens a backdoor—and you're breached."

"How is the transformation effected?"

She pursed her lips. "It's more of an unfolding. Some of the code is hidden." She curled her hands together, knuckle to knuckle, then opened them like a flower. "It comes to the surface, and other parts, the ones that look like they don't do anything, get rearranged."

He sat back and let out a long breath. "Then we're facing another wizard who has technological expertise."

She thought, then shook her head. "I don't think so. The Trojan wasn't built the way I built that worm of mine. Theirs looks like more of a cut-and-paste job, like they started with the code, then put the magic on top of it. I don't know if they even seriously expected it to succeed. It feels to me more like a probe. Or a beta program."

He nodded slowly, then cleared their plates and poured fresh tea. She took a sip and toyed with a wrapped fortune cookie. She used to enjoy reading the fortunes, saving the good ones for luck. Now she had no desire to see it.

"I've been thinking," Jas said. "And I have an idea." He paused, as if awaiting an explosion.

Amethyst waited, too.

"What you've been doing today," he said, "studying that code. I'd like to make it official. Put you on the payroll."

The dullness evaporated. "What? No."

He waved a hand. "Then I can 1099 you. We'll call you a consultant."

"No."

"Anyone looking in my direction won't know what I am, but they will know I'm a wealthy and powerful man. They won't be surprised if I hire a wizard. It's extra protection for both of us. If I'm known to have a wizard at my disposal, they'll think twice about trifling with me. If you're known to have a patron, they'll be less likely to attack you."

"No."

"Amethyst—"

"No."

"*Amethyst*. Do you enjoy being hounded and hunted? Am I really such a terrible alternative?"

She hadn't asked the question, what she was supposed to do. Still, he'd answered it. And the idea made perfect, depressing sense.

She put her head in her hand. "How long have you been planning this?"

There was a beat of silence. "I first considered it when you came asking my help. I began to seriously consider it when I discovered the virus."

Then before Talys—before what happened. *If* Jas was telling the truth.

She raised her head. "What would you make me do?"

He gave her an exasperated look. "I wouldn't *make* you do anything. As far as I'm concerned, we'd be partners."

"Say that with the Truth-O-Meter turned on." She wiggled her fingers as if casting a spell. "Like you did when you first told me about the virus."

He sighed. "I swear I will treat you as an equal."

The little magical bell of truth rang. She nodded.

He cocked a brow. "Which is what you *should* have asked me. Partners aren't necessarily equal. If you ask for truth, make sure you have your terms precisely defined. Just like with a contract."

She rubbed her forehead. "Why this proposal, Jas?

Just...why?"

"I told you—"

"I know what you told me," she said. "But with you, it's always something else."

She was pushing him, but he only paused before replying.

"Wizards form partnerships only rarely," he said. "Generally, there's too much rivalry between us."

"No!" she said. "Really?"

"But when they do," he went on, "they're formidable." He cupped his tea between his hands. "I know you can't trust me, Amethyst. But I trust you. You're exactly what you seem. If you ever decided to turn on me, you'd tell me."

She gave a breath of a laugh. "I can't turn on you, Jas. I'm not on your *side*."

"I'm asking if you will be."

They could go round and round with this all night. The bottom line was that she didn't—couldn't—trust him. *Now*, he proposed this. *Now*. When, yes, she was vulnerable. When even trying to decide what to eat and what to wear was a heavy lift most days. And he had to know it. Yet every argument he offered was blindingly reasonable.

Did she dare risk agreeing? Could she afford *not* to?

"Okay," she said. "But only if there're no bindings involved."

Something flickered across his face—relief? Satisfaction? "A binding would make us stronger." He held up his hands. "No, I'm not proposing it."

She nodded once. "Good. So can I go home now? Maybe go back to *indulging* myself?"

"I'll take you home, but no. No more wallowing. If this is going to work, you have to be seen working for me."

Three or four arguments occurred to her, but she was just so tired. He would be challenging her, badgering her, *feeding* her again, for godsake. But that was tomorrow. He wouldn't know if she spent tonight...wallowing.

Jas stood. After a breath, she did, too.

"No wallowing tonight, either," he said.

Damn him! "I thought you were going to treat me like an equal."

He gave one of his crinkly, charming smiles. "I rely on you to do the same for me if I ever begin neglecting myself."

"Oh, don't worry," she muttered. "I will."

CHAPTER 15

J as didn't want her to wallow? Fine. But if he thought she'd just quietly accept this partnership with him, he was only outsmarting himself.

Amethyst paced the length of her back patio, past the resin chairs, cold orange in the streetlight, the frost-killed pots, the trellised honeysuckle bush, its leaves blackened and dying. The house lay dark, the back windows blank, reflective eyes. Caramela sat in the dining room, perceptible to her wizard's senses as a watching shadow on the other side of the sliding glass door.

A breath of air came from nowhere, chilly with fall. It curled around her waist, smoothed her hair back from her face. The leaves of the mulberry tree in the corner of the yard rattled; a few fluttered down. One came to rest at her feet. The breeze sighed and wandered away. She bent and picked up the leaf: yellow, with a pattern of dark spots. She pressed the cool leaf against her cheek. The slight astringent smell wafted to her.

If only Talys was here, she wouldn't be vulnerable to begin with. She wouldn't even consider an alliance with Jas. If only…

She stopped, stared into the darkness. If only she could find Talys, bring him back.

Spells lay like coins at the bottom of her mind. She sifted through them. Healing, for the wound in her. Shielding, to protect herself. Fending, to drive off the evil that beset her.

A summoning, to call spirits.

Amethyst caught a swelling breath. Hope shouldered aside the ache in her gut.

She studied the spell. It was formal, layered with ritual gesture, ritual words, as if the wizard she'd gotten it from had been medieval. The spell was also powerful, powerful enough to call a living soul across vast distances and past most obstacles. Powerful enough to call a spirit from other planes—or back from the dead.

Magic that strong demanded a price. She didn't care what it was. She'd pay it.

She built a barrier around the backyard, a bubble that would contain the magic—and keep the neighbors from noticing any strange lights or noises while working it. Magic ran through her like a burst of adrenaline, hot and cold at once, for an instant carrying with it the neighborhood's life: Caramela, worried and not understanding why she was locked inside; Heather doing yoga to New Age music; Gary and his girlfriend, Emily, making out in the backyard; a cat slipping along the alley wall after some small prey. The barrier settled and sealed, and Amethyst was alone.

Power moved through her. The temperature of the air and ground dropped as she borrowed heat energy for the barrier. She'd need to save as much of her own power as possible for the spell.

She opened her arms to the four cardinal points. She sang the words, Latin syllables with the cadence of a traditional Catholic mass. The unfamiliar words formed images in her mind: Tapestries breathing against stone walls. Beneath a groined ceiling that swallowed shadow like a demon's mouth, hooded figures surrounded a kneeling man clad only in a loincloth. Smoke curled from braziers gripped by bronze gargoyles. The man's arms rose, candlelight moved over his skin. The air shimmered with power and he collapsed, a wasted scarecrow between one instant and the next—

The vision vanished, stone walls replaced by concrete block, shadowy ceiling by the hard glitter of the high-altitude night sky. Her mouth was dry, the memory of the man crumpled on the stones a cold knot in her gut. The power in her faltered.

She pushed the image aside. The magic was far more potent now than it had been then. And she was a different kind of wizard, born to survive handling rough, half-feral magic. She wouldn't abandon Talys because she was scared. She wouldn't give up without even trying.

She gathered power again, molded the magic to the shape of the spell. Energy poured out of her like blood. Her hands and feet went cold, then numb. Her knees buckled. Pain spiraled around her backbone, ribs, the bones of her arms and legs. Her stomach and guts cramped. Her heart fluttered like a moth against glass, but she clenched her jaw and held the shape of the spell.

Physical bonds broke like cables snapping, the energies that held reality together. A shimmering line appeared in the air, split apart like a ripping seam. Night streamed inward, feathers of darkness against light of no color she could name. An otherworldly wind plucked at her shirt and whipped her hair forward, around her face. Energies crackled, drew the hair on her arms straight up. A sense of impossible vastness, of unending infinity tried to suck the bobbing spark that was Amethyst into itself. She held onto the pain that beat through her, the laboring of her lungs, the shudder of her heart.

She held her arms wide in a gesture of welcome. "Talys, I summon you!" she cried.

The light pulsed, then glared bright as a trumpet call. The polarity reversed. Light and wind spilled out. Imminence gathered, approaching.

On her knees, Amethyst threw back her head. "Come!"

She opened the throttle to her power as wide as it would go. Magic tore out of her in a white-hot burst. She screamed and toppled. Her face hit the ground and darkness clamped over the light.

❖❖❖❖❖❖

Something fluttered around her. Flakes of silver against the dark, slivers of a whispering voice.

A-A-A-A-m-m-m-th-th-th-th—

Points of warmth touched her skin, like snowflakes in reverse. A thread of energy wound through her.

Amethyst opened her eyes. Dim blades of grass marched away in her view.

"Talys?" Her voice came out as a bare creak. She felt like a whole hillside had slid and landed on her.

What had happened? Had she been in a wreck? She tried to get her hands under her, push herself up, but couldn't. Her guts clenched, so hungry they hurt. She must've been doing magic. That was the only thing that could make her feel so empty and drained. Where was Talys? He should be here, not letting her lie on the lawn like a bird that hit a window.

"Tal—"

She stopped. The spell. The summoning. She struggled to get up again. Thumping and scratching came from somewhere nearby. The warbling cry of a distressed dog. Caramela.

Amethyst rolled her head in the grass. Caramela jumped and clawed at the patio door. The spells must've collapsed when Amethyst had. She wanted to stretch out a hand to the dog, to put a calming thought in her mind. Neither hand nor magic responded.

"What's that?" a woman's voice said.

"Sounds like a dog." That was a man. Gary. It was Gary's voice. He and Emily had been in the Griegos' backyard.

"Is it Amethyst's dog?" Emily's voice said. "Gary, you'd better peek over the wall. It sounds like something's really wrong."

"I don't think—"

"I'll do it, then." Nothing for a moment, then, "Oh my god! Gary, somebody's lying on the grass. It looks like Amethyst!"

The voices went away, but Caramela kept hurling herself and digging at the glass door. Amethyst's front gate creaked. Footsteps and voices approached.

"Crap, Emily!" Gary said. "Oh, crap!"

Footsteps tapped on the patio, hurried through the grass. Feet appeared in her view.

"Amethyst?" Emily said. Her voice shook. A hand touched her.

"Caramela," Amethyst whispered.

Two breaths went out—they must've thought she was dead. Gary's legs walked toward the house, then Emily rolled her over and she couldn't see him anymore.

In the streetlight, Emily's face was a pale blur surrounded by wisps of curls. "What happened? Did you faint?"

Dog nails scrabbled on concrete, then Caramela pounced on her, whining, sixty pounds of pit bull muscle and frantic tongue. Amethyst could scarcely turn her head away.

Emily looked up at Gary. "You better call 9-1-1."

"No," Amethyst said. "Food."

"What?" Gary said.

Amethyst wasn't sure she could get the word out a second time. She closed her eyes and concentrated on breathing.

"I think she said 'food,'" Emily said. "Is she diabetic or hypoglycemic or anything? I think they're supposed to drink juice or something like that. Check her refrigerator."

Amethyst drifted a moment, then Gary was jostling her, propping her up.

Emily put a glass to her lips. "It's orange juice."

Amethyst drank. Much of the juice dribbled down her chin. Emily offered a banana. Amethyst could barely chew, although swallowing was becoming easier. Caramela snuffled her, still whining.

"What do you want us to do, 'Thys?" Gary said behind her. "Can we call anyone?"

"Melodie," Amethyst rasped out.

"Where's your phone, Amethyst?" Emily said. "In your purse?"

She wasn't sure if she told Emily where to find her purse, but then Emily was kneeling beside her again, a phone pressed to her ear.

"No, sorry," Emily said into the phone. "This is Emily Keener. I'm calling on Amethyst's phone. She fainted. No. Yes, she's doing a little better, but she asked us to call you."

Emily continued her conversation. Amethyst cranked her eyes up to Gary. He looked worried.

"Thanks," she breathed.

A strained version of his grin appeared. "Any time."

Emily thumbed off the phone. "We should get her in the house," she said to Gary. "Do you think you can carry her?"

Gary gathered up Amethyst then staggered to his feet, awkward and off-balance with her in his arms. She knew she was going to be mortally embarrassed sometime in the next day or so, but that time wasn't now.

Gary got her settled on the couch. Caramela climbed up beside her. Amethyst drank more juice and closed her eyes again.

Voices and movement made her open them. Melodie stood by the front door as if she'd zapped there by magic. Amethyst blinked, disoriented, then Melodie came and knelt by the couch, her lips thin and brows crooked. Marl seemed to be debriefing Gary and Emily. Marl glanced at Amethyst, invited the other two outside and shut the door.

"Jesus Christ, Amethyst," Melodie burst out. "Have you eaten at *all* since—" She closed her mouth.

"Not you, too," Amethyst said. Her voice still came out in a creak.

"What do you mean, me too? You look like a Holocaust survivor. Your house is a wreck. I thought you needed some space. If I'd known you were going to try to kill yourself—" Her voice caught.

Amethyst's chest squeezed. She wanted to take Melodie's hand, but couldn't reach that far. "It was…" She took a breath. "…the spell."

Melodie frowned. "What spell? I've seen you work magic, and if you expect me to believe it did this—"

"I tried to bring him back."

"Oh God," Melodie breathed and sat back. "Talys? You tried to bring Talys back?" she put a hand over her face, then dropped it. "What are you thinking, Amethyst? He's gone. What would you bring him back *to?*"

"Anything! The car. My phone. Me. Like before."

Melodie's eyes went round. "I'm calling your mom. Where's your phone?"

"No!" Amethyst put some force into the word. "No! You don't understand." She closed her eyes, but tears pushed up, rolled hot down her cheeks. "I failed. The strongest spell I ever worked. I couldn't find him. He wasn't there."

She turned her head and sobbed, weak, painful sobs that wouldn't stop.

CHAPTER 16

*A*methyst had to get home somehow. She didn't have a car. It'd take hours on foot, and there were some bad neighborhoods to go through. She took a breath, set her jaw and started walking.

She knew the streets, but they didn't go where they were supposed to. One, lined with dingy storefronts interrupted by menacing alleys, grew narrower and grimier and dimmer as she went on. She faltered, then turned and backtracked, hurried down a side street that was a little less daunting than the alleys.

Her feet hurt, but she kept walking. This street was headed into one of the bad neighborhoods. It'd be crazy to try to go through there on foot. She stopped, breathing hard and almost in tears.

Grey, forbidding buildings crowded a cracked sidewalk littered with broken glass. Silver light beckoned a block up. She couldn't see where it came from, but she went that way. She turned the corner. A little apartment tucked itself into the frowning buildings. Silver light flickered through the casement windows and open door.

She didn't know why, but the light soothed her distress. She stepped through the door—

Into darkness. She couldn't feel her feet on the floor, the clothes on her body, the blink of her eyes, even her breath. She was nothing, floating in nothingness. Fear beat in the absence of her heart.

A flicker of silver came. She turned, moved through the darkness toward it. Another, like the brief, bright flash of a falling star. She followed its fading trail. A silver spark danced ahead. She ran toward it, but it winked out. Another flared. She darted forward, reached and caught it between cupped hands.

The flake of silver warmed her fingers, made the edges glow red. She held her cupped hands to her heart, and she felt the beat of it now.

"I can't get home," Amethyst whispered. "Everything is wrong."

The spark between her fingers was warm, like something alive, and sent warmth into her. A flurry of silver burst in the darkness, like a log suddenly settling in a fire. Sparks rose, twisting, edging the shape of her hands and arms and body. The mote she held bumped the inside of her fingers as if trying to escape. She held it tight, following the glowing trail of one of the sparks—

The doorbell rang. Amethyst started awake. Caramela, at the end of the couch, raised her head.

Amethyst blinked and wet her dry mouth. Mouth-breathing. Ugh. The bowl of soup in her lap tilted at a dangerous angle. She straightened on her pillows, righted the bowl and wobbled it to the coffee table.

Mama—who Melodie had called, no matter how much Amethyst argued—stood at the front door talking to someone outside.

"She's resting," Mama said. "She's very sick."

Then Jas' voice: "May I see her? We'd made arrangements to start work on a project today."

Amethyst cursed silently. This was bound to happen. If not here, then at his office if she could've dragged her pale, bony, magic-fried self to the office—no way around it.

Mama looked over her shoulder at Amethyst, stepped outside and closed the door. No point in trying to follow the discussion outside with wizard's senses. If anyone could get past the gauntlet of Mama, it was Jas.

"Mama," Amethyst called.

No reply. She probably couldn't hear her through the door. She tried again.

"Mama!"

She'd use a little magic, just a touch, to get Mama's attention. She reached for her power. It was like groping into a dark pit. She closed her eyes, let out a breath and tried again—

Mama opened the door. "*Mija?* Jasper said he heard you call."

Of course he did. "Uh—yeah. It's okay, Mama. He can come in."

Mama studied her, then turned back to Jas. "Okay,

just for a minute. But you have to promise not to tire her out or upset her."

"You have my word," Jas said and stepped inside.

His gaze fell on her and his usual charming smile disappeared. "What," he said in a dangerously even tone, "have you done now?"

"Jasper!" Mama said.

He turned. "I'm sorry, Mrs. Rey. I didn't expect to find her in this condition."

She noticed he didn't say anything about her not looking like this yesterday.

Mama folded her arms and gave him the level look that used to tell Amethyst and Alex Junior that they were –this– close. "No badgering. She's been worried about it all morning."

He drew himself up. "I have no intention of badgering her."

Mama's well-shaped brows twitched. "I'm sure you don't, Jasper." She looked past him at Amethyst. "Call if you need anything, Violita."

"Okay, Mama," Amethyst said and gave Jas a look that said, *I'll do it, too.*

Mama nodded once and took herself into the kitchen.

The magic stirred and a spell slipped into being.

"What did you just do?" Amethyst said.

"I don't particularly want her to overhear our conversation," he said. "Do you?"

Amethyst couldn't reply for a moment. "You're in *my* house. And you just cast a spell on my *mother*."

She opened herself to her power, to break Jas' spell.

Nothing happened. Like turning a key in the ignition and not even getting the click of a dead battery. She groped around in the place within her that could touch the outside world. It was dark. Dead. Her heart ramped up. Heavy cold knotted in her middle. The magic teased her, shimmering, bent to the shape of Jas' spell, but nothing in her moved to touch it. She clenched her jaw. Her power was there. It had to be, just like it had been even before she'd known what it was. It couldn't just be *gone*—

"Amethyst." Jas, bent over her, gripped her shoulder. "What's wrong?"

His slim, strong fingers bit into her shoulder blade. She focused on him, the mismatched brows drawn into a frown. Caramela gave a whine that faded into a growl. He let go, but still frowned. Amethyst touched the dog and she settled again.

"I can't do it," Amethyst whispered.

"Can't do what?" Jas said.

She found herself shaking, her pulse fluttering in her throat. "I can't work the magic."

Jas just stood over her. "What do you mean, you can't work magic?" He gestured, taking in her condition. "What happened?"

She hesitated. "I tried something." It wasn't any of his business. Except under the circumstances, it was. "A— a summoning."

"Good God, Amethyst." Finally, he sat in one of the chairs that flanked the coffee table. "I won't bother asking what you intended to summon." He didn't say anything for a long, uncomfortable moment. "I don't understand you.

You agree to an arrangement that's to our mutual benefit, one that will make both of us less vulnerable. Then you do something to achieve the opposite."

"Do you think that's what I intended?"

He gusted a sigh. "A spell like that could've killed you," he said at last. "I'm surprised it didn't. I was wrong to have taken you so lightly when we met."

Yeah. You were, she wanted to say. Instead, she gave a one-shouldered shrug.

"I don't know what to expect after working a spell like that," he went on. "There weren't many wizards left in my time, and by then, most of us were fairly restrained."

"Talys—" Her throat knotted. She swallowed. "Tom told me once I could go into a coma. He never said anything about…" She waved a hand over her wasted self.

Jas put knuckle to lips. "If you can still see the magic," he said slowly, "I expect your power will return as you recover strength."

She shook her head, then a thought sent iced spikes through her. "The only magic I've worked was when Tom was around. What if—" She couldn't tell if the feeling that churned in her was dismay…or relief.

"Don't be ridiculous," Jas said. "You're a wizard. Forgive my bluntness, but you don't *need* a familiar to work the magic. If you're trying to get out of your agreement with me—"

"Goddammit, Jas," she flared. "Everything is not about you!"

"Then what were you thinking when you worked that summoning?"

She opened her mouth, but nothing came out.

"Just say it," he said in that even, ominous tone. "Tell me you have no intention of working with me."

"I never said I was backing out. I told you I'd help you, and I will."

She'd only hoped to do it on her own terms.

"I'm glad to hear it," he said. "In the meantime, while you're convalescing from magic that likely killed the last wizard who attempted it—"

"Look, I'm sorry, okay? I—"

"Do you think," he said, "you could allow me to finish without assuming the worst?"

She clamped an arm over her middle and gave a little wave of her free hand.

"Thank you. I was going to ask what you intend to do."

"I—" She stroked Caramela's head. "I don't know."

He folded his arms. "Because at the moment, you're no use to me, yourself, or anyone else. And don't give me that look. One of us has to be practical. To begin with, I'll reinforce your protection spells, since I know you won't agree to something sensible like staying with me until you recover."

"You know," she said pleasantly, "last time I checked, I already have a dad."

"And while you're busy undermining yourself," he went on as if she hadn't spoken, "your enemies are moving forward. I'd strongly advise you to get your family and friends out of the line of fire as soon as you can crawl off that sofa and take care of yourself."

She went cold again. "You don't think—"

"No," he said. "*I* think. It's you who aren't thinking."

"Damn you, Jas. If you think you can maneuver me—"

"I wish you'd stop cursing me. I'm your best hope."

She cracked a laugh. "Not if I don't have any power. You said it yourself—I'm no use to anybody. Not to you—and not to whoever thinks they can strong-arm me into working for them."

"Ah, that's where you're wrong. Only I know you're no use—and here I am, still helping you. Do you think the individuals who've been applying increasing pressure will believe you can no longer perform? Don't you think they might press you for proof of your helplessness?"

She sat back in her pillows, queasy.

"Yes," he said. "Now you see." He stood, brushed short, caramel-colored dog hairs off his trousers. "I'll see to those spells."

"Jas."

He paused, raised his brows.

"Why *are* you helping me?"

"Would you rather I didn't?"

She folded her arms. "You're a pragmatist, remember? Helping others out of the goodness of your heart doesn't fit the job description."

He sighed and sat again. "For godsake, Amethyst. I'm doing everything I can to show you I want to start over. Can't you accept that?"

"No," she said.

He raked a hand through his hair, leaned elbows on

knees and stared at her. "You're the most damned unforgiving woman I've ever met."

"Then the ones you've met only cared about good looks and charm," she shot back.

He blinked, then grinned suddenly. "Thank you. If I can get a compliment out of you, I know I'm making progress."

"It wasn't—!"

Mama came through the kitchen doorway. "That's enough now."

Jas didn't start or look guilty. Amethyst looked for the spell he'd cast to keep the conversation private, and sure enough, it was gone.

Mama stepped between Amethyst and Jas and picked up the half-full soup bowl. "You didn't eat this," she said to Amethyst. "Just like you haven't eaten the rest of the food I found in your refrigerator. I'll bring you some more, but you need to finish it this time." She turned to Jas. "You promised you wouldn't badger her."

"I admit it, Mrs. Rey. I was trying to make her aware of how her choices affect the people who care about her."

"That's good," Mama said evenly. "But—"

"Mama," Amethyst interrupted. She gritted her teeth, then said, "He's right. I can't keep doing this to all of you. It isn't fair. It isn't right."

Mama made a sharp, annoyed gesture. "You talk like you've been pouting because your boyfriend forgot to call you. Look at you. The last time I saw you like this was when Nani passed away."

Amethyst stiffened. Nani was her great-grandmother,

a *curandera*—folk healer. Northern New Mexico had long tradition of *curanderismo*, but Nani had been something more than the usual herbalist or midwife. Amethyst had been closer to her than anyone except Dad. Then, when Amethyst was thirteen, Nani died. That year was like a dark dream, only dim, raw snatches of memory. Being taken out of school to be homeschooled. Turning her back on the mysticism and magic Nani had taught to instead spend hours alone in her room with her computer, something logical and predictable and as far away from magic as she could get.

She came out of her memories. Jas watched her with curious interest. An echo of old pain and worry drew a line between Mama's brows.

Amethyst shook her head and reached for Mama's hand. "I know, Mama. I'm sorry. I won't do that to you again. In fact, as soon as I'm up, I want you to go home. You shouldn't have to keep interrupting your life, leaving Dad, having to come take care of me."

"I promised your husband I'd be a good friend to her," Jas said to Mama. "I'll watch out for her."

"I don't—" Amethyst began.

"In any case," he went on first, "we still have that project to work on, which I admit is important. I have a vested interest seeing her well."

Amethyst resisted the impulse to knot her fingers in her hair. "Please, Mama. I promise I'll be good. I can't stand having two of you…um…*fuss* over me."

Mama eyed Jas. "*Badger*, you were going to say."

He made a little 'oh, well' gesture.

"Don't bother trying to make him feel bad about it, Mama," Amethyst said. "I don't think a nuclear bomb could stop Jas. But if you go home, you won't have to hear the explosion."

Mama gave a wry smile, bent and kissed Amethyst. "When I hear you talk like that, I know you're getting better."

Amethyst turned her head and kissed her cheek.

"I should get back to the office," Jas said, then, "I'll call you later, Amethyst. All right?"

She held in a sigh. "Yeah, Jas. Sure."

Mama's gaze went from one to the other of them, her brows raised ever so slightly, her lips pursed just the least bit.

He said his goodbyes and let himself out.

Mama settled in the chair he'd been sitting in and folded her hands over one knee. "Eat that chile verde."

Amethyst had a feeling she had something to say. Jas might be out of the house, but that didn't mean he couldn't still hear. Funny, it almost seemed that Mama had the same instinct.

Amethyst ate, fighting the exhaustion that made her arms and head feel ten pounds heavier than they were. A car started. Mama turned to look out the living room window. A well-tuned purr diminished down the street. Caramela, who'd raised her head when Jas got up to leave, plunked it down on Amethyst's shins, a heavy, solid weight.

Mama turned back. "Be careful, *mijita*."

A prickle ran up Amethyst's neck. "Of what, Mama?"

"Of that one." She tilted her head toward the front door.

Amethyst made noise halfway between a cough and a snort. "What?"

"Tom is barely gone, and here he is. 'I'll watch out for her,' he says. 'I'll be a good friend to her,' he says. I see the way he looks at you. If he thinks he'll replace Tom—"

"Mama." Amethyst rapped the spoon on the edge of her bowl. "Stop. If you think I'd let him—"

"What is this 'let'? You said yourself you can't stop him when he decides something. And now he's convinced you to send me home, hasn't he?"

Amethyst only opened her mouth. She shut it, tried again. "He made the suggestion, yes. But I'm not stupid, and I'm not totally helpless. And I'm here to tell you, I'm sure not going to let him hear me admit he's right if I don't really think he is."

Mama pressed her lips together. "Maybe he is, but I don't like it. Caring about you, that's one thing. I understand that. But he should give you time. What he's doing…" She frowned. "It's disrespectful of the dead. And it's disrespectful of you."

If Amethyst had the power to disappear right then, she would have. As it was, it felt like someone had dragged her shirt in a patch of tumbleweeds before she put it on—burning prickles all over.

"If that's all you're worried about, I think I can safely assure you that Jas will *not* get his way."

"You don't have to promise that. But if anything happens and you feel uncomfortable, you tell me. You pick up the phone and call me, and don't worry about anything else. *That*, you promise me, Violita."

Amethyst had to smile at the idea of Mama facing off with Jas. Without magic, he didn't stand a chance. Even *with* magic, it could be a close thing.

"I promise, Mama. Jas will not take advantage of me."

CHAPTER 16.5 - OPPOSITION

Wind moaned around the old farmhouse, rattled the seedy windowpanes in their frames. Branches skritched at the fieldstone walls like undead souls seeking entry. The oil lamp on a much-rubbed desk of rosewood guttered in a stray draft.

A man sat in a brocade chair by the desk, reading. The title of his book was *U.S. Government and Politics*. Stacked on a table beside him were more books. *Investment Banking. Big Data. Hardball: How Politics is Played.* He raised his ash-colored head and looked toward the dark windows. The rattling window quieted, the skritching stopped and the lamp flame calmed, burning tall in its glass globe.

Somewhere in the room, a bell chimed. The man—the wizard Char—gusted a sigh and put down his book. A sheet of linen paper lay blank on the desk. Char frowned down at the page, waiting for the message. Dark marks like ink slowly bled into the paper, creating words:

Your bane must've worked. There's been a death—the live-in boyfriend. Family and friends were staying with her, but she's alone now. She stayed out of sight for several days, but is now leaving the house. I'm ready to move, but need advice.

Char hissed in annoyance. The powerless had been far more respectful in days gone by, not pestering with questions and demands. This one would learn better—very soon. But for the present, this was work well done. The son of Robert need not know it benefited Char as well as himself.

He picked up a quill, trimmed the tip and dipped it in the inkpot:

Her home and travel conveyance will be warded. You will not approach her there. Personal wards and shields are likely as well.

No reply appeared on the paper. Char gave a thin smile. He could imagine the man cursing the difficulty of wizards. He tutted softly. Such a pity.

At last, a reply appeared: *Then I'll need help.*

This time, Char hesitated. The woman who destroyed the Dragon would be formidable. He, too, was formidable, yet still the Dragon had taken him, sucked him dry of power and left him imprisoned, an empty, tormented shadow of himself. He had no wish to tempt such a fate again.

He swept the quill's feather back and forth across his chin, thinking. The bane had removed the woman Amethyst's escort. How had that weakened her? Unless her escort had been something more. Possibly, but he had no intention of being the one to discover the answer to that question.

Find help elsewhere, Char wrote.

If Robert's son could indeed take her…

Well. Then Char would decide what was best to be done. In the meantime, he had greater concerns. He picked up *U.S. Government and Politics* and began reading again.

CHAPTER 17

S tanding at the open closet, Amethyst took a long, shaky breath. Talys' things hung on one side: black jeans and trousers, black shirts, a black suit. Black sneakers and boots and dress shoes on the floor. Mama had offered to take care of it all for her, but Amethyst wouldn't let her. It was stupid, really. The body that had worn these clothes was probably out in some Four Corners desert—

She stopped the thought.

No matter what, Talys wouldn't need the clothes again. Even that thought hurt. What if she'd managed to call him back? If he returned as a car again, or a black dog or a raven? How would she feel? He'd been her ally when he was a car, a sure, steady presence. What he'd been afterwards—the man's form he'd inhabited—had enabled him to be so much more than just her familiar.

She took the clothes out of the closet, laid them on the bed and began folding and packing them into boxes. The closet stood painfully empty. She quickly slid the door closed, picked up a couple boxes and carried them through the house.

Her arms were full and the laundry room door closed. She reached for the magic to open the door—

And almost ran into it. She stopped, clenched her jaw, closed her eyes. Tears rushed up with the wrenching violence of vomit. She sank to the floor, still clutching the boxes. Hunched over them, she pressed her forehead to the cardboard. A whiff of Talys' scent came, a faint musky spiciness. Caramela tapped across the linoleum and snuffled her. Amethyst put an arm around her, held the boxes close with the other.

Talys, gone. The magic, gone. No way to bring him back now.

Her phone rang, a few bars of Spanish guitar. She jerked up her head, wiped her face on her t-shirt and got up to answer it.

Jas Harker, the screen said, with a picture of him. She didn't remember adding him as a contact or uploading his photo. She sniffed and swallowed.

"Hi," she said. Her voice quavered even on that short word.

"Are you all right?" Jas said.

She choked back the impulse to snap, to snarl, to say something irrational and unreasonable.

"Fine," she said instead.

He didn't say anything for a second, then, "You don't sound fine."

She just breathed. "I was packing up Tom's stuff. Before that, I was writing thank-you notes to everyone who sent flowers and food. Sorry if I'm not sounding properly cheerful."

"Amethyst—" He stopped, started again. "Are you still coming in?"

She was pretty sure if she said 'no,' he'd come and fetch her. She sighed. "Give me half an hour, okay?"

"I'll see you then." His photo winked off the screen.

She put the phone back on the kitchen peninsula, opened the laundry room door and carried the boxes of clothes through and into the garage.

Four days after the summoning, the bones of her hands and wrists still stood out, but at least her jeans stayed on without a belt now. And yes, Jas was feeding her. Yesterday it was pastries and hot chocolate from Satellite for breakfast, a turkey sandwich and French onion soup from Le Peep's with Cake Fetish cupcakes for dessert. She had a strong suspicion that was a lot of the reason he expected her to come in. Even worse, she was beginning to have traitorous feelings of gratitude about it.

The unfinished window for Jas' building still occupied her garage. It—along with her other unfinished commissions—accused her like dogs left outside in the snow. Everything loomed, each obligation an insurmountable task. She turned her back on the glass and slid the boxes of clothes onto storage shelves. *Do* not *cry*, she told herself. *One thing at a time. You can do it.*

Glancing back once at the boxes, she made herself shut the door to the garage. It was okay. After all, Talys had lived in the garage when he was a car. She went into the bedroom to change, Caramela trotting behind her.

"I should just show up like this," she told Caramela.

Amethyst was wearing sweats and one of Talys' black t-shirts, big enough to hang mid-thigh. She sighed and took her hair out of its ponytail.

"But I'd probably regret it later."

She made sure Caramela had water, locked the house and got in the car. She took Eubank to Indian School. Up in the Heights, Indian School was a funny street; it was one of the major east-west streets, but much of it ran through residential neighborhoods. It was a slower drive than, say, Lomas or Menaul, but with the parks and front yards, more pleasant. Plus more or less a straight shot to Magus in Uptown.

Today was one of those brilliant late-fall days, all blue and gold and breezy with a glitter of white from last night's snow on Sandia Crest. All she could think was that Talys wasn't here to share it with.

She cruised past Eubank Elementary School and Snow Park, no school zone lights flashing to slow her down. Past Wyoming, it was all houses until Taylor Park and Inez Elementary. Cars filled the school's parking lot on the opposite side of the street. The sound of a horn came through the rolled-up windows. One car, parked by the fence, flashed its lights. Amethyst glanced toward it.

Movement flicked in her peripheral vision on the right. She jerked forward again. In the street in front of her, a small running figure, a glimpse of an open mouth and wide eyes.

Amethyst yanked the wheel to the left and slammed on the brakes. The car slung crosswise, tires screeching. She stiffened for the sickening thump. Instead, a small form, arms and legs outflung, flew away, repelled by the wards on the Subaru.

Amethyst tumbled out of the car, ran around to the

front. A child lay face-down on the pavement a few feet away, a little girl. She didn't move.

Oh God, oh God. It's not real. I'm having a nightmare. I'll wake up, and it'll all go away.

Her chest heaved with ragged breaths or sobs. She looked around wildly. No one in the park, or in the school parking lot across the street. The little girl remained motionless on the pavement. Amethyst had to get her off the street. But if she moved her, she might hurt her worse.

She turned one way, then the other. Oh God, what should she do?

She found herself kneeling on the cold asphalt in front of the car, small stones pressing into her knees through the fabric of her jeans. The radiator fan buffeted her with warm air from the engine—she hadn't turned off the key. The child wore jeans and pink sneakers and a pink jacket with an applique of a cartoon hippopotamus on the back. One arm lay under her. The other was flung across the pavement.

Amethyst covered the child with her own jacket, pressed her phone to her ear. Had she dialed 9-1-1? She must've. The dispatcher was asking questions, giving instructions. Amethyst didn't understand anything she said.

"Get the paramedics," she told the dispatcher. Her voice came out high and panicked. "She's not moving. Where're the paramedics?"

Too long, everything was taking too long. She threw down the phone and held her hands over the child's still form. A spell came without thought, one of healing, of taking away pain. She reached for the magic. Nothing. She clenched her fists, threw back her head and screamed, reached again.

Nothing.

Sirens wailed. Cars were stopped all up and down Indian School Road now. People crowded around. Someone touched her shoulder, spoke to her. Her face was cold, wet. She tried to be quiet, to settle down, but she couldn't breathe, there wasn't enough air.

Beneath the noise of sirens and voices, the chords of a Spanish guitar played. Her phone, there on the pavement beside her, showed Jas' picture.

Jas. *Jas. He* could still use the magic.

She snatched up the phone. "There's been an accident," she gasped. "I hit—"

"Where are you?" Jas broke in.

"Indian School by Taylor Park, but—"

"Ma'am," a man's voice said behind her. "Are you the driver?"

Still on her knees, she spun. An APD officer towered over her. The cop car, light bar flashing, sat in the opposite lane blocking traffic. Another cop ushered bystanders to the sidewalk. Amethyst scrambled to her feet, shaking so hard she could barely stand. A second car, black and unmarked, lights flashing behind its windshield, pulled up behind hers. Two men in civilian clothes got out.

"Where's the ambulance?" Amethyst said. "She needs an ambulance!"

"Turn around and put your hands on the car. You're under arrest."

No no no no... "The little girl! You have to help her!"

The cop grabbed her, spun her, shoved her hard against the car. Her head snapped and her face slammed the door frame. It should've hurt. It didn't. Only the shock of hitting something solid.

Her phone skittered across the hood, slid off the other side. Her arms were wrenched behind her, handcuffs snapped on her wrists. A hand caught her by the collar of her shirt, by the arm, hauled her around, propelled her toward the unmarked car. One of the plainclothes opened a rear door. Amethyst stumbled forward. *No no no no no...*

One of them pushed her head down. Dizziness swept her. The sounds of voices and sirens fell silent. She staggered. The motion tore her free of the grip on her arm. Hands cuffed behind her, she pitched headlong toward the side of the car. Someone caught her arm, circled her waist and pulled her back.

The world wheeled, or someone turned her, and she found Jas standing in front of her.

She stared at him, uncomprehending. The guy in plainclothes right behind him held one hand cupped over an invisible head. The other hand gripped a non-existent arm. Another guy stood on the far side of the car. He seemed to look right at them, but didn't move, didn't say anything. The cop who'd slammed her against the car hung mid-stride, one foot raised. Amethyst turned her head. Onlookers stood frozen on the sidewalk. Cop car lights glared steady, no longer flashing. As if the world had stopped, all one more twist of the nightmare.

Jas looked her up and down, took her by the shoulder, turned her and struck off the handcuffs. They hit the street with clink, glowed red, then orange, white, and vaporized. Pale smoke whirled upward. A puddle of melted asphalt marked where they'd lain. He looked angrier than she'd ever seen him, brows pulled down over blazing black eyes, lips thin and pale.

He grasped her shoulders again. "What happened?"

Amethyst tried to talk, but only gulping sounds came. She stopped, took a shaking breath. Wetting her lips, she tasted blood.

"She ran right out in front of me! I didn't see her. I-I-I hit her." She gripped his arms, shook at him. "Jas, you have to help her. You said you can heal people. Please, Jas."

He took her by the wrist, pulled her along to the front of her car. Somewhere in the distance, a siren wailed. The little girl still lay under Amethyst's jacket. Jas knelt, reached out a hand, then drew back.

Amethyst's stomach knotted, cold and sick. She clenched her fists against her mouth.

Jas pushed to his feet again, gazing down at the child. He cursed and kicked her.

Amethyst screamed and launched herself at him. She got in a couple of punches, then he caught her wrists and wrestled her back against the car.

"Stop it, Amethyst. Enough, stop it!" He pinned her against the car's side. "It's a simulacrum. It isn't alive, only an object animated by magic. You didn't hit a child. You didn't hurt anyone."

"She ran out in front of me! I saw her face!"

"Look." He pulled her up, dragged her forward,

flipped her jacket off the child. "No blood."

He turned over the body. Amethyst flinched away.

"Look at it, Amethyst." Jas shook her wrist.

She turned back, but saw only the oval of a face, a spill of hair.

"It isn't alive," Jas said. "It never was alive. Magic moved it. Illusion made you see what you expected to."

She shook her head. All she'd seen was the horrified face, then the little body lying there, so still.

"You were set up," he said. "Someone engineered this to get you out of your warded car, to keep you from defending yourself." He narrowed his eyes and scanned their surroundings. "We can't stay here." He straightened, pulling her up.

Her head spun. Everything still seemed nightmarish, unreal. She wanted to close her eyes, curl into a ball and disappear.

"Jas, the cops just arrested me. I can't leave. It'll be ten times worse!"

He steered her around the Subaru and opened the passenger door. "I very seriously doubt these are police officers." He pulled out his phone, snapped photos of the cops, of the patrol car and the black unmarked one. "What worries me is the wizard who spelled that simulacrum."

He urged her into the passenger seat, circled around and got into the driver's.

"What—"

"Did you call 9-1-1?" he said.

"Yes, but—"

"Then the real authorities will be here any moment.

The evidence needs to be gone when they do."

He backed up the Subaru. The sad heap lay there at the end of black skid marks. Jas gestured, and green fire crawled across the heap. Amethyst dug her nails into her knees. Green flames blazed up then collapsed. White ash whirled upward on a column of superheated air. More green fire spidered across the asphalt. Blue smoke rose from the tire tracks, leaving behind an almost invisible grey blur.

"That should take care of the blood, too." He spun the wheel, pulled down a side street.

"Blood! You said—"

He looked at her strangely. "Yours. The airbags didn't deploy, so I know the car's wards absorbed the impact. Who hit you?" His voice was tight.

She shook her head again. Everything after she'd gotten out of the car was a smeared streak of horror.

"Nobody hit me."

He reached out, touched her lips and showed her his fingers. They glistened red.

"You're in shock," he said. "Listen to me. All right?"

"Okay," she said.

Shock. Was that why nothing seemed real? Why she could taste the blood on her face but not feel what had made her bleed? Adrenaline. Her body shutting out everything but fight or flight.

He braked at a stop sign, made a right down another quiet residential street.

"I'm taking you up to my place."

"But all those people. They saw you. People will see

my car driving away!"

"Amethyst, please. Stop crying. It's very distracting."

"I'm not crying." Her hiccupping voice said different. She sniffed and gulped and tried to stop.

"I heard what was going on over the phone. Besides the spell of stillness, I took the precaution of casting ones of concealment and diversion. No one will have seen me, and the car driving away from the area will appear to be a '95 Ford Bronco with a primered right front fender. As far as everyone back there is concerned," he waved a hand generally behind them, "the moment I released the spell, you, your car, and the child vanished into thin air. Let your friends the counterfeit police officers attempt to explain it."

She tried to process it. "What if someone took pictures or video?"

He sighed. "The simulacrum wasn't the only evidence I took care of."

Her mind insisted she'd killed a child. "Are you sure, Jas? You're not lying to me again, are you? *It looked like a little girl.*"

"If you hadn't been panicking, you'd have realized what it was. As a ruse, it was very well done."

She was breathing too fast. An image of the child's face in front of the car rose again. Jas' green fire consuming the still little body. "If it wasn't real, why did you destroy it? What would there be to find but a…a *thing?*"

"What would happen when the real police and paramedics show up and find what looks like a body in the street? They'll take photos, interview witnesses, write reports. They'll look for a woman of your description driving a car like yours."

"Those witnesses can *still* describe me and my car!"

"And say what? Someone hit a child? Where's the child? Where's the car? If they find you, where's the damage to your car from the impact?"

"But I *did* hit her!"

He shot her a sideways, exasperated look, reached across the console and gripped her wrist. "Amethyst Maria Rey," he said. "*Go to sleep.*"

"Are you—"

Darkness crashed down on her.

CHAPTER 18

*A*methyst *knelt by the little girl's body.* Sobs wrenched her. The girl's face was a blank oval without eyes or nose or mouth. Green fire crawled over the body. Like burning paper, it crisped and curled and whirled away, pale ash rising in the air. She scrambled to catch the flying bits, but her fingers were gone, leaving only the paddles of her palms. People surrounded her, muttering. *She killed him. She killed him.*

Amethyst turned, and the body at her feet was Talys', the empty baseball cap lying by his head, his empty hands slack on the ground beside him. Dark wind tore at her clothes, her hair, her self. She tattered, scattered, grew smaller, thinner. She squeezed her eyes closed as the last of her shredded, only fragments of grief and pain on the wind.

Amethyst, a voice whispered.

Out of the darkness, silver light gleamed. The scraps of her spun, gathering out of disintegration.

Go back, the voice whispered. *You don't belong here.*

A hot cocoa-and-cinnamon voice, familiar. Talys. She

gravitated toward it.

Go home, he whispered. *Be whole.*

She was whole again, herself, kneeling in the dark, a silver rain falling around her. "How?" she asked him.

The silver rain slowed, sputtered to a stop. She leapt to her feet. "No! Don't go! Don't leave me!"

She ran, calling, tripped and fell headlong. She flung out her hands to catch herself—

Amethyst jerked and woke.

On a sofa. In a high, bright room. She'd never seen either one before.

She wrenched upright. An icepack and an afghan slid into her lap. Jas sat by her in a chair, his sleeves rolled up. His tie lay, a puddle of green silk, on a slate-topped coffee table next to a washcloth streaked with blood.

Her brow and cheekbone and lip throbbed. She put a hand to her face. "Ow."

"You have a split lip and the beginnings of a black eye," he said. "Other than that, how are you?"

Everything came rushing back. The dark wind of her dreams blew out to fill the room, dimming the sun streaming through its tall windows. It shouldn't be Jas sitting by her asking that question.

The stupid tears surged up again. No. *No.* Damned if she'd cry anymore, especially in front of Jas.

She took a long breath, let it out. "I'm totally screwed."

He gave a small smile. "Only roughed up and badly

frightened. I can help with the roughed up part, if you'll let me."

She considered the offer for an instant, then thought, *Oh, what the hell.* She nodded.

"Lie down again," he said.

"Why?"

"Because the magic makes most people dizzy," he said patiently. "And some lose consciousness."

It was weird lying down as he asked. The smell of the couch's leather enveloped her. It was even weirder when she realized that he must've carried her in from the car.

A visceral memory of the binding he'd laid on her last year flashed, his arm around her, his fingers sliding through her hair, and she, unable to move, to think…

She shivered and resisted the impulse to start back up.

Jas perched next to her on the edge of the couch, laid a gentle hand on her face and bent his head.

Magic swept her, a pressure in her head like a sudden change in altitude. Heat like the burn of chile on the tongue, an effervescent prickling ran under her skin. A wash of green slid across the room, a color that sounded like wind in treetops, that smelled like a damp forest meadow.

Every muscle in her body went slack. The green intensified to a glow, then a flare. Panic boiled up—

The room returned. Jas sat back and lifted his hand.

"There," he said. "Does it feel any better?"

She quickly pushed herself upright, touched where his hand had lain. "It doesn't hurt."

"Good. The magic won't change the way it looks, but you'll mend more quickly." He returned to his chair. "I did a little research while you were asleep. Your police officers actually come from the opposite end of the spectrum. Three have extensive histories of violent crime. One is ex-Army Special Forces, dishonorable discharge."

He picked up a tablet from the end table beside him and turned it so she could see. It would've been easier if she scooted to his end of the couch, but she stayed where she was.

A photo of a man in APD black showed, with name and vital statistics beneath. Amethyst didn't know if it was one of the cops who'd arrested her—well, the pretend cop, she supposed. Jas slid images across the screen, the photos he'd snapped of the four men and matching mug shots.

"Facial recognition software is a technology I've come to appreciate," he said. "I ran the plates on the cars as well. They're skip plates—untraceable. Someone has experience hiding data trails. I'll keep digging, but I suspect magic will be necessary to bridge the gaps created by cash transactions and clandestine meetings."

He tapped the tablet a couple of times and handed it to her. The photos he'd taken of all four men showed on the screen, two uniformed cops and two plainclothes.

"Which one hit you?" he said.

"Nobody hit me." Hadn't she told him that before? Why did he keep asking? She thought, trying to remember. It still seemed like a nightmare, one she hadn't yet awakened from. "It must've been when they pushed me against the car." She handed back the tablet. "One of the uniforms. When they put the handcuffs on." She shuddered, wrapped her arms around herself. "The Anglo guy, I think."

He nodded, studied the tablet a moment and blanked the screen.

She just sat hugging herself and shivering. "I can't do this anymore, Jas."

He set the tablet on the end table with a soft click. "I agree. Over the years, I've learned when it's time to fall back and regroup. I think it's time. Until we know who's behind this and why, we'll be continually on the defense."

She stared around the living room—something real, not the nightmare. This real place was beautiful. Windows showed a glittering sweep of Albuquerque down to the Rio Grande then back up again to the dark line of the volcanic escarpment. Rounded kiva fireplace built into one corner. Tiffany lamps that looked like they might be the real thing, not some Malaysian knock-offs. None of those belonged in the nightmare. *Nichos* in the walls holding antique porcelain figurines—

Wait— "We? What *'we?'* I don't have any power. I tried to use magic. I couldn't touch it. I'm no use to you."

He looked up as if praying for patience. "I'll dispute that. I'll also point out that you're of even less use snatched up and spirited away somewhere that would take a great deal of effort and considerable messiness to retrieve you from. So." He leaned elbows on knees. "We're going out of town for a while."

She closed her eyes. "Jas, please."

"I need to make a few calls first, but we can be on

our way after lunch."

"You have a company to run. A company with problems."

"I also have access to the Internet. There's a new concept called telecommuting. Perhaps you've heard of it."

She wanted to ask why he couldn't have thought of that *before* dragging her to the office, but just put her head in her hands.

He laid a hand on her shoulder. "Rest. If you like, you can use the guest bedroom."

She pushed to her feet. "I'm going home."

"Do I really need to point out that home is the worst place you can go right now? In any event, your dog is already on her way."

"What do you mean, she's on her way? Dammit, Jas! You can't just summon a pit bull across town!"

"It's only a few miles, nothing for a dog. I have her spelled. She'll be fine."

"And my commissions." She waved her arms. "What about *them?*"

"Your accountant already called your clients and explained that you were in a serious auto accident. He'll be happy to ensure their deposits are refunded until you're able to complete the work."

"What accountant?" she squeaked.

He put a hand on his chest. "Jacob Arken, CPA."

She gazed at him, marveling. "My dog is gone, I can't go home, and now I don't have a source of income. Holy Mary mother of God." She dropped to the couch and put her head in her hands again.

"Yes, but you're going on vacation courtesy of Magus Corporation," he said. "Think of it as a sign-on bonus. Nothing unusual for a tech firm wooing talent."

She wondered if *Jas* had been the wizard who spelled that simulacrum. He was just devious enough for it. He'd known when she was on the road, likely what route she'd take. He'd *called* her, for godsake, right after it happened. Had it been more than the half hour she'd told him it would take to get to office?

No, he couldn't have been behind it. He already had her in his clutches. Didn't he?

Or he could be what he seemed, a friend who came through when she was most in need. The only problem was knowing for sure which was the truth.

CHAPTER 19

Telling her parents and Melodie was the most gruesome part of the plan. After all, she couldn't just disappear on everybody. And the first thing everyone asked was, "You're not going alone, are you?"

Melodie was only her best friend—about all she could do was yell, "Are you insane?" Mama and Dad were another matter. Worst of all, she had to face them in person.

She had to give Jas points for coming in with her when she dropped off Caramela at her parents' house in San Cristobal, rather than waiting in the car. Dad got a grim, angry look on his face Amethyst had almost never seen and promptly invited Jas outside. Amethyst started to follow, but Mama caught her, hauled her into the kitchen, made her sit down and lit into her, half in English and half in Spanish.

"I know, Mama," was all Amethyst could say, and, "You're right, Mama."

Dad came and rescued her eventually. He didn't look angry anymore, but he did look glum. Apparently Jas' charm had its limits.

She kissed Mama. Jas had already tucked spells of protection and homefinding and soothing around

Caramela before they'd gotten out of the car. Amethyst had to content herself with giving her a kiss on top of the head before making her escape.

Dad walked her to Jas' green (of course) Range Rover, his arm around her shoulders. Their breath plumed on the air. The sulfur-yellow blooms of the chamisa lining the driveway had faded to the color of straw. Fall's purple aster had turned to little white puffs of seed heads on brittle stems.

"I don't like it, Thistle," he said. "I agree it's not a good idea for you to take off alone right now. But if you need a change of scenery, you can stay here."

Oh, wouldn't she give anything to do that. "No, Dad, I can't. You've been dealing with my problems enough lately."

"We're your parents, Amethyst." When he called her by her real name, she knew things were serious. "We're supposed to deal with your problems."

Not these problems, she thought. "I know. But I'd still feel guilty and imposing and all. And that would sort of defeat the purpose of getting away, wouldn't it?"

He sighed. "I suppose so." He glanced toward the Range Rover. Jas sat in the driver's seat, waiting. "He's persuasive, I'll give him that."

Amethyst grinned, surprising herself. "Guess it's part of the corporate magnate job description."

Dad grunted a reluctant laugh. "Probably." He stopped, turned her to face him. "Do you trust him?"

Oh, yes, absolutely! She hated lying.

"He's seen me at my worst and still come through for

me," she said. "I can count on one hand the number of people who'll do that."

He studied her, then nodded slowly. "That'll have to be good enough. I wouldn't normally get involved, but I know this is a rough time for you, Thistle. I don't want to see you hurt worse than you already are. Okay?"

"Okay, Dad. Thanks." She hugged him.

He kissed her cheek and held her shoulders. "Keep in touch. I expect you to call if you need us."

"Mama already made me promise."

"Good."

He hugged her again and walked her the rest of the way to the car. She got in.

Dad leaned in the door frame. "Drive safely," he told Jas with a nod, unsmiling. He shut the door.

Jas started the Range Rover, swung it around and crackled down the gravel driveway.

"It's been a long time," he said, "since I've had to convince anyone's father that my intentions are honorable."

She smacked her forehead. "Do not say another word."

He grinned. "I see where you get your formidable sense of What is Right. I think I'll never again cross a Rey."

"Good idea. And remember, I have a brother, too."

He gave an exaggerated shudder.

She had to resist grinning back at him. The three-hour drive to San Cristobal from Albuquerque had let the nightmare begin to fade away. The familiar road following the Rio Grande, whitewater through its gorge, then cutting through the sagebrush flats around Taos, had reminded her of other trips, other days looking forward to seeing her parents, seeing the house under its bare cottonwoods, Dad's blue heeler, Caballero, inspecting her to make absolutely *sure* she was who she was supposed to be.

"By the way," Jas said. "Thank you for the vote of confidence."

"What—? Oh." Damn wizard's senses. She scowled at him. "Didn't your mom ever tell you eavesdropping is rude?"

He shrugged. "I generally ignore rules when it's of benefit to do so."

"I bet," she muttered.

❖❖❖❖❖❖

A hand shook her knee. Amethyst started up, blinking. Night pressed against the car windows. The headlights showed a narrow road, an old church on the left, a bridge overhung with bare cottonwood branches ahead.

"What?" She rubbed her neck. "Where are we?"

"Ojo Caliente," Jas said beside her.

She woke up the rest of the way. Jas, his face illuminated by dash-light, steered the Range Rover across the bridge.

"Sorry," she said. "I guess I fell asleep."

He gave a soft laugh. "The snoring suggested you might have."

She groaned and leaned her head in her hand.

"I'm not surprised," he said. "Crisis will do that."

A sudden uprush of gratitude almost choked her. This was *Jas*. He wasn't supposed to be so damned kind and understanding. She swallowed until she was relatively sure her voice would be steady.

"I wasn't really snoring."

"You certainly were. With your mouth wide open. I'd never have taken you for a snorer."

"God."

"Not to worry," he said. "I've already seen you at your worst, remember?"

"No. *Now* you've seen me at my worst."

He turned to look at her. One brow arched provocatively, he drew breath as if to say something, then shook his head and faced forward again.

Amethyst's face burned. He hadn't said a thing, and she still wanted to crawl under the seat. She didn't want to think about exactly *what* he'd been about to say.

The headlights illuminated a rock fountain, drained for the winter, with a spiral carved into it. Jas turned left, pulled into a gravel parking lot and parked at the end of the old hotel. He turned off the engine. The lights illuminating the brick-paved walkway along the front of the hotel spilled through the windshield, showed his reflected profile against the tinted driver's window.

"Before we go in, I should tell you." He still held the steering wheel, tapping it with the fingers of one hand. "We'll be sharing a room."

Amethyst drew an outraged breath.

"I can place shielding and protective spells," he said before she could speak. "But I'm uneasy about what's been going on. I'll feel much more comfortable if we remain close. I know you're going to argue that we'll do fine in neighboring rooms, but the fact is, your power is damaged at the moment. If you do run into more trouble, you have no way of protecting yourself. I booked Casa de Ojo, you'll have your own room and bathroom. You don't have to worry—I'll be a perfect gentleman. I swear to you, I don't have any ulterior motives—"

"Jas," she interrupted. "You're talking very fast. Why are you talking fast?"

He drew a long breath. "I'm trying to keep you from arguing with me."

She nodded, thinking. "You could do the same kind of voodoo zombie magic you did on me last summer, and I *couldn't* argue with you. Right?"

A knot appeared in his jaw. "Amethyst, I—"

She held up a hand and he stopped. "Right?" she said.

"Yes." The word came out clipped.

"If you did, I couldn't do anything to stop you. The fact that you're arguing instead of doing voodoo zombie magic, which would be a lot easier, tells me that you *will* be a perfect gentleman. But if you aren't—"

"I don't," he said, "need magic to persuade women to sleep with me."

"I'm sure you don't, Jas. Charm is probably enough."

"Usually."

She snorted.

He reached over and touched her face.

She jerked back. "You said—"

"The illusion. The one I placed on you at your parents' home. So they wouldn't freak out…" He made air quotes. "…when they saw your face. The magic needs to be renewed from time to time."

She knew that, of course. He also didn't necessarily need to touch her to do it. Although she had to admit that touching made a stronger, more convincing illusion.

"And that's all?"

"What else?" he said, perfectly innocently.

Damn, he was good. Whether he intended only what he said or something else, she'd look unreasonable if she balked at his touch. And even though it was only Jas, she didn't like the idea of looking stupid.

She sighed, made a little 'go ahead' gesture and closed her eyes. His fingers came to rest on her face again, a light, almost ticklish touch, then magic feathered her skin. She twitched but didn't pull away.

"There," he said. "You should be good for another few hours."

She looked out the windshield a moment, fiddling with the hem of her shirt. "I never said thank you. For everything. So thank you."

"Of course," he said quietly.

She slid out of the Range Rover without looking at him, snagged her coat from the backseat and shrugged it on.

An odd tingle started in her feet. They must've fallen asleep. She walked with Jas along the front of the hotel. A couple of women sat in rocking chairs on the hotel's veranda, talking quietly. The tingle crept up her legs, less like a tingle now and more like a humming vibration. A strange sense of…of drawing in, of being at the center, bore down on her, as if the world had opened an eye and taken notice of her tiny, insignificant self.

It was like those times she'd worked big magic, where for a few moments she actually became part of it, open to everything, connected with everything else. A faint silvery sound brushed her, a warm flicker of being. She reached out to catch it—

A hand grasped her arm. "Amethyst?" Jas said.

She blinked. They stood at the bottom of the steps to the hotel's main entrance. Jas held her elbow.

"What is *that?*" she said. "I feel like I'm standing on top of a generator."

"Wait," he glanced toward the women on the veranda and guided her up the steps and into the lounge. A murmur of voices came from the adjoining restaurant, but they had the lounge to themselves.

"The magic is very strong here," Jas said and gave her a curious look. "Haven't you been to Ojo before?"

"My Nani brought me here when I was a kid, when it was a funky little half-run-down place and you had to change in the old bathhouse."

The historic hotel had been built somewhere around 1920. The bathhouse was even older, and there was a Pueblo Indian ruin on the mesa above the hot springs that showed people had been drawn to the place for centuries before *that.*

"Melodie and I used to come at least once a year,"

she said. "I was planning to come over Christmas—"

Her voice dried up. She'd wanted to bring Talys then.

"Then you haven't visited since your power manifested."

She just shook her head.

"You'll be more sensitive now. This is a place of power. I thought if you'd heal anywhere, this would be it." He studied her in the lamplight. "Will you be all right?"

She made an internal assessment. She certainly didn't feel *bad*, just...caught up by something enormous. She let herself relax, and found she could sort of float in it.

"I'm okay," she said.

He nodded. "Let's get something to eat, then we'll check in."

As always, the food was excellent. Jas paid (always the gentleman—well, usually), and they made their way along a wide brick walkway to the spa entrance, their breath unfurling white in the mountain air.

Lights glowed along the front of the pueblo-styled building with stepped Southwestern arches, carved porch posts and corbels and tall oak-and-glass entry doors. Jas went to the registration desk to check in. Amethyst gravitated toward a fountain in the form of a slightly twisted column of granite.

He finished, came over and handed her a key. It was attached to a safety pin, so you could pin it to your bathing suit while using the hot springs.

"You should find bathing suits in the gift shop." He nodded toward the shop off to one side of the entrance doors.

She faced him. "Jas, I weigh about a hundred pounds right now. I can go out in public as long as I'm wearing jeans and sweatshirts. Anything less than that..." She folded her arms. "Let me put it this way. If I was a dog and people saw me with you, between the bruises and the bones, they'd accuse you of abuse and neglect."

He made a strange sound that might have been a laugh caught back at the last instant. "But as you aren't a dog, people will simply see a woman who's been ill coming to take advantage of Ojo's healing waters. And it would be a shame if you *didn't* take advantage of them. Don't you agree?"

She sighed. "Yeah, a matter of fact, I do."

He pulled out a money clip, peeled off a couple of bills and handed them to her. They were hundreds. "We're on a strictly cash basis for the time being. I'm sure I don't need to remind you to leave your phone off. It's too easy for someone with the right connections to locate you."

If they hadn't already talked about it, the realization would've made her queasy. As it was....

Well, it still made her queasy.

"Thanks for the reminder," she said.

If he heard the sarcasm in her voice, he ignored it. "I'll get our luggage settled in the room and meet you back here," he said. "Will you wait for me?"

Which meant, under the circumstances, *I expect you to wait for me.*

"Either here or in front of the fireplace outside." She held the hundreds between thumb and forefinger. "You know I'm paying you back, right?"

He gave a little wave that could've been either agreement or dismissal then pushed back through the entrance doors.

Looking at the bathing suits was more fun than trying them on. It was even less fun changing into the one she bought, praying the other women in the locker room didn't catch a glimpse of her. The Ojo Caliente t-shirt she pulled over the suit didn't match the pretty sarong in violet and teal, but the two together mostly disguised the fact that she had no boobs or butt left whatsoever. Not that she'd had much of either *before* she worked the summoning.

Being so thin now, she got cold easily. *More* easily. Even rotisserie-ing herself in front of the outdoor fireplace with its fragrant, snapping piñon logs, she was shivering by the time Jas came out, dressed now in a beige hotel courtesy robe. He looked her up and down, raised his brows, no doubt at her eclectic attire, and held another robe open for her. She slipped into it. Behind her, a small man with a black ponytail and worn denim jacket threw another piñon log on the fire and rearranged it with a poker.

Jas' hands lingered on her shoulders and magic rippled over her, almost as warm as the fire: spells of protection, shielding, ward. She slid a glance at the little man with the poker, but he seemed absorbed in what he was doing.

She gave Jas a questioning look and mouthed, *Spells?*

"Just a precaution," he said. "I booked an hour at one of the private pools. Ready?"

A couple of young men trotted hand-in-hand down the steps. The man with the ponytail hung up the poker and, a little stiff-legged, also descended the stairs, headed across the courtyard toward the main bathhouse.

"Jas," Amethyst said. "We're not on a weekend getaway."

He shrugged. "No, but the pool comes with the room. So why not enjoy it?"

Damn. He'd snatched her out of a very bad situation. Put up with a browbeating from Dad. Booked a whole house so she wouldn't have to share a room with him. And now she wanted to argue about sitting with him in a hot spring?

Oh, hell. "Why not?"

He gestured toward the bathhouse.

Along with the spa reception building and some of the lodgings, the main bathhouse was part of the improvements made to the property over the last ten or fifteen years. This building was in the Northern New Mexico style, with a pitched metal roof instead of a Pueblo-style flat roof. A porch with round posts topped with carved corbels sheltered the entrance. An old man almost as bony as Amethyst sat on the carved bench outside the door. He made her feel a little less conspicuous.

The bath attendant, the little man with the ponytail and denim jacket, greeted them with a gap-toothed smile. He looked Native American, and had some kind of accent. It sounded a little like some of the Pueblo peoples had, but not quite. Amethyst had seen him here as long as she remembered. A flash of memory came of Nani, her great-grandmother, talking quietly to the man in Spanish. What had Nani said? Amethyst couldn't remember, wasn't even sure if it was a real memory.

The man led them to one of the private pools under the mesa's cliffs, unlocked a wooden gate and held it open. "I'll knock after forty-five minutes. You do the wrap afterwards?"

"We'll let you know," Jas said.

The attendant nodded. "Come to the bath house. I take care of you."

He stepped out and the gate clicked shut behind him.

It was all very cozy—small pool full of steaming green water, ramada made of raw juniper logs and roofed with the slim sticks of latillas, both with the bark still on, kiva fireplace in the corner with more crackling piñon logs.

Jas took off his robe, hung it on a hook by the fire and slid into the water.

Before this, she'd never seen him in anything other than business wear. He was pale and slim with flat, defined muscles, a little dark hair on his chest and legs. Very different from Talys' Navajo build that hid all his strength under smooth, deceptively rounded torso and limbs.

Amethyst stood at the edge of the pool, hugging her robe around her and concentrating on the tiles that lined the pool, the rolled towels by the fire, anything to keep away the blush that was trying to push into her face. Jas raised his brows at her.

She took a breath, slipped out of the robe, then the t-shirt and sarong. She plopped into the water as quickly as she could. Well, if nothing else, she'd have absolutely nothing to worry about now that he'd seen her in a bathing suit.

Mercifully, Jas only closed his eyes and leaned his head back on the pool's edge. Amethyst sat tense for a while. The warm water coaxed her to relax.

She laid back her head, enjoying the contrast of warm water around her body and cold air on her face and shoulders. Stars glittered past the edge of the ramada, sharp as shards of ice in the high-altitude night. Piñon smoke curled its earthy, spicy fragrance around her.

The magic felt even stronger in the water, like it was seeping into her, pushing out pain and emptiness. She let herself float, traced the spring green and earth red and vibrant blue energies as they wove through her, branched along her nerves, pulsed with her blood through her veins.

A splash came, and the water lapped against her.

"That's enough for me," Jas' voice said from somewhere far away. "Do you want to stay?"

She found her way along her body, made her muscles move, her head nod.

"Stay as long as you like," he said.

The slap of wet feet on concrete came, a clunk of wood, the spatter of sparks. The click of a latch. The magic drew her in again, cradled her and rocked her and soothed her wounds.

A wave of energy rolled over her. Amethyst let it furl away. It came again, a throb like an underwater explosion.

From somewhere, a pulse of magic.

CHAPTER 20

Amethyst's eyes snapped open. The fire had died down to red embers pulsing in a charred log. She turned her head, listening. No trace now of whatever force had moved through the magical ether, but vague unease shivered through her.

She dragged her arms out of the enveloping water and levered herself to her feet. Water streamed off her skin and hair, but the magic still clung. She climbed out of the pool, drew in a deep breath of cold, smoke-spiced air. Goosebumps prickled her skin. She snatched up her robe and belted it on without drying off first. She unlatched the gate and stepped out.

The two pools by the bathhouse were empty, green eyes glimmering up at the sky, water splashing from the upper pool into the lower. The courtyard beyond was just as deserted, lounge chairs and hammocks vacant, Adirondack chairs and wood tables dreaming under dim ramadas.

Amethyst frowned. Where was Jas? He'd made such a big deal about keeping an eye on her, and now he was nowhere to be found? She padded across icy concrete to the bathhouse entrance. The bath attendant had said something about coming here for a wrap. She stepped inside, into warm yellow light. The attendant's station was empty.

A powerful urge to call Jas' name swept her. She bit it back and pushed aside a curtain. Beyond, a hall led deeper into the bathhouse.

Her heart beat too hard. She turned her head one way, then the other, searching. She found no trace of Jas. *He's probably gone back to the room, damn his conniving self.*

She turned to go back. A breath of cold air breathed across her face and neck, a silvery ripple of power shivered over her.

She froze. "Tal—?"

No. Not Talys. Something in her middle gave a painful squeeze. But it had *felt* like—

She looked back down the hallway. The cold, dense air seemed to urge her that way. She shivered, took a step, then another. Something drew her on, past the men's locker room and showers, still and quiet, past deserted massage rooms and empty private tubs. She found herself moving faster, her breath coming as quick as her heartbeat. She pushed through a door.

Six narrow beds, almost like massage tables, lined the room. Jas lay on one, swaddled in some heavy, drab green fabric.

Amethyst let out a breath and propped fists on hips. "What happened to 'we have to stay close'?"

He lay there, eyes closed. A prickle ran up her back and down her arms.

"Jas? Are you asleep?"

He didn't move, not even a flicker of eyelids. The

prickle turned cold.

"Jas!"

She lunged across the room, took him by the swaddled shoulders and shook him. His head lolled from side to side. He was hot, too hot. His face and lips were grey, his eyelids so pale they looked translucent.

Her throat was so tight her breath went through her teeth in little whimpers. She tore at the thick fabric that bound him. It might've been molded on him. She cast around, for a knife, scissors, anything to get it off. Nothing. Nothing. She grabbed him and rolled him over. He slithered off the table, but the wrap never loosened its grip.

She wrenched at the edges around his throat. "Not again. Not again. Please, Jas. I can't do this again!"

The heat of awareness burned into her back. She whipped around. Door closed, no one in the room. But behind the door—

She threw herself at it, flung it open. The bath attendant stood outside. Amethyst seized him by the jacket and jerked him inside.

"Get it off him!" she snarled.

"What you doing, lady? What's wrong? I don't do nothing!"

She shoved him away, raised her hands, and not thinking, reached for her power.

The magic suddenly, impossibly poured through her, so strong it knocked the breath out of her. It hit the man, splayed him flat against the wall. His eyes and mouth flew wide.

Fury and power burned through Amethyst. "Take—it—off!" she snarled and tightened her grip on him.

His eyes bulged. His dark face turned darker. His mouth worked.

She turned the magic on Jas, spells of opening, of unlocking, counterspells against binding and imprisonment and harm.

The fabric around Jas fell open. Amethyst pounced on him, tore it away. She eased the pressure on the little man but still held him, then bent her mouth to Jas' and started CPR.

His color... Oh god, his color...

"Don't you die, you bastard." She jammed the heels of both hands down on his mottled, too-hot chest.

The magic coiled like a dragon, hot and just as huge. She caught a wisp of it, molded a vitalizing spell and sent it into him with each thrust.

Jas' eyes flew open, his back arched and he sucked in a breath. She almost sobbed in relief, then his dark eyes blazed. His hands whipped up and a blast of magic hit her.

Force hurled Amethyst across the room. She smacked into the wall, lost her grip on the magic that held the bath attendant.

"Not me!" she shouted and began to call a protective spell.

The magic suddenly slipped away, like water down a drain. Jas, up on one elbow, thrust a hand spread-fingered at her. His teeth were bared, feral. She put up her hands, useless defense, but this time, no magic hit her.

"Not me, Jas!" She made a wild gesture at the bath

attendant, scuttling out the door. "Him!"

Reason came back into Jas' face. He reached out, made a grab at the air, but once more, no magic followed.

Damn! What the hell was going on? What happened to the magic?

She thrust away from the wall, toward the door. Her shoulder and side, back and hip screamed with pain, but she launched herself through the door, hit the bath attendant from behind, knocked him flat.

Her lungs and heart stopped.

She writhed over, clawing at her chest and throat. Glittering greyness narrowed around her vision. Jas shoved her aside, grabbed the attendant and slammed his head into the tile floor. His eyes fluttered. Jas punched him in the face, one quick, vicious jab. The man went slack.

Amethyst's heart thundered suddenly. She sucked in air with a whoop, but the greyness still pressed down on her. Hands grabbed her, pulled her up. She tried to fight them, but only fumbled.

"No, Amethyst," Jas' voice said, echoing and hollow. "I won't hurt you."

Light and color seeped back in. Her face was pressed to a chest. Arms clenched tight around her. She flailed, suffocating again—

"No, no, I won't hurt you again. I'm so sorry—"

"I can't—breathe—" she gasped.

Jas held her in his arms, both of them on the floor. He shifted, raised her, cupped her face, looking anxiously down at her. "You are breathing. Are you all right?"

She dragged in another shuddering breath, pushed it

out again. She felt like there wasn't enough air in the world to satisfy her lungs.

"Are you?" she managed to get out.

He, too, was panting. "Yes." He closed his eyes as if fighting dizziness. "Yes, I think so."

"I'm okay." Well, more okay than a minute ago, anyway. "I felt…" *Talys.* "…something wrong. I didn't know. But…" She took another breath. "I had to come. You just lay there. Then I felt him watching…"

"Amethyst, I swear to you, I didn't mean to hurt you. And you couldn't even protect yourself from me—"

"The magic just disappeared." She shook her head. "It was there, then it wasn't—" She stopped, gripped his arm. "Jas. I used it. When I found him outside the door. *I used the magic.*"

His arms loosened suddenly and she slid into his lap. He slumped over her, caught himself, one hand braced on the floor. She extricated herself, holding him by one shoulder. His skin, so hot before, now felt cooler than it should. She glanced at the attendant, but he was still out cold.

Jas' head drooped. "Sorry."

She never would've imagined he had so much apology in him. "You weren't breathing for longer than I wasn't." She wondered if both of them wouldn't benefit from bottled oxygen. "I had to give you CPR."

He made a strange wheezing sound. "And to think I wasn't conscious to enjoy it."

She let go of his shoulder and pushed away. "Well, I didn't get to enjoy pounding on you, either." She winced and rubbed her own shoulder. It was starting to really throb. The way her ribs and back and hip felt, she'd be walking like an old lady tomorrow. "And I'm here to tell you, your protective spells don't work worth a damn."

"Against my own power? No."

"Not against his, either." She tipped her head toward the bath attendant.

Jas sat up. "That's right. When I threw those spells at you," he grimaced, "the magic didn't respond. I couldn't touch it." He studied the man.

"No, Jas," she said. "We're not going to kill him."

He glanced up. "Did I say anything about killing him?"

"You have a look on your face like a coyote eyeing a chicken pen."

"He tried to kill you. He tried to kill *me*."

"And don't you wonder why? Neither one of us did anything." She climbed to her feet. Her head swam. "We need to either get out of here, or do something to keep unwitting civilians from stumbling on us assaulting the staff."

She carefully opened herself to the magic. It was still there, still rushing like a river through a narrow channel, but she didn't have the strength to grasp it properly. Being bounced off a wall and forcibly put into cardiopulmonary arrest couldn't have helped things much.

"Wait," Jas said, and his power unfurled, joined with hers, molding a barrier spell, spells of repelling and concealment.

Mixing her power with another wizard's was very

different from working with Talys, who had simply amplified and directed her own power. This was more like some intricate Regency dance, and less like revving up an engine.

Jas' head drooped again.

Amethyst, bracing herself against the hallway wall, bit her lip, wondering how much help he'd be able to give her.

"We still have to keep him from doing something to us when he wakes up."

"Yes," Jas said, his head still hanging.

Okay, no need to get alarmed yet. Between the two of them, they could still work the magic. Barely.

She ran spells through her mind. *Ah.* One that didn't require a lot of power. Perfect.

She unpinned the room key from her bathing suit. *Don't think about it*, she told herself. *Just do it.*

She took a deep breath, held it and scratched the pin across the back of her hand.

"Shit!" she hissed.

Jas' head snapped up. "Amethyst!" He caught her hand.

"Hold still." She turned her hand over, gripped his and did the same. Blood from the scratch on her hand ran over his.

"What are you doing?" He snatched his hand away.

She scratched a line across the bath attendant's forehead. He groaned and his eyelids flickered. She grabbed Jas' hand again, pressed it to the bleeding line on the attendant's forehead.

"I'm working a binding." She mixed her own blood

with the man's then called the magic.

First chance she got, she'd better do some kind of germicidal spell. She didn't know if wizards could get AIDS or hepatitis, and she didn't want to find out.

She straightened, jammed the pin through the fabric of her robe and re-tied it. The cut stung. So did pretty much everything else.

"Can you help me drag this guy back into the room? I think I might have a cracked rib."

That got Jas to haul himself up. He swayed, put a hand to the wall to steady himself, then bent and caught one of the bath attendant's wrists. Amethyst gripped the other, clamped her arm to her sore side and pulled.

Ow, ow, ow. Things really needed to lighten up. She wasn't sure how much more beating she could take.

"First the summoning, now this," Jas said, panting. "I hope you know how close you're treading to black magic. What was your familiar thinking, teaching you such spells?"

"I didn't learn them from Talys. Besides, it's *old* magic, not black magic. And didn't you say the morals were different a long time ago?"

The bath attendant blinked, rolled his head and mumbled something in some language that wasn't English, and wasn't Spanish. They pulled him into the room where she'd found Jas, then Amethyst limped around him and shut the door. Jas crossed the room and retrieved his robe from a line of pegs.

The man suddenly wrenched upright. He winced, blinked, touched his head. He looked down at the blood on his hand. The magic around them wavered, then sank away.

Jas, leaning on one of the tables and looking a little grey again, stiffened.

"Bet you're glad now I used blood magic for that binding," Amethyst told him.

The magic used for the spell resided in the living blood. No need to tap the magical ether after the spell was set.

She said to the bath attendant, "In the interest of full disclosure, whatever you do to us, you'll do to yourself. So unless you're suicidal, you probably don't want to try to kill us again."

She wondered if he'd try something anyway. She flashed on Jas, lying so still on that table and kind of hoped he would.

"I don't try to kill nobody," the man said. "He's having a heart attack or something! I'm going for help and you jump me. What's the matter with you?"

Jas started to say something, but Amethyst said first, "You tried to kill him. I'm sick and tired of seeing people killed, and if you think you can sit there and play dumb and I'll believe it, when you stood outside, *watching* while he—"

Jas had crossed to her and now touched her shoulder. She held up her hands in a gesture of surrender and folded her arms, shaking with anger and reaction.

"Why did you try to kill me?" he quietly asked the man. "I'd done nothing to threaten you."

The man's dark eyes moved from one to the other of

them. "Why'd you come here? What you want?"

"We—!" Amethyst began.

"I brought her here for healing," Jas interrupted.

"Lots of people come here for healing," the man said. "When your kind comes, you don't come for healing."

"What do you mean, *our kind?*" Amethyst said.

"*Magos*," the man said. "Mages."

"Our kind has been coming here for years," she said. "My great-grandmother was a *curandera*. She used to bring me here all the time."

Something flicked through the bath attendant's eyes. "Which one? What was her name?"

"Rosalinda Romero. From San Cristobal."

"You are Rosalinda's great-granddaughter?"

"Amethyst Rey. Yes."

Beside her, Jas had grown very quiet.

"Then you should know," the man said. "She would tell you, go see Pico when you go to Ojo Caliente. Don't use *la magia* unless you talk to the guardian."

"I *don't* know, because Nani died. Somebody killed her when I was thirteen."

"*Killed* her! How?"

Amethyst hesitated. The memories were like a dream, a nightmare. She'd hidden from them for so long.

"I didn't understand then. I only knew it was something to do with magic. Nani had been afraid, working magic on me, on herself."

"Me and Rosalinda, we spoke of this," the man— Pico?—said. "She said *el diablo* hunts. She said to me, '*Mi bisnieta*, my granddaughter, I fear for her.' I told her, 'Bring *su bisnieta* to me. If *el diablo* comes here, the earth will take his magic.' Why didn't she come?"

Amethyst shook her head. "I don't know. Maybe she didn't have a chance. All I know is one day I felt—" The image came of Nani lying on the floor, powdered herbs smeared on her cold forehead and chest. The look on her face—

Amethyst shivered, then realized she and Pico had been speaking Spanish. She switched back to English. "Everybody kept telling me she was old. They said she'd had a heart attack or stroke, but that wasn't what killed her. I think now she'd been drained of her power."

"What do you mean," Jas said suddenly, "the earth will take his power?"

Pico stomped one foot. "This place, it's where the magic lives. I live here a long, long time, guarding it. Maybe I can't do nothing to you now, but you won't use the magic unless I say so."

"What, *anywhere?*" Amethyst burst out.

Pico made a sharp downward gesture. "The magic goes down into the ground. No more magic."

"Too bad she won't be able to remove that blood bond, then," Jas said.

Pico's dark gaze slid between them. "You think I'm stupid? I let you use the magic, you try to kill me."

"Look, Pico," Amethyst said. "If we wanted to kill you, we could've done it while you were knocked out." She shot Jas a look. "No magic necessary. Just—" She mimed throttling someone. "And second, that blood bond works both ways." *I think.* This time it was Jas who shot her a look. She ignored him. "Would I have laid a binding like that on you if I intended to do you any harm?"

Pico only glared and wiped the blood trickling down his forehead.

"Mexican standoff," Jas said.

"Actually, no," she said. "Because I have a history here. Right, Pico? My great-grandmother trusted you to watch out for me. And you know what? You let her down. She died trying to keep me safe, and you let her down. You knew she was in trouble, and you never came looking for her *or* me. And when I show up, hurt and sick, you try to kill the man who brought me here to help me. You tried to kill *me*."

"How am I s'posed to know who you are? You come talk to me first—"

"Maybe it's you who should've talked to somebody first," she said. "Instead of just trying to kill them."

"You think I'm some kind of animal, just killing people? No." Pico shook his head hard. "Indian people, they leave their weapons on the other side of the river and come here for the magic. Español and Anglo *magos*, they want all the magic for themselves. I tell them no, the magic belongs to the earth, and what the earth gives belongs to everybody. They don't like that, so they try to kill me. So I don't give them no chance no more."

"Take the magic for themselves," Jas said slowly. He had that coyote-eying-the-chicken-coop look again. "Are you saying other wizards have tried to tap into the magic here?"

Pico got a dark glitter in his eyes. "They try. I don't

let them."

"How many—" Amethyst began.

"When did you last face a wizard?" Jas interrupted.

Pico hesitated. "A long time."

Amethyst could see the devious wheels turning in Jas' head. It was scary.

"The point is," she said, "we're here, we didn't try to take the magic, and we didn't to do anything to you—" Pico opened his mouth, but she said quickly, "Before you tried to kill us. And to be honest, even afterwards, I was extremely restrained." She nodded at Jas. "As my friend will be the first to say." She folded her arms, unobtrusively holding her probably-cracked rib. "Do you think we can call a truce?"

Pico was silent a long moment. "Rosalinda was a good woman," he finally said. "A very strong *curandera*. I'm sorry she's gone."

"The wizard who most likely killed her had been stealing other wizards' power," Jas said. "He tried to steal Amethyst's, as well. She defeated him."

Pico looked at her with new respect.

How the hell had Jas known that? She'd never told him what happened. "Not by myself," she muttered.

Pico nodded. "Okay."

The magic came flooding back, humming up through her feet. She abruptly felt less worn and battered. Oh, everything hurt just as much, but she didn't have to pull the will to keep standing from the roots of her teeth. Jas' chest rose with a breath and a little of the tension in him seemed to unwind.

"Thank you, Pico," Amethyst said.

"Now you take off *la maldición*, the curse," he said, gesturing at his bleeding forehead.

Uh-oh. "Um…" She shifted from one foot to the other and glanced at Jas.

He raised his brows.

"I'll have to find the counterspell first," she said.

Pico looked like he was ready to do his life-force suck thing again and worry about the blood bond later.

She held up her hands. "I'm sorry. Really, I am."

"I suppose we can all consider it insurance," Jas said.

"If something happens to you, something happens to me," Pico said. "Then who will guard this place?"

Amethyst gusted a sigh and rotated the sore shoulder. "If something happens to us, I'm guessing it won't be long before this place is next." She drew a breath. "We're on the same side, Pico. My friend and I aren't too happy with what other wizards are doing right now, either."

"And what you doing about it?" Pico said.

Hiding. Under the circumstances, that wouldn't be the best thing to say.

Jas set a hand on her shoulder. "Amethyst already set protective spells on the Albuquerque petroglyphs when another wizard attempted to tamper with them."

Her brows went up. She was beginning to think he'd kept a closer eye on her than she'd ever guessed.

"Sacred lands," Pico said. "Very old. Lots of power there, too. The *magos* didn't like that, huh?"

She thought of everything that had happened since. She thought of Talys and swallowed hard.

"No." Her voice came out small and unsteady. She cleared her throat. "Look at it this way. If something happens to you, we'll know about it. And then we can make sure this place is protected, too."

Jas looked like a lightbulb had popped on. That was scarier than the devious wheels.

Pico studied them. Finally, he grunted. "Sometimes the magic does things. I'm old. Nobody's come to take care of this place. Maybe the magic brought you."

Oh, *no*. "I—" Amethyst began.

"It's entirely possible," Jas said first.

Thanks a lot, Jas. She didn't let herself glare at him. What the hell was he up to now?

CHAPTER 21

*G*limmering *light shone through curtains.* Moonlight? No. The light was silver, not white. Amethyst blinked around an unfamiliar room. The light wasn't behind the curtains. It was in the room.

She sat up in bed, her heart pounding. "Talys?"

She scrambled up. Warmth furled around her, warring with a disembodied sense of disapproval.

Amethyst, what are you doing?

She reached out to the light. "You came back!"

No.

"Yes. I can see you! It was you at Ojo, wasn't it? You took me to Jas."

You can't do this.

Her hands drooped. "What?"

I'm not there. I'm not the same.

"You are here," she said. "I'm talking to you!"

No. Go back. Let go. Let go and find strength.

"No! I won't let go. I've found you, and I'll bring you back."

You cannot.

Pain jabbed her. She winced. "I can. I can and I will."

No, he said again. *Go now. Gather strength.* Again the pain came.

"Talys, don't—" She swung out of bed, reaching for the silver light of him—

And opened her eyes to an ordinary motel room. A blur of orangish light seeped around the edges of the curtains. Air hushed through a vent somewhere.

"Talys?" she called, her voice rising. She spun, searching the dim room. Her hand knocked into something on the nightstand. Water splashed her, then the something—a glass—thudded to the floor. "Where are you?"

The door snapped open.

"Amethyst?" Jas' voice came from the shadow in the doorway. "What's wrong?"

"Talys," she said. She stumbled barefoot across the low-pile carpeting, groping ahead of her. "He's here. I talked to him. *He isn't dead.*"

Jas, wearing a t-shirt and boxers, came into the room. The dim light glowed on the planes of his face, leaving his eyes in darkness.

"It was just a dream," he said gently.

"It wasn't! It wasn't!" She turned, turned again. "He was here. He led me to you at Ojo." Jas stood by her now, a hand under her elbow, urging her back toward the bed. She set her feet. "I'm not dreaming, and I'm not crazy. He's—somewhere. Not here. But he wasn't destroyed,

Jas." She gripped his arm, warm and wiry under her cold hand. "I've been dreaming about him almost every night. And every night he's a little closer, a little more real."

"Of course you've been dreaming about him. But that's all it is, Amethyst. Dreams. Because you miss him. Because you want him back."

He clicked on the bedside lamp. The warm reds and creams and dark woods of the bedroom of their suite at the Santa Claran Hotel sprang into view. He urged her onto the edge of the bed and sat beside her.

For obvious reasons, staying at Ojo had been out of the question. So she and Jas had piled their mutually battered selves back into the Range Rover and Amethyst, as the least wiped out of the two of them, had driven them to the hotel on the Santa Clara pueblo, just outside Española.

She slumped, pressing her arm to her side where she'd hit the wall earlier. The same pain that had invaded her dream—had it really been a dream?—jabbed at her now. Since she'd smacked into the wall mostly on one side and been slammed face-first into the car on the other, there wasn't much of anything that *didn't* hurt.

"But at Ojo—"

"You've been through a lot in the last twenty-four hours. You're in pain." He made a face and raked a hand through his hair. "I'm sorry, Amethyst. Truly, I didn't mean to hurt you. My reaction was just…instinct."

"It's okay. Don't worry about it."

"I also didn't thank you."

His gaze was intense and serious. She couldn't meet it

for long. She shrugged the non-sore shoulder. "I'd say we're even, but to be honest, I've lost track."

He shook his head, then said, "Have you found a counterspell for that binding?"

"Um... I don't know if there was one. If there was, I don't seem to have it." She shifted again. "You know, there's something I don't understand. The way you talked, you've been going to Ojo for years. Why did Pico try to kill you this time? Especially when he said it's been a long time since he had to deal with wizards. It's not like he'd suddenly be on high alert."

Jas shrugged. "Apparently I never used magic when I visited before. Unless I did, he'd have no way of knowing I'm a wizard."

Her back and hip were really starting to jab. She finally got up from the bed to sit in a chair. It also gave her a moment to figure out how to phrase her next question. There didn't seem to be a good way.

"This is going to sound rude, but why didn't you ever try to take over that...that power spot?"

He smiled. "The way I tried to take you? Believe it or not, I did have a worthy motive in your case."

"Huh."

"All right, not entirely," he said. "But I didn't want to see another wizard disappear into whatever Bermuda Triangle had been swallowing them. To answer the question you actually asked, I was more concerned with remaining incognito than with amassing power. And before you feel the need to ask another uncomfortable question, no, I haven't changed my priorities."

"Okay, so how about another uncomfortable question. I'm pretty sure going to the bathhouse for a wrap doesn't constitute effective guarding of a powerless companion. How in God's name did he convince you?"

"I went to arrange some extra time in the private pool. The attendant—Pico—told me it was already booked and I'd need to talk to the manager. I followed him, then—" He frowned. "Honestly, Amethyst, after that, I don't know. And that makes me extremely uneasy. Considering I've lived in New Mexico for almost a hundred years, I seem to be encountering native magical traditions with dismaying frequency lately."

She rubbed her eyes, hissing when she brushed her sore, swollen cheekbone.

"Come on," Jas said abruptly. "We need to get you some pain relievers." He pulled her up. "And as soon as I'm able, I'll work on mending what I damaged."

She eyed him. What was with all the concern? Guilt?

Jas? Feel guilty? Nah. Something else was going on.

They descended from the quiet of the hotel to the smoke and video-game noise and lights of the casino. Jas seemed preoccupied, his head turning from side to side.

Amethyst watched him, curious. "What are you looking for?"

"Hmm?" He studied a young Spanish couple at the roulette table. "Nothing in particular."

"Nothing. Right."

"There's the gift shop," he said.

It was a neat change of subject, but she was too tired and too uncomfortable to call him on it. She took a tiny, overpriced bottle of Aleve to the register and paid.

"You need something in your stomach before you take that," Jas said.

Amethyst slanted him a look. "You're trying to feed me again. Every time you try to feed me, you're up to something."

He sighed. "Then let me put it another way. I'm hungry."

The fare at Burgers and Brews probably wasn't Jas' usual, but at one in the morning, there was no being picky.

Amethyst chased the Aleve with a cup of oversweet hot chocolate, gritty with undissolved sugar, then dug into a Frito pie. Jas started on a green chile cheeseburger.

"I have to admit," he said. "I'm worried."

"About what?"

"Pico's place of power. That magical nexus."

She shrugged. "Why? It's been there, what, pretty much forever? And even you didn't know about it until now."

"No, not what it truly is. But…" He gestured as if searching for words. "Northern New Mexico seems to draw sensitive people. Artists. Writers." He raised a brow. "Wizards. Even your familiar was here, waiting for you— or someone like you, at any rate. Doesn't it seem strange that so many of us are here? New Mexico is even called The Land of Enchantment."

"Well, yeah, poetically."

He shook his head. "It's more than that. When I came in the 1920's, Albuquerque and Santa Fe were tiny towns with dirt streets. At the time, I thought the only things to recommend the place were the light and the views. And the isolation."

Jas looked somewhere in his mid to late thirties. It was strange to think of him maybe knowing people like Georgia O'Keefe, D.H. Lawrence, Ansel Adams. *And how old were you then?* she wanted to ask.

"None of those exactly seem like they'd be a draw for you," she said instead.

"The isolation was. Or so I thought then. Remember, I was fleeing whoever was making wizards disappear. Eventually, even he followed. I thought he might've followed the spoor of my power. But Pico spoke of having to defend the nexus against wizards. How did they find out about it?"

"I assume the same way people found native villages or gold or anything else they wanted. But you're saying the magic itself drew them?"

"It's subtle, and we may not realize it, but I'm beginning to think so. And once a wizard actually sets foot on that nexus—"

"We can feel how strong the magic is."

"And how much stronger it makes us. Even when we don't realize exactly what it is."

She blew through her lips. "And you think it's only a matter of time before somebody decides what a great idea it would be to take it over. But Pico seems to have been good at keeping that from happening."

"We confronted him yesterday and bested him. How, when he's been guarding that nexus for so long?"

"There were two of us, and he wasn't expecting—"

She stopped. "Oh."

"You see the problem," Jas said. "Pico might've withstood individual wizards."

"But there're a lot more now than there have been for a long time," she finished. "At least since the 1600's, when Europeans came, right? And if they decide to gang up on him…"

The Frito pie was suddenly less appetizing.

He took a long breath. "We're going to need help, Amethyst."

She rubbed her forehead. "Where have I heard that before? And why does it give me such a bad feeling?"

"Possibly because enlisting the help of other wizards is always a chancy proposition."

"I guess it depends on how you go about it," she said, deadpan.

Surprisingly, he smiled. "That's where you come in. You'll lend legitimacy to our endeavor."

She made a skeptical face. "Me. How?"

"Your honesty. Your sincerity. Those qualities I appreciate in you."

She tapped her fork on her plate, *ting-ting-ting*. "Why?" she said. "Why do I let you talk me into things?"

"Because I'm plausible and reasonable."

"Jas, so help me God, if I ever find out you're using some kind of sneaky magic—"

"Why would I use magic," he said, "when convincing you the ordinary way is so much more satisfying?"

Chapter 21.5 - Opposition

R obertson clenched a fist and leaned close to his laptop screen. "What the hell do you mean she *disappeared?*"

On the screen, Darnell shook his head. "We had her in hand. Fisk was putting her into the car, then *poof.*" He waved his hands. "She was gone. Her car, too. Even that—that—"

"The dummy she hit?" Robertson offered.

"Yeah. That." Darnell smoothed his buzz-cut head. "It was like nothing happened there."

Robertson drummed his fingers on the table. The city skyline spread outside his office windows, gradually blurring away into thin snow.

"Witnesses?" he said.

"Oh, plenty saw it. But—"

"But?"

"Jesus," Darnell said. "What're we supposed to say? We ended up doing damage control. Thanked 'em for their participation in the shoot. Told 'em we'd be letting them know when the movie comes out. Shit."

"And no one," Robertson said dryly, "took a picture with their phone."

"We checked. Apparently not. Even the ones who thought they had."

"Shit," Robertson said in turn.

Darnell wet his lips. "You'd better know."

It was like one of those late-night commercials: *But wait! There's more!*

"What?" Robertson said.

"Gore's in the hospital. The car died. He was under the hood, checking things out, and the hood fell on him. Bashed his head into the engine. Broke his shoulder. Busted his face all to hell. He just came out of surgery."

Robertson relaxed. He thought it'd had something to do with magic. "I'm already covering expenses. What else do you want?"

"There was no way that hood should've fallen," Darnell said. "He put up the hood support rod. I watched him. When we got the hood up, that rod was bent like a giant hand had shoved down on it."

Robertson bit back a curse. "So what're you saying? Somebody had it in for Gore and tried to make it look like an accident?"

"I don't know," Darnell said. "But Gore got kinda rough with that chick. Knocked her face into the car, bloodied her up a little. It just seems funny…"

Robertson shoved to his feet, walked away. Funny. No it wasn't funny. Not at all.

"Mr. Ragman?" Darnell said.

Robertson came back to the desk, back into range of the webcam. "You were Special Forces. Find her. Isn't that what you guys do?"

"Begging your pardon, Sir, but we have been looking for her. She hasn't gone home. Even her dog is gone."

"She has family. She has friends. Ask them."

"We tried. We can't get anywhere near 'em. Bugs don't work. Nothing works." Darnell did the head-smoothing thing again. "I seen a lot of shit, but I've never seen anything like this. I don't know what the hell is going on here, but whatever it is, I don't like it. We talked, me and Fisk and Garcia, and we decided. We're out. Cover our expenses, keep the rest. But we're out."

Robertson ground his teeth. "Look, Darnell. What happened to Gore was just a coincidence," he lied. "You know it as well as I do. If it's more money you want, just say so. Don't try to lay this woo-woo bullshit on me."

"It isn't the money—"

"Then do the job I hired you for. You say her family is out. Fine. My intel says she's doing something for Magus Corporation. Use that. Unless you can't. Is that the problem?"

Darnell sat silent a moment. "We can *do* the job, but—"

"Good," Robertson said. "You said you were the best. That's what I'm paying for." He lowered his voice. "I need this woman on board. Bring her in and you'll be able to pick and choose your jobs. Or retire, if that's what you want." He paused. "But bailing now won't do your rep much good. Will it?"

"No, Sir."

"Then we're still on with this? I'm counting on you."

Darnell sighed. "Yeah. But Gore's out. I'm going to

need a guy to take his place."

"I'll rely on you," Robertson said. "Just one thing, Darnell. Find someone with more restraint. If I didn't make it clear before, I don't want the goods damaged. Understand?"

"Yes, Sir. It won't happen again, Sir."

"Good." He closed the chat window and slammed down the laptop screen.

"Fuck!" He fought the impulse to throw the computer through the window.

Everyone he threw at her, the bitch scared off. More time, more effort, more money. But he had buyers lined up. Buyers he'd had to stall, who were *done* being stalled. It was embarrassing. And nobody embarrassed him in front of a client. Nobody.

Wizard or no wizard, she was about to regret her lack of cooperation.

CHAPTER 22

Amethyst didn't get bored easily. But sitting beside Jas all morning, watching the dice roll, the chips slide across the table, she was utterly, inexpressibly bored.

Not to mention annoyed.

Jas threw the dice. The woman sitting on Jas' other side squealed and clapped and bounced in her seat. Since she was wearing a cami top and a skirt that barely covered her crotch, there was a lot of bouncing going on there. A Spanish woman with dyed blond hair and a dress with a lot of boobage leaned over him, her hand on his shoulder.

The dealer slid him a pile of chips. Bouncy Woman leaned close, put a French manicured hand on Jas' thigh and whispered something even Amethyst's wizard's ears couldn't make out over the surrounding clamor.

He smiled, then turned and offered the dice. "Here, Amethyst. Roll me an eight. I'm counting on you."

Bouncy Woman pouted. A ridiculous spurt of gratitude went through Amethyst. She took the dice. Then narrowed her eyes.

Great. Now she had a choice of refusing and looking like the flirting was getting to her, or being complicit in what Jas was doing here.

He'd been using magic. Sometimes he let himself lose, but the magic was enough to increase his winnings. It was part of the reason she stayed, no matter how bored and annoyed she got—to keep an eye on him.

Jas' brow and one corner of his mouth gave the slightest lift.

"Straight up," she said and rolled the dice. In other words, *no magic.*

An eight came to rest on the table. Bouncy Woman and her friend squealed and clapped and hugged Jas. Amethyst struggled not to roll her eyes.

"My lucky charm," he said, giving Amethyst that damned crinkly, charming smile of his. He grabbed her hand and pulled her to her feet. "Come on. Let's see how you do at the roulette table." He nodded to his two admirers. "Good luck, ladies."

It was the smoothest brush-off she'd ever seen. The women looked like they were trying to figure out if it *was* a brush-off.

Jas kept hold of her hand. Amethyst thought about pulling away. But if he was going to be gallant, she wasn't going to discourage him. Most guys, when faced with two hot babes hitting on them, would've forgotten the existence of their skinny, not-much-to-look-at companion.

She did *not* like feeling like a starving dog he'd just tossed a tidbit.

"What, exactly, are we doing here?" she said.

He slid her a look. "Aren't you having fun?"

"Watching you…" Conscious of casino surveillance, she waggled her fingers as if casting a spell. "Or watching you flirt with only-legal-this-year bimbos?"

He threaded his fingers with hers and leaned close. "Jealous?"

"Please." She extricated her hand. "And you didn't answer my question."

"Nothing works on you, does it?"

She turned, met his eyes and said drily, "Yeah. As a matter of fact, there is one thing. Honesty. It makes me totally fall into men's arms."

Damn. She wished she hadn't said that. But the look on his face made it almost worth it.

"Oh," he said. "Well then. I need to keep a ready supply of cash."

"Uh-huh. And?"

"And," he drawled, "We're hunting."

"Hunting *what?*"

"Anyone doing exactly what I've been doing." He waggled his fingers the way she had. "By definition, a wizard making a living that way will be interested in remaining a free agent."

She stopped, turned to face him. "And tell me, Jas. After you find this wizard or wizards, *will* they remain free agents?"

He heaved an annoyed sigh. "What do you think?"

"I think," she said, "you're asking the wrong person that question."

His eyes flashed, then he threw up his hands. "Why do I even bother?" He stalked away.

She swallowed an impulse to laugh. The next was to feel bad. But dammit, what did he expect? For all she knew, this show of temper was all an act, too.

She watched his retreating back. She was half inclined to just let him go back to Dos Chi Chi Girls and call Dad to come pick her up. Except besides being petty and immature, it would also be extremely stupid.

Damn. If this was an act, he'd expect her to go running after him. Well, she wasn't about to abuse her self-respect that way.

She reached out a staying spell. Jas slapped it away and spun.

Amethyst sauntered her way through the cigarette smoke and waitresses carrying trays of drinks and Spanish grannies clutching their buckets of pennies. Jas steamed toward her rather more quickly.

He looked about like he had when he found her in handcuffs. "Don't you *ever*—"

"Are we going to have a wizard's war in the middle of the Santa Clara Casino?"

He drew a swift breath for some reply then slowly let it out. "You're trying to irritate me, aren't you?"

She raised her brows. "Me?"

It looked like he'd mostly mastered his temper. Mostly. "You know what your problem is, Amethyst?" he said. "You have trust issues."

She stood speechless for a moment, then barked a humorless, disbelieving laugh. "*Trust* issues! Sweet Mary in Heaven. If you think—"

A few heads turned.

He grabbed her arm. "We're not having this conversation here."

"Then why did you start it?" she shot back.

He towed her through the flash and *ding-ding-ding* of the slots and into a wide, carpeted hallway at one end of the casino. Amethyst called a fending that should've knocked him flat, but it bounced around his protective shield in a rush of air that rattled a wall sconce in its socket. He steered her into an alcove in front of double doors to a conference room. Behind him, the dark bubble of a surveillance camera hung from the ceiling. Let *him* worry about what the screens back in security were showing right now.

She jerked out of his grip. "I can*not* believe you. Accusing me of having *trust issues*." She spat the words. "If you think you can play the good guy for two or three weeks and expect me to buy it, you've got a way higher opinion of yourself than I thought you did."

"What do you plan to do?" he said. "Question every move I make? Analyze my every word for hidden meanings?"

"You must think I'm an idiot." She shook her head. "Yes, as a matter of fact that's exactly what I'll do. Because—gosh, so sorry to disappoint you—I'm *not* an idiot."

"Don't be ridiculous. You know perfectly well I've always respected your intelligence."

"Right. That's why you've been running con jobs on me from the minute I met you."

He paced a step away, turned back. "All right. I've apologized. I've explained myself. I've told you I was wrong. What else do you want? Payment in blood?"

The anger went out of her. "I've told you what I want, Jas. But you won't hear me."

She brushed past him.

"Amethyst, wait." He touched her, but didn't grab.

Good choice. She turned back.

He let out a long breath through his nose. "I *do* hear you. But I can't change what happened last year. And if nothing I do can ever convince you—" He gave an angry shrug. "I'll take you home, and you and I will face the coming storm each in our own way."

She narrowed her eyes. *Now* he was trying guilt and regret on her—

She stopped herself. "Okay."

His face didn't change, but a flicker of something— worry? disappointment?—went through his eyes.

That wasn't the 'okay' she meant. She broke from his gaze. "You're right." Again. "I *haven't* been giving you a chance. But I don't— I have trouble— How do I know you won't—" ...*hurt me again*. She took a breath, pushed it out. "—you won't do something like that again?"

She'd never seen a look like that on his face before, one so...so open. So *honest*.

"You don't," he said quietly. "I can only show you, and show you again. However many times it takes, until you believe it."

She couldn't catch her breath, like all the air had been sucked out of the building. She tried to swallow and couldn't.

"Okay," she whispered.

Tension went out of him almost visibly. "Come on,

then." He held out a hand. "Let me tell you what I have in mind."

Amethyst bit her lip, then put her fingers in his.

✦✦✦✦✦✦

The lounge in the adjoining hotel was empty except for the two of them. Jas had woven a spell that made sure it stayed that way, a little glamor of aversion, just enough for anyone passing by to feel a strong reluctance to impose on their privacy.

They sat side-by-side on the tan and turquoise cushions of a *banco* beside a kiva fireplace. Amethyst was pretty sure the Indian rugs underfoot were hand-woven. The tin wall sconces with Pueblo Indian motifs were probably handmade as well.

"The nexus could be the solution to our problems," Jas said.

The 'our' was the only thing that kept her from exploding.

He held up a hand. "No, I'm not planning on taking it over."

"I didn't say anything."

"You didn't have to. Your face said it all."

"*Now* who can't win?" she muttered.

A smile flickered across his face. "Ideally, we'd get Pico on board. Under the circumstances, I'm not optimistic about that, and I have the feeling we don't have a great deal of time to waste."

"Ideally," she repeated. "That sounds like your idea

might be something Pico wouldn't agree with."

"I want to create a nexus of our own."

"Jas——!" She took a deep breath, let it out again. "Okay. So we increase our powers while controlling what other wizards can do. Do you want me to point out how many *more* problems that will create?"

He leaned back, extended an arm along the back of the *banco* behind her. "You aren't taking into account that a nexus already does exist. What do you think will happen if it falls into the hands of the kind of wizards Pico protected it against for the last four hundred or so years?"

She rubbed her temples. *Gather strength*, Talys had said. Was this what he was talking about?

"I don't like it."

"Why?" Jas said. "Because I'm the one proposing it, and you still don't trust me?"

"Well..." She gave an unhappy shrug. "Partly. Sorry."

"Fair enough." He bent his head in that old, slightly regal way she'd noticed when she first met him. "That's why we'll be looking for help. Besides the fact that we'll need the power, the more people involved in the project, the less likelihood for abuse."

She drummed her fingers on a cushion. "I thought wizards were contentious. Hardly ever joined forces."

"Yes. Because we have power, and someone else with power can pose a threat. But if faced with a common danger..."

"You're optimistic."

"I prefer to say visionary."

"Huh. But I don't know how you plan to persuade

anyone to help set up a fail-safe that can be used against *them*, too."

"We'll simply have to convince them that the pluses outweigh the minuses."

"*We* aren't particularly good at convincing people who don't necessarily want to be convinced. That's *your* specialty."

He laughed. "True. But will you help me?"

She wasn't a cunning person. No matter how she followed the threads of logic, Jas could tie her up in knots so tight she'd never get unraveled.

She rubbed her head again. "Understand I'm battling my default reaction here. But I still have to ask—and remember, you're the one who said you're a pragmatist—what's in it for you?"

For just a second, it looked like his temper flared again, then he seemed to shake it off.

"All right. Then I'll answer that I have absolutely no desire for the general population to realize that *yes*, magic and wizards really do exist. Modern skepticism is too great an advantage to give up. I have a vested interest in maintaining the status quo, which has worked for me for a long time."

"I can't believe it," she said. "We actually are on the same side."

He flashed her a disgusted look. "I thought we'd already agreed on that."

"No, you thought I was on *your* side. There's a difference."

"I don't see it."

"No, I guess not. But that's okay. I'll come along for the ride."

"That isn't quite a vote of confidence," he said.

"It's the best I can do right now. And you promised to show me that I can trust you, remember?"

"That I did. And I will. But the plan will be a hard sell if you aren't behind it."

Amethyst pushed to her feet, all the aches and pains accumulated over the last day or so protesting. "Let's worry about that *after* we find a wizard to sell it to."

CHAPTER 23

Magic feathered along Amethyst's nerves. She stopped and narrowed her eyes, listening, scenting. The flash and clamor of the casino around her faded, but after her experience at the State Fair, she knew better than to open wizard's senses. If another wizard was here, she'd have to search the old-fashioned way.

Jas was off on his own search. For all she knew, it was his magic she sensed.

She sighed and wove around the line waiting outside the buffet. Maybe he had the patience to troll casino after casino in search of wizards, but she didn't. The Inn of the Mountain Gods casino was—what?—the seventh casino she and Jas visited? Eighth? They'd all begun to blur together after a while. Some of them were small, others bigger; some had table games, others nothing but slots. By the time they'd reached Albuquerque, Amethyst had had enough.

You've already dragged me through every casino down the Rio Grande, she'd told Jas. *Well, if I'm going to get dragged through another one, we can go to Ruidoso. I'd like to see some scenery I haven't seen 147 times already.*

With Dad's side of the family living in California,

she'd been down I-40, where there were at least three or four more casinos, a *lot*.

Jas had done his damnedest to convince her otherwise, but she was done being convinced. Besides, it was fun watching him fume and mutter. And it felt kind of good to win an argument with him for a change.

Amethyst waded her way through the press of bodies and cigarette smoke, searching for the table games. She wasn't sure how long card games had been around. Long enough for them to be more familiar to most wizards than any slot machine—electronic or otherwise.

Finally, she found them. A noisy group surrounded the craps table. A couple of middle-aged women sat at one blackjack table, a slim man with slicked-down, straw-blond hair at the other. Amethyst prowled the edges of the area, watching the people, scenting for magic.

Nothing. That was the problem identifying wizards: as long as they didn't use magic, they seemed just like anybody else.

But that blond guy...

Maybe it was the hair, slicked down like she'd seen in pictures from the turn of the last century. His clothes, too—high-waisted trousers, a pinstriped vest and narrow tie, loosened. All he needed was a bowler hat and handlebar mustache.

Amethyst must've paused, because he turned to glance at her. No, not he. *She.* The blond guy was a woman.

Amethyst called up a smile and pretended she hadn't been staring at him—*her*. "Hi. Mind if I watch?"

Okay, it was lame, but if she'd really been considering joining the game, that's exactly what she'd do.

The woman gave a half-shrug, then the dealer nodded. Amethyst stationed herself a respectful distance away.

Her heart was fluttering in her throat. She would've asked herself why, except she'd been attacked by every wizard she'd encountered so far—including Jas. She wasn't looking forward to being attacked by another one.

She glanced around. The one time she'd be glad to see Jas, he was nowhere to be seen. And using magic was out, because the minute she did, whoever *else* was using it would know they weren't the only wizard around. Damn.

She forced herself to take slow, even breaths. No point in getting upset yet. She had to pin down the wizard, first.

The group at the craps table cheered and clapped. The atmosphere around the roulette table had the gravity of an operating room.

"Five of spades," the blond woman said in a pleasant alto voice. "Change."

Amethyst snapped her attention back to the table in front of her. "Excuse me?"

The woman waved a long-fingered hand. "This card. Interruptions. Surprises."

The back of Amethyst's neck prickled like hackles rising. Her heart beat harder.

"Really?" she said.

The woman tapped the table. The dealer turned up the five of clubs.

The woman's light brows went up. "Change again. New alliances. Time to make new plans."

She tapped two fingers on the table and laid a second pile of chips beside the one in front of her. The dealer reached across the table and separated the two fives then flicked down two new cards. The ace and nine of spades.

"Damned foul spread." The woman cocked a brow at the dealer. "Not a red card in the deck, eh? Two death cards. Endings. Beginnings. More change—forced change."

Amethyst concentrated on looking politely interested while ignoring her dry mouth. The dealer's only reaction was a slow blink and a twitch of his lips.

The woman tapped the table again.

The card that appeared was the queen of clubs.

"A dark woman," the blonde said with another sideways glance at Amethyst. "Powerful." Her head snapped up. "The agent of change."

She shoved to her feet, raised her hands.

"Don't," Amethyst said, holding out her own hand. "Not here."

The woman's eyes narrowed and the magic rippled, touched but not shaped to a spell.

Yep. I thought so.

On the other side of the blackjack table, the dealer stiffened, reached under the table.

Amethyst changed her staying gesture to the offer of a hand to shake. "Hi. I'm Amethyst. Can I buy you a coffee?"

The magic quivered like a drawn bowstring. It took

everything Amethyst had to keep from calling up wards and shields. That would *so* not improve the situation. She kept the friendly smile plastered on her face and her hand extended to shake.

The woman looked down at her cards. "Five of diamonds. Start new projects." She rolled her eyes. "Finally. A red card. And it has to say the same thing."

"Blackjack," the dealer said as if nothing untoward had happened, sliding chips across the table.

Amethyst stuck her hand in her jeans pocket but didn't relax. The woman scooped up her chips with a practiced hand.

The magic surged.

Amethyst called up a spell of stillness at the same moment, the same thing Jas had done after the incident with the simulacrum. It didn't stop time, but it did the next best thing—stopped everything and everyone within range.

Including the blond woman.

"Hell," Amethyst breathed, suddenly sweating.

Well, she was about to find out just how much she could do without a familiar.

She took a deep breath, set her feet, worked a couple of protective spells and separated the woman from the spell of stillness.

The woman's eyes flared wide and she slammed her with some kind of force spell. It collided with the shield Amethyst had conjured with a jolt that went to her bones.

Amethyst held out her hands. "Look, I swear, I just want to talk—"

The other woman vanished.

Cursing, Amethyst opened herself to the currents in the magical ether. There, that eddy, where something had dived through the magic—

Amethyst zapped herself after. She winked into the world again in a parking lot at one end of the resort, the huge building looming on one side, dark pines and the black satin of the lake under starlight on the other. The blonde still stood in front of her.

"Damn you!" the woman spat and grabbed for the magic again.

Amethyst called up power. She punched it into the magic, churning it, turning it hot and caustic. This was what the magic had been like when her powers first came, before the wizards returned. She could handle it. Most older wizards couldn't.

The blonde's breath hissed through her teeth in a plume of white. She cursed again, obviously not appreciating what Amethyst had done.

"No spells," Amethyst said. "Not unless you want everyone to know what you are and what you can do. There'll be camera surveillance out here, too."

The zapping here was going to cause enough problems.

The woman clenched her fists at her sides. "Who are you?"

"I told you. I'm Amethyst." She hesitated, wondering if telling her would make any difference. "I'm the one who got your power back."

"Why?"

Amethyst held in a sigh. The same damn question

every wizard asked. "Because at the time, I was battling for *my* power, too. And once I won that battle, the rest of you happened to be on hand to take back your own." She spread her hands. "Nothing I decided to do, just the way things worked out."

Of course, it had been more complicated than that, but the wizardly view seemed to be that if you got power, you kept it. If you didn't, you must be up to something. Judging from the woman's face, she thought Amethyst was up to something.

Hard shivers wracked Amethyst. She rubbed her arms and tried to keep her teeth from chattering. A spell to warm things up would've been nice, but she didn't dare waste the power under the circumstances.

"Amethyst?" Jas' voice came from behind her. "Is everything all right?"

He stepped out of the shadows, a slim figure etched out of night and the orange glow of the parking lot lights. She never thought she'd be relieved to see him.

"Well, I'm honestly not sure," she said, then to the blonde, "Is it? Because I'd sure rather have this conversation inside where it's warm."

Jas came and slid his jacket over her shoulders. "I agree. And I suspect you'll need something to eat."

The woman's eyes narrowed as she looked back and forth between them. "Who are *you?*"

"He's my—"Amethyst stammered a moment. *My what?*

"Her very good friend," Jas said with steel.

Amethyst angled him a glance. Maybe he hadn't liked

her fumbling over what to call him.

"This is getting absolutely nowhere," Amethyst said. "If she's not interested in keeping away from the guys who're after me, there's no reason to stay out here and freeze."

This time it was Jas' eyes that narrowed. He gave a blonde a long, hard look.

What—? The conspicuous gallantry, the show of concern— He'd also thought the woman was a guy. Amethyst struggled between laughter and disgust.

"Why should I care about who's after you?" the blonde said.

Amethyst shrugged. "You shouldn't. Not until they find out about you. Then you'll wish you'd've sat down with us over a cup of coffee and let us tell you what we know."

Keeping that blocking spell going, she could feel her power sucked down like fuel for an engine shoved full-throttle. She wished Jas would help, but suspected he was pretending to be a civilian.

She dropped her spell, conjured a good, strong ward then turned and started back toward the resort, Jas right beside her.

"Wait," the woman said. "Why would you want to help me?"

Amethyst waved a hand and kept walking. "We're going inside. If you want to ask more questions, you can ask them there."

Surprisingly enough, Jas didn't say a word. Amethyst nudged him with an elbow. He glanced aside at her, barely turning his head. She waggled her fingers: *do some magic*. His lips made a disapproving twist but she gave one, insistent nod and waggled her fingers again. If they were going to convince this woman to join them, they couldn't surprise her with the fact that Jas was also a wizard.

The way you surprised me, she wanted to tell him. He must've been getting good at reading her, because he made a little gesture of acquiescence.

Warmth bloomed around her, seeped into her. Her shivers even in Jas' jacket eased.

She let out a breath. "Thanks."

"Happy to do it," he said. "I already took care of the security feeds."

"Good," she said on an outrush of breath. "I was kinda tied up."

"I see that. Are you all right?"

Amethyst could almost feel the woman watching them.

She made a disgusted noise. "All I can say is I better not've lost any more weight."

Jas made a noise of his own, something that sounded halfway between a laugh and a snort. "We'll have to do something about that."

"Yeah. *You* can introduce us to the next wizard we meet."

"Are you sure you trust me to do that?" His lips were quirked in a little smile.

"Mmph. Damned if I do, damned if I don't," she grumbled.

He laughed.

An ordinary person would've still been able to hear their voices, but not their words. Being a wizard, the blonde would be able to hear every one. The knowledge gave Amethyst a self-conscious prickle. She and Jas sounded like...very good friends.

Eeech.

She kept her own wizard's senses tuned behind her. The woman must just be standing there watching them walk away. If she had any interest in making their acquaintance, she would've called out by now. So much for Amethyst's skills of persuasion. She was surprised Jas hadn't stepped in.

It was a long way back to the casino, and seemed to get longer with every step. Yesterday's aches and pains reasserted themselves, and she was limping by the time they rounded the front of the casino.

Jas touched her elbow. "Shall I transfer us?"

Oh, wasn't that tempting. "Better not. One of us should stay at full strength."

He nodded. His hand stayed under her elbow, not quite supporting but ready to.

It was a shock going from the chill, glittering dark of the mountain night to the casino's warmth and garish racket.

"You'll want the buffet," Jas said.

"Oh, yeah," she breathed.

There was a line at the buffet. A long line. Amethyst kept herself from groaning. Jas gave her another glance, worked some spell and started guiding her up the line.

"Jas—" she began.

"Yes, yes," he said. "I know it isn't right. But we aren't hurting anyone, and you can't wait."

He slid into line in front of a big young woman with candy apple red hair and piercings in nose and lip and eyebrow. Amethyst braced for a loud objection, but right then the girl's plate and silverware slithered off her tray and hit the floor with an awesome crash.

Jas took two trays and loaded them with utensils and plates, then slid over to the soup and salad bar.

"Soup?" he asked as if none of the commotion taking place six feet away existed.

She leaned close. "You made her think we were already in line in front of her, didn't you?"

"Why use mind-magic when a simple distraction will do?"

Amethyst snorted but didn't argue, pushing her tray along the buffet line and loading up with tortilla soup, ambrosia, meatloaf, tamales, and two twice-baked potatoes. She loved twice-baked potatoes.

She picked up her tray and turned to find a seat in the crowded dining area. The tray wobbled in her hands, splashing a brown, fizzing puddle of Coke. Overexertion. Exactly why they'd cut to the front of the buffet line. But if Talys was here—

Unexpectedly, tears blurred across her vision. She gritted her teeth and fixed her attention on keeping her tray steady. *Stop it*, she told herself. Talys *wasn't* here. She couldn't keep sniveling every time something reminded her of the fact.

Jas' hand closed on her shoulder.

Blinking hard, she scowled. "I'm *fine*—"

He wasn't looking at her, but past her, at one of the booths nearby. She followed his gaze.

The blonde in her man's vest and tie sat there, working on a plate piled as high as Amethyst's own.

With a sideways glance, the woman cocked her head. "You said you wanted to talk." She took a bite of tri tip and gestured with the fork at the empty seat across the table. "So talk," she said around the meat.

Amethyst just stood for a minute, trying to change mental gears. Jas gave her an odd look and nodded. She gathered herself and slid into the seat.

The blonde studied them and chewed. Jas arranged his food in front of him, obviously waiting for Amethyst to take the lead. *Thanks, Jas.*

Amethyst took a little time to arrange her own plate and utensils. And snarf down a few bites. She was *not* about to tackle another wizard while woozy with magic-induced hunger. The ambrosia was just what she needed right now, sweet and creamy and fruity. The slightly floral scent of the green chile smothering the tamales urged her to sample it next.

Finally, she said, "What do you want to know?"

One sharp, pale brow rose. "Why you're here. What you want."

Here we go. "We're here looking for you—or someone like you, anyway. What we want…" She let out a breath and glanced at Jas. "We want help."

The woman sliced open a baked potato, applied butter, salt, pepper, sour cream. "Earlier you said someone was after you. Why?"

"Because somehow, they found out what I am. They apparently want me to work for them. And they won't take 'no' for an answer."

The woman stared at her, her fork hanging still over her plate, then turned the look on Jas.

He'd been quietly working on a crusted catfish fillet and rice pilaf. He made a helpless gesture with his free hand. "She has a stringent set of ethics when it comes to dealing with ordinary folk."

The woman laughed. "Well then, that's your problem."

Not again!

Jas bumped her knee with his. Amethyst kept her mouth shut.

"Actually," Jas said, "it's a problem for all of us. Drawing too much attention is rarely desirable, as I'm sure you'd agree. And at this stage, things are beginning to happen that will draw attention."

Two lines appeared between the woman's brows. "So how does this involve me?"

"It doesn't, yet," Amethyst said. "But whoever is after me wants me badly enough to out me."

Jas lowered his voice. "There are fools out there who know just enough about us to realize we can be useful. They also haven't thought through the ramifications of using our abilities—or if they have, they don't care." He took a sip of coffee.

"Go on," the woman said.

"I've been around a long time," he said. "I've seen

the changes as we grew fewer and fewer. We've never been wholly invulnerable to ordinary folk, and nowadays we don't have the advantages we once did. The one we do have is that most people no longer believe in the abilities we possess. If that were to change, they have the numbers—and the means—to do us a great deal of harm."

"I play a quiet game," the woman said.

"So do I," Jas said. "And I intend to make sure the game stays quiet."

The woman had very chilly grey eyes. Those eyes shifted from Jas to Amethyst and back again.

"How?" she said.

"I think we need something to keep things private, don't you?" Amethyst said. "Would you like to do it, or should I?"

The blonde made a little dismissive gesture and a spell shimmered into being.

Amethyst touched it, a permeable bubble around them. A baffling spell, she guessed, something that would allow people to hear them talking but not what they said. She nibbled the inside of her lip, considering, then added a little energy to the magic.

"What was that?" the blonde said, suspicious.

"Something to work on any electronics watching us," Amethyst said. "No lip reading."

"I hope that's all it is," the woman said with a hint of threat.

Amethyst held in a sigh.

"The way we see it, we have three problems," she said. Better to convince her how big those problems were.

If she heard the solution first, it would all be over. "First, we need to keep the public at large from knowing about magic and wizards. I know you've been…" How to phrase it politely? "…away for a while, but trust me when I tell you that people now wouldn't take it well."

The woman looked like none of this was news to her. Okay, good.

"Second," Amethyst went on, "the people who think they can use us need to realize they can't have everything they want. It just messes things up for everybody else, including us." She gestured to include the three of them sitting at the table.

"Which brings us to reason number three," Jas said.

"The wizard involved in your troubles," the blonde interrupted.

Amethyst's brows shot up.

"Wards and talismans and such would be enough to take care of the measures commoners might use against you. If you're here looking for help, that means wizards are the problem." At Amethyst's surprised look, the woman shrugged. "I'm a card sharp. If I can't guess my opponent's strategy, I don't win."

"You'd make a heckuva programmer," Amethyst said.

"You're strong enough to defeat the one who overcame me," the woman said. "But you can't take action without revealing yourself—and all of us. That means what you do to keep the game quiet requires more power than you have between you." She took a bite of baked potato. "I'm waiting to hear what it is."

Jas told her. The woman *was* a card player—her poker

face was perfect. In fact, she kept right on eating while Jas explained his idea.

"You're offering to deal me in on a high-stakes game," she said when he finished. "Why?"

"You're here," Jas said. "Not plying your skills for the highest bidder. That means you're not interested in being a hired hand—or a puppet master."

The woman smiled. "Or maybe no one has offered good enough terms."

Jas nodded thoughtfully. "What we're offering is the option."

"The terms?"

"To continue to make the choice of what you'll do."

This time, it was Amethyst who kneed Jas.

He didn't break from the blonde's gaze, which had gone chillier than ever.

"What he's saying," Amethyst put in, "is sooner or later, someone will find out you're a wizard. Then you'll be in my position, which let me tell you, is not at all a happy one."

She gestured at her face, wiping away the illusion that hid the bruises.

"The ones who did that now regret it," Jas said mildly.

Amethyst kept herself from glancing at him, tried hard to keep a *what the hell?* look off her face.

The blonde's own face stayed just as unreadable as ever. "And once I help you create this nexus? How do I know it won't be used against me?"

"Because I won't let it be," Amethyst said.

Again, that thin, pale smile. "Did you ever think he might be playing us both for rubes?"

Amethyst was very conscious of Jas beside her. "We discussed it. The thing is, if anyone involved in the project tries to cut out the others, he—or she—is going to have some mad wizards to deal with."

"Who likely *still* won't want to give themselves away," the woman said.

"I imagine two or three of us could come up with a quiet way to deal with the miscreant," Amethyst said.

"Ideally, we'll want a trustworthy guardian," Jas said. "One we can all agree on."

Again, Amethyst barely kept herself from reacting. She envied the other woman's control.

The blonde toyed with her fork, studying them again. Finally, she said, "The cards have spoken of change for a while now. I thought at first it was the obvious—much has changed since I returned." She stabbed a last piece of meat. "Then tonight while I played, all those fives…"

She took the bite, wiped her mouth and extended a hand across the table. "I'm called Lottie. Lottie Golden."

"Amethyst Rey."

Jas shook her hand in turn. "Jasper Harrek."

All those aliases rolled awfully easily off his tongue. But that one in particular… She'd heard it before. Where?

"Now we're all introduced," Lottie said. "What next?"

"Now," Jas said, "we gather strength."

Amethyst couldn't help starting at the echo of Talys' words. Lottie's gaze flicked to her, but if Jas noticed, he didn't react.

Amethyst waved a hand. "Just something I heard before," she explained.

"Do you have a phone?" Jas asked Lottie.

She produced a flip phone from her pants pocket. Jas took out a little notebook and a pen and wrote down his number, then hers.

Paper. How quaint. Amethyst wondered if that was an old-wizard thing, or a matter of staying under the radar.

He tore off the half with his number and handed it to Lottie. "I don't know how soon we'll be ready. It depends upon how quickly we find more associates."

And what our non-associates are up to, Amethyst thought. No, better not bring up any looming problems.

CHAPTER 23.5 – OPPOSITION

I t was like a voice whispering in his head, calling him to this one, certain house.

Benny, Benny, paint the pretty colors on me! the house said, a little flat-roof thing with a single-car garage in an old neighborhood. *Color my sky!*

He hadn't done it in a while. Last time, when he did that carport, he'd almost been caught. There it had been, a grainy surveillance picture of him in his Isotopes ball cap and lucky red shirt, plastered across the ten-o'clock news with the voiceover: *If you recognize this man, call 242-COPS.*

He almost shit himself. He'd called in sick to work and holed up in his apartment until the food ran out, then stuffed the cap and shirt in the bottom of a garbage bag and dumped *that* in a trash can at the dog park. Nobody would be picking through a can full of dog shit for aluminum or anything. And then he promised himself he'd never do it again.

Then the dreams started. First the sweet smell of smoke. Then the warm crackle of sparks. The heat pressing against his skin like a lover's hands. The leaping colors of the flames, red and orange against the night. And best of all, the wail of sirens and kids and even grown men and women, watching helplessly as God took everything away.

He'd wake up, all sweaty and panting in bed, scrub his face and remind himself of that news report. No. Fuckin'. Way.

So it was weird when he found himself driving out of his way after his shift at the Easymart, through that old, not-quite-run-down neighborhood with all those ugly gravel yards, looking at the all the little houses. Especially *that* one.

Next thing he knew, he was parking his car and getting out to walk past the house. Except every time he looked at it, licking his lips and getting the prickly sweats thinking about it, his mouth would go dry and the sweats turn cold and it was all he could do to keep from running back to his car.

Benny, Benny, come paint the colors on me!

He knew better than to stand in the middle of the sidewalk staring at the place. He shuffled along the alley behind, his hood up, hands jammed into his pockets against the cold night air. Concrete block walls rose on each side. Wooden gates, closed and locked. He slowed when he got close to the place, only sneaking little glances past his hood.

Nothing. Okay, good. He bent down like he was just tying his shoe, looked up and down the alley, then went for the gate.

Bam. He found himself against the wall on the other side of the alley, his head spinning.

Benny, Benny...

He paced up and down, panting, shaking, sweat

trickling from his underarms down his ribs. It was bad, bad, like drugs or something. He wanted to leave, but couldn't. He could *see* the flames licking, the black billows of smoke lit red from underneath, the smell of burning wood and wires and plastic....

He blinked, shook his head and it was all gone, just the night, a dog barking a couple of yards away, the sound of cars going past the alley mouth. He wet his lips, looked away, anywhere but at the back of that house. His gaze fell on the other houses.

Well, hell. What was wrong with one of them? They'd all burn just as pretty as this one, right?

He slid one more glance around, made a running start across the alley and scrambled over the concrete block wall.

CHAPTER 24

"**D**id I ever tell you," Amethyst said, "I don't like surprises?"

It had taken her this long to even catch up to the question. After dinner last night, she'd barely managed to peel out of her clothes before crashing in the hotel room. Even this morning, she'd still only been firing on three cylinders. Minor magical duels, it seemed, did that to a wizard.

Oh, yeah. Not to mention the encounter with Pico and the whole business with the simulacrum day *before* yesterday. If this was falling back and regrouping, she didn't want to see what confronting their enemy would look like.

Now they wheeled along Highway 70 between Ruidoso and Roswell. The slopes and pines of the Sacramento Mountains had quickly given way to rocky hills sparsely dotted with juniper, then to not much more than desert scrub. Pretty soon even the hills disappeared. Now they drove along a monotony of gently rolling sand blotched with some kind of dryland grasses.

Jas sighed. "What have I done now?"

She ignored the pained tone. "'We'll want a trustworthy guardian,'" she quoted, repeating his words to

Lottie.

"You don't agree?"

"Of course I agree! But that isn't the plan we discussed. When I agreed to work with you, you promised we'd work as equals. And here you go making unilateral decisions."

"There are times I'll have to make decisions on the fly, Amethyst. So will you. So you *did*, confronting Lottie on your own, then showing her that your enemies were able to hurt you, which I personally felt was the height of foolishness. And I haven't berated you. We'll have to trust one another's judgment if we expect this partnership to work."

She folded her arms and looked out the window, mostly to keep him from seeing her face.

"Okay, you're right," she grumbled. "But who do you plan to get for a guardian? Pico sounded like he was talking retirement. And we'd better get clear right now, *I* have no intention of following in his footsteps."

"I hadn't considered it."

"Good." She tapped her foot on the floorboard. "I wonder if you're thinking of volunteering for the position."

He shot her a disgusted look.

She held up her hands. "Okay. But then I don't think it's a good idea to make promises you can't keep, either."

"I hope you noticed that I never promised a guardian. I said we'll *want* one, which you just agreed we will."

"But you implied we'd produce one!"

"If someone assumes something I never said, how is

that my fault?"

Amethyst smacked her thigh. "This is exactly the problem I have with you. Why can't you just be straight with people?"

This time he turned to face her. "I'm straight with you."

Are you? she thought.

"You asked for openness," he said, turning back to the road. "And I trust and respect you enough to give it to you."

That set her back. He seemed to be doing that a lot lately.

"But others—especially other wizards—" He shook his head. "No. I'll proceed with caution, and I'll protect myself and my options."

"But if you expect them to trust you—"

"I don't need them to trust me," he said. "I need them to work with me. You said you'd defer to me in negotiations. Have you changed your mind?"

"And *you* said you wanted me along for... How did you put it?" She put a hand over her heart. "For my honesty and sincerity. How can I back you up if I don't feel *you're* being honest?"

He drew breath to argue, then let it out. "All right, I see your point. But I hope you see mine, as well. You and I have an understanding. The relationship we have with other wizards won't be at the same level. You can't expect it to be."

"I *get* that. But I don't like misleading people."

"Understood and noted," Jas said. "But frankly, that's

the way things work in this type of transaction. When something new comes up, you have to think on your feet." He took a hand off the steering wheel to make a swooping motion. "Ski the leading edge of the avalanche."

Amethyst shuddered. "Eeech. I'll stick to honesty. It's easier."

He *tsk-tsked*. "Where's your sense of excitement? Your confidence?"

In a box in my garage with Talys' stuff, she thought. But she didn't want to say that to Jas.

"Anyway," she said, "what's with the *names?* Jacob Arken. Jasper Harrek." She made air quotes.

"I'm sure you've gathered that I'm a little older than I look. I can hardly keep the same name throughout my life."

"So what *is* your real name?"

He gave a little quirk of a smile. "Perhaps someday I'll tell you."

She rolled her eyes. "I can't wait. Then what was that about the guys who did this…" She gestured at her face. "…regretting it?"

He gusted a sigh. "*Nothing* gets past you," he said. "That was what I won't berate you about—never show weakness during negotiations. It doesn't inspire confidence in your abilities."

Her face heated. She would *not* feel stupid. "Well, did they? Regret it?"

His mouth twitched, and not in a funny way. "I certainly hope so."

Dammit. She really should pursue it. But if Jas *did* do

something about the guys who manhandled her, she wasn't sure she disapproved. In fact, she was pretty sure what she felt was a certain amount of savage satisfaction. But she wasn't going to tell Jas *that*, either.

She turned to the passing scenery, such as it was. Smooth jazz came softly over the Range Rover's speakers. A satellite station. Most of the over-the-air stations they could pick up seemed to be either country or Christian.

Metal buildings and signs advertising motels and restaurants soon sprouted from the desert, then an orchard or two. In front of a mobile home dealership sporting a 20-foot-tall blowup alien, complete with big, slanted eyes and silver suit, Jas pulled over to activate his GPS. A map of Roswell appeared.

"Feed stores and Pentecostal churches," he told it.

Red dots broke out across the map.

"Should I ask?" Amethyst said.

"Not unless you want to spoil the surprise."

"You mean we didn't come to look for alien wizards?"

Jas didn't dignify that with a reply.

Roswell was the UFO capital of America, with an annual UFO Festival over the Fourth of July weekend. Amethyst and Melodie had gone one year while they were still at UNM. The parade had been the best part, the people, even dogs dressed up as aliens; cars and bikes tricked out with blinking LED lights and unlikely silvery appendages.

The town of Roswell really exploited the alien theme. The old-fashioned streetlamps were painted with slanted alien eyes. The Walmart sported the likeness of a flying saucer crashing into the wall. A sign at Arby's proclaimed "Aliens Welcome!" Even the McDonalds had been built in the shape of a silver and neon flying saucer.

Amethyst waved a hand at another *UFO PARKING* sign in front of a t-shirt shop. "The UFO museum is up ahead, I think. Let's stop."

"Amethyst—"

"Please, pleasepleaseplease? You can drop me off while you visit your feed stores and churches."

Jas assumed a stern look. "We are not on a pleasure jaunt," he said in the same voice he might've used to say, 'Don't make me come back there.'

"Funny," she said. "I seem to remember someone telling me I was going on vacation courtesy of Magus Corporation. And I haven't had much fun yet."

He glanced over at her. "It's good to see you smile again. It's been a long time."

She instantly wiped the smile off her face.

"It's all right to smile, Amethyst," he said. "It's all right to enjoy things. It doesn't dishonor or betray Tom."

And just like that, the tears came again. She struggled with all her strength, but they tore through her as uncontrollably as a seizure, as impossible to stop. She turned away, horrified and humiliated.

Jas pulled into a parking lot and turned off the engine. His hand fell on hers, held it tight.

It took a while before she could wrestle her grief under control. Jas offered a handful of tissues. She blew her nose and cleaned her face but stayed facing the window, away from him.

"All right," he finally said on a sigh. "If it's that important, I'll take you to the UFO museum."

A laugh wobbled out, as unexpected as the crying. She coughed, cleared her throat.

"All right now?" he asked.

"Yeah. Thanks." She wiped her face again. "Sorry." She crumpled the tissues in her hand. "You know, I don't usually cry this much."

"No need to apologize. It's hardly surprising." He started the car again, pulled back onto the road. "We'll stop at the feed stores, first. I need to pick up a few things."

His brisk attitude was the only thing that kept her from wanting to curl up in a ball and disappear. Although she didn't know why she should care what he thought of her. It was only Jas.

The GPS giving its directions kept any awkward silences at bay.

The first feed store was pretty bare-bones—bags of feed stacked around, salt blocks, some shelves displaying chicken feeders, fly spray and horse tack. Jas looked around, asked where the bulletin board was and made a beeline in that direction. Amethyst bought some pig ears for Caramela.

The second place was a Tractor Supply. This time, besides looking at the bulletin board, Jas wandered through the men's wear section, disappeared into a changing room with a selection of items and came out again dressed in jeans, cowboy boots and a Western shirt in black, grey and sage green plaid.

Amethyst, an Indian-print sleeveless top in hand, blinked at him.

He finished tucking in the shirt and rolled the sleeves. "Things always go more smoothly when you fit into the environment," he said with a passable southern New Mexican twang.

Surprisingly enough, he wore the outfit well—no hint of the dude about him.

He nodded at the top she still held. "You might as well pick up a few more things. Give me the tags and I'll pay while you change."

She wanted to argue, but how could she? It wasn't like she had a suitcase full of clothes out in the car.

After one more feed store and two churches, Jas was looking grim.

"What," Amethyst said, "are you looking for?"

He pulled into a parking lot in front of an attractive newer church with lots of big windows. Topiary junipers trimmed into twists as tight as drill bits grew along the front.

"I'll tell you when I find it," he said. "Right now, it seems I'm not looking in the right places. Or things have changed more than I'd realized." He opened the door and climbed out. "I'll be right back."

A few minutes later, he came barreling out of the church. Amethyst stiffened and opened herself to the magic, ready to blast whoever had sent Jas Harker running.

He piled into the Range Rover and slammed the door. "Pay dirt." He waved a slip of paper. "We're just in time. Today is the last day."

She let out a breath and pulled back from the magic. "What is it?"

He handed her the paper—a flyer. It read:

Tent Revival

Join Reverend Nathaniel Sonshine by the Pecos

Everyone welcome under the big
yellow and white tent
For two inspirational days of singing,
gospel preaching and worship

Come let Jesus change your life!

Salvation! Healing Miracles!

Friday and Saturday, November 6 & 7,
starting 1 PM sharp

On Mary Lou Road, Hagerman, New Mexico

Amethyst lowered the flyer, incredulous. "You've been looking for a tent revival? Are you serious?"

"Absolutely serious." He tapped the flyer. "'Healing Miracles.' Does that bring anything to mind?"

"Jas. You do remember the Prophet of Doom? You remember the Fundamentalists from Hell who camped in front of my house for a couple of weeks? People like that do not like people like us. They think people like us should die and burn in Hell for all eternity."

"Ah, that's where you're mistaken," he said. "They like people like us perfectly well—as long as they don't know what we are."

"No," she said. "No, no, no. No *way* are you getting me to go into that lion's den."

Jas started the Range Rover, backed out of the space and pulled back onto Roswell's main drag, heading south. "I understand. Where would you like me to drop you off while I reconnoiter?"

She thought about Jas cursing the Prophet of Doom. She imagined Jas loose among dozens of revival attendees and wondered who would be more dangerous to whom. The whole situation would be a bomb waiting to explode.

"Okay, fine." She folded her arms and turned to the window. "I'll go."

CHAPTER 25

I f the big yellow and white tent hadn't been a dead giveaway, the cars parked all up and down the otherwise isolated rural road would have. Actually, there were at least four pickup trucks for every car, most coated with a patina of New Mexico dust.

Jas parked at the tail of the line of vehicles. It was a long walk back to the tent, roadside grit crunching under their feet, the lemony scent of some weed tangy in the air.

"You're going to be regretting those boots before too long," Amethyst said. "Trust me."

It was his turn to look incredulous. "Amethyst. Don't you use magic for anything?"

"Well…" She brushed imaginary dust from her jeans. "Sometimes. When I think about it."

He shook his head.

Here, the Pecos River wasn't much more than a running arroyo fringed on each bank with a single line of the usual invasive salt cedars. The tent rose from the river's naked flood plain. People milled under and around it, some sitting on folding chairs under its shade. The men were mostly dressed the way Jas was—good jeans, boots and cowboy hats—although there were a few polo shirts and ball caps. A lot of the women wore skirts. Fortunately, there were a few in dressy Western wear.

"At least what I'm *wearing* won't stand out," Amethyst muttered.

"The flyer said 'Everyone welcome,'" Jas said.

She made a skeptical noise. "Yeah. Range Rovers that stand out like a ballet dancer at a rodeo, northern New Mexican Spanish girls, wizards and all."

"No illusions, I'm afraid. Not even the one to cover your bruises." He swept a hand in front of her face. The magic rippled as he removed the illusion. "We'll just have to come as we are."

Amethyst had raised a hand to take off her sunglasses, but made a face and left them on. She didn't want everyone who looked at her wondering if Jas was the one who beat her. It would be degrading.

"What happened to not showing vulnerability?"

"It depends," he said, "on how you go about it."

Yellow and white balloons marked the path to the tent. Jas, ever-gallant, gave her an unnecessary hand over the guardrail, then down a couple of feet of gravel to the dirt. They walked through an open farm gate. The smell of mud, an uncommon one in desert New Mexico, grew stronger as they approached the river.

Even in November, the air was warm. Music rolled over the landscape, keyboard and tambourine and guitar coming over speakers. Suns adorned the tent's white stripes, doves the yellow ones. The things that looked like puffy clouds with eyes and little stick legs must've been lambs.

Amethyst and Jas strolled to the rearmost rank of

people. A middle-aged man with a huge cowboy hat and even bigger belly stood and offered her his seat. She stammered, caught off guard, but Jas smoothly guided her into the offered chair.

He tipped his hat to the man, thanked him and stood behind Amethyst's chair. She was conscious of his hands resting on the back and forced herself to sit normally, not lean away from them. Clapping and swaying, the big-bellied man beamed at them both, and in a not-bad tenor, belted out the song coming over the speakers.

She expected to be as bored as she'd been at the casino, but found herself tapping her feet to the music.

After the song, an amazingly top-heavy woman introduced the next one. The big-bellied man turned to Jas.

"Have you heard Reverend Sonshine preach yet?"

Jas shook his head. "Can't say as I have. When I saw the flyer, I thought I'd show my fiancée a good, old-fashioned tent revival like we used to have when I was a young man."

Amethyst barely kept from choking. *You are so doomed, Jas Harker,* she thought. *So doomed.*

The other man laughed. "You're still a young man! Where you from?"

"Deming, way back when," Jas said. "But nowadays, I find myself travelling a lot around the oil patch."

Amethyst tried not to stare at this twangy, casual-talking version of Jas.

"You in the oil business?" the other man said.

Jas nodded and touched the brim of his hat again.

"It's been good to me."

Huh. Something else made up spur-of-the-moment? Then again, it wasn't outside the realm of possibility that Jas really *did* have some oil investments.

A stir came from one side of the tent, scattered clapping, some cheers. Amethyst turned to look.

"And here he is," the top-heavy woman's voice came over the speakers. "Everyone, let's welcome Reverend Sonshine!"

The cheering rose in a wave, people turning, craning to see.

A big 1970's-vintage American car of some kind came idling into view across the dirt, sunlight flashing on chrome and glass and what must've been some kind of glitter paint job. A little closer, and Amethyst saw it wasn't a paint job. Every inch of the car's sheet metal was covered with bits of mirror, little suns, lambs, doves and fish in ceramic, metal, plastic, painted wood.

Amethyst blinked, staring. The door swung open and a man stepped out of the car, waved and greeted the crowd.

He didn't look like anything special—mixed-race, with skin a couple of tones darker than her own, kinky light brown hair, slightly round face. He should've looked ridiculous in the bright yellow jacket and white slacks and suspenders he wore. Somehow, though, this guy carried it off, radiating energy and joy and enthusiasm.

He stopped in front of the car and held up his hands. "Welcome, y'all!" he called.

It was the most amazing voice Amethyst had ever

heard, rich and resonant even with a Texas twang stronger than any southern New Mexican one. A voice like that could sing opera.

"Welcome, and bask in the joy of the Lord," he went on. "Lift up your hands. Let me hear your voices!"

"Praise the Lord! Praise Jesus!" people called back, raising their hands.

The big-bellied man beside them leaned close. "I thought it was a funny name," he said. "But after I heard him the first time, I figure he can call himself Reverend Twinkleshins for all I care."

The music started again. People began singing and clapping to another energetic gospel song.

After the Prophet of Doom and his disciples, Amethyst should've been nervous. Instead, she found herself feeling happier than she had a few minutes ago.

Jas bent close to her ear, on the side opposite the big-bellied man. "'Reverend Sonshine,' indeed. He's good."

Amethyst stopped bopping. "You mean that's….?" She gave a little wiggle of her fingers, then opened wizard's senses, scenting. "I don't feel anything."

"No, you wouldn't. It's…" He fell quiet a moment as if thinking. "You might call it charisma." His breath whispered against her ear. "We all have it, to some degree. Some of us more than others."

"Some of us more than others, right," Amethyst said just as quietly.

He gave her a sideways look as if trying to figure out if she mocked him or herself, but only straightened.

People parted to let Reverend Sonshine through, then

closed in again behind him. He held up his hands again. The excited voices quieted. He bent his head a moment as if praying, raised it once more and began his sermon.

After Nani died, Amethyst hadn't had much use for religion. People talked about God's love, God's mercy, God's plan. She hadn't seen love or mercy or any kind of plan in snatching away a kind, generous, loving woman whose life had been devoted to helping and healing others. In the fifteen-plus years since, she still didn't. Especially after Talys.

Listening to Reverend Sonshine preach, she almost forgot about that. When people shouted out their praises, she caught herself wanting to join in. It was eerie.

She looked up at Jas. He wore a look like he was enjoying himself as much as everyone else. But his dark eyes held calculation that made the back of her neck prickle. He looked down and met her gaze. The calculation faded, replaced by a crinkly, conspiratorial smile.

She glanced away again. He trusted her. The man she wouldn't trust to save her seat while she went to the ladies' room, and he trusted her to have his back. He'd said so, of course, but she'd assumed it was just another Jas con.

More preaching, more singing as the sun slid through afternoon into an early sunset. She glanced back once to see Jas intently texting on his phone.

The low, coppery light gilded and haloed Reverend Sonshine as he raised his arms again. "Let those who suffer come forward. Let those who despair come to me. Let the power of Jesus Christ our Lord fill you and drive away your pain and sickness."

The grief that constantly clenched under Amethyst's heart, a black, aching stone, urged her to stand up and follow the others who edged their way to the aisles and moved forward. She crossed her arms and tucked her chin to her chest.

The congregation had fallen silent. Reverend Sonshine's amazing voice came over the speakers, calling on the Lord for healing. He'd taken off his yellow jacket some time ago and stood on the stage now in suspenders and a white shirt with the sleeves rolled up, his palms pressed to a woman's head. His eyes were closed, his head tilted back as his prayer rolled out over the speakers.

The magic wrenched, like a daydreamer poked to attention. Amethyst leapt to her feet as if someone had poked her, too, standing on tiptoes to see better. The woman on stage stiffened as if in a seizure, then went boneless. Two men in suits—assistants, Amethyst guessed—caught her, lowered her to the stage. Amethyst's wizard's eye saw the glowing swirl of magic around the woman, a pulsing, shivering iridescent white and glittering gold so thick and vibrant she was surprised it wasn't visible to ordinary eyes.

Jas leaned close, a brush of warmth against her back and arm. "I told you it makes people lose consciousness," he murmured in her ear.

On the stage, people swarmed around the woman, propping her up, chafing her hands. She opened her eyes, lifted her head and smiled with awe and worship at Reverend Sonshine. With the aid of his assistants, he helped her to her feet, letting the assistants guide her off the stage. Excitement buzzed throughout the tent. An old man climbed the steps the woman had just stumbled down, two middle-aged men—sons, probably—steadying him.

"Holy crap, Jas," Amethyst whispered, turning, not caring how close he stood. "Did you see that?"

"Impressive," he said. "We've obviously come to the right place." The calculation was back in his eyes.

"Jas—" she began, warning.

"Don't worry," he said. "It'll be fine."

Fine. Right. But she couldn't argue with him here. She only had to hope that the same thing that kept her silent would make him behave himself. She did *not* enjoy the idea of fending off a snarling mob.

People crowded around the steps to the stage now. The assistants held the mic as they announced ailments. Cancer. Autism. Kidney failure. Stroke. Again and again, the magic leapt at Reverend Sonshine's touch. He had to be feeling it by now, using that much power, but his voice came just as strong as ever, his back remained just as straight.

The sun made a fiery arc along the horizon, then disappeared. Late fall twilight deepened quickly and lights came on under the tent. The crowd around the stage dwindled.

Jas touched her elbow and nodded in that direction. "Let's go."

The big-bellied man had wandered away some time ago. People, no matter how enthused they were, had to eventually go home to take care of things there, so the tent was quite a bit emptier than it had been in the afternoon.

Amethyst had taken off her sunglasses after the sun went down. Leaving them on would've been more obvious than just letting the bruises show. And she wore a long-sleeved denim shirt. She'd only look thin, not like she was about to succumb to some wasting disease. Plus no one was looking at her, anyway.

Walking toward the stage and Reverend Sonshine was another matter. She stayed a little behind Jas, trying not to imagine neon arrows pointing at the bruises on her face.

Roadies—was that what you called them when it was a tent revival and not a band?—were breaking down sound equipment. Reverend Sonshine had come down off the stage and was speaking quietly to a small group.

Amethyst walked slower, falling back from Jas. He glanced back and tilted his head: *come on.*

Reverend Sonshine looked up, straight at her. "Did you want to speak to me, miss?"

His voice wasn't resonant now, but gentle, so gentle, like a man calming a frightened animal. Amethyst's nervousness and self-consciousness drained away.

'Charisma' wasn't the word for it. She suddenly understood how all those Jonestown cultists had drunk the poisoned Kool-Aid.

Swallowing hard, she stepped forward, squelching the instinct to call spells against enchantment and entrapment and illusion. They wouldn't do any good, anyway. The guy wasn't using the magic for this.

"I, ah—" she stammered like an idiot.

The people the reverend had been talking to drifted

away. Behind him, the roadies carried cables and speakers out of the tent, presumably to a waiting truck somewhere.

"You're hurt." The reverend's gaze flicked to Jas where he stood by her and back again. He stepped toward her. "Do you need healing?"

He thought Jas was the one who'd hit her. She fought the impulse to defend him.

"I— No, thank you," she said. "It's been taken care of." This time it was she who glanced at Jas.

Reverend Sonshine took another step and swept an arm around her, neatly blocking her from Jas. Jas didn't visibly react, but tension suddenly shimmered off him like heat waves. If Reverend Sonshine noticed, he didn't show it.

"This is healing," he said, spreading a hand in front of her face. "But not this, I think." He touched his own heart.

She stood, stunned. How the hell could he know that? *Duh, Amethyst. Magic, ya think?*

The pressure of his fingers urged her toward the stage, away from Jas. One of the assistants was coming their way.

Amethyst tensed, then it clicked: he thought she needed help getting away from a wife-beater. She mentally kicked herself. *Woman*-beater. *Woman*-beater.

She set her feet and laid a hand over her heart. "You're right about this. But everyone tells me time has to heal that wound." Extricating herself as politely as she could, she added, "Thank you, though."

She glanced at the man in the suit, who suddenly looked a lot more like a bouncer than an assistant. Things were *not* going well.

"Remember," Reverend Sonshine said, searching her face. "The Lord is a shepherd willing to protect his flock."

"Um, yes." She edged toward Jas and raised her voice enough for the bouncer to hear. "But really, I'm okay. I appreciate your concern."

"I'm called on to share the gifts the Lord gave me," the reverend said.

Jas' smile was utterly devoid of its usual charm. He stepped close to the reverend. "O shepherd, what would your flock think if they knew where those gifts really come from?"

Amethyst rounded on him. "Dammit, Jas—"

"You know how it works," Jas continued as if she hadn't spoken. "A word here, a whisper there..." He switched back to the twang. "And then they're runnin' you outta town on a rail. Just ask my friend here. She'll tell you all about it."

Amethyst gave Jas a look that would've crisped his hair if she'd been using magic.

He ignored her. "You didn't think it was I who beat her, did you?" he said in his normal accent.

Reverend Sonshine leveled a hard look on him. "I think a man who threatens a man of God might be capable of anything," he said in a voice loud enough to carry.

The people remaining in the tent turned, aghast. The roadies looked around at them, suddenly tense. The man in the suit moved toward them more quickly than she'd expect for a man that size. His partner stepped into the tent lights, also steaming their way.

Jas waved a casual hand. A spell sprang into being,

and everyone suddenly developed a peculiar disinterest in what was going on.

Reverend Sonshine fell to his knees. "Lord, protect me from evil!" His voice filled the tent, even without an amplifier. "Save me from the machinations of the Enemy!"

"You've been using a great deal of power, Nate," Jas said. "I suspect you're in no state to contend with us."

"Lend me your strength," the reverend prayed, eyes closed and hands clasped. "Let me drive off the shadows that beset me!"

"The Lord helps those who help themselves," Jas said. "And the best help for you is to deal with us."

Amethyst crouched beside him. "Reverend, please. I'm sorry. Really, we only want to talk to you."

He kept on praying.

She gave Jas another dirty look. He met her eye unapologetically. Maybe he was going for good cop/bad cop. If he was, she didn't appreciate being made a part of it.

"I know it sounded bad, but he's right," she said. "People could hurt you because of your power. People who don't believe it comes from God. That's why we want to talk to you. To stop people like that."

He abruptly stopped praying. "'People like that'?" he repeated. "People who would whisper lies to destroy a man's good work?"

Amethyst winced.

"I see," Jas said, addressing Amethyst. "If what he does is only lies, I suppose that makes him a charlatan. I don't feel any regret exposing those who prey on the gullible and desperate. Do you?"

Reverend Sonshine shoved to his feet. "The Devil speaks out of your mouth, twisting my words!"

"Am I twisting them?" Jas said.

Amethyst also got to her feet—painfully. Reverend Sonshine started to offer a hand to help her, but let it drop. A twinge of guilt went through her.

"Neither of us believes you're a charlatan," she said. "I saw your power, all white and gold. Beautiful."

The reverend's gaze darted between her and Jas, an *Oh, shit* look dawning on his face.

"You too?" he whispered.

Seemed Jas was right about wizardly alliances. They were rare. And scary.

Amethyst sighed. "Me, too. And I too just wanted to live my life in peace. And now someone has made that impossible."

Reverend Sonshine's eyes cut to Jas, questioning.

"No, he wasn't the one who outed me," she said. "I thought so at first, because we hadn't been on good terms. Sometimes we still aren't." She gave Jas a significant look. "But I decided to help him because I don't want people controlling my life. I also don't want them controlling the lives of ordinary people."

"I strongly suspect you feel the same," Jas said. "If not..." He shrugged. "I suppose it won't matter what I do."

The reverend faced him. "The Lord will protect me from evil."

"Well," Jas drawled, "that leaves me safe."

She felt like banging her head on something. Except at the moment there was nothing nearby to bang it on. Plus it would just make her face hurt worse.

"I hope we're not evil," Amethyst said. "It's not our intention."

"I don't think *you* are evil," the reverend told her. "But I greatly fear you're being led astray."

Amethyst gave a humorless laugh. "Sometimes I fear it myself. But I've got a fair amount of evidence that the guys who did this…" She gestured at her face. "…are the ones I have to worry about."

"I think you'll agree, Nate," Jas said, "as far as evil goes, talking to us is the lesser."

Reverend Sonshine glared. "It seems I have little choice in the matter."

Jas gave that same thin, dangerous wizard smile. "You might be right."

CHAPTER 26

Amethyst didn't usually have much of a temper. She wasn't much into yelling and screaming and throwing things.

Right now, she felt like all three.

The highway stretched straight ahead as far as the headlights reached, railroad tracks paralleling the road on one side, telephone poles flashing by on the other. Amethyst stared out the windshield, arms folded and wishing she were anywhere else. No, that wasn't quite right. Wishing she was with any*one* else.

"Amethyst." Jas broke the silence like dropping a glass on concrete. "I know you're angry—"

"Angry!" she burst out. "The way you treated Reverend Sonshine— That was low, even for you, Jas."

"*Even* for me."

"Oh, excuse me. I didn't mean to offend you," she said. "You didn't even give the man a chance! Just went straight for the threats."

"He wouldn't have listened to any other argument."

"He was a good man! He didn't deserve what you did."

"You have no idea what kind of man he is," Jas said. "He heals people. Good for him. It doesn't necessarily follow that he's possessed by only the best of motives. Would you like me to detail where that rescuing-the-battered-woman performance might have led?"

"You'd know."

"Oh, no, no." He shook his head. "One accusation at a time."

"You're right. Why go down *that* rabbit hole? How about this, then? Do you have any idea how bad you made me look? How you…you…" She spluttered. "How you *sullied* me?"

"Sullied!" he said on a startled laugh. "That's a word I haven't heard in conversation in a long time. I hardly sullied you. At worst, you looked like a trusting fool. More likely you seemed the reasonable and rational one of us."

"I guess that's the way you do business. But not me. You want to strong-arm any more help, you're on your own. I'm done."

"Now *that's* a mature, productive attitude."

She narrowed her eyes. "You know, Jas, that's the third time you've called me childish. Forgive me if I haven't had a hundred years or so to get into the habit of treating people like convenient tools."

His nostrils flared. "Did it ever occur to you that I might have a reason for what I did?"

"Oh, yeah. You always have a reason, don't you? Somebody's about to get devoured." She waved her hands. "The world as we know it is about to end. You know what? I don't care."

"Don't be melodramatic, Amethyst. It only makes you sound foolish."

She gave a disbelieving laugh. "You think this is for effect? Then you really don't know me as well as you think you do. Here, let me lay it out for you. I'm still going to help you with your damned nexus, because the alternative is worse. But I won't be part of your schemes. And so help me God, if you try to play any games with that nexus—"

"Don't," he cut in, "bother with threats you won't carry out. I know you well enough to know *that*."

She wanted to hit him. It took every scrap of self-control she had left not to.

"Stop the car."

He laughed and kept driving.

She clenched her fists and ground her teeth. "Stop the damn car, or I'll stop it for you."

"Don't be ridiculous."

She just shaped the magic and cast a barrier spell in the road ahead.

The Range Rover lurched to a stop as if it had run into one of those runaway truck sand pits on mountain grades.

He whipped around, reaching for her. "Amethyst—"

She flung up a shield. Purple sparks spat around his fingertips in a crackle and squeak of energy. He cursed and snatched his hand back. Amethyst grabbed her purse, shoved open the door and flung out.

"What are you—?" he began.

She slammed the door, ran across the road and started walking into the night.

It was usually a good idea to have a plan before slamming out of somebody's car in the middle of nowhere a couple hundred miles from home.

Amethyst didn't have a plan.

Well, one beyond storming along some road toward the airport lights visible a couple of miles off across the barren flats. And where there was an airport, there'd be a car rental. Maybe. If it was a big enough airport. And if the car rental places weren't already closed.

Damn Jas! Every time she thought she might be able to work with him, if not trust him, he did something like this. Turned into a complete bastard who'd do anything, absolutely anything, to get what he wanted. She should've known better. How pathetic that she'd fallen for his 'I'm such a good friend' routine. Pathetic and stupid.

She didn't know if he'd come after her. The first thing she'd done was work the same spell she had at the petroglyphs, with Talys. Her own saliva, a bit of dirt, the stiff stem of some weed that let her fade into her surroundings, just a breeze through a tuft of grass, a brush of shadow in the moonlight. She could've zapped herself to the airport, but a splash that big in the magic wouldn't exactly be unobtrusive.

There were, she was relieved to discover, car rental outlets. Normally, a walk of a couple of miles wouldn't bother her. But normally people didn't slam her into cars and bounce her off walls. By the time she trudged up to the door of the Hertz place, she was limping and her rib felt like it was trying to drill through her lung.

The woman inside was just locking the door.

Amethyst stopped outside, not trying to hide her dismay. "I'm sorry, I know I'm too late," she said through the door. "But I really, really need a car."

The woman took one look at her, unlocked the door and pushed it open. "Are you okay?"

"I had a fight with my—" She couldn't believe it. Her voice was actually shaking. Amethyst cleared her throat. "With my boyfriend."

Boyfriend. It was all she could do to choke it out.

The woman's face went hard. "Son of a *bitch*," she said, biting out each word. "You should call the cops."

"I know. But all I want right now is to go home. Can I still get a car? Please?"

Showing up at 9:00 at night on foot, with a limp, a black eye and a split lip seemed to be the magic ticket.

She had to use her credit card—no way around that. That didn't mean that the car anyone saw rolling down the road had to be the same one listed on the rental agreement. So what left the lot as a silver Kia Rio turned onto Highway 285 as a black Mustang. The license plate read *TALYS*.

For the first 80 miles or so, anger and upset and the need to keep the illusion in place over the car kept her awake. Then everything over the last few days started dragging at her.

Amethyst rubbed her eyes and punched on the radio. This far out in the boondocks, seek-and-scan rolled up and down the dial without stopping much. She finally picked up a talk radio station that faded in and out with the terrain.

Whatever radio blowhard was on the air was annoying enough to keep her from running off the road. At 11:00, a news spot came on. Static swelled over the announcer's voice and she started to drift. Shaking her head, she turned off the car's heater and switched the control to vent.

The radio station faded back in. "...Magus Building in Albuquerque's Uptown area still cordoned off."

Amethyst snapped straight, all traces of sleepiness gone. "*What?*"

She turned up the volume.

"...After five this evening..." Static.

She cursed and slammed the steering wheel in frustration.

"...Eleven victims have been rushed to area hospitals, two of them in critical condition. APD hasn't yet issued a statement. It's unclear at this time if terrorism is..." The signal dissolved into static once more.

"Damn! Damn! Damn!" She punched the seat.

That must've been around the time Jas was texting. He *knew* what happened—of course he did. No matter how far under the radar he was flying, he'd have a way to find out about something like that. And then the way he'd dealt with Reverend Sonshine, quick and ruthless—

Did it occur to you I might've had a reason for what I did? he'd asked her.

And she'd said she didn't care.

Guilt almost choked her. He'd known what had happened at Magus, known people who worked for him had been hurt, and sat there while she ripped him a new orifice over his treatment of some stranger.

Because *once*, he'd grossly miscalculated in his dealings with her, and she still couldn't forgive him for it.

She reached for her purse, for her phone inside then stopped. No, she'd already made enough mistakes. If she was serious about helping Jas, about repairing what she so totally, horribly screwed up, she had to think. She had to find out what exactly was going on.

And who was responsible.

CHAPTER 27

Amethyst powered up her phone the minute she saw the aluminum yucca at the mouth of Tijeras Canyon, the lights that shined on it shifting from purple to magenta to red to tangerine orange. The *Welcome to Albuquerque – "Bienvenidos!"* sign flashed past in the headlights.

She tapped the GPS app off—no point in making it easy for anyone looking for her. Her text message alert tone sounded. Then sounded again. And again.

Her stomach curdled into a cold, hard knot. She pulled to the shoulder of the freeway and brought up the texts.

From Melodie early this morning:

call me

A little later:

ur house is ok dont worry

And another:

Heather in hosp they want to keep her ovrnite

Heather. Boobilicious, Daisy Duke-wearing Heather from next door.

Another:

Heathers cousin sez fire dept thinks its arson

Amethyst's heart beat so hard she was queasy. She kept scrolling through texts.

Melodie this afternoon:
WHERE R U? CALL ME

The last one was from Jas, sent about an hour ago:
Call me. Don't do anything foolish.

She put the phone on the passenger seat and gripped the steering wheel, staring straight ahead through the windshield. The city spilled down to the Rio Grande and back up again the other side of the river, lights caught in a glittering net. She could even make out the Uptown area from here, the tall buildings blocks of light and shadow against the shimmer of city lights.

Something had happened at the Magus Building. Something happened at home. Only two data points, not enough to draw a pattern, she reminded herself.

Her gut, sick and clenched and cold, told her different.

Someone was sending a message: *Come out, come out, wherever you are.*

Don't do anything foolish, Jas had said.

He'd probably think what she had in mind was foolish. He'd probably be right. But she was pretty sure what was going on wouldn't stop by unplugging the magic—something that would take time. Too much time.

Amethyst hiked into the Sandia foothills, her shadow

stretched long over the pale ribbon of trail by the descending moon.

She found a secluded hollow surrounded by rounded granite boulders. The mountain rose maybe hundred yards away, a wall of darkness against the night sky. If not for the hum of the city, subdued by the late hour, she could've imagined herself deep in the wilderness.

She swept weeds and bits of vegetation off the decomposed granite dirt, then placed stems of sage, a pinon twig and a mourning dove feather on the ground in front of her. Not what the spell she'd found called for, but the symbolism was what counted. She hoped.

Shivering, she spared enough power to call a cocoon of warmth around her. November in Albuquerque was quite a bit colder than in lower-altitude Roswell.

She touched a thought to the ceremonial objects. The piñon twig flared into a spicy-scented flame. The sage and feather sent up coils of smoke, one earthy and herbal, the other sharp and acrid.

It was hard, hard with her heart mercilessly slugging her breastbone and her stomach making snaky knots in her middle. But she closed her eyes, breathed deep and slow and concentrated on the mingled smells of burning, on the shape of the magic forming.

She let the magic lift her, dissolve her, whirl her into it and away. She felt herself become the smoke, weightless and insubstantial.

She swept upward in a dizzying rush, the mountain a moon-etched darkness below her, ever more of the city visible in a circuit-board maze of lights. Considering that she wasn't actually hovering a thousand or two feet in the air, her nonexistent lungs couldn't catch a breath and her nonexistent stomach swooped and dived at the height. She pushed the imaginary sensations away, concentrated on where she wanted to be and *moved*.

Like zapping from place to place, it was only a matter of being *here* one moment and *there* the next, but lightly, as easily as touching a thought to the magic.

At this hour, she found herself in a bedroom, one only big enough for a twin bed, a chest of drawers and the space needed to get from the door to each piece of furniture. The window, set deep into foot-thick walls, spoke of an old adobe house. A shape lay under a blanket woven with a pueblo motif of diamonds and bands in contrasting yarns, only shades of grey in the dim light.

"Pico," Amethyst said from the foot of the bed.

He sat straight up, his black hair loose around his bare shoulders. "Rosalinda's great-granddaughter." His eyes narrowed and he frowned. "You're spirit-walking? How?"

She shrugged. "It's an old spell I found. I'm gambling any wizards who might be around are less likely to sniff it out."

He still frowned as if that were no answer at all.

"I need to talk to you, and I don't have a lot of time." She wet lips she didn't have. Funny how that worked, how closely tied consciousness was to a body.

"I think things are about to get ugly," she went on, "and I don't know how to break that blood-bond between us. Do you have any ideas?"

He shook his head. "I told you, sometimes the magic does things. I think this is one of those things." He pulled the blanket around his shoulders, shifted to sit cross-legged, back against the headboard. "What you gonna do?"

She wanted to fidget, but it seemed sort of beside the point. "I don't know yet. People are getting hurt—ordinary people, who don't have anything to do with all this." She gave a vague wave to take in the magic around her. "But we—Jas, the man who was with me—and I have been working on a way to protect—" *the nexus*, she almost said. "The magic here—well, there. At Ojo. We feel the same way you do—we don't want wizards to be able to use it any way they want."

The frown was back. "How you gonna do that?"

She took a long breath. And told him.

Pico leapt out of bed, shaking with fury. "You, you're the same as the rest of them!"

"No, Pico, I swear that's not it." She held out her hands, pleading. "Jas realized that when the two of us were able to overcome you, others would be able to do the same. And if they do... Well, let's just say we can't let that happen."

He stared hard at her for the space of three slow breaths. Amethyst just stood, trying to project earnestness. Finally, he made a frustrated gesture and muttered something she didn't understand.

"I saw what happened when the Spanish came," he said. "With their guns and their horses, they were stronger. There were more Indian people, but we didn't see the danger until too late. The world we knew ended."

"Yes," Amethyst said. "Yes, exactly. Three, four hundred years ago, most of the wizards were already gone. But they're back now, and they don't think anything of using the magic the way they once did. To increase their own power. To increase the power of anyone who pays them enough. Your world was destroyed then. I don't want to see mine destroyed now."

"You will not stop this without many *magos*."

"I know," she admitted. "But after we left Ojo, we went looking for others like us, who just want to be left alone, who don't want to see everything screwed up."

"How many?"

"There are four of us now. Jas wanted your help, too, but didn't think you'd be willing."

He folded his arms. "He's right."

Shit. "If I…if I'm not around, he'll only have two other wizards. I'm pretty sure that won't be enough to create a nexus. So basically, you have veto power. If you don't want this to happen, you don't help." She bit her lip. "What worries me is that blood bond. If something happens to me—"

"No guardian," he finished.

"Right."

Pico gave her another long, dark stare. "Rosalinda would never threaten me to get something. It makes me sad that her granddaughter will."

"I'm not threatening you, Pico! I'm telling you the honest truth. If I could, I'd break the blood bond. I can't, and these people know who I am. They know how to get at me. How long do you figure until they catch up to me?"

Indians were *very* good at the inscrutable thing. Not even any betraying body language.

"If you weren't so young," he finally said, "if I didn't see you hurt, I'd think you were as clever as Coyote."

You didn't grow up in New Mexico without picking up at least a nodding acquaintance with Native American mythology. Coyote was the North American Indian trickster deity.

"Jas is Coyote," she said dryly. "Not me."

Pico nodded. "I think so too. You can't trust Coyote."

"No," she drawled. "You can't."

He nodded thoughtfully. "Coyote brought people many good things."

"Usually for his own selfish reasons."

"You know that." He grinned. "Good. Rosalinda didn't bring up a stupid girl."

You wouldn't say that if you'd known me last year, Amethyst thought.

"In this case," she said, "I think his reasons align with mine, which is enough to go forward. If you're involved, you'll keep him more honest than anything else I can think of."

He nodded again as if reaching a decision. "You and me, we'll feel each other's hurts. But we share power now, too. You can use my power, and I can use yours."

"*What?*"

"I'll help you against your enemies, who are my enemies now."

Amethyst scrambled, reassessing the situation,

processing possibilities that hadn't existed a moment ago.

"Thank you, Pico. That's—" She shook her head, dazed. "That's more than I could ever have hoped for."

"Now I know you're telling the truth," he said. "If you knew, you could've taken my power without asking, like you could've hurt me without caring, leaving the magic's home open to any who would take it."

The programmer's mind clicked in, following the logic. She'd also mixed Jas' blood with Pico's. "Then...Jas..."

"I won't tell Coyote what I told you."

That Jas had access to Pico's power any time. Damn. She'd never planned that.

"No, I guess not," she said. And Pico could control Jas in ways other than just unplugging the magic. Damn again. "You know Jas isn't your enemy, either, right?"

Pico gave a small smile. "As long as he doesn't do things an enemy would do."

She nodded slowly. How could she argue with that? But it felt so...so *wrong* to know of such a vulnerability and keep it from Jas. Like betraying him.

"You're a good woman, Amethyst Rey," Pico said. "Your great-grandmother would be very proud."

"I sure hope so," she muttered.

❖❖❖❖❖❖

A methyst returned to herself, cold and stiff, in the hollow among the boulders.

If she couldn't break the binding she'd set on Pico,

she owed it to him to protect him. That meant protecting herself, too. Which definitely wasn't a bad thing.

She sat thinking, sifting through spells. She had a feeling that combining old spells with modern magic might help baffle other wizards.

The really old spells had a flavor all their own. Finally she found one she liked, one that had been made for a king. It turned aside weapons, counteracted poisons and repelled curses and magical attacks. That king had obviously intended to be invulnerable, but even magic couldn't manage that. There were always loopholes. But if she couldn't have invulnerable, Amethyst would settle for well-protected.

She splayed a hand on her thigh and called the magic. A shiver of alarm brushed her.

Her head snapped up. "What?" she said aloud.

It was almost as if someone had spoken. She held her breath, sent wizard's senses into the night.

No one was there, of course, only the sharp glitter of stars overhead, a horned owl sweeping by on silent wings. Could it have been Talys? No... It hadn't felt like him. She waited, listening, but all remained quiet. She returned to the magic.

The spell had originally been imbued with the wizard's own power—a good failsafe, in case the king grew displeased with the wizard. Amethyst modified it, powering it with the earth's magnetic field, something that was always present. The magic pulsed, bending to the shape of the spell.

She lifted her hand. She'd worked a small making in

addition to the talisman of protection. A tattoo of a stylized raven now marked the outside of her left thigh. The fingers of her hand formed its wing, her thumb its head. The raven's body, where her palm had lain, contained the spell's protective symbols disguised in a pattern of black lines.

She admired it for a moment then pulled her jeans back up. She liked the idea of a raven. Talys had been a raven in one of his past embodiments.

In the parking lot, she cast the lightest, most inconspicuous spell she could find on the Kia, a little spell of disinterest. People would still see the car, but wouldn't really notice it, just a small car leaving the Sandia open space parking lot and rolling along the city streets, totally unremarkable.

At almost two in the morning, Amethyst's neighborhood was dark and quiet. Her house sat peaceful and untouched. Heather's house next door—

Soot blackened the walls above empty, shattered windows. Debris littered the front yard. Grass and shrubs lay trampled and broken.

Amethyst slowed down, cold and sick. Heather was in the hospital tonight. Only for observation, from what Melodie's text had said, but seeing that house, it could've been worse. Much worse.

She drove on up the street and around the corner, the cold in her middle gradually turning hotter. By the time she reached Eubank, its traffic signals turning over six almost-deserted lanes, she was throttling the steering wheel so hard her hands hurt.

Forcing herself to keep to the speed limit, she headed for Uptown.

She wasn't surprised to see a swarm of activity in the Magus Building parking lot. Yellow police tape, mobile crime lab, cop cars marked and unmarked, flashing lights.

Under ordinary circumstances, someone from the variety of agencies at the scene would've stopped the Kia and questioned her. But she just pulled into the driveway and parked on the far fringe of the lot.

A hundred yards or so away, activity surrounded the burned-out shell of a van. Five or six other cars sat nearby, their windows blown out, the sides facing the van blackened. Pebbles of tempered glass and shards of metal glittered in the blaze of portable lights set up around the area. Generators chugged away. The stench of burned rubber and plastic, a sharp stink of explosives still hung in the air.

Obviously Jas' wards didn't extend over the entire lot. And someone had known it.

She pulled out her phone, turned it on and hit the speed dial icon. The call went to voicemail. Damn.

"Jas," she said. "I'm sorry. Really, really, really sorry. My next door neighbor's house burned, too. I just pulled into your lot. I'm sure you're here, I'm going to try to get in to see you."

She ended the call, wrapped that little attention-diverting spell around herself and got out of the car.

The world winked out.

CHAPTER 28

The wail of a train's horn dragged her up out of darkness.

The weight of some spell pushed down on her, trying to hold her. Amethyst couldn't move, couldn't even open her eyes, but magic raced through her like a grass fire, a hot, ragged red edge burning out the spell that held her.

Thoughts, memory finally took shape. Pulling into the Magus parking lot, the image of blackened cars. Calling Jas' number, getting out of the car.

She would've bolted upright then, but her muscles only twitched.

"She waking up?" said a man's voice with an Eastern-sounding accent. "I saw her move."

"She won't wake until I waken her." Another man's voice, this one with an accent that sounded vaguely Italian. "How could she?"

Magic still seethed through her, eating away at the spell—a sleep spell? How could she have worked a counterspell in her sleep—? Oh! The raven tattoo on her leg. The protective talisman she'd conjured on the mountain.

She sent tendrils of wizard's senses into her

surroundings. Cold, still air. Smells of dust and old grease and metal. A hard surface beneath her, the weight of something—a blanket, maybe—over her. The train's horn came again, echoing in a big, empty space.

"When she wakes," the second man said, "she'll try to use magic. The binding spell I placed will prevent that."

A wizard. Of course. Couldn't he sense her spells—?

No. That talisman wasn't using her power. And he must be assuming the magic in flux was due to his own spells.

"Well, let's roll," Eastern Guy said. "You ready?"

"Very well." The wizard worked some spell. Magic touched her.

Hell with this, Amethyst thought. She reached for the magic to zap herself out of there—

And ran into the binding, locked like steel bands around her power.

The wizard's counterspell swarmed over her, dissipating the sleep spell he'd set, the one the talisman had already dissolved. Why hadn't it worked against that damned binding?

Because it was made to protect an ordinary mortal, not a wizard's power. Shit.

She opened her eyes and sat straight up, snapping her hands up defensively.

Her wrists were bound with a zip-tie. Halogen lights glared in her eyes. Two men stood over her. Her heart ramped up, beating so hard she could feel it in her lips and fingertips.

She sat on a cement floor, old, cracked and

crumbling. Banks of small-paned windows rose two stories, faint light gleaming through the rectangles of broken green and yellow glass. High above, overhead cranes spanned the building's width, hulks of rusty metal, cable and hooks against a fretwork of roof support trusses sketched dim across the shadows.

A train horn blew again. She knew this place. She'd been here for a crafts market. The old Albuquerque Rail Yards.

Amethyst swallowed down the strangling tightness in her throat. Waking up bound, body and magic, in an abandoned industrial building with two men standing over her was not a recipe for assurance.

She shaded her eyes from the light to see the men. One looked like somebody's kindly uncle, mid-forties or so, tall, with a high forehead and slightly thinning hair. He wore a long wool coat over a button shirt and slacks. The other one, short, slightly stooped, with a hard face and dark, curly hair—

Something in her middle tightened. That one, she'd met. Once. He'd shown up in her living room asking why she'd done something as unheard of as returning the wizards' power to the rightful owners.

"Ms. Rey." Eastern Guy, the kindly-uncle-looking one, raised his hands in a calming gesture. "I'm Hal Robertson. I'm glad to finally meet you. Before you try to do anything, let me explain the situation here."

Well, now she knew who'd been after her. And who was behind Talys' death. Anger burned out the fear. Anger was a much better feeling.

She swung her glare to the wizard. "Your manners are just as bad as the last time I saw you. Did you tell your boss I threw you out of my house then?"

The wizard gave a thin smile. "Ah, *bambina*. You speak so boldly for being caught in my binding."

"And you seem pretty sure I won't break it."

Spells whispered through her mind, spells of unlocking, unbinding. Spells of pure power that would sear through anything in their way.

"Before you start a pissing contest, that's the situation I need to explain," Eastern Guy—Robertson—said. "There are several men placed around us."

He gestured toward the corners of the huge building, doubly dark after the glare of the lights. Amethyst sent out wizard's senses again. He wasn't lying—there were four men, three in various corners and one up high, on one of the cranes.

"The moment you try to cause trouble for Stregone here," Robertson went on, nodding at the wizard, "their orders are to shoot you. Not to kill, of course—that would defeat the purpose. But I'm told it hurts like hell, and makes it hard to concentrate on other things. So why don't we just sit here and talk like civilized people."

She'd rather let them shoot at her. *That* was something the talisman should work against. But besides not being particularly eager to test it against bullets, she had to admit that sooner or later, she was going to have to do something about these jerks. Under the circumstances, it looked like it'd have to be sooner.

"*Civilized people* don't kidnap and tie up people they

want to talk to," she said, clenching her fists above the zip-tie. When she'd tried to move her legs, she discovered her ankles bound, too.

She remembered how Jas had vaporized the handcuffs she'd been in not too many days ago and pushed at Stregone's binding. He looked at her, raised a brow and shook his head. Uh-huh. So he'd be able to tell if she tried to break it. Damn.

"Sorry about that, but you've been hard to catch up to." Robertson didn't sound sorry at all. He didn't move to cut the zip-tie, either. "I wanted to make sure you'd stick around long enough to talk. But that's all water under the bridge now." He waved a hand and crouched so he wasn't looming over her. "I wanted to meet you because I have a proposal for you. A job offer, in fact. With your talents, I can promise you'll be able to name your terms."

"Good to know, but I already have an employer."

"Magus, right." He shrugged. "Tell them you got a better offer. I'll make sure of it."

"We have a contract."

Stregone laughed.

Robertson smiled a little. "I really doubt Magus' lawyers will take you to court for breach."

"Maybe not," she said. "But I'm still not interested. Thanks anyway."

"Well, that's too bad," Robertson said. "That's really too bad."

"You know, Mr. Robertson," she said, "this is stupid. You've got me tied up, spelled up and under the gun. For me to do whatever job you have in mind, you're going to have to turn me loose. Whether I tell you yes or no, you aren't going to trust me once I'm free. So what's your leverage?"

Robertson grinned and leaned an elbow on one knee. "You're one smart lady, I'll say that. Okay. If you don't like the idea of a lucrative, comfortable job, I should just mention that certain government agencies would be extremely interested in someone like you. They might want to see what they could do with a wizard—or they might just want to find out what makes one tick."

The drop her stomach took was worse than when Melodie had brought up the idea months ago. Because then, it had only been an idea.

Robertson swept a hand to take in the huge, decrepit building. "Did you think I brought you here for the dramatic effect? Railroad cars get hauled all over the country. No one ever thinks about what's in them or where they end up. As a matter of fact, there's a car out there on a siding right now. All I have to do is put one tied up, spelled up, under-the-gun woman in it, make a call, and off it goes. Who knows where it'll end up. Or we can discuss job offers. I know you'll find one you like and will stay with, because if you don't, I can make that call any time." He shrugged again. "Up to you."

"Seriously?" she said, pure bravado. "You'd try to disappear me when my current employer is a data security company? Somehow I don't think that would work out quite as well as you think."

"Even Magus Corporation doesn't want the government breathing down their necks. The IRS. The

FTC. Hell, even the CIA and the NSA, for all I know. I don't think your boss would take much convincing to drop the matter."

Would he? Jas had said he was a pragmatist. And the most pragmatic move would be to just cut her loose.

Her stomach, already in free-fall, turned into a cold, gluey knot. She really was on her own in this. Until now, she hadn't realized she'd counted on having Jas at her back. Stupid, wasn't it, because Jas wasn't exactly the type you could count on for anything.

She slumped.

Robertson nodded. "Good. Tell you what. Let's get you untied now. I imagine you're getting pretty cold and stiff by now."

"Fine, whatever," Amethyst said.

And slammed the full force of her power against Stregone's binding.

Stregone shouted a curse in what sounded like Italian and staggered a step back.

Robertson scrambled to his feet. "What's going on?"

The wizard yelled again, still in Italian, gesturing. He flung a spell of force, something that should have swatted Amethyst flat. Instead, magic flared around her in a shock wave of aurora borealis colors, a hum of electromagnetic energy—the talisman reacting to an attack.

She wanted to shout in triumph, but kept cranking power, straining to form a counterspell against that binding.

It was like a turbocharger suddenly kicked in. Her power abruptly expanded, shredding the binding. She reeled for an instant. How—?

Pico's power. She must've accessed it. It swept through her in waves, foreign... Yet somehow familiar?

"Shoot!" Stregone shouted. "Tell them, shoot their guns!"

Amethyst disintegrated the zip-ties around wrists and ankles and rose to her feet, flinging away the blanket that covered her.

Robertson's eyes went wide. He scrambled backward. "Fire!" he shouted over his shoulder. "What the fuck are you idiots waiting for? Fire, goddammit!"

A muffled *thwack* sounded. Something flashed white, then disappeared, swallowed by that aurora shimmer. More flashes—bullets? They were shooting at her, but the talisman's protection vaporized the bullets, like meteorites burned up in the Earth's atmosphere.

"Do something!" Robertson shouted at Stregone.

More of those throttled coughs, and a flurry of bullets flashed white all around her. Magic pulsed behind her.

She wheeled to face Stregone. The concrete under her feet gave way. She windmilled her arms, sinking into a surface suddenly turned semi-liquid, like hot quicksand. She jumped, jerking up her feet like she did when jumping some obstacle on her skates, and sucked the energy out of the transformation. The air went cold enough to freeze the hairs in her nostrils. She landed on an icy surface of gritty powder, all that was left of the concrete.

He must've figured out that direct attacks wouldn't work.

"Very good, *bambina*," Stregone said in a lull between

gunshots. "But how long can you expend that kind of power? Stop now, before your shield fails and one of those bullets finds you."

I can keep it up longer than you think, asshole.

The lights went out. Utter darkness plunged down. Not even streetlight glowed through the windows, as if the power had gone out for blocks around.

"What the hell?" Robertson yelled more profanities, his voice cracking. "Get the goddamn lights back on!"

The bullets kept coming, bright flashes and the shield's answering shimmer in the darkness. The gunmen obviously had night-vision goggles.

She called a pulse of energy strong enough to burn out electronics, punched it outward.

Curses echoed from far corners of the building, more suppressed gunshots, the flare of muzzle flashes, the zing and whine of ricochets. No more flashes against her shield, though. She'd taken out their night goggles.

"Come on, Stregone," she called into the darkness. "I kicked your butt once. Is this guy paying you enough that you have to let me do it again?"

Pop-pop-pop, and white stars burst around her again as they aimed toward the sound of her voice. Well, that was dumb.

She sent wizard's senses out into the dark. The gunmen were scrambling, zig-zagging through the darkness toward her, the one overhead creeping along one of the cranes.

The aurora glow of her shield showed Robertson stumbling backward. He tripped on the cord to one of the halogen lights. It fell with a crash and a spray of broken glass. She cast a staying spell toward him.

A ward batted it away. She cursed. Her breath was suddenly coming hard, but it still felt like she couldn't get enough air. Sparks flickered against the darkness. Her muscles started trembling. Her thoughts slowed, syrupy, slithering away before she could catch them.

You're suffocating! That thought came clear as if someone had spoken it aloud. She stumbled, fell, catching herself on one hand and knee. She sank to the floor, groping for the magic.

Without willing it, her hands rose. Power ripped through her and wizard's fire exploded outward, a writhing ring of electric-arc purple and thundercloud violet threaded through with flashes of green. Wind blasted outward. There was a crash, the sharp chime of glass shattering. Someone screamed.

She could breathe again. Lying flat on her back, she gasped, gasped again. Sparks peppering her vision, still panting, she pushed herself up.

She had to end this. If Robertson got away, she'd only have to go through it all again later. The big problem was Stregone. With her borrowed power, she should be able to outlast him. But she didn't have time.

Time. Yes.

Once, someone had cast a spell on her that took her just a little bit out of time, shifted her a tiny fraction off the plane of reality. She riffled through her mind for magic that would do that.

There. That spell was close, but it was arcane,

convoluted, a surrealist latticework of energies that twisted time and space into the impossibility of an M.C. Escher drawing. It was big medicine, maybe as big as that summoning she'd used to try to call back Talys. Fortunately, she had access to more power than she had then.

She closed her eyes and opened up the throttle.

She felt another shift in her power, a sudden increase, like when she'd burst Stregone's binding. This time it felt strange, a flow of earthy water weaving through her wizard's fire, not mixing, but complementing it. Gathering the magic, she shaped it to the spell.

The darkness shimmered into a thousand different colors, smells, sensations. Stregone was a twisting knot of salmon red, sticky strings of power pulling at the magic. The men were bright flashes bobbing in the rich, shifting colors of the magic. Her talisman's undulating aurora of protection unfurled around her from the tattoo on her thigh.

She hesitated, confused. She hadn't expected the spell to manifest this way. It was as if she swam through the magic itself, that ether visible to wizards' eyes. Something to do with using Pico's power?

She willed herself forward, toward the flare that was Robertson, then extended the spell, wrapped it over him. He flickered from flame to flesh, solid and present within the swirl of magic.

He gave a yell, turned, turned again, wild and terrified. "What the fuck have you done?"

"Taken us where we won't be bothered." Amethyst

folded her arms. The magic rippled and eddied with her movement. "You've given me a lot of grief these last few months, Hal. You won't be giving me any more."

He made a gesture, quickly repressed. "Look, Ms. Rey. Put us back. I'm sure we can come to an agreement." He took a step toward her, hands held open placatingly.

She shook her head. "The only agreement I want to make with you is to *leave me alone.*"

"I'd do that if I could," he said. "But even if it isn't me, it'll be someone else. You're just too valuable."

"Oh, but I bet there isn't anyone else. If I'm so valuable, you'd make damned sure no one else knows about me. When someone can buy direct, why bother with a middleman?"

He chuckled. "You're right. On the other hand, I don't think you realize the reach some of my clients have. I might not be able to offer the goods, so to speak, but information is almost as valuable. Once certain people find out about you, how far will you be willing to go to maintain your independence? Underground? Overseas?"

He was hitting every fear that had come up since all this started. *Is this why you guys will do whatever it takes?* she'd once asked Jas. *Because if you don't, somebody will do it to you first?*

She forced a laugh. "You know, I've been exercising a lot of restraint lately. I think it's given you the impression that I'm helpless." She shook her head. "I don't think *you* realize how simple it would be to stop you. There wouldn't even be any blood. I can leave you here, in this otherplace. I can put you inside the mountain." She leaned toward him and whispered, "I can reach into your mind and burn out everything you know about me."

"Honey," he said. "If you were going to do any of that, you wouldn't be telling me. You'd just do it." He stepped toward her, offering his hand. "Now come on. Let's quit playing games and face reality."

And the reality was that she was going to have to do something ugly. She couldn't see any other choice.

If only none of this had ever happened. If only she could be like Jas, a wizard quietly living in the ordinary world—

Memory flickered, Jas on the sidewalk in front of her house, the Prophet of Doom fleeing. *A good curse can work wonders*, he'd said.

She set her jaw, trying to ignore the queasy sinking of her stomach. "Just remember, you said it."

She molded the magic to the shape of her will. "Your plans will fail, Hal Robertson. Your plots will unravel. Your schemes will backfire, and you'll be discredited and ignored. When you're motivated by greed, when you attempt to trample the wishes and feelings of others, you will be impotent."

The curse settled around him, sank into him.

Oblivious, he smiled and shook his head. "And you'll wish you'd been sensible, Ms. Rey. Because from here on out, you're a lab rat."

He moved, reached for her. She flung up her arm in a block. His other hand came out of his coat holding a gun. She shoved it down.

The gun crashed. A burst of white light flared.

Something punched her in the leg and her protective magic winked out. The same instant, Robertson screamed and fell to his knees, clutching his wrist.

Her heart slammed as sharp and hard as the gunshots. She backed up, coughing on blue smoke and the peppery smell of gunpowder, the stench of blood and burned flesh.

What—? Robertson hunched over his hand—what had been his hand. What was left was a bloody, mangled mess. The gun lay on the floor by him, a twisted lump of metal.

Pain finally hit her, like a dog had sunk its teeth into her and torn out a chunk of flesh. She gasped, clamped a hand to her leg and looked down.

Her thigh looked like a piece of raw meat. Blood covered her hand, soaked the leg of her jeans. The pain built, waves of it, each pounding her harder than the last. She clamped her jaw on a scream, staggered and collapsed to one side, tears of agony pouring out of her eyes. She couldn't breathe, only panting raggedly. Robertson had stopped screaming, now gabbling profanities, now cursing her.

The world slid and swam in front of her. *Oh, God, please let me faint.*

The magic slithered out of her grasp. The spell frayed away and the darkness of the ordinary world slid across the colors of the magical ether.

CHAPTER 29

Men shouted. The blue-white beams of flashlights slashed the darkness. One found her, pinned her to the crumbling concrete. "What the hell happened?" "Muthafucka. Gun exploded." "Shut the fuck up, asshole. Get down here and help me get a tourniquet on him. She's gonna need something, too."

"I'll take care of her," Stregone's voice said.

Magic struck like a truckload of sand, crushed her to the floor.

Stregone walked up. This time the magic writhed over her, worming into her leg. "*Il capo* won't want you to die, so I've stopped the bleeding." He leaned elbow on knee and bent over her. "Where you're going, it will be a long time before anyone sees to that. A long time hurting," he whispered and smiled.

She wished she could spit in his face. She only lay on the concrete shaking. It was all she could do to breathe. The pain swallowed everything. Everything but the terror.

The magic rippled as he gathered it, preparing to shape it to a spell. She groped for her power, also fumbling for the magic—

It drained away.

Stregone stiffened, his eyes going wide. "What did

you do, *puttana?*"

The *thwop-thwop-thwop* of a helicopter sounded overhead. Light, bright as daylight, blazed through the broken-paned windows, through the holes in the roof, illuminating the blue haze of gunsmoke.

"ALBUQUERQUE POLICE," a voice over a loudspeaker said. *"THROW YOUR WEAPONS OUT AND COME OUT WITH YOUR HANDS IN SIGHT."*

More shouts, curses, men scrambling. Gunshots. One of them grabbed her, hauled her up. A gun's barrel jabbed into her neck under her jaw. Adrenaline shot through her, cold and hot at once. The pain roared up from the wound in her leg and swept over her.

Pain. Noise. Lights stabbing her eyes. Someone dragging her. A scream tore out of her throat. Then she floated, carried away by a tidal surge of pain.

A vague wash of sound and movement, then a man's voice said, "Lie still, Ms. Rey. The paramedics are here now."

Panting through clenched teeth, she blinked up at the face that leaned over her, a Spanish man with close-cropped salt-and-pepper hair. *Paramedics?* she wanted to ask, but the only sounds that came out were sobbing whimpers.

"…area secured…" another voice said.

No more gunshots. The squawk and beep of radios, the wheeling of red and blue and white lights against a distant wall. A man's voice nearby sobbing obscenities. The lights and voices blurred, faded, drifted.

Another flurry of movement, jostling. The stab of a needle in her hand. Someone took hold of her wounded leg.

Amethyst's eyes flared wide. She howled and clawed for the magic, but nothing, nothing, nothing there. A man and woman in blue leaned over her. The man pressed a dressing to her thigh. The woman was setting up an IV.

Amethyst wrenched her hand away. More pain. "No! No needles!"

She tore out the IV needle. Blood poured out. She didn't care.

The man pounced on her, pinned her shoulders. Amethyst fought, her heart pounding icy fire through her veins.

"Some help here," the man shouted.

Hands grabbed her, held her down, held her arm while the woman inserted the IV in her other hand.

"Ms. Rey, calm down," that first man's voice said. "We're APD. You're safe, you're okay. They're going to give you something for the pain, okay?"

"No!" she gasped again, writhing and bucking under the hands that held her.

Her leg, oh God, her leg, but she couldn't let them drug her, couldn't let them put her on that train. She'd rather die.

Through the confusion of moving people, she saw another paramedic tending to Robertson. His kindly-uncle face was twisted with agony, tears running down his cheeks. There on the floor almost close enough to touch, at the feet of three men in helmets and fatigues and body armor, lay a guy in black combat gear in a pool of blood.

The IV trickled cool sleep into her veins. She fought it, but everything grew soft and distant and finally wisped away.

✧✧✧✧✧✧

Amethyst opened her eyes. Acoustic panel ceiling. Stainless steel bed rails, curtain in soft watercolor hues. An antiseptic smell, the soft beep of machinery. IV line running to her hand.

She wrenched upright, her heart clawing up her throat.

"Whoa, whoa!" A chair gave a sharp scrape and clatter, then Dad was leaning over her, his arm around her, half comforting, half restraining. "It's okay, sweetheart. Thistle? Hear me? Everything is okay now." He held her, stroked her hair. "You're going to be fine. Relax."

She clenched her fingers on his arm. "Dad?" She looked around wildly, rigid and quivering in his grasp. "Where are they? Where are we?"

"We're at UNM Hospital," Dad said. "You had surgery a little while ago. The cops took care of the men who kidnapped you. Nobody's going to hurt you now."

"Dad, don't leave me. Don't let them take me away." Tears were running down her face.

Dad's arm around her shoulders tightened. "Nobody's going to take you away. Now that you're awake, the police will want to talk to you. But I promise I'll stay right here. They want to take you anywhere, they'll have to go through me first. Hear?"

Sniffling, she nodded hard, the tears still gushing out like she was five years old. Dad sat on the side of the bed and just held her. She finally stopped, wiped her face, blew her nose and sat up.

"Better now?" Dad said. "They said this might happen when you woke up. Said you were pretty panicked while the paramedics were working on you. What happened, baby?"

She just breathed for a minute, trying to take herself out of that dark, echoing building, away from bindings and threats and pain. *No magic*, she told herself. *Don't say anything about magic*. But she could tell him the rest.

He sat quiet and let her talk, nodding and holding her hand, the one she'd ripped the IV needle out of. It was bandaged now. With whatever drugs they'd given her, it didn't hurt at all.

Her leg still hurt. A lot. Like something was trying to chew a hole through it.

Dad sat quiet when she finished. "Amethyst," he finally said gently. "This is the second time in a year or so you've ended up in the hospital. What's going on?"

She looked down where his hand held hers. "I don't know."

Again, that moment of silence, painful silence that plucked at her to say something. Then, "I'm going to ask you something, and I want you to answer me honestly. Okay?"

Something tightened in her chest. She nodded.

"All this stuff that's been happening to you lately—it

seems pretty strange. Things like this don't happen to most people. But maybe you're not like most people." His pause seemed to pulse. "Are you like your mom's grandmother?" He spoke slowly, as if he hated to ask as much as she might hate to answer. "Are you like your Nani?"

Surprise jerked her eyes up to his. She couldn't talk. What was it that clamped its hand around her throat? Relief? Gratitude? Fear?

She gave one, jerky nod and looked down again.

The breath went out of him. "Thank God." He hung his own head, his eyes closed in relief.

"Thank...God?" Amethyst echoed.

He raised his head again. "I was afraid it was drugs or something like that." He gave a wry laugh. "Too much *Breaking Bad*."

She gave a weak smile.

"Rosalinda told us this would happen," Dad said. "Said you had what she did, but she thought it was something different. Maybe something more. I saw enough of what Nani did to at least halfway believe in it. Your mom was raised with it, though. She didn't have any question. She's been waiting fifteen years or so for this to happen. But it was like whatever Nani'd seen in you, you locked away in a box after she died."

Amethyst pleated the blanket. "I don't know, Dad. Maybe I did."

"And then last spring, when you came to visit? When you were upset. Remember?"

She nodded. "Talys—Tom…"

She hesitated. Jas was the only one in the world who

knew what Talys had been. *Well, it doesn't matter now, I guess*, she thought. Her chest squeezed and she cleared her throat.

"I'd met Tom not long before, and he had abilities of his own." Her voice came out thin but steady. "He saw what I was—am. I didn't want any part of it. I just wanted to live my life."

"But what you are has a habit of catching up with you, doesn't it?"

She nodded again.

Dad nodded in turn. "And Jas Harker. Does he know?"

Uh-oh. "Um... Yes?"

"I guess I'll have to have another chat with him, then."

"Dad—" she began to protest.

Voices and footsteps came into the room. A short, solid, businesslike woman walked in. Dad stood and faced her.

"Mr. Rey, I'm Detective Moreno, APD," she said. "I need to speak with Ms. Rey."

Dad shifted his weight. "We've been expecting you," he said. "But I really don't—"

Detective Moreno smiled and made a patting gesture. "Don't worry, I already had the lecture from the on-duty physician. I'll just get a statement for now, then she can rest."

Dad turned back to Amethyst. "I'm right here, Thistle, don't you worry. You won't be going anywhere until it's time to take you home."

He took a chair at the foot of the bed and crossed his arms, watching over her. Detective Moreno sat by the bedside and started asking questions.

Amethyst said "I don't know" and "I can't remember" a lot and then complained about how much her leg was hurting and how tired she was, all of which was true. Then the terror came roaring back and next thing she knew, she was crying again, which was almost as bad as telling what really happened, magic and all.

Dad got up and went out and the nurse came in, shot something into her IV line and it was lights out.

When she woke up, she shot straight up in bed again, jerked up her hands in defense. Magic prickled at her fingertips, raced across her skin.

"Okay," Dad said beside her. "I'm going to give you a week of that kind of behavior. If it isn't better by then, you need to see somebody about it."

She panted, let go the magic and tried to settle her heart back in her chest. "It isn't paranoia if someone's really after you."

"That's true," Dad said, flipping the cover over his tablet and setting it aside on the bedside table. "But you can't spend your life waiting for 'em to come and get you, either."

A knock came at the door.

Amethyst squeezed her eyes closed. "Please. No more cops."

Whoever it was came into the room. Dad stood up, placing himself between the visitor and the bed.

"I've come to minister to Amethyst Rey," said a half-familiar voice with a Texas twang, rich and resonant even speaking softly. "Is she able to see me?"

Surprise shot through Amethyst. Dad looked back and raised his brows at her. He knew her attitude about religion.

"He's okay, Dad. I know him."

Dad turned back. "I'm Alex Rey, Amethyst's father."

"Reverend Nathaniel Sonshine."

He stepped into view, shook hands with Dad. He was a little more toned-down than when she'd seen him at the tent revival, wearing an aspen-leaf yellow sweater over a white shirt. She wondered if that amazing car of his was off glittering somewhere in the hospital visitor's lot.

He turned his eyes on her—brown, with gold rims. She hadn't noticed that when she'd talked to him at Roswell.

"May I sit with you?"

"Amethyst?" Dad asked.

"It's okay," she said again, though paranoia was clawing at her insides. Dad was right. She was going to have to get a grip on that pretty soon, or it'd take over her life. "Is Mama here? Why don't you two take a break, get some breakfast." She glanced at the clock. "Oh. Dinner, I guess. Sorry."

Dad made a dismissive gesture. "If you're sure…"

She nodded, called up the most lying smile she'd ever put on and gave him a little wave. He stepped out.

Reverend Sonshine settled into the chair Dad had been sitting in. "How are you?"

She shrugged. "Not at my best." She wet her lips.

"Reverend Sonshine, you are about the last person I would've expected to see here."

He gave a small smile. "The Lord loves all his children. I strive to do the same." He scooted the chair closer. "I hear you took a bad wound. Can I help?"

She blew out a breath. "The surgeon was talking about shrapnel from the exploding gun and risk of infection and additional surgeries to repair the damage to my muscles. So yeah, I sure hope so. But I can't—" She bit her lip, spread her hand above her thigh, where the bandage was. Right where the talisman had been. How could this have happened? "I don't have any way to repay you, Reverend."

He waved a hand. "Did our Lord Jesus ask for payment when he healed the sick? I didn't come to create a debt. God gave me a gift. It's up to me to share it with those who need it."

She gave him a sideways glance. *And maybe once I'm able to help Jas make his nexus, he'll leave you alone.* No, that wasn't fair.

"I told Jas you're a good man."

"I know," he said cryptically and clasped hands between knees. "May I touch you?"

A little shiver of unease went through her. Really, she *didn't* know him, and he didn't have any reason to feel goodwill toward her. In fact, the most sensible thing for him to do would be to remove her as a threat, or use her as leverage with Jas or—

Stop it, Amethyst. You're getting to be like every other wizard you've met. Is that really how you want to be?

She took a long breath. It shook, and didn't do much to calm the clamoring fears.

"Okay," she said.

He leaned forward and placed his hands on her thigh. Reverend Sonshine closed his eyes, bent his head and prayed.

Jas' healing magic had swept over her like a wave when he worked it on her. Reverend Sonshine's hit like a flash flood, slamming into her and through, drowning her in its strength. It was like charged particles streaming out from the sun, energy that could burn her alive, explode her into an assortment of loose atoms floating through the air.

Terror should've spiked through her, but she only felt warmth and ease, the pain and the wrongness of damaged tissues fraying away under a blaze of molten gold and rippling pearl. That energy expanded, filling her, as if she were a glass humming in tune to the note that would shatter it.

Then there was nothing at all.

CHAPTER 30

J as slid Amethyst's rented wheelchair into the back of the Range Rover. The hatch glided down automatically as he came around and got in the driver's seat.

She'd noticed him limping when he came into the house. He was limping now.

"Are you okay?" she asked.

"I strained a muscle playing tennis. I'll be fine." He slid the key into the ignition and started the engine. "I didn't think your folks would let me take you. They don't seem to feel you're ready to talk to the police yet."

"It's my fault," she said. "I didn't do great when I talked to the detective yesterday. And I haven't— Well, I've been a little…jumpy. But I just want to get it over with. Maybe then I won't have to keep thinking about it."

"It's a good idea for you and me to talk before you talk to anyone else. We need a cover story."

"I know." She concentrated on picking a tuft of lint off her sweat pants. "I didn't expect to see you, Jas. I wouldn't blame you if you hadn't come."

"I got your voicemail." He bowed his head. "Apology accepted." He paused, then said, "I'd've come sooner, if I could."

Jas hadn't come to the hospital, and Amethyst had to

admit it bothered her. She wasn't quite so ready to admit how glad she'd been when he showed up at her house today.

Fortunately, she'd only had to stay at the hospital one more night, and that was only because it'd been too late to discharge her. The wound hadn't magically disappeared, but the doctors didn't need to know that the pain was bearable and it wouldn't require any more surgeries. Only time to finish healing. The surgeon could scratch his head over that when it came time for the follow-up appointment. Or maybe she just wouldn't go.

"I know you had more important things to deal with," she said.

Jas shot her a glance, started the engine and pulled away from the curb. "I had *other* important things to deal with."

She didn't know what to say to that.

"Having a horde of investigators in and out of the building all day and night," he went on, "hasn't been conducive to working on our project. We'll have to wait until things calm down. But after recent events, I suppose we all need time to recover our strength."

"How are your people?" she said. "The ones—the ones injured in the bombing."

"All but two have been discharged from the hospital. One who was in critical condition has been upgraded to serious but stable. The other..." His lips went to a thin line. "She didn't make it. Reverend Sonshine has a powerful gift, but he can't create true miracles."

Her heart squeezed into a cold, hard knot. "Oh my

god, Jas. I'm sorry."

"Sorry," he repeated. "Is that sympathy, or guilt? It had better not be guilt."

"But it was because—"

"*You* are not the one who set that car bomb," he interrupted. "You did not go out and purposefully antagonize these individuals. Someone is definitely responsible for what happened, but it isn't you, Amethyst."

"But I—"

He held up a hand. "No."

She shut up.

He turned right, made another right onto the street that led to Lomas. The GPS wasn't turned on. Seemed he knew her neighborhood pretty well.

"What happened after you called me?" he said.

She told him, waking up at the Rail Yards, the binding, the gunmen.

"That was smart," he said when she explained about the talisman. "Not tying it to your own powers. That gave you an edge. Spells like that are never as all-encompassing as they're billed, but they're still useful. What finally made it fail?"

"I was wondering that myself for a while, since it vaporized every bullet they shot at me. I think what happened was when Robertson's gun fired right against my leg, the talisman made the bullet explode inside the gun, so of course the gun exploded."

"The talisman still should've protected you."

"That's what I thought, too. But I peeked under my bandage this morning. There's gunpowder embedded all over my leg there." She waved a hand over the spot and made a face. All those little black dots peppering her skin, like dirt. "I think the gunpowder must've messed up the talisman's symbols so it wouldn't work anymore. Or else it didn't work against the exploding gun itself, and when my leg got turned into hamburger..." She shrugged. "There went the talisman."

"That makes sense, although I'm leaning toward the first explanation. From the fireworks I saw down there, I assume you managed to break the binding." He gave her an odd look. "It takes a good deal of power to break a binding from a standing start."

What was that look about? The binding *he'd* laid on her? She definitely wasn't planning on mentioning it. Especially not now.

She plucked at her sweats where they pulled against the bandage. "Well, I think I had help."

He raised his brows in a question and pulled around an old man in an ancient Buick doing 25 in a 40 MPH zone.

Should she tell him, or shouldn't she? She'd been worrying about it, caught between something told in confidence and this partnership—or whatever it was— with Jas. But not telling him felt like a cactus spine in her skin, one of those fine, tiny ones you can't even see but that still prick and irritate.

"Remember the blood binding I put on Pico?" she said. "Well, with things going south, I thought I'd better give him a heads-up. And he told me something I didn't know."

"That the binding links power, as well," Jas said.

"Oh." The tension went out of her. "He told you?"

"No, but many bindings have that effect. Still, I appreciate your telling me." He kept his eyes on the traffic stretching and compressing like a Slinky from light to light.

"Maybe you can explain something else," she said. "I figured the lights going out was something you did to the power grid, and somebody might've heard all the gunfire and called 9-1-1. But the guys on the SWAT team called me by name. They knew I was there. Did *you* call?"

"No," he said. "You did."

"I— What?"

"Emergency dispatch got a call from a woman who identified herself as Amethyst Rey. She'd managed to get hold of a cell phone while her captors were otherwise occupied and reported that she'd been kidnapped and was being held at the Albuquerque Rail Yards. GPS pinpointed the location of the call."

Amethyst just sat with her mouth open.

Jas smiled, more smug than crinkly this time. "I have the recordings, if you'd like to hear them."

She shut her mouth and squeezed her eyes closed. "God. No."

"Amethyst." He gripped her fist where it clenched on her knee. "I'm sorry, I wasn't thinking."

She shook her head, opened her eyes, made herself look at the streets in the bright November sun, the dealerships full of shiny new cars, the traffic carrying people to lunch, shopping for Thanksgiving dinner, running errands, whatever ordinary things they had to do this day. It didn't help.

"Don't say sorry," she said. "If you hadn't done that—" She took a shaky breath. "Robertson said he'd give—*sell* me to the government to—to study."

Jas' hand tightened on her fist.

"This isn't over, Jas. He can still tell them. Stregone, the wizard working with him, *he* can still tell. The guys with guns—they'll tell what they saw, all those bullets they shot at me going *poof*, like little wishing stars, the shield, the fire I blasted at Stregone—"

Jas gave her hand a shake. "Listen to me. You work for *me*, and Magus Corporation does certain things for certain agencies. I hold information that makes what Edward Snowden leaked look like a child's tattling. I can promise you, no one in the government wants to get on my bad side."

"He said they'd put pressure on you—"

"And I'd shrug my shoulders and forget I ever knew any Amethyst Rey? And you believe that?"

"You keep telling me you're a pragmatist!"

"God in heaven." He drew a hand down his face. "Not only are you the most unforgiving woman I've ever met, you're also the most literal-minded."

He turned onto a side street and pulled to the curb next to a park. Low-slung, 1960's-vintage ranch houses with xeriscaped front yards lined the opposite side of the street, perfectly ordinary.

He shut off the engine and turned in the seat to face her. "All right. Let's say I'm that kind of pragmatist. I'm also a wizard who can't use anything more than the most subtle, untraceable magic without exposing myself to any other wizard in a thousand mile radius. Does it make any sense at all that I'd be willing to discard the one person I can reliably use as cover? And don't look at me like that. You're the one assuming I think that way."

"Well, don't you?"

"I'll let you decide. While your friend Hal Robertson—who by the way, has four aliases I've discovered so far—awaits arraignment on charges of kidnapping, aggravated battery with a deadly weapon, conspiracy and several other felonies, I will be busy. By the time I'm finished, his every problematic association, every dubious dealing, every questionable dollar of income, inflated expense, doctored account and inaccurate income tax filing will be revealed. I have no doubt much will prove interesting to his clients, not to mention the appropriate authorities. Furthermore, every incident from his personal life that might potentially cause humiliation will be spread far and wide for all to see. If by some miracle he manages to beat every charge brought against him, he'll quickly discover that he's too toxic to touch."

"Oh." Even on the one word, Amethyst's voice came out unsteady. Who needed curses when Jas Harker was on the job? Or maybe Jas was part of the curse.

"Meanwhile, as for the men who aided and abetted your kidnapping—those who survived the SWAT team, in any case—" He paused and gave a smile that sent a cold thread slithering down Amethyst's neck. "Well, we both know what happens in jail to men believed to be snitches and child rapists. I'll be surprised if they make it to trial," he added with cheerful glee.

She was shaking her head. It wouldn't be that easy. "What about *Stregone? He* won't stay comfortably locked up in MDC. When will I wake up and find him leaning over me again?"

She was going to see that in her nightmares for a long time. Caramela would be sleeping in bed with her for a while.

"You're panicking," Jas said. "Calm down."

She didn't realize how fast she was breathing until he said it. She took two or three deep breaths, let them out slowly.

"Okay. I'm calm."

He raised a skeptical brow but didn't argue. "Stregone saw you break his binding while scarcely batting an eyelash, work at least one spell that would drain most wizards dry, then, when he thought you wounded and helpless, you sucked all the magic out of the air."

"I *was* wounded and helpless. And it was Pico who sucked out the magic."

"But Stregone will think it was you. If he's willing to go anywhere near you after that, he's an idiot. In the meantime, while the magic was offline, he was arrested and his photo and fingerprints taken. And unfortunately for him, I have copies of both. As well as access to data worldwide."

She hadn't been able to shake the sense that disaster was only hiding, still waiting to pounce on her. For the first time in...god, how long?...the worry and fear lightened.

All that time she'd been mad at him, all the times she'd been at cross purposes with him, she'd never stopped to consider that Jas might make a very, very bad enemy. It was amazing to discover that he also made a formidable friend.

"You just want to hear me say 'I'm sorry' again, didn't you?"

"Are you saying it?"

She scowled. "And here I was feeling all friendly and good about you. I wasn't even going to ask about Reverend Sonshine, because I was afraid to spoil things."

He laughed. "I suppose you want to know how I convinced him to come heal you."

"I haven't had my dose of righteous indignation in a couple of days." She sighed. "Go ahead. Tell me."

"I began by apologizing abjectly. I told him my friend was so angry over my treatment of him that she'd gotten out of my car ten miles outside of Roswell and walked off into the dark. And made sure I couldn't follow."

She put a hand over her face. "Okay, I'll say it. I'm sorry, I'm sorry, I'm sorry."

"Amethyst. You were right. I told him so. I also told him that it was because of me that your enemies had caught and hurt you. And you didn't deserve that."

She swallowed the sudden thick feeling in her throat. "You know I'm going to ask him."

He gave one of his best crinkly smiles. "I wouldn't expect anything else."

CHAPTER 31

Amethyst lay in bed, eyes open, wizard's senses extended into the night. In the neighboring houses, someone watched late night TV, a couple made love. A rabbit nibbled the few remaining green blades in the Griegos' lawn and a coyote trotted along the arroyo to the north. Most people lay asleep, their dreams floating like luminous flecks in the shift and swirl of the magic.

All quiet, nothing to worry about. But she still couldn't sleep. Yes, the leg still hurt even after the healing, and it wasn't comfortable to sleep on her left side, but that wasn't the problem. Or not all the problem, anyway. She hadn't been sleeping well since the Rail Yards. If it wasn't lying tense, feeling through the magic for danger, it was nightmares, or jolting awake to throw spatters of purple sparks into the dark.

Caramela lay spooned against her, her heavy head pillowed on Amethyst's arm. Amethyst kissed her head and stroked her short, soft fur for comfort. Caramela turned, gave Amethyst a little lick on the chin and heaved a contented sigh.

Well, if Caramela could be comfortable, there was no reason Amethyst couldn't be, too. She closed her eyes, cuddled the dog and concentrated on relaxing her tight muscles one by one. She drifted, dipping in and out of sleep, then finally sank into dark and quiet.

A silver sun glowed on her, the only light in an infinity of darkness. It pulsed slightly as if with a heartbeat, giving off a familiar warmth.

Amethyst hugged herself. "Oh, Talys. Please come back. How can I do without you?"

You'd once have done most anything to be rid of me. His voice carried an echo of humor.

It might've been funny before. Now, she turned aside. "Don't talk about that. I need you, Talys. Don't leave me alone."

Are you alone?

She thought about Jas, a friend…or a friend only to the extent of his self-interest?

"But you're the one I trust. You're the one I knew I could always count on."

Trust is a gift.

A gift. Something you gave. She turned it over in her head. Something you gave, knowing once you'd given it, it belonged to someone else. To value—or not. She shied away from the idea.

"I just want you back."

I can't come back. I've told you, I'm no longer what I was. The bond between us is broken.

"If you—" It was suddenly hard to go on. She forced herself. "If you don't want to be my familiar anymore, just say so. Don't hide behind a bunch of magical crap."

The silver sun dimmed. *What I want is of no matter. But should it bring you comfort, I would return if I could. Yet this isn't possible. I can no longer manifest outside the magic. I am the magic.*

She shook her head, not understanding. But an idea unfurled at the bottom of her mind, a pale thread tiny as a poppy seed sprouting.

"Where are we now?" she said slowly. "It seems empty."

Another plane. An idea of a place.

"What do you do here?"

Be. Think. Speak with you, when you come.

The idea quivered upward toward the light, opening fragile leaves. "At Ojo, it was you, wasn't it? I felt you. You led me to Jas. If you can't come into the world anymore, how were you able to go there?"

I wasn't. I felt you, as I do when you call to me, but you were here, in this thought.

There it was again. Thought. Idea. "Are you in my head again, Talys?"

No. Evasiveness shimmered in the answer.

"Ohmigod. I put the pieces of you back together, like

Frankenstein's monster, and now you don't exist anywhere unless I think about you." She put her face in her hands. "I couldn't let you go, so I've trapped you."

No, Amethyst. I'm no more trapped than any mortal creature in its body.

"But you're not a mortal being. You could change bodies the way we change clothes, go anywhere, live as long as you wanted. I've taken that away from you."

My existence was taken. You gave it back.

Tears ran cold down her cheeks. Again, again. When would she ever stop crying?

"It's my fault you died. If I hadn't been so stupid, if I hadn't been so sure I knew the right way to handle everything—"

Do any who live in the world know better? I was far older than you, far older than you know. Yet I could not avert what happened. If I could not, how could you expect to? Guilt is pointless, useless. Corrosive. Don't allow it to destroy you, for it will, it will. It surely will.

She wiped the tears with the heels of her hands. "I have to try to fix this. But I'm afraid I'll just make it worse."

Life is groping forward into the dark. If you remain still, frozen with fear, you won't truly live.

Amethyst blinked awake, her cheeks cold and wet.

"Talys?" she said into the quiet of her bedroom.

She expected to see him hovering there, a silver sun glowing in the dimness. But the only light came from the streetlight, pale orange stripes angled on the wall.

Disappointment cut her, like shards of glass in her middle. She willed it down.

Caramela twitched against her in a dream, making little whimpering barks. Breathing deep to ease the ache in her chest, Amethyst smoothed the dog's ears until she quieted.

❖❖❖❖❖❖

A methyst checked the time on her computer screen. Again. 4:38. Well, she might as well give up pretending to be productive. She wasn't getting much done checking the time every three minutes.

She didn't quite know how she'd gone from refusing to work for Jas to working for Jas. She had her own office. With a window. One with a fabulous twentieth-story view of the Sandia Mountains. Today snow clouds rolled over Sandia Crest like overboiling milk. An early snowstorm was probably whitening the east side of the mountains.

It was very weird. She had *commissions* to finish, for godsake. Yet here she was, driving down every day for the last week to the Magus Building to look at code, searching for malicious spells in worms and viruses, Trojans and malware, inserting wards and guards in the firewalls, fendings and bindings, the more esoteric and arcane, the better. If the other Magus employees wondered why her office smelled of herbs and boasted a smudge pot and mortar and pestle, about the most comment she'd gotten was a blink or the side-eye.

Then again, most computer types tended not to notice a lot of things.

She logged out of her secure account and put the computer to sleep. Unhooking her cane from the arm of her chair, she levered herself to her feet. She felt conspicuous using it, but it was better than hunching along the corridors on crutches. So she made her slow, halting way to the top floor.

Sylvia, Jas' executive assistant, greeted her with a smile.

"I'm early," Amethyst said.

Sylvia checked the screen on her desk. "He's free now. Go on in."

Amethyst gave a nod of thanks, smoothed her skirt and hair and opened the door to Jas' office.

"Amethyst—" he began, then took in what she wore and straightened.

Broomstick skirt in shades of violet and merlot, silver concho belt, ankle boots and an amethyst and garnet bead necklace over a cotton fine-gauge sweater. Real dress-up for her, when her usual style was jeans, sneakers and a cable sweater.

Jas straightened his tie, came around the desk and helped her sit down at the round table in front of the windows.

He took the chair next to hers. "I wondered about your request for a meeting. Now you have me really curious. What's going on?"

She hooked her cane on the edge of the table and folded her hands in front of her. "I have a proposal."

He nodded, suddenly all business magnate, a side of him she'd never seen. It was more than a little intimidating. She couldn't afford to be intimidated.

"Go on," he said.

"First of all, what's going on with the nexus? Maybe we've got my problem solved, but I get the feeling what I've been doing lately is just....busywork."

"Not entirely," he said. "As for the nexus, I've been involved in negotiations."

She shot him a look, but refrained from pointing out that by all rights, *she* should also be involved in any negotiations. She had a feeling she hadn't been because she wouldn't approve of his tactics. Or maybe he was just worried she'd be a loose cannon. Maybe she would.

"Ah," was all she said. "Let me guess. Pico exercised his veto power."

"Not yet. But whenever he deigns to communicate with me, I'm anticipating he will."

She nodded. "I've been thinking about your idea about a guardian. Let me tell you what I have in mind, because I think it'll help in your negotiations."

CHAPTER 32

Everyone had been cleared out of the Magus Building. Security sweep, they'd been told, and working at a company like Magus Corporation, most people just sighed, gave a resigned nod and submitted to the body and e-scanners on their way out.

It was a security sweep, all right, but this one didn't only sniff out people and electronics that didn't have any business there. It also looked for unwelcome magic.

The last of the security team left, the doors closed and the light at the entrance flashed four times, then glowed a steady red: locked. Amethyst, ignoring the little coil of unease in her belly, dropped the camouflage spell that hid her.

She limped over to Jas, her sneakers quiet against the floor of river-smoothed pebbles. Only about a third of the lobby's lights were on. The green glass gave the illusion of being underwater. The burbling echoes of the fountain, an enormous granite boulder that looked like it had come straight from the face of the Sandia Mountains, only reinforced the impression.

"That's it?" she asked.

"That's it," Jas said. "How do the spells look?"

She looked at the magic with wizard's senses. Ward

and shield spells rippled and shimmered like a lake under mountain skies, a humming crystalline blue streaked with sunset orange against Albuquerque's night sky. A reversing spell added a layer that sheened like a snowboarder's sunglasses. It made a faint crinkling sound and smelled like a furnace. If anyone sent anything their way, their spell would be reflected right back at them.

"They look good." She turned to Jas. She couldn't put her finger on it—why was she so nervous? "You trust me to do this?"

He gave her an odd, intense look. She'd been seeing that same look from time to time lately.

"I know you won't rest until you try—here, or somewhere else. And I'd rather you do it here."

She turned a hand palm-up in agreement.

He watched her with that dark, intent look, standing very still. "Amethyst…"

The hairs on the back of her neck stood up. A wave of goosebumps swept up her arms. *That* was what it was.

She stood with him in the deserted lobby. Doors locked, alarms engaged. She'd stood here with him once before, exactly like this, the fountain murmuring and chuckling in the background. *Damn. Damn, damn, damn…*

"What?" she said.

When had she decided to trust him enough to be here alone with him, no one else in the building, trapped behind his wards and shields, in this place that was his?

She unsheathed her power, touched it to the magic.

He felt it. He made a move as if to reach for her, but caught himself.

"No." His own power remained contained, out of sight, as if he were an ordinary man. "I need to tell you something."

"What?" she said again.

The sense of déjà vu was so strong she glanced past him, out the windows, expecting to see headlights barreling toward the front of the building.

"We're bound," he said.

A shield. Call up a damn shield. She didn't. Why not?

"No. We're not."

"Yes, we are," Jas said. Patiently. Calmly.

An echo of pain brushed her, like a sub-audible rumble of distant thunder. "How could you do this to me again, Jas? You told me I could trust you. You told me—"

"No, Amethyst." This time he did move, reaching out to her. "I didn't do it. You did."

She jerked back. "Don't lie to me. At least do me that courtesy."

"I'm not lying to you. It took me a while to determine how it happened. Before you put the binding on Pico, you held my hand to cut it. Our blood mixed, too. Yours and mine."

In her mind's eye, she saw herself catching his hand, drawing the pin across it. How the blood had run across her hand and over his.

It was hard to breathe. "How long have you known?"

"Since that first night, when we stayed at the Santa Claran. I was feeling your pain—literally." He paused. "That's why I didn't come to the hospital. After you were shot, I hurt too much to hide it."

He'd been limping when he picked her up for her interview with the detective. And said he strained a muscle.

"And you didn't tell me? You didn't think this was something I ought to know?"

He raked a hand through his hair. "I knew you wouldn't like it. I was trying to find a way out of it."

"I'm bound? To you? You're damn right I don't like it."

"And I to you."

"Oh, that makes it ever so much better."

"Without the binding between us," he said, "you wouldn't have broken the one Stregone placed on you. You certainly wouldn't have had the power to go on to work some of the magic you did while fighting those people."

"That was Pico's power."

"That was *my* power. Believe me, I know. I was meeting with some FBI field agents when you drew it out of me. That was my first indication you were in any kind of trouble. I can't remember the last time I've had to end a meeting so abruptly. So yes, on the whole, I do think it makes it better."

She folded her arms and stared at the fountain for the space of several breaths.

"Okay." Her mind churned. She struggled to calm down and think. "So I guess you couldn't figure out a way to break it, either. What now?"

"As I told you a while back, a binding makes us stronger. Unless we find a way to break it, or it fades on its own, I say we take advantage of it. Much that happens in magic isn't random. Some underlying purpose is often involved."

"Talys told me something like that a long time ago." So had Pico, for that matter. "Unfortunately, this particular binding also makes us more vulnerable. It's not exactly helpful if when I get shot, you go down, too."

"I'm not so sure that isn't—"

The lockpad by the lobby doors flashed and beeped. Jas turned. A man and woman waited outside.

"We'll talk more about this later." He studied her. "Are you all right?"

She stood quiet a moment. "I wasn't thrilled at first about having a familiar, either." She puffed a breath through her lips. "I guess I can learn to get used to this, too."

A smile flickered across his face. "That's enough to be getting on with."

He walked to the doors and stood in front of a smart phone-sized screen for a retinal scan. The light flashed green. He pushed open a door and Lottie Golden and Reverend Sonshine stepped inside.

Lottie wore a duster over her man's vest and narrow tie. Only in the Southwest could you get away with dressing like that. Amethyst had to admit the other woman looked seriously cool, even if she didn't swing that way. Or go for blondes, for that matter. Reverend Sonshine was less impressive in a puffy down jacket. Something yellow peeked out under the zipper.

"Come on in." Jas led the way.

Amethyst walked to meet them.

Lottie took in her limp with the same bland face Amethyst had seen at the Inn of the Mountain Gods. "What happened to you?"

"I got shot," Amethyst said.

"Shot!" Lottie stared, then started laughing. There was nothing bland about that laughter. "My lord," she said at last, still chuckling. "You are young, aren't you?"

Embarrassment and anger burned through Amethyst.

"Amethyst," Jas murmured beside her.

She ignored him and stalked (okay, limped) to the fountain. Taking a deep breath, she called the magic. It crackled through her, as hot as the anger.

Talys had once guided her through a transformation spell. She worked it now, weaving it with one of her own, the first magic she'd ever wrought—a spell of making. She swept both over the fountain, a sizzling surge of energy that went straight to the atoms of the granite that formed the fountain, breaking atomic bonds, restructuring crystalline matrixes. The making did things to the minerals that didn't happen naturally.

The huge boulder of rough, greyish stone was now glossy, night-black granite shot through with stars of mica scintillating with color, like tiny, embedded bits of stained glass.

She turned to Lottie. "Yeah," she said. "I'm young."

Transformation was big medicine. So was a making. She probably should be saving her power for the nexus, but she'd been planning to do this anyway.

"If you don't like it," she said to Jas, "I'll change it back."

He looked like he was trying to hold back a grin. Or maybe it was a grimace.

"I already told you I appreciate your work," he said.

"I'll call Pico, okay?"

He shrugged. "Go ahead. He hasn't been answering my calls."

This spell was easy. She just closed her eyes and tapped along the binding to him. When she opened them again, he stood in front of her, as solid and real-looking as if he were there in the flesh, looking around the lobby like he'd never seen such a sight before. He probably hadn't. She suspected magical nexus guardians didn't get out and about much.

"Pico," Amethyst said. "I don't think you've met Lottie Golden and Reverend Nathaniel Sonshine. They'll be helping us."

"So," Pico said. "Coyote wants to build the place of power in his own house."

Amethyst winced and cast an apologetic glance at Jas, whose brows gave a sardonic lift.

"It's a very safe place," she told Pico. "Hard for enemies to breach."

Pico nodded. "Very hard for enemies." He didn't say it approvingly. Like he was thinking 'enemies' would be whoever Jas decided they'd be.

"When the magic is concentrated enough, I'll call the guardian," Amethyst promised him.

"Your place," Lottie said to Jas, then turned to Amethyst. "Your guardian. And you expect us to help you."

Amethyst's temper finally got the better of her. "Tell you what, Lottie. We'll be happy to accept a contribution from you. Just name it. Maybe you could lay a spread and tell us if we'll have success in our venture, or something."

Lottie mimed closing and laying down a hand of cards. "I fold. You might be young, but you're not afraid to call a bluff." She grinned, an expression that made her sharp features even sharper. "And I already did lay the cards. I wouldn't be here if I hadn't."

Amethyst gave a grumpy nod.

Reverend Sonshine had been quiet since he'd greeted Pico. Now he said, "I have something to contribute."

He took off his down jacket. Under it he wore a tawny-brown sport coat nicely set off by the butter-colored sweater vest under it. He opened the coat and took something small and rectangular out of an inside pocket.

"The truth," he said and put the thing—a book a little smaller than an ordinary paperback—in Amethyst's hands. But this book was hardly ordinary.

Stamped on an old, crinkled cover of real leather was a cross surrounded by an ornate pattern of leaves and tiny, four-petaled flowers in silver. The book's pages were brown as breakfast crepes, the edges as fragile and cracked. A fancy brass clasp speckled with age held it closed.

And magic hummed in it, almost as sentient as in the petroglyphs, if not nearly as old.

"Oh," she whispered to the book, "you are beautiful."

"Yes," Reverend Sonshine said, smiling that smile

that had people cheering and surging forward just to bask in it. "The man who brought me to our Lord Jesus gave me this. No lie will stand in its presence. It turns evil from its path."

"Reverend Sonshine—" She stopped. Was he really giving them this?

Then the old logical brain started ticking over again, *click, click, click.*

"This is a precious thing," she said slowly. "I'm sure you never let it out of your sight."

"I do always keep it with me," he said, his eyes glinting like he knew exactly what she was thinking.

He'd known she and Jas had been telling the truth. And they weren't up to anything nefarious.

"You can't mean to leave this here," she said.

"It might come back to me in time. For now…" He put his hands over hers where they held the book. "I think this is best place for it."

She looked over at Jas. His chin might've been tucked a little, but she couldn't read his expression.

A tiny wavelet of worry went through her. "Sound good to you?" she asked him.

"It will be useful," he said. Something about the way he said it—

She sent him a questioning glance, but he didn't respond.

"Pico?" she said.

He was laughing silently, but nodded. "Good for me."

What the hell was going on with everybody? Heat rose into her face. They were probably laughing at the kid trying to play grown-up wizard. She'd get mad about it later.

She sent a protective spell through her hands and around the ancient Bible, then carried it to the fountain. With a gesture, she stopped the water and opened a pocket in the pebbles at the fountain's base, then tucked the book inside, the water shimmering like a crystal box. Another flick of magic and the pebbles and water swept back to cover it.

She put a hand on the cold floor to lever herself to her feet, but Jas was there. She took his offered hand and let him pull her up.

Stashing the book under the fountain must've made everyone decide this was the focal point of the nexus. The five of them (well, four and one spirit sending), stood around the fountain at equidistant points. Amethyst could see the shape of the pentagram. Wonder how Reverend Sonshine felt about that? It must be weird for Pico, too. Four was the sacred number for a lot of Native Americans.

Then the magic started moving, and she stopped thinking about anything else.

Thundercloud violet and emerald green, pale champagne and pearl white with rich gold all rose and twined together in a blazing knot of power. Another flow traced a triangle of power, this one a fluid, transparent skein, from her to Jas to Pico and back to her again.

They wove spells of opening, spells of calling, and some spell that built a lattice of shapes and angles that would, she guessed, allow the magic to concentrate here. She wasn't sure what Pico was doing, but the magic suddenly shifted, as if the *majordomo* had opened a gate on an *acequia*, letting the water rush into a new channel.

The magic surged, bubbling up through her feet, singing through her blood and bones and flesh and bursting out of her, following the command of their combined powers, racing along the lines of the matrix created for it. Amethyst peeled away enough awareness to begin the summoning.

Power tangled suddenly with hers.

She blinked her way out of the magic. On Reverend Sonshine's other side, Jas' dark eyes met hers. *Not like that*, she could almost hear his voice say in her mind.

She frowned: *What?*

His power guided hers into the shape of another spell, one lighter and more elegant than the power-sucking ritual monstrosity she'd used before. Abruptly, she could see how the spell worked that he'd begun tracing for her, as if it had been one of mass of old spells jumbled in her mind, one she'd simply missed.

She nodded and swept her arms open in a gesture of welcome.

"I summon you out of darkness into light. I summon you from nonbeing into being, from nothingness into form. Break the boundaries of the plane that holds you and enter this one. Be free to swim in the magic. So I summon you. Come, Talys!"

The inaudible roar and imperceptible rush of powers fell silent. Darkness snuffed the blaze of magic. She stood once more in the void, the warmth of Talys' silver sun glowing on her.

"Will you come?" she said. "I should've asked you before, but I didn't have it figured out yet. Why you were able to manifest at Ojo."

I didn't.

She shook her head. "You told me you're part of the magic now. The magic is concentrated there, so you were able to come even though I hadn't called you."

He didn't reply, only pulsing gently in the dark. That silence was unreadable, unsettling.

"We've made another place like that," she said into it. "A nexus of magic."

Why?

"I know you've been around a long, long time, Talys, but I haven't. From what you and Jas have told me, things are very different now than they once were. Like I told you before, I don't want a bunch of wizards coming in and rearranging the furniture to suit themselves."

Wizards like you have always existed. They have always struggled against the unscrupulous.

"Sure they did. When people still believed in magic. Nowadays it's pretty hard to be a wizard struggling against the unscrupulous without attracting a whole lot of awkward attention. You tried to warn me, but I wouldn't listen to you."

I can't help you now, Amethyst. You must trust in your own strength.

The familiar knot twisted in her throat. "I know. I'm trying to. But you can still help. If you're willing to. If you're willing to come back into the world."

How?

"The guardian of the nexus at Ojo is old. No one has come to replace him. But you, Talys, you're not mortal. You can protect the nexus we're creating, keeping the magic safe, keeping anyone from taking it all for themselves. You can't be swayed or bribed or tricked or threatened. You'll be the perfect incorruptible guardian."

Even in this dark nowhere, power beat in her like a second heart. She waited, biting the inside of her lip.

Very well, he said. *I will come.*

A strange combination of relief and triumph surged through her. She reached for him.

The black ache under her breastbone wailed for her to fill it, to take the essence that was Talys and fill that hollow, where she could carry it with her forever. No more pain. No more emptiness. Simple.

She wouldn't do that to him, no matter how desperately she wanted him back. She loved him, and that wasn't the kind of thing you did to someone you loved. Amethyst closed her mind and heart to the keening of grief, wrapped Talys with the power of her summoning and unfolded her awareness into the world once more.

Magic surged like an approaching thunderstorm, crackled across her skin like static electricity. Like it had at

Ojo Caliente, it now filled the Magus Building.

Amethyst shook her head. The magic was almost overwhelming, like drinking a shot of pure whiskey when you were only used to sparkling wine. After the power she'd expended, on the fountain, the creation of the nexus, the summoning, she should've been flat on her back. Maybe even worse.

Instead, she felt good. Powerful. Like the future was a jewelry box, and she held the key. Jas and Lottie and Reverend Sonshine looked dazed— No, more stunned and giddy. Drunk. Drunk on magic. They could do—anything. Have—anything. Nothing would stop them—

Where is the guardian?

Amethyst peeled herself out of the magical updraft, no longer sailing above the world, possibilities whipping through her hair.

Pico's spirit-sending met her eyes. His voice whispered into her mind again: *Where is the guardian?*

Her heart suddenly pounded. The magic rushed just as rich and intoxicating, but no longer enticing.

"Talys?" she said aloud. She twisted one way, then the other, searching for him. "Where is he? Talys!"

Amethyst could suddenly think again, reason again. The magic was still there, still booming like a flash flood through the building, but somehow, she'd found a place to stand.

She turned to the fountain, looking just as she'd left it. She'd expected to see his silver energy shining out of that gleaming black boulder shot through with color. But there was nothing. Nothing but the murmur of water, the underwater-green light, Jas and the others watching her.

"He said he'd come." Her voice squeezed into silence on the last word.

Jas had moved from his place in the circle. Now he stepped close to her.

"You can't summon a dream, Amethyst," he said gently.

He wasn't a dream, she wanted to tell him, but only trusted herself to shake her head.

She reached out, touched the water that spilled over the boulder. It ran over her fingers like tears.

Another voice whispered into her mind, burbling like the water: *I'm here.*

She felt Talys' familiar warmth expand, pouring through the nexus, a brilliance spreading out from the fountain to fill the building.

She would've flung her arms around the boulder, but Jas' hand fell on her shoulder.

"He's here! Do you hear him? Can you feel him?" she babbled. "I told you, I told you he wasn't just a dream."

Jas stared at the fountain, looking as surprised as if…as if it had just spoken to him. Now she could see the edge of silver in the water's ripples. She pulled free of Jas, plunged both hands into the water running like mercury over her skin.

"Oh, Talys, you're back! I've missed you. I've missed you so, so much."

"What the hell is this?" Lottie's angry voice said, but it was nothing, nothing Amethyst cared about.

Reverend Sonshine said something in reply, but

Amethyst didn't hear it.

I'm here, in the magic, Talys' voice said, no longer hot cocoa, but a liquid purl. *This is my place.*

Her hands fell, out of the water.

"Yes," she whispered. She swallowed, swallowed again. "That's right. To guard..." She couldn't go on.

To guard the nexus. To keep the magic for all.

"Yes." This time, her lips and tongue only shaped the word.

Pain stabbed, stabbed again. This was no longer her Talys. She thought back over the times she'd talked to him after the summoning. Had he ever called her 'love,' the way he used to? If he had, she didn't remember it. Only her name.

She'd remade the fountain for him—black, what he'd liked to wear. Just another form for him to inhabit, if not as mobile as the others. But he wasn't her familiar anymore. He'd told her, but she hadn't wanted to listen.

"You did good," Pico said to her. "This spirit will be a good guardian."

He looked sad and sympathetic, as if he knew what Talys had been to her. Maybe he did.

She cleared her throat. "I know he will. He always was for me."

She felt Jas' gaze on her, but couldn't look at him. Everything was over—the people who'd been after her stopped, the magic protected, Talys made whole again.

She slumped, suddenly exhausted. "Looks like I'm done," she said. "I'd better go."

Her voice came out dead, dull.

As she turned, Jas touched her. She started. His arm circled her shoulders, drew her to him. He cupped her head with his other hand.

She should extricate herself, but somehow, it didn't seem to matter all that much. Heaving a shuddering sigh, she rested her head on his shoulder and let him hold her.

Footsteps tapped on the floor, moving away, Reverend Sonshine and Lottie's voices gradually fading into the echoing murmurs of the fountain.

Amethyst closed her eyes, Jas' shoulder warm and solid under her cheek. She thought about Reverend Sonshine's enchanted Bible, lying not three feet away under Talys' fountain: *Lies and evil can't stand before it.*

"Well," she murmured. "I guess that's enough to go on with."

ALSO BY KATHLENA L. CONTRERAS:

The Land of Enchantment

Familiar Magic

Do You Believe in Magic (short story)

Crooked Magic

This Magic Moment (short story)

Could It Be Magic

Fated Magic – a Land of Enchantment novel

Also…
Shadowbound

Kathlena L. Contreras writing as
K. Lynn Bay:

Blackthorne

ChanceShaper

Springtime in Hades

For reading samples and book descriptions,
go to FlyingTigerPress.com

To hear about new releases by Kathlena L. Contreras and K. Lynn Bay, you can sign up for my mailing list at FlyingTigerPress.com. I promise I won't spam you, and I'll never share your information with anyone.

If you enjoyed this book, please take a moment to write a review on your favorite site. Your opinion can help other readers decide to try a book by an author new to them.

Thank you for reading!

Check my Flying Tiger Press page on Pinterest for images from *Crooked Magic.*

ABOUT THE AUTHOR

Kathlena Contreras has been writing since the age of eight, when while hanging out at her dad's office one summer, she typed out a story about a saber-toothed tiger that encounters a time machine. The story was three paragraphs long.

Many years and many paragraphs later and here she is, still writing about weird things. In between writing, Kathlena has been the owner of a successful small business, an assistant medical librarian, a database manager and a pusher of paper in countless offices. She's also been a copy editor for three nationally distributed rodeo magazines and the editor of a local literary magazine.

She currently lives with her husband, five dogs and assorted livestock on the edge of the woods above the valley east of Albuquerque, New Mexico, USA, the Land of Enchantment, a place where the view goes on forever.

Kathlena L. Contreras also writes as K. Lynn Bay.

Stop by and say hi at FlyingTigerPress.com

To hear about new releases, you can sign up on my website. I promise I won't spam you, and I'll never share your information with anyone.

Email at kathys.wizards@gmail.com
Flying Tiger Press on Pinterest
Kathlena L. Contreras on Facebook
K. Lynn Bay on Google+